To Melissa!
Enjoy your
journey to your
next Destination!
Lori Beard
10

DESTINATION D

A Novel

By Lori Beard-Daily

Destination D

This is a work of fiction. All of the characters, names, incidents, organizations, and dialogue in this novel are either the products of the author's imagination or are used fictitiously.

Published in the United States by BQB Publishing
(Boutique of Quality Books Publishing)
www.bqbpublishing.com

Printed in the United States of America

ISBN 978-0-9831699-7-0 (p)
ISBN 978-1-937084-35-6 (e)

Library of Congress Control Number: 2011936657

Book design by Darlene Swanson • www.van-garde.com
Photo by Reggie Anderson
Cover design by Dion Jefferies

Acknowledgments

It is hard to believe that in 1998 I originally wrote *Destination D* as a play. Back then, it was entitled *Plane As Plain Can Be*. Four years later, my best friend, Shree, suggested that I turn the play into a novel. So, I did. Now, nine years later, the book is finally completed.

Writing a book is something that I have wanted to do for a very long time. I just didn't have any idea that it would take me this long to get it out. Just like the title, the book has had many destinations. It's been on a long journey of editors, agents, publishers, and even television executives. Everyone had an opinion about how I should write the book, and I listened to them all—for nine long years! In the end, it was finally my voice that I decided would have the final say.

I have been very blessed to have had a lot of supporters along the way. Now, I finally have the opportunity to let them read the finished product and thank them for the part they played in the book's completion. If I have missed anyone's name, please know that it was not intentional, and I hope you will accept my sincere apology.

I want to say thank you to the following:

God for giving me the gift of creativity and the faith to continue to believe in Him and myself.

My husband, Bryon, for always supporting me—even on days when I didn't deserve it! He read my manuscript over and over again. He helped me brainstorm ideas, edit, and even did some rewrites. Even when he was too tired to work on his own projects, he was always there to help me with *Destination D*. I love my hubby!

My daughter, Erica, for praying every night of every year since she was four years old that the book would be published. She is now thirteen. See, God does answer prayers. I appreciate your faith, Erica!

My daughter, Erin, for staying positive and keeping me encouraged on a daily basis. Thank you for having an everlasting bright side!

My son, Eric, for doing his best in trying to keep his distance from me during my rewrites and just trying to help with whatever needed to be done. You have been quite a trooper!

My mother, Gwen Beard, and my father, Israel Beard, PhD, for never discouraging me. It really paid off!

My in-laws, George and Elizabeth Daily, for supporting me on all of my writing projects. I couldn't have married into a better family!

My best friend, Shree Sullivan, who initially encouraged me and put the idea in my head to write a book. You have always been there for me, and I'm so grateful for you.

My colleague and friend, Angelo Omari, for giving me the gift of friendship and referring me to the Clark Atlanta University's graphic design class that worked with me on book cover design.

My angel, Lin Sun, PhD, a college professor at Clark Atlanta University whom I've never met. She had her talented graphic design students enter a contest for the cover of my book. She managed the project and—poof—the cover was born!

My winner for the cover design contest, Dion Jefferies. I appreciate you for hanging in there and giving me the exact graphic that I wanted for the book.

My friend, Theron Barney, for giving me great ideas on how I could make this a better book and being a wonderful sounding board. His wife, Valerie Benning Barney, for introducing me to her talented husband and allowing me take up his time to work out the kinks in rewriting *Destination D*.

My friend, Shawn Evans Mitchell, for encouraging me in more ways than she'll probably ever realize. I admire your wisdom, journalistic skills, and, most of all, your friendship.

My friend and Spelman sister, Florence Greer, for being the first person to buy my book even before it came out. Flo, you are the best, and I really appreciate you!

My homegirl and dear friend, Denise Robinson, who never stopped believing in my talents.

My friend and advisor, Denise Whiting Pack, for giving me the additional networking resources I needed during a time when I needed to keep things moving. She gave me the encouragement to believe that I could do this.

My publisher, Terri Leidich, of Boutique of Quality Books Publishing Company, for really believing in my story and allowing me to tell it in my own words.

My friend, Gary Yates, who has been there for me through all of my playwriting days and remains one of my biggest supporters. Thank you for your LA agent referral when the manuscript was being considered for a TV series.

My colleague, Sandra Weber, for liking the storyline so much that she gave me an opportunity to pitch *Destination D* as television series for TBS, Inc.

My colleague, Bruce Kirton, for working with Sandra Weber and answering my questions as I went through the TV pitching process.

My coach, Chandra Russell, for encouraging me and instilling in me that anything is possible if I believe.

And I definitely have to mention Margaret Fernandez, Esq.; Loretta Lyle, PhD; Lencola Sullivan-Verseveldt; Thonnia Lee; Angela Benson; Ivan Yuspeh; and Rico Pena. Some of you were involved in the initial stages of the book and others toward the end. If it has been a while since we have spoken, I wanted you to know that I haven't forgotten how you helped guide me with one or more of the following: editing, character development, advice, or personal referrals. I truly appreciate your time and efforts.

Check-In

Dee sat straight up in the oversized stuffed leather chair with her eyes fixed to the beige coffer ceiling, counting all the quadrangles. With heightened anxiety, her pupils swiftly scanned the room and gravitated toward the floor-to-ceiling windows. Staring back at her was a picturesque view of snow-capped mountains rising just a little higher than the clouds. There lay her comfort zone.

I can do this, she whispered. Her heart thumped so fast she was sure that its reverberation could be seen through her red cashmere sweater that was now sticking to her back from beads of perspiration. *C'mon, Dee you can do this.* And before she knew it, the words tumbled out of her mouth like a toddler taking its first steps.

"I am . . . a . . . li . . . liar, and I can't be trusted. And I wouldn't know what the *truth* looked liked if God himself showed it to me." She held her breath, then gently released it and felt a surge of relief envelop her tall slender body. *There, I said it.* She breathed in again and slowly exhaled. Her large mink brown eyes were now brimming with tears that struggled not to fall.

Dee continued staring out of the window and with a slight turn of her bottom lip, she stammered, "My friends call me Dee. I have a BA in political science from Spelman College and a JD from Columbia University. As a matter of fact, Simon and Garfunkel named a song after me," she said, with an evasive tone that the doctor couldn't tell if she was serious or trying to be funny.

The doctor paused from his note taking. He raised his left eyebrow and curiously leaned forward in anticipation of what she was going to say next. Dee turned both of her lips slightly upward, trying hard to simulate a smile.

"You know the song, 'Bridge Over Troubled Water?'"

He answered with only a nod so he would not interrupt her flow.

"Well, *I'm* that bridge." Her voice cracked slightly as she struggled to speak. Dee anxiously folded her arms across her chest and nervously tapped her fingers as she waited for his response.

The doctor's sapphire blue eyes caught a brief glimpse of her, and she quickly shifted her attention toward the window. Even with all of the tension that was mounting inside of her, somehow his smile felt like a warm blanket that comforted the chill that slowly crept up her spine.

"Why are you smiling at me like that?" Her eyes darted to and from his again.

"Ms. Bridge, I find it quite interesting that the first word you use to describe yourself is 'liar.' You also have a quick wit and sense of humor that I think is quite positive." His voice was as smooth as a gracefully aged Italian Merlot wine. He looked up at her again hoping to gain her eye contact, but she continued to resist.

"That's because it's the truth—and please call me, Deirdre," she said, still in deep thought about the incredulity of her confession.

"Well, Deirdre, that may be, but you have quite a few accomplishments. You're a college graduate, and you have a law degree from one of the most prestigious law schools in the country. There is obviously more to you than just being a liar."

"Yes. One would think."

"How do you feel about taking into consideration an accomplishment you've made each day? You'll probably find there's a lot more positive about your life than you realize. Every day we should learn something we didn't know the previous day."

Dee listened while she got up from the chair to walk over to an opposite window that was so transparent she felt she could reach out and touch the Salt Lake City skyline. Her flawless skin glistened as the morning sun beamed through the window on her cinnamon brown face, placing her a little at ease. The thought that this would be the first of many visits here made it even more difficult to come to grips with just how serious things really had become.

Her fingers trembled as they gently massaged her temples. Too many thoughts had caused her head to throb. *I can't believe that I've gotten the nerve to come . . . and to a psychiatrist's office, for God's sake!* Flying over 2,000 miles to see *this* doctor because she didn't want to take a chance of running into someone she knew back home in Atlanta. It was a bit over the top, even for Dee.

Usually, Dee's outward appearance radiated elegance and charm, and her inner beauty was just as appealing. But today was different. As she gazed out the window, she saw the reflection of a woman who was a mess both inside and out. Each passing day was a reminder that her life was like a kite without a hand to guide its sail. And if she didn't stop the lying, she would never be able to get back on course and—just like a kite—she would be lost forever.

Prepare For Take Off

It was Friday at 11:30 a.m. Thirty minutes before quitting time. Bill McKesson popped his narrow head through Amanda's doorway. Oblivious to his presence, Amanda continued keying in the information from the stack of papers that consumed the majority of her desk. Her fingers clicked away at the computer as Bill pushed his gray bristly eyebrows together and frowned as he strained his eyes to see the small Roman numerals on her clock. He pulled out his wire-rimmed glasses from his jacket pocket and perched them at the top of his nose.

"Amanda, what are you still doing here?" he asked, his voice bold with southern charm.

Amanda jumped. Her chubby arms knocked over some of her paperwork, spilling it onto the floor. "Oh, Mr. McKesson, I didn't see you standing there."

"You still haven't answered my question."

Amanda smiled and looked at Bill sheepishly while she bent to pick up the papers. He had folded his arms deliberately across his chest. His look of discontentment made her feel even guiltier that she had not taken the whole day off instead of just half of it.

Her fingers meticulously organized the piled case files on her desk. "Sir, it's not noon yet."

"Oh, hell! Amanda! What are a few more minutes? Go on and leave. You've certainly earned it," he said, waving his platinum-Rolex–laden wrist toward the doorway. "C'mon Amanda, VAMOOSE!" He motioned his head in the direction of the hallway, shifting his salt-and-pepper toupee a little toward the left.

"Yes, sir!" Amanda nodded as she neatly stacked some more files and returned them to her filing cabinet. Her auburn curls bounced across her face, helping her mask the laughter through pressed lips. "I'll be leaving in about ten more minutes."

"Always here to the bitter end. Just see that you're outta here before noon, today—*please!"* he said, waving a warning finger at her.

Amanda nodded as she thought about how nice it was of him to stop by. Bill knew how often she stayed late, and that was thanks to one particularly shrewd, self-absorbed attorney. But Bill was unlike any attorney that she had ever worked for. He *really* cared about his clients.

Bill interrupted her thoughts and firmly patted Amanda on the shoulder and turned to leave. "Oh, I almost forgot! My wife picked up a little something for Tracey." His age-worn hand fumbled eagerly through the blue lining of his double-breasted suit pocket. He hastily pulled out a small box wrapped in gold foil paper with a jewel tone ribbon neatly tied around it.

"Tell that daughter of yours that we all said congratulations. That's a mighty fine accomplishment," he said placing the gift on her desk.

"Oh, tell Mrs. McKesson she didn't have to do this!" Amanda's smoky gray eyes danced as if she was just handed a personal trophy.

"Oh, yes she did. She does exactly what I tell her to!" They both laughed. Everyone knew that even after thirty-five years of marriage and three grown children, Evelyn McKesson was the boss in the family—not Bill.

"Well, I can tell you that anyone who gets into Hampton University on a full scholarship has made a major accomplishment. And that says a lot about you as well."

Amanda blushed. Her face turned the same scarlet red as her loose fitting floral print polyester dress. "I don't know what to say, Mr. McKesson."

"Oh, go on, Amanda! Have a good time at the party!"

Amanda smiled at the present. Yes, Bill was definitely one of a kind. No wonder he was the highest paid partner in the firm. His charisma alone was worth millions.

"Thank you, sir. I will."

It was 11:45 a.m. and she meticulously began stacking the files and then stopped momentarily to look at her daughter's picture. She briefly remembered when she was her daughter's age. An honor student as well, Amanda also had selected Hampton University as one of her college choices. But that was where her and Tracey's similar paths ended. Amanda picked up her purse and pulled out an old photo that she kept buried in her wallet. It was a reminder of a past that she kept hanging onto, but she knew she needed to let go. She smiled and put the picture back and immediately got back to work.

Reminiscent of a master working a Rubik's cube, Amanda swiftly and skillfully continued to place all of the file folders in alphabetical order in the file drawer behind her. Next, she double-checked her briefcase for the work that she had planned to do over the weekend and eyed the present from Bill that still lay on top of her desk. Not wanting to wrinkle its ribbon, she gently placed it on its side in her briefcase and carefully zipped it up. Amanda looked at the clock again. It was exactly noon. She heaved a sigh of relief. "*Now*, I can leave."

She turned off the lights in her office and pulled the door handle behind her. The telephone rang, breaking her stride. Amanda dutifully re-entered her office, but paused before answering the phone, thinking it might be Tracey checking to make sure she was leaving on time.

"Hello, this is Amanda."

"Hi Amanda, it's me."

No, not you! Amanda scowled at the thought of who was on the other end of the line and rolled her eyes. She wanted to kick herself *hard* for answering the phone. Amanda's face dropped and a cloud seemed to cover her. It was just a matter of time before the sun would drop out of sight and the rain would come pouring down.

She gripped the edge of her desk trying to maintain her disposition. But the sound of that woman's voice on the other end of the phone made her stomach do flips and her voice fell silent.

"Amanda? Are you there?"

"Yes," she whispered, feeling as if someone had just knocked the wind out of her.

"Listen, Judge Ferguson just called to tell me that the two cases in front of ours settled so the whole docket has been moved forward. The court date for the *Johnson v. Tyfish Systems*' case is in two weeks. I need those files that you were working on by the end of the day, today."

"But, I'm leaving early today. Hello, are you there?"

There was silence at the other end of the phone, and then Amanda heard a loud sigh. She knew it was the beginning of her orchestrating a guilt trip.

"I told you last month that I needed to take a half day today because of Tracey's graduation party," Amanda said.

"Yes, I remember," she answered with a hint of bitterness in her voice. Amanda imagined this woman confidently propping her high-heeled Christian Louboutin pumps on her mahogany desk as she always did when she got irritated when the person on the other end of the phone was telling her something she didn't want to hear.

"But I can get it to you by the end of the business day on Monday. Is that all right?"

Agitated, the attorney flung her chair around, abruptly removed her feet from her desk and was now at full stance. "Listen, Amanda, I knew at some point this was going to happen. Don't make us go down this road today, okay? I see resumes come across my desk every day from paralegals that are just itching for the opportunity to work with this law firm. Now, if you can't handle a little extra work load, I can give one of them a call."

"But . . ."

"Gotta go, I have a call coming in. See you at 5:00!" The attorney abruptly slammed the phone in Amanda's ear.

"I can't stay . . . hello?" Click. "She hung up on me!" Amanda stared at the receiver. Her hands trembled as she attempted to place it back in its holder. She looked at the clock: 12:05 p.m. She closed her eyes and ran her fingertips gently up and down the back of her head in hopes that the pain and the thought of that woman would both go away.

I've been planning this party for Tracey for months, and now the day has finally arrived, and it took her all of five minutes to ruin it. She clinched both fists, raised them above her head, and violently shook them as she screamed in silence.

Pamela Madison was the firm's only black female attorney. She'd graduated in the top ten percent of her law class at Columbia University and was known for her intimidating tactics in the law firm as well as in the courtroom.

Pam's reputation preceded her. Moving from a prestigious law firm in Chicago, she quickly learned many effective yet unscrupulous tactics, making her well sought after by several prominent law firms across the country. Sterling, Mathis, and Silverman nabbed her with a lucrative bonus and a six-figure salary that primed her to be the first black female partner in the firm.

Although Pam could be ruthless, you had to admire the singular quality that put her a cut above the rest: Pam knew how to get what she wanted. The problem was that she didn't care who she hurt in the process. She was the first attorney to arrive at the office each morning, and the last to leave every night.

Always poised to strut her credentials confidently, Pam was notorious for un-leveling the playing field with the prosecuting attorney that was going up against her in the courtroom. And once she found the person's weak spot, she was merciless. One case in particular was a widely publicized sexual assault.

Pam had stood next to her client in the courtroom. A small smiled played across her lips. She leered at Allison Hughes, the opposing attorney who was decked out in her finest courtroom attire. Her exquisite tailor-made pantsuit gave the impression that she was at the pinnacle of her game, but Pam knew that Allison was no match for her. In an icy tone, Pam had whispered to Allison, "I hope you're getting plenty of rest, because you're going to be worn out after you *lose* this case."

Allison's face turned colorless. "Excuse me?"

Pam was silent. Her eyes spoke volumes, and she knew Allison got the message. *You heard me. I didn't stutter.*

Allison bit her lip, put on her best poker face, and directed a pensive look toward the judge.

"Judge Hampton, may I approach the bench?" Allison had asked in almost a whisper.

"Yes, Miss Hughes. Is there a problem?"

Pam couldn't help but stifle a laugh as she watched Allison walk pointedly over to the judge. She could tell that Allison was getting more and more worked up by the second.

Pam, on the other hand, had three parts to her courtroom strategy. Number one: Getting the prosecuting attorney rattled before the trial. Unbeknownst to Allison, she had just fallen victim.

Allison shot Pam a deliberate cut of her eyes as she assertively turned to face the judge. "Well, Your Honor, Counselor Madison seems to think that making threatening remarks before my opening argument is going to shake me." Allison waved her finger accusingly in the direction of Pam as she proceeded to tell the judge what Pam had said.

"Is that true, Ms. Madison?"

Pam approached the bench, unfazed by Allison's allegations. A devilish grin spread across her face as she pretended to make peace with Allison.

"On the contrary, Your Honor, I was simply expressing to Counselor Hughes that I hope she had plenty of rest for this case. It's going to be a long one, and I know that she has had some personal difficulties. I was only implying that . . ."

"Implying what? That I *can't* try this case?" Allison had blurted out. The blood vessels in her forehead were making a well-defined V in the middle section of her eyebrows.

"*I* didn't say that," Pam had calmly insisted, knowing that Allison Hughes was as high strung as they came. Recently, rumor had it that Allison's newlywed husband was found in bed with another man. It was just a matter of time before the network got wind that her Fortune 500 executive husband was really a closet homosexual. Pam shuddered at the thought of the embarrassment it would cause Allison. And although Allison was doing everything she could to try and have some sense of normalcy, it was obvious that she was clinging to the edge of a dangerous cliff, and Pam was ready to push her right over it.

"I know your tactics, Counselor, and I will not allow you to intimidate me," Allison said, trying to contain the pent up frustration swelling inside of her. Pam knew at that very moment Allison was teetering on the brink. Any sudden collapse would push her right off this case.

Judge Hampton intervened. "This is a courtroom, and you are both professionals. So let's act like professionals."

Allison tried hard to keep her composure, but the perspiration from her underarms was already making a dark puddle on her light gray blazer. She resumed her position with her client and took a tissue from her briefcase to wipe the perspiration that was now falling profusely from her brow. She smoothed her thick honey-blonde hair back in place and began perusing over her notes, nodding as her client whispered in her ear.

Pam was as smooth as she was alluring. She walked coolly back to her seat with a smirk on her face and gave her client a reassuring wink as she slowly *broke down* her opponent. This was strategy number two.

"Counselor Hughes, will you be giving opening arguments?" asked Judge Hampton.

"No—I mean yes, Your Honor." Pam's sedate green eyes honed in on Allison as if she was putting her in a trance. Allison slowly began to speak, stuttering over her words. "Your Honor . . . Mr. Fielding . . . has . . . uh, been . . . a . . . excuse me, Your Honor."

Allison had looked up at Pam and scanned the room with her eyes, as if she was lost. She picked up the glass of water that was sitting on her desk, and as she drank, her hands shook, causing the water to trickle down the sides of her mouth.

Perspiration slid from her forehead, landing on her cheeks, and down her neck to her silk blouse. Allison removed her suit jacket, unaware that her undergarments could be seen through her soaked blouse.

Pam had carefully observed the scene unfolding before her. Her intimidating gaze distracted Allison so much that she forgot her opening arguments altogether.

Judge Hampton frowned. "Ms. Hughes, are you all right?"

"I'm sorry, but I'm just really warm . . ."

"Court will be in recess for five minutes. Ms. Hughes, I want to see you in my chambers."

Allison's body language was that of a clumsy moth that had accidentally flown too close to a spider's web. She'd attempted to catch a glimpse of her client's eye to reassure him that she was still in control, but Pam could tell that it was too late. She had already lost his confidence and it was evidenced by the defeated looked on his face.

This was the grand and final strategy, number three. Pam's plan was working better than she had expected. It was obvious that Allison was incapable of trying this case. Furthermore, Pam knew that it would take a while to get the case reassigned to another attorney, and this would give her even more time to plan a new strategy. Pam looked at her client again, and gave another assuring wink while Allison's client sat looming in regret and fear.

Although Pam stood only 5'4" tall, in the courtroom, she was a titan with fifty-four trials under her belt. She had never lost a case, and that one appeared to be no exception.

Rough Air

Dee climbed into the hotel van and said, "I'm really getting a bad feeling about this trip."

"Dee, you've been getting some bad vibes for a while now," Birdie answered back.

"Yeah," Jodie chimed in. "Maybe you need to take some time off."

Birdie turned and nodded at Jodie. "You may be suffering from burnout. And we all know how that goes."

"Sure do," Jodie laughed. "Whenever I feel a case of burnout firing up, I immediately take three days off, whether it's calling in sick or just moving a trip around so I can go lay on the beach for some simple R and R. I come back ready for my next trip, and I'm good to go."

Oh, but I'm way past the burnout stage. Well, well past it, Dee thought. A faraway look appeared in her eyes as she watched the snow-capped mountains appear larger as they neared the airport. A tear slid down her face, and she swiftly wiped it away, hoping no one could see her agony.

Birdie looked over at Dee and noticed how unusually quiet she was. They had been flying trips together for the past two weeks; it seemed as if every time they headed back to the airport, Dee grew very solemn.

"Dee, are you all right?"

No, I'm not all right. I'm tired of living out of a suitcase for three days. I'm tired of the dumb questions passengers seem to come up with all of the time, and most of all, I'm tired of this smelly uniform and having to be with all of you every week!

Dee cleared her throat. "Yes, I'm fine," The last thing she needed was to let them know what she was really thinking. Unless she wanted her business to hang out on the line, she couldn't tell another flight attendant how she was really feeling.

"Look at those mountains!" the pilot shouted. "They're even beautiful in the dark. I think I'm coming back here next week to do some skiing."

"That sounds like a great idea, Mike. Dee, are you back on this line again next week, too?" Jodie asked. Dee stayed wrapped inside her own world and continued staring out of the window as Jodie tapped her on the shoulder.

"Hey, Dee, did you hear me?"

"I'm sorry, what did you say?"

"Are you on this trip again next week?"

"Um . . . I don't know. I can't remember my schedule. I might have swapped it for a turnaround."

"Hey, why go up and back in the same day when you can layover for three days?" Jodie giggled. Her perkiness was starting to get on Dee's nerves.

"Sometimes, I just need to get back the same day, you know? I just need to get this over with," she mumbled under her breath.

Impatient passengers crowded around the ticket counter in the gatehouse waiting to see if their names could be added to the standby list on the flight from Salt Lake City to Atlanta, and on to Miami. The flight was sold out, and several people were hedging bets on how many people would have to watch the plane take off without them. The people with confirmed reservations were seated, calmly reading newspapers while others made pallets of luggage on the floor, preparing for a long night at the gate.

Once the boarding began, passengers clutched their tickets as if they were holding the winning numbers in the state lottery. When their row numbers were called, they scurried on board as if prize money was being given away.

On the plane, seas of navy blue blankets were cast across the seats. Several passengers immersed themselves in them and drifted to sleep. The plane was silent except for a group of college students sitting in the back of the plane. One of them was a freckle-faced young man with auburn hair. He was wailing loudly to Jay-Z playing on his earphones.

"Shhh! Would you please keep your voice down?" Jodie said, in a gentle yet firm voice. Her charcoal ponytail swayed between her shoulder blades as she briskly walked by. "You're going to wake the other passengers," she scolded.

"What'd you say?" Jackson asked at the top of his voice. His bright red hair and clean-shaven freckled face made him look too young to be up at this early hour.

There were two girls seated on either side of him. The girl on the right giggled as she pulled one of the earphones out of his ear and whispered loudly in it. "She said to keep it down, you wannabe 50 Cent!"

"In other words, shut up with the singing. You're being a nuisance to the other people on the plane," the younger-looking girl on the right snapped back.

Both girls were wearing Hampton University sweatshirts and looked young enough to still be in junior high school, especially the girl with the chestnut hair and slanted eyes. She was seated on his left and wore braces and small wire-rimmed glasses. The girl on the right looked a little older. Her dark wavy hair was tied up in a blue scrunchie. Her complexion was a smooth mocha brown with little need for make-up.

Jodie rolled her eyes at him as she strolled past to check on the front of the cabin. Jackson mouthed "sorry" and nodded that he would comply.

Dee tried to get comfortable, but after two hours, it was impossible. If there was one thing she disliked more than being a flight attendant, it was a long flight. Either you stayed busy the whole time or you did nothing the whole time. Dee decided she preferred neither as she began strolling down the aisles. She paced up one side of the middle cabin and back down the other, purposefully avoiding the back cabin. The exercise kept her from falling asleep. A flight attendant call button finally broke the monotony. *Great, something to do,* she mumbled bitterly under her breath as she walked toward the light.

"May I help you, ma'am?"

An old woman looked up at her and smiled. "Yes, dear. Can you tell me where we are now?"

The ludicrous questions had already started, and they were only halfway through the flight. Dee liked to call these questions "101 ways to *not* get a flight attendant to *ever* answer your call button or a.k.a. The Dumb List," because people were always *dumb* enough to ask flight attendants questions like that. In her mind she would answer: *How do I know where we are? I'm 30,000 feet in the air just like you. What do I look like? A walking compass?* But instead she answered, "I'm not quite sure. The pilot will be making an announcement shortly."

The old lady nodded in satisfaction and patted Dee on the shoulder. Her frail fingers could barely hold up the five carat ruby ring on her fourth finger.

Dee rolled her eyes hard as she walked toward the front of the airplane. She was careful not to trip over one man's foot that had made its way into the aisle while he lay sleeping. *If you don't get those big boats out of this aisle . . . Man, I wish I had a dollar for everyone over 6'3" who does this. I should just pop his feet one good time with the beverage cart. It would serve him right for not putting his long cheap behind in a first-class seat!*

"Ladies and gentlemen, we are about forty-five minutes outside of Atlanta," the pilot announced over the intercom. "We are expecting some tail winds, which may put us in a little earlier than the ETA. So, just sit back, relax, and let Atlanta's finest flight crew assist you with having an enjoyable flight." Dee winked at the elderly lady whose destination question had just been answered. Dee was happy to hear that they were so close to landing because she couldn't wait to get off.

The passengers stirred a bit. Their arms stretched out of blankets and eyes fluttered as they gradually began to wake up. Jodie and Birdie started moving the beverage carts toward the galleys in preparation for landing. Suddenly, out of nowhere, a jolt smacked the plane. The outside force was so unsettling that it tossed the plane about like nunchucks being used for the first time by a martial arts amateur.

Jackson's head plunged into the back of his seat. His arms flailed in the air, hitting his face and causing his earphones and MP3 player to plummet to the floor. The girls that were seated next to him were no longer giggling, but had turned pale from horror as the plane bobbed and weaved.

"Ladies, and gentleman, this is your captain speaking, we have just hit a patch of rough air. We are working with flight control to get us into some smooth air, but it may be a little bumpy for a few more minutes. I want the passengers and the flight attendants to remain seated with your seat belts securely fastened."

"Oh, you don't have to tell me twice," Dee said as she turned to rush back toward her seat. But before the pilot could finish his sentence, one of the beverage carts came hurtling down the aisle, charging in the direction of the man's foot that had been sticking out. He had managed to stay asleep while the other passengers numbed themselves into a glazed state of denial. Dee saw the cart and ran after it. She caught it by its handle with the tips of her fingers and reeled it in toward her palms and clutched her fingers around it.

"Oh, my God! That was a close one!" She wiped the pellets of perspiration off of her forehead with her sleeve, and the plane jerked again. The 70-pound cart began to slip out of her grasp and was inches away from crashing into the man's foot. "Hey, wake up, mister!" Dee yelled. "Hey, can somebody please wake this guy up? I can't let this cart—oh no!" she mumbled breathlessly, trying not to frighten the passengers who were now searching Dee's face for some symbol of protection. She stretched out her long legs and hunted for the brake with her foot.

"Uggg, pl-please . . . just let me stop this from . . . going into this man's foot," she prayed and within seconds, she found the brake and pressed it down.

The passenger awoke just in time to picture his foot being snapped off by the weight of the cart. Dee looked at him and shook her head in disbelief. *Okay, now you wake up.* "That was a close one, huh? Glad we were able to save that foot!" Dee said as she let out a fake smile. *You idiot!*

As the plane continued to jostle back and forth, Dee became exhausted, but her adrenaline allowed her to pull the cart back up the aisle and into the galley with the help of Birdie. *I knew I had a bad feeling about this flight.*

"Thanks, Birdie," Dee said, panting like a novice runner.

"Can you believe this turbulence?" Birdie asked with a petrified look on her face.

"See, I told you I had a bad feeling about this!" Dee was still trying to catch her breath while she latched the cart back in its holding place.

"Yes, you did, didn't you?" Birdie said, as she immediately sat down. "I don't *ever* remember being in anything like this."

Birdie had been flying for more than thirty years and usually flew international trips. But this month she'd decided she wanted a change in routine and flew domestic instead. Little did she know that this might be the flight that would help her finalize her decision to retire.

Dee heard whimpering coming from the back of the plane as she sat down and buckled her seat belt. *What now?* She turned around as the whimpering became louder. *No, I don't want to do this, but . . .* Dee thought to herself as she unbuckled her seat belt.

"Dee, what are you doing?" Birdie asked.

"Unfortunately, I'm going to have to get up and try and talk to that passenger. The last thing we need is to have the person freak out the other passengers and cause total pandemonium on the plane."

"Be careful, Dee."

Dee looked at Birdie out of the corner of her eye and mumbled to herself, "So you say as you sit *securely fastened* in *your* seat belt." Dee managed to maneuver her way over to the college students and placed her hand gently on the girl's shoulder in an attempt to console her. The young girl was crying so hard that she was choking on her tears. Her friend seated next to her had pulled the blanket over her head, and all Dee could see was a formation of a body trembling in the blankets.

"Don't worry, the pilot will find some smooth air soon and everything will be all right."

Recognizing Dee's voice immediately, the girl quickly peeked out of her blanket and looked up at her. She grabbed Dee's hand as if it were her only lifeline.

"Tracey! Oh my God . . ." Dee shouted, as the plane tussled some more. Dee held fast to the back of her seat with one hand, while Tracey tightened her grip on Dee's other hand. Before Tracey could respond to Dee calling her name, Jodie's fretful voice interrupted her.

"Dee, take your seat, now!" Jodie shouted from her jump seat. The other students' faces looked even more disturbing as Tracey's moist gray eyes pleaded with Dee's not to leave them alone.

"It will be okay, really, it's just a little rough air," Dee said, trying to sound convincing enough to believe it *herself.* The plane unexpectedly dropped down and Dee fell to her knees causing her hand to unleash from Tracey's. The plane shook even harder. *This is definitely more than a little rough air,* Dee thought. "Hey, Tracey, you and your friend just remain calm. I've *got* to get back to my jump seat." Dee looked composed, but was just as frightened as everyone else.

Dee gripped the frayed carpet with her hands and knees as she took tortoise steps up the aisle toward her seat. Small droplets of perspiration trickled down her forehead and trailed down her neck and chest, causing her white cotton blouse to stick to her. For every move she made forward, it seemed like the turbulence caused her to take two steps backward.

"It's going to be fine, Dee. Just a few more inches . . ." Jodie encouraged.

"Grab my hand!" shouted Birdie as she tried to reach for Dee's hand.

"Oh my God! Birdie, I can't!"

The plane took another dive and she lost her grip, causing her to fall back down to the floor and bump her head at the base of a cabin seat. Still a little dazed from her fall, she closed her eyes and slowly moved her head around to regain her composure. When she opened her eyes, she saw the plane was filled with a morbid silence and the smell of fear permeated the air. Now there wasn't a sleeping eye in the entire cabin.

Her heart pounded louder. And just when she was about to lose faith in her own calming words that she had said to the college students, the man whose foot she had saved struggled to make his way up the aisle toward her. The force was pulling him back so hard that he had to grab onto the back of each seat to keep his balance. When he finally made his way to her, he reached out and took her hand and lifted her off of the floor.

"Th-thank you, sir," she said, rubbing her head.

"One good turn deserves another," he replied shakily while holding onto the seat back. His dark eyes kept rapidly moving back and forth as if he wasn't sure what direction he should take. The jerky movements of the plane bounced him up and down, making him look like a neatly dressed pogo stick on top of a pair of stilts.

"How's your head?"

Hopefully, it's a concussion so I can forget about this nightmare and take some time off. "Just a little bump. Nothing serious, though."

"You may need to get it looked at, just to make sure." Suddenly the bumpiness came to a sudden halt, and the plane started to ascend.

"Ladies and gentleman, this is Captain Douglas. I apologize for that bumpy ride. We ran into a few unanticipated storm clouds. They've moved to the north and we anticipate smooth flying from here on out . . ."

"Like I was saying . . . I'll be fine," Dee said, as a look of relief spread across her face and her voice returned to normal.

"Flight attendants, prepare the cabin for landing." The captain's voice rang loudly through the intercom.

"Well, that's my cue, you better get back to your seat," Dee said as she tried to manage a warm smile. *Other than the fact that he could probably sleep through a tornado, he seems like a nice guy,* Dee thought as he smiled back at her.

Now that the flight was about to land, Dee didn't miss a beat as she walked down the aisles checking seat backs and collecting empty cups. She made her way back to the college students who also had a tremendous look of gratefulness. Tracey had already unbuckled her seat belt and was getting up. "Auntie Dee! Thank you." Dee pointed to the seat belt sign and winked.

"Oops! I'm sorry."

"One thrown flight attendant is enough." Dee laughed. "Your mother would have a fit if you got hurt—and especially on one of my flights!"

Tracey's face became a little flush from embarrassment. "I know."

"What were you doing in Salt Lake City?"

"Mimi has an aunt who lives out there," she said, pointing to her friend sitting next to her. "We just hung out with her aunt for a few days. Mimi, this is my Auntie Dee."

"This is your aunt? Miss Dee, thank you."

"No need to thank me, Mimi. I'm just glad you are okay."

"And that's our friend Jackson," Tracey said, pointing to the young man with the MP3 player.

"Yeah, nice meeting you, and thank you. We didn't know what hit us," Jackson chimed in as he pulled his headphones out from underneath his seat.

"See, I told you everything would be fine," Dee said, relieved that everything really *did* work out okay.

"Now, you know that since we're landing you can't play that—"

"Don't worry, ma'am. I've learned my lesson. It's going in my carry-on."

"Auntie Dee," Tracey interrupted, "do you think you'll have some time to talk when we land?"

"I'm headed onto Miami after we land, but I'll be back in Atlanta in three days. Why don't you give me a call or text me, so we can catch up, okay?"

Tracey let out a long sigh. "Okay."

Dee smiled, but she could see there was something pressing on Tracey's mind. She glanced out of the window and saw the plane headed for touchdown and rushed back to her jump seat. When she sat down, she started thinking about her session with her doctor. Just like a rerun of a bad movie, his voice played over and over again in her head: *I should look at my job as being important. I have to feel proud of my accomplishments and my chosen field. Okay, here goes: I am proud to have helped some distressed people feel more comfortable today, and I am proud to have prevented someone from having a severe leg injury.* She took a long deep breath and closed her eyes. *And the lesson that I learned today: I've got to find another occupation—and soon!*

Clear Skies

After finally reaching Miami, a Renaissance Hotel van pulled up in front of the airport and all eight crewmembers loaded their luggage on top of the luggage racks and settled back into the high-back jade green leather seats. When they arrived at the hotel, there was a crew sign-in sheet at the front desk with everyone's room number. After the crew signed in, the hotel representative gave each person a small white envelope with a key card inside.

"Dee, what floor are you on?" asked Doug, one of the pilots who immediately noticed she was not moving off with the rest of the crew to the fifth floor.

Dee nonchalantly looked down at the room number on her envelope. "Um, it looks like I'm on the twenty-fifth floor."

"It's strange that they would put you so far up from the rest of the crew," Jodie replied apprehensively.

"Maybe they just ran out of rooms. I'll be fine." *Hey, after a day like today, they could put me on the roof just as long as I'm not on anybody's airplane.*

"Will we see you at dinner tonight?" Birdie asked with the same tone of concern.

"Hey, I'm a big girl. Really . . . I'll be fine. Listen, I'm really beat. I'll see you at check-out in the morning, okay?" Dee said, putting on her best reassuring smile.

Jodie finally relented. "Okay, I'll call to check on you later to see how you're feeling. And by the way, don't worry, I wrote an incident report about you bumping your head. I'll turn it in to your supervisor when we get back to Atlanta."

"Thanks, but I'll be fine. Really. Goodnight." Dee waved goodbye until the elevator doors closed. She leaned leisurely back against the elevator rail and rode it for the next twenty floors. Once she got off, she walked down a long winding hallway and saw that her room was in a flight attendant's dream location—tucked away in a corner far away from a raucous icemaker and the relentless opening and closing of an elevator door.

As she slid her key card into the door slot, she grinned at the thought of how she lucked out on the hotel running out of rooms. Her grin turned into a quiet gasp as she stared in awe of the room's beauty. This was a slice of heaven, and she quickly forgot about her plane ride from hell.

"I don't believe this!" she said, as she rolled her suitcase through the doorway and closed the door. The suite was decorated with traditional mahogany furniture. Dee strolled through the living room that was decorated in beautiful hues of jade, salmon pink, and ivory. An eggshell white sofa sat in front of the stacked stone fireplace. Its pencil thin stripes matched the salmon-colored walls. The sofa's clawed feet were identical to the ones on the round end tables sitting on both sides of the sofa.

In the bedroom, there was a four-poster king-size bed accented with a lovely jade satin bedspread that cascaded to the floor. The bed stood three feet above the ground and came with its own three-step wooden stool. Across from the bed, a thirty-two-inch flat screen television was enclosed inside a striking armoire unit. Its panels were etched with intricate carvings of palm trees.

A fully equipped kitchenette with white granite countertops and a mini-bar sat discreetly on one side of the suite. The bathroom was Dee's favorite. A double vanity sink with brushed metal faucets and a dual towel warming rack was located across from the marble sunken Jacuzzi tub. There was also an eighteen-inch flat screen TV that hung from the ceiling. Behind the bathroom door hung a beautiful blue velvet monogrammed robe that looked comfortable enough to spread onto the floor and use as a coverlet in front of the fireplace.

She could hear the faint sounds of her favorite neo-soul artist, Maxwell, wafting throughout the suite. She followed his pleasing melody out to a private balcony located just outside the French doors of her bedroom.

"This view is breathtaking. If my crew could see this, they would no longer *worry* about me; they'd be *envious* of me!" Dee laughed as she pictured herself calling them up to join *her* for dinner in her lavish suite. She would pay for a full price airline ticket just to see the look on their faces.

Dee sat down at the small patio table for two and marveled at the spectacular view of the Atlantic Ocean. She was in awe looking at the crystal blue waves casually drifting back and forth on the sand. A quiet sea breeze tap-danced across her face and down to her tired muscles. She felt her muscles relax as she laid her head back on the chair and soon she was dozing.

The morning rush hour traffic twenty-five floors below was nonexistent as the faint sound of a buzzer disturbed Dee's tranquility. "Where in the world is that buzzing coming from?" Dee awakened out of her peaceful slumber and realized that the sound was coming from the phone in her room. "I told them I would be fine!" she said, as she went inside to answer it. "Now, what? Hello, Jodie?"

"No, this is not Jodie. Try again, Desiree," the sexy baritone voice answered back.

"Oh my, goodness! Chris?"

"What other man would know your room number?" Chris teased, pretending to be jealous.

"Just you, baby, but . . ."

"What time did you get in?"

"Just a few minutes ago."

"But, how'd you know . . . I mean . . . I didn't tell you . . ."

"Slow, down girl, first things first. How'd you like my gift?"

"You bought me something, but where is it?" Dee asked while her eyes scanned the room.

"You're standing in it!"

"Standing in . . . oh my! Chris, that was you?"

"You like it?"

"Do I like it? I love it. I should have known that you had something to do with this romantic view and exquisite suite."

"Nothing but the best for my baby. See, you already forgot that you told me you were flying into town today for a meeting. And I know you stay at the same hotel every time you come to Miami. So, it wasn't hard to figure out."

"You devil!"

"Yeah, I want to be *one* with you. What time can I come over?" Chris whispered seductively.

"Ahhh . . . I'm looking at my watch now, how about an hour?"

"Too long, baby, I'll be there in thirty minutes," Chris purred before she could answer.

"Ah, okay, I can't wait to see you, either," Dee said, chuckling into the dead receiver.

Chris Dickerson was Dee's Miami lover. He was a linebacker for the Miami Dolphins and had a $5.2 million contract. Although he scored high in charisma and looks, her lover lost points when it came to intellect. Nevertheless, his extremely sexy style and the way he made Dee feel in bed dropped his brain to secondary importance.

Just the sound of Chris's voice made Dee quiver. His voice was so deep, mellow, and smooth that it made the late Barry White's voice sound like a canary. Chris couldn't walk into the same room without Dee wanting him to take command of her body and make love to her. His small, dark eyes could take control of her, and his lashes were long, especially for a man with a 6'4" 225-pound frame. The smoothness of his bronze skin gave the appearance that it had never been introduced to a razor, and his upper body was cut like a middleweight wrestler. His physique began with six-pack abs and ended with firmly sculpted buttocks and solid, muscular thighs.

Dee met Chris six months ago when they were seated in first class on a flight from Atlanta to Miami. She was elegantly dressed in a stunning blue Ralph Lauren silk wrap dress. Chris looked very stylish in a short sleeve black Polo shirt, emphasizing his bulging muscles that were resting on the shared armrest between them. His straight cut Levis fit his thighs and butt perfectly. He politely asked the lady sitting next to Dee if she would exchange her aisle seat with his. She obliged, and Dee and Chris talked for the entire flight.

"So, do you always look this beautiful when you travel, or are you going someplace special?" Chris asked as he flashed his impeccably straight white teeth in a teasing grin.

"Yes, I always look this beautiful," Dee grinned. "*And* I'm going to a wedding."

"I hope you are not the bride-to-be."

This guy is too smooth for words, Dee thought. "The bride is a good friend of mine."

"Whoo! That's a relief." Her seatmate flashed his pearly Chiclet teeth again and held his brawny hands playfully to his heart.

"Very funny! So, where are you going once you land?" Dee asked, secretly hoping that they could meet again while she was in Miami.

"To work."

"I see," Dee said trying not to sound too nosy as she coyly glanced at her watch. "Well, it's a little late to be starting a work day unless you're working a third shift."

"Well, let's just say that sometimes I have to work late, and then there are other times when I have to go in a little early."

Dee had recognized the famous football player as soon as he entered the jet. She was intrigued by the thought that he wasn't arrogant, and he didn't start their conversation by bragging about his job like a lot of other professional football players she knew. Dee was flattered at the idea of *him* wanting to get to know more about *her*.

Chris's eyes ran the length of Dee, taking in every curve and every bit of her delicate beauty from head to toe. "So, now that you know my work schedule, what is yours like?"

"Same holds true with me. Sometimes I work late and sometimes I work early," she teased back.

"*Touché*!" he said, as he lifted his water glass and took a sip. His smile was so irresistible that she momentarily pictured herself caressing his lips with hers. And for a moment, he looked as if he was thinking the same thing, too.

"Excuse me, sir," interrupted a short, stocky flight attendant. She had managed to maneuver her way from the rear of the airplane to first class. She did her best to lean over gracefully and gently whisper in his ear. "Aren't you Chris Dickerson with the Miami Dolphins?"

Chris looked a little embarrassed as Dee gave him one of her "you got busted" looks.

"Guilty as charged," he said, politely.

"Well, I hate to bother you, but my little boy is a huge fan of yours, and I was wondering if you would sign an autograph for him?"

"Sure, I'd be glad to." The flight attendant's face lit up like a child's on Christmas morning as her brown stubby fingers handed him a pen and a piece of paper.

"What's your son's name?" Chris asked as he neatly wrote his signature.

"Michael Canton," she said breathing deeply while trying hard to keep her eyes from roving all over him. She extended her hand flirtatiously, "And *I'm* Barbara."

"Well, it's nice to meet you, *Barbara*," he said, shaking her hand and handing her his autograph.

"Thanks so much."

"No problem."

"May I get you anything?"

"Bottled water will be fine."

She turned to Dee unenthusiastically, faking a half-hearted smile. "And you?"

"I'm fine, thanks," Dee responded politely as she watched the woman walk back to the galley. She was so relieved Barbara didn't know her.

"So, Mr. Dickerson with the Miami Dolphins . . ."

Chris interrupted before she could finish her sentence. "All right, you got me. I apologize. It's just that I didn't want to, you know."

"Know what?"

"Didn't want you to think . . ."

"Think?"

"Okay, you're not going to give a guy a break, are you? Please, let's just start over."

Dee gave him the once-over and was about to read him like a best-selling novel until she stared into his gentle eyes. Barbara walked back over and poured water for Chris into an ice-filled glass.

"If there is anything else I can get you, Mr. Dickerson, please don't hesitate to call me," she smiled seductively.

"Thank you."

Barbara glanced again at Dee and gave her a stiff smile as she returned to the main cabin. Dee shook her head and chuckled under her breath at her immature behavior.

"So, as I was saying, before we were interrupted," Chris joked as he raised his bottled water in salute. "I'm Chris Dickerson, and I'm very glad to be sitting here with you. Would you mind telling me your name?"

Damn, he's good. "Desiree Bradshaw," Dee lied, coming up fast with a pseudo name while trying to sound indifferent, but not too forgiving.

"Desiree Bradshaw . . . Desiree Bradshaw . . . hmmm . . . Ms. D." The richness of his voice made her feel as if she had just been crowned the Duchess of York. However, she wasn't ready to let him off the hook that easily.

"My *friends* call me that."

"What . . . D?"

"Yes," she said coolly, as if he was being too presumptuous.

Chris decided to change the subject. "So, *Desiree*, how long will *you* be in Miami?"

"Just overnight. I have to fly back again in time for a conference." *Oops! I'm doing it again.*

"A conference, huh?"

Oh, please don't ask.

"Would you mind my asking you what type of conference?"

I knew it! She already regretted her lies. "Why do you ask?"

"Well, depending on what type of conference it is, I was thinking that I could meet you there."

"My, my, my . . . aren't we feeling overly confident?" Dee teased, loving every minute of the thought.

"No, not really, I was just hoping you would let me see you again."

"Hmmm, I'll think about it."

Chris glanced at his watch. "Well, based on our estimated time of arrival, you have about thirty minutes," he said, flashing his beautiful ivories again.

"I don't know; I may need more time to make my decision," Dee quipped.

The pilot's voice came over the loudspeaker. "Flight attendants, please prepare the cabin for landing." They both raised their seatbacks and put up their trays as the flight attendants began walking through the aisles.

"Fifteen more minutes, Miss Bradshaw," Chris said, trying hard to sound serious as he added more bass to his already baritone voice.

Dee laughed. "All right. All right. I'm going to a lawyer's conference, but I won't have much time to socialize."

"I see, an attorney who is strictly business."

"No, that's not it," Dee said as she breathed deeply, detesting herself even more for what she was doing. "I mean, I just don't want you to travel somewhere to meet me if I won't have time to spend with you."

As usual, Dee managed to justify her lying. After all, she *did* have a law degree. And although she had not gotten her nerve up yet to take the bar—that *small* factor was only a mere technicality.

"Okay, I can appreciate that," Chris said sounding somewhat disappointed in Dee's subtle rejection and turned to look out of his window.

Dee could see the defeated look on his face and did not want him to think for a minute that she meant that they could not see each other from time to time when she was in Miami. The flaps of the plane began to go down. Dee knew she needed to come up with something quick and clever, or else her chances of ever being up close and personal again with this incredible man would be slim-to-none.

Thinking fast, she discreetly unfastened her purse, and as if she had timed it perfectly, the plane landed with the contents of it conveniently falling in his lap.

"Oh, I am *so* sorry," Dee said as she began to gather up her belongings, all the while praying that he would notice the wedding invitation with the directions to her hotel sitting in the corner of his seat.

As the plane stopped, the passengers began to gather their luggage. Chris looked back at his seat to make sure he had retrieved his belongings. "Hey, Desiree, I think this belongs to you," he said, examining the invitation and innocently handing it to her.

"Oh thanks! I don't know what I would have done if I'd lost this. I'd have no idea on how to get to my hotel without them."

"Is someone picking you up at the airport?"

Excellent, Dee thought. *He fell hook, line, and sinker.* "No, I told my friend I would just catch a cab."

"Would you like for me to take you there? I mean, if that's not being too presumptuous. It's on my way home."

Of course I want you to take me to my hotel. And if you act right, I might even invite you up to my room for a special treat. And if you are a real good boy, I might give you a taste. Dee smiled seductively at his offer.

"Well, if you're sure it's not too much trouble."

"It would be my pleasure."

"All right then. I'll take you up on your offer."

Now, six months later, they were still seeing each other, and he was *still* clueless about her real identity. As she hung up with Chris, Dee's psychiatrist's voice rumbled in her head like a storm cloud about to burst open and rain on her charade. "*There is more to you then just being a liar; you are very accomplished." Easy for him to say*, she thought. *This is not the right time for me to come clean, especially not today. If Chris knew what I really did for a living, it would instantly change how he feels about me. I'm sure of it.*

Dee began rummaging through her suitcase and selected a provocative black-laced nightgown trimmed with black pearls. Matching thong panties completed the look. *This will definitely ensure a replay of the last time when we never set foot outside my hotel room.*

A loud knock cut her thoughts short and she nervously looked at her watch. "It can't be thirty minutes already!" She ran to the door with great anticipation and saw a distorted image of Chris's good looks through her peephole. "I'll be right there!" she yelled as she made a mad dash to the bathroom and flung off her uniform and undergarments. She stuffed them into a plastic bag and tossed them underneath the bed. In her haste, she ripped her stockings and pitched them in the trashcan.

Next, she grabbed her work shoes, threw them into her suitcase, and shoved them underneath the bed. She removed the velvet robe from the hook on the bathroom door and draped it sensuously over her naked body, exposing her shoulders. She pulled the rubber band holding her ponytail and let her golden brown tresses free fall off her bare shoulders, then shook her head from side to side. A sinful little smile cast across her lips as Dee carefully surveyed the room, making extra sure there was no airline paraphernalia in view. Becoming Desiree once again, Dee whispered, "Now, let the good times roll . . ."

Early Departure

Amanda twisted her hands together until they were sore. Her nails were bitten down to the quick, and her vision was blurred from the tears welling in her eyes. She traced her finger around the gold leaf frame holding her daughter's picture and laid it face down. A single tear ran down her cheek and hit the back of the frame's cardboard, staining it miserably.

"I can't believe my baby's graduation party is tonight and I have to work late again," she sniffled, trying not to break down completely as the phone began to ring.

"Hello, this is Amanda," she said, clearing her throat.

"Hi, Mama, I'm baaaaack!"

Oh God, not now . . . Tracey will never forgive me. Amanda's hands began to shake, and the receiver twitched in her hand as she tried unsuccessfully to maintain control. She strained to sound upbeat. "Hi, baby, I was just thinking about you."

"Mama, is everything all right?"

"How was your trip?"

"Great! Salt Lake City has the most gorgeous mountains! We had some really bad turbulence on the flight back home, but Auntie Dee was working the flight, so she looked out for us. "

"Dee? What a coincidence. Dee and I haven't spoken in a while."

"I know."

"Did Melvin call?" Amanda's tears streamed steadily down her face as she made a valiant effort to change the subject.

"That's why I was calling. He said he wanted to make sure you had the light fixtures for the basement."

"That was on my to-do list to pick up today when I left from work."

"Well, the basement looks great!" Tracey said, trying to gauge her mother's reaction.

Amanda wiped the tears from her eyes. "Yes, Melvin and his crew did a great job in finishing it."

"And right before the party, too! So, what time should I tell Melvin to meet you here?"

Amanda looked at the clock. It was almost one, and she had no idea when she was going to finish the documents that Pam wanted. Her voice became solemn. "Tell Melvin I'll call him."

"You don't sound like yourself, Mama."

Amanda felt nauseous and needed a drink of water. "Hold on, baby." She wiped her eyes again and took a tissue from her briefcase and blew her nose. Before stepping out of her doorway, Amanda looked around to make sure there was no one around to see her in her miserable state. She walked briskly down the hall, dabbing her eyes while pretending something was in them. Finally, she reached the water cooler and chugged five cups of water before she felt like she could walk back to her office and speak with Tracey. When she regained some composure, Amanda picked up the phone.

"Tracey, are you still there?"

"Yes, Mama. You were about to tell me what was the matter."

"Well now, it's nothing . . . just something I needed to handle at work."

"Mama, no . . . not again. You promised!" Tracey cried out, knowing good and well where this conversation was leading.

The last thing Amanda wanted to do was break her promise. The relationship she and Tracey shared had become inexplicably strained over the last few months, and she wanted to have the party to celebrate her daughter's accomplishments and hopefully bring them close again. She hoped Tracey's road trip with her friends would bring her back more relaxed.

"I know, Tracey, but . . ."

Tracey's voice quivered as she tried to force back her own tears. "Oh, Mama, I can't talk about this right now, okay? I'm going out for a little while."

Here she goes again with her evasiveness. "I understand, baby, I do. Where are you going? You just got back in town!"

"I just need to get some air. That's all, Mama," Tracey sniffled.

Why does she do this every time we talk lately? I'm too upset right now to get into this with her. "I'll see you when you get home." Amanda's voice was barely audible.

"Bye, Mama."

Amanda held the receiver to her ear until the phone went dead. Tracey's elusiveness was killing her. Feeling mentally drained and powerless, she gently placed the receiver back in its holder and walked over to close the door, then sat down to gain strength. The flood of tears that had been building up was now flowing freely as Amanda sobbed uncontrollably.

"I've got to pull myself together," Amanda whispered as her voice started to crack. She wiped tears from her face and made an attempt to smooth her unruly locks and straighten her dress. Moving sluggishly to her desk, she unpacked her briefcase and began to work on the attorney's case.

It was 3:15 p.m., and Amanda was still at her desk finalizing everything for *that woman*. Pam Madison. Ugh. It was as if she always had something to prove. How could such an intelligent woman be so effortlessly bitter and hateful toward people all of the time? No wonder she was still single.

Everyone in the firm knew that Pam Madison's ultimate goal was to become the first black female partner at the law firm. The case that Amanda was working on just might be the one to get her there. The client was Titus Johnson, the CFO of Tyfish Systems Inc. The board of his company was accusing him of misappropriation of funds in excess of $15 million. If Pam won this case, it would be a huge coup. As Amanda thought seriously about where Pam's career could be headed, she dreaded the thought of her having even more power. She was already incorrigible. The idea of one more boost to her ego was more than Amanda could bear. *Hmmm, I wonder what would happen if I accidentally left two . . . say, maybe three pages out of this document. The perfect spot would be here, toward the end,* Amanda plotted with herself as she crafted a way to take the exceptionally self-absorbed attorney's blind ambition down a notch or two.

Pam's superior attitude had been wearing on Amanda for some time now, way before Amanda even started working for her. After being her legal assistant for three years, and handling more than forty cases, Amanda still couldn't understand why Pam used intimidation to deliver her point—*especially* with her, of *all* people. Well, Amanda also had a point—a breaking point—and this time it was Amanda's turn to deliver.

Undisclosed Crash Pad

I don't know how much longer I can stand this, you know?" Tracey said as she paced the hardwood floor. Her black high heels sounded like mice scurrying back and forth. She was dressed in a red form-fitting knit dress featuring a small V-neck. She looked every bit of twenty-one instead of the ripe young age of seventeen.

"Just a little while longer and then we'll tell her," he said as he pulled Tracey toward him, bringing her uneasy strides to a standstill. His soft cotton shirt felt good against her face as it rested on his chest. She could hear his heart beating fast and knew that he was just as nervous as she was about their situation. His dark brown pupils were so trusting and confident that he appeared uninhibited on the outside, but just like her, he carried all of his feelings deep inside.

"She's not going to understand. She's too busy working every night to even listen to me," Tracy cried as mascara ran down her cheeks.

"I just want to be honest with her, Tracey. This secret has been going on for too long and she deserves to know," he said as he placed his arms around her, rocking her like a newborn baby.

"I just want to stay just like this. You know? I always feel so comforted by you—so secure. I just don't want anything to spoil what we have."

A long, slow breath came from his mouth, then he lifted Tracey's chin to meet his eyes. "Here, let me get you a tissue." He walked to the bathroom and came back with a tissue and handed it to her. "Let's just give it some time, okay, then maybe we can tell her together," he said, rubbing her shoulders.

Tracey pulled back brusquely, causing her hair to fly wildly in her face. "No way! Together? She'll feel like she's been ambushed!" She started pacing frantically again, blowing her nose to the beat of her steps. "Mama would be so devastated. Besides, I already told you how she feels about you!"

"I know," he said, walking toward the window. He was feeling almost as hopeless as Tracey looked. The rain had just started, sounding like pellets being shot from a BB gun as it hit the windowpane. The noise was distracting at first, but it quickly became no more than an afterthought. After all, the rain would eventually go away. The issue with Amanda would not. "But your mother is a logical woman," he said, trying to sound encouraging as he continued watching the rain, now beating harder.

"Not when it comes to you—believe me! Melvin knows it, too! He eggs her on. He can't stand you, and his attitude just makes it worse."

"Well, that's why they both need to learn the truth. Right?"

Tracey shook her head. "Wrong!" Her pace slowed down as she made her way over to a plush leather chair. She sat down, and her body soon melded into it. Feeling a small sense of comfort, she smoothed her hair out of her face and let it hit the back of the chair as she exhaled.

"I just wish . . ."

"Wish what?"

Tracey was silent. He bent down and sat on the arm of the chair. "Stop! You can't change the past, Tracey. What's done is done. You've got to move past that."

"Well, she hasn't, and from where I'm sitting, it doesn't look like you have either!"

"Look, your mother loves you very much, and she doesn't want to do anything to tear your relationship with each other apart."

"Yes, but if she makes me stop seeing you, then what?"

"Your mother won't."

"But what if . . ."

"She and I will work it out. I promise, Tracey."

"But, so much time has passed already!"

"It doesn't matter," he said reassuringly.

"I just wish it didn't have to be this way." Tracey sounded very despondent.

"What matters is that I love you, Tracey."

"I love you, too," Tracey answered as he wiped the tears from her face. She closed her eyes and laid her head on his knee hoping he was right.

Clear Exit

It was 3:30 p.m., and Pam had just returned from a client meeting. She stepped into the oak-paneled elevator, looked straight up at the mirrored ceiling, and smiled to herself. To her, the mirrors symbolized strength—her strength—and represented every glass ceiling she had to crash through to get to where she was today. She was so close to being a partner at Sterling, Mathis, and Silverman, one of the most prestigious firms in Atlanta, that she could taste it. And the flavor was delicious.

As the elevator reached the fiftieth floor, she inhaled deeply, closed her eyes, and breathed out as a rush of adrenalin flowed through her body. The bold bronze letters spelling out the firm's name were located behind the receptionist's desk. Italian crystal chandeliers hung from the domed ceiling in the marble foyer. Chippendale furniture flanked the waiting area and several expensive paintings hung throughout the corridor, while beautiful Persian rugs warmed the dark-stained parquet floors.

"Good afternoon," Carol Ann, the front receptionist, remarked.

Carol Ann thrived on her position as guardian of the gate. Her stance was upright and stiff and her mannerisms reflected all business. The partners often joked that they couldn't tell what she enjoyed more—her job or the "perks" that came with it.

There was no reciprocal response.

Carol Ann was used to Pam being rude. "May I get you some coffee?"

"No, I'm fine, thank you."

"He called again," Carol Ann said, handing her a message.

"Not again." Pam looked at the message and quickly crumbled it up in her hand. Carol Ann looked at her sympathetically. The man had been calling this woman non-stop for the past three weeks. He was always extremely polite, but there was something about his voice that sounded desperate. Carol Ann wondered *why* she was so hell-bent on avoiding all of his calls.

"Hey, I know it's none of my business, but . . ."

Pam held up her hand in front of Carol Ann's face signaling her to stop. "You're right, and let's keep it that way." It was obvious that Carol Ann was privy to everything going on at the firm and made it her business to know everyone else's business.

"I didn't mean to pry . . ."

"Listen, Carol Ann, I realize you have your sights set on *higher* plateaus, but stick with what you do best. I realize Hugh Richmond is a senior partner, and *he* may like you showing him your professional and *personal* skills, but I prefer you keep everything totally professional with me and stay out of my *personal* affairs. Is that understood?"

"Yes, ma'am," Carol Ann answered timidly, wishing she could crawl underneath her desk until she recovered from her stinging blow.

"Now, have you seen Amanda?" Pam asked coolly.

"Yes, as a matter of fact, I have," she answered sheepishly, hoping this bit of news would help redeem her from the *faux pas* she had just made.

Carol Ann leaned over the front of her desk to whisper something to Pam. Her bright ruffled crimson blouse revealed just enough cleavage for Hugh to enjoy and for the firm *not* to consider it inappropriate business attire.

"Rumor has it that she's been feverishly working to finish that *Johnson v. Tyfish Systems* case so she can make it home early for her daughter's graduation party, tonight. Poor thing."

"Thanks, Carol Ann," she replied dryly.

Pam headed back toward her office and found three stacks of papers sitting neatly on her desk. She eagerly massaged her hands together. "Well, well, well, what have we here?" she said under her breath. She closed her door partway and sat down. As she carefully sifted through each page, a slight grin came across on her face.

Unbeknownst to her, Amanda was watching her every move through the cracked door. *Just look at her salivating like a wolf that has been left with a flock of sheep! The nerve of that . . .*

"Amanda?" Pam called out. She felt someone's eyes watching her and decided to investigate to see who was checking up on her.

Amanda paused briefly to give herself a moment to regroup. "Yes, it's me. I see you've had a chance to look over the files for *Johnson v. Tyfish Systems*."

"Yes, I'm still reviewing them. Come on in and have a seat. How long have you been standing there?"

Amanda was getting more infuriated the longer she watched her. She thought: *Long enough to see you decide how you're going to go about taking all of the credit for all of my hard work.*

"Oh, I just walked by to check to see if you were back in your office yet," Amanda said as nicely as she could. She had changed her mind about leaving out the last few pages of her documents. If she had done that, then it would have made her as evil as Pam, and the slightest thought of ever being like that woman only repulsed her.

"Please close the door behind you and sit down."

"All right," Amanda complied.

"Let me start by saying that you did an excellent job in gathering the information that I requested."

"Thank you."

Pam pushed her chair away from her desk and carefully placed her forefinger on the side of her face while she contemplated her next sentence. Amanda began to feel uneasy and shifted her body around in her chair. She clutched her sweater tightly and casually looked down at her feet as the attorney stared at her.

"Amanda, I don't like playing games with people, so let me get right to the point. I'm *not* satisfied with the mediocre attitude you displayed today. I also think you've been slacking since you found out you would not be working with Bill McKesson on this case and would be working with me instead. I don't appreciate, nor will I tolerate, inappropriate behavior from you or anyone who works for me."

Blocking out the sound of her voice had become an art form for Amanda. She knew that her boss would go on and on until she felt like she had pummeled Amanda's self-esteem into the ground. Amanda had gotten to the point where she could read her lips without listening to her. Sometimes, she made a game of it by starting the second hand on her watch and checking to see how many seconds it would take her to finish her insults. So far, it had been only thirty seconds, but Pam was just getting started.

"Amanda, you knew about this case several weeks ago, and today you had a hard time making a decision as to whether or not you would give me the information that I needed. In this business, things are always subject to change. We have to go with the flow whether we like it or not. Understand?"

Amanda nodded like a child who had just been reprimanded as Pam continued her rant.

"I think it's only fair to tell you that I'm going to report your insubordination to Pete and let him make the decision on how to handle this. After all, as it appears that you'd rather work for the big boys anyway, perhaps he can find you a place with one of them. Of course, I doubt very seriously that they would put up with your antics as much as I have. As a matter of fact, I know they wouldn't, and you do too, which is why I don't understand why you are not more grateful and solicitous to me."

Amanda paused. "I'd like to say something, if you've finished."

"Yes, as a matter of fact, I do believe I am," she retorted arrogantly as she held her hands out and stared at her nails, debating whether or not she needed a manicure.

Amanda took a deep breath before she spoke. She didn't know exactly what she was going to say, but whatever it was, it was long overdue.

"First of all, I find it very insulting that you can sit across that desk and talk to me like I'm a nine-year-old child. I realize I was a little hesitant at first, but I did stay. It seems to me like you have forgotten about all the other times I have spent nights with you until 9:00 and 10:00 assisting you with other cases. Have you ever taken a look around you and noticed that you are the only attorney who takes twelve cases at a time? I am the only paralegal who works sixty or more hours each week."

"I see." Pam folded her arms deliberately across her chest and leaned back in her chair.

"Most of the attorneys around here at your level are only assigned five or six caseloads, and their paralegals work only fifty hours or so—if that! Why do you always get overloaded? Please don't misunderstand me. You are an excellent attorney, but you just take on more and more and they just keep giving it to you.

You stay here all hours of the night while everyone else goes home. I've been here and listened to the other lawyers talk about you."

Pam raised her eyebrows at Amanda's comment. "Really, now. And what are these *other* lawyers, saying?" She couldn't have cared less if she were the talk of the entire Bar Association. The bottom line was this: She was there to win cases and get paid—period!

"They say, 'When they don't want to do something, they just turn it over to the black girl. She'll do anything. You know how *they* are. Always trying to prove something.' I've heard them over and over again, laughing at the many hours you put in. Even though you make six figures, you are still underpaid in comparison to them. They work fewer hours than you do, bill fewer hours, and still make more money. Even with all of the brains you have and the legal finesse you possess, it will never be enough for any of them to respect you."

Pam moved forward over her desk. It took everything in her to not reach across and grab Amanda by her throat. She held back her comments in reserve and kept what was really on her mind to herself.

How stupid does she really think I am? And who in the hell does Amanda think she is, coming into my office telling me what these white boys think? I thought she was upset because she had to work late, not about the people who talk about me. Does she think I'm that naïve and don't know what they are saying behind my back? Why is she saying this now? Oh! How I wish she would just shut up and stick with what she gets paid to do around here.

"Amanda," she said coolly.

"Please, let me finish. I know I'm sticking my neck out here."

Pam stared at Amanda condescendingly. Amanda was right about one thing: she was stepping out of line. Way out of line.

Hmmm . . . what is it with her today? Pam fumed. *All of sudden, she's gotten downright bold and saying things to me as if she doesn't expect it to have any consequence. She's confident to the point where she's borderline insubordinate. Well, good for you, Amanda—you're finally speaking up for yourself after all these years. But I'm not the one to practice your newfound identity with today or any other time. Please, go talk to someone who really gives a damn!*

Pam sucked in her cheeks and bit down hard on the inside of her jaw so she wouldn't go postal on Amanda. She was no fool; she knew she needed Amanda's assistance for this case. Despite her disdain for Amanda's family issues, she was one of the best paralegals in the firm. Of course, she would never tell her that. But for now, she would hold her tongue until *after* her big trial was finished, and then after that, Amanda would be too!

Amanda talked so much that Pam's ears became numb. The pain spreading from her cheek was relentless and made her even angrier as Amanda's utterings continued to ramble.

"You have no idea how they feel about you. And then the people who try to support you, like me, working with you all of the long hours . . . The one time I need to leave early, and the one time I decide to put my family first and my job second because my *only* child is about to graduate from high school, you force me to work. For months you knew about this celebration. Now, because of this one instance, you decide I'm lazy. You berate me and try to make *me* feel guilty! No wonder people around here call you the evil-eyed tiger. You sure know how to chew 'em up and spit 'em out when you are through with them.

"And one more thing," Amanda's voice became low and somber. "I know we made a pact that we would never discuss this."

"I told you earlier I did not want to go down that road with you! So let's not break that pact!" Pam sneered.

Amanda started to shake. "Oh, you broke it long ago," she said, holding back her tears. "I just never did anything about it. But, I can't and I won't be silent anymore."

Pam abruptly stood up. Her papers flew across the desk and startled Amanda. "Damn you!" she whispered as she slowly managed to win back her composure and sat back down.

Amanda's voice quivered at first, but she managed to speak very deliberately and quietly. "Let's drop the formalities for now, okay, PAM?" Those three letters hadn't come out of her mouth in so long, she'd forgotten what it sounded like. *What happened to the person who I knew at Spelman, huh?* Amanda thought, still fighting back her tears.

"I'm *Ms.* Madison to you in this office! Which by the way, don't think I haven't noticed how you purposefully avoid calling me that! The *Pam* that you knew at Spelman did what she said she would do and became an attorney!" Pam struck back in her most haughtiness tone. "But, you on the other hand . . ."

"Yes, I got pregnant! I had an illegitimate child and couldn't finish law school like you and Dee. I couldn't hold up my end of the bargain for the three of us to become lawyers together, and you haven't let me forget it, have you? I don't know what has happened in your life that would make you become so bitter, cruel, and self-righteous."

"You are so ungrateful, Amanda! This is exactly why I didn't want you assigned to me. I'm the one that got you this damn job, remember?"

"And you have never let me forget that, either! How many times do I have to thank you? I'm not ungrateful, PAM! But, YOU certainly are!"

"It's MS. MADISON!"

"Get over yourself, okay!" Amanda yelled as Pam rolled her eyes at her audacity. "I have worked long and hard for you, and I'm one of the best paralegals this firm has—if not THE best! But, have you ever once said, 'Good job, Amanda!' This was supposed to be a short-term assignment. I had no idea that I would end up working for you all of this time. Oh my God, if only I had known that this short-term assignment would turn into long-term hell. My God! We used to be best friends . . ." Amanda's voice dropped as she regained her composure and rose from her chair. "I'm done with this," she said calmly and waved her hands in the air. She got up to smooth the wrinkles in her dress.

Pam finally released her bite and managed to smile awkwardly as the pain continued. She had let Amanda have *her* say and decided it was now *her* turn. They hadn't been friends since Amanda started working for her; after today's episode, there was no way they would ever have that relationship again. She sharply pushed her chair back from her desk and stood staring straight into Amanda eyes.

Amanda interrupted her next move and spoke confidently. "You can't intimidate *me* anymore, Pam! So save your courtroom drama for the courtroom. Effective today, I am resigning from Sterling, Mathis, and Silverman. Here is my notice," she said as she quickly slid her resignation letter across the desk.

"And for the record, I'm glad things turned out the way they did. I'm a wonderful mother with a beautiful daughter. I have a man in my life that loves me for me. I can truly say that the people around here will miss *me* when I'm gone. But, it's sad you can't say the same thing. Now, I can finally really enjoy my daughter's celebration—guilt free! Best of luck to you, because *you* are certainly going to need it!"

Layover

Chris sat on the edge of the Jacuzzi tub wearing only silk gray boxer shorts while he watched Dee enjoy her warm bubble bath by candlelight. He thought of everything for a romantic evening and brought twenty lilac-scented candles and carefully showcased them throughout the suite, leaving a brilliant glow in each of the rooms.

"Ummm . . . this is so divine," Dee said as Chris poured her a second glass of champagne. She sipped from the fluted glass and closed her eyes, leaning into the soothing jets.

"Well, it should be at over $400 a bottle," Chris chuckled.

Dee's eyes opened wide. "What kind of champagne are we drinking with that kind of price tag?"

He carefully lifted the bottle out of the champagne bucket and turned the label toward him. "Let's see now, it's Dom Pérignon Rosé champagne," he said, with the worst imitation of a French accent Dee had ever heard.

"Really, I didn't know you were such a champagne connoisseur," Dee said, trying to control her laughter.

"I'm *not,* but one of my buddies on the team is, and when I told him what my plans were this evening, he highly recommended it." They both roared with laughter.

"Well, here's to good friends!" Dee chimed her glass against his.

"And here's to good friends with *expensive taste!*" He clinked her glass back and playfully wrapped his wrist around hers as they slowly sipped the other's champagne.

"So, what kind of case are you working on now?"

"Huh? Ow!" Dee cried as she bumped her head on the back of the tub. She was so caught off guard by his question that her champagne went down the wrong way, causing her to cough uncontrollably.

"Baby, you all right?" Chris asked as he firmly patted her on the back. The patting was making her cough worse as she struggled to catch her breath. Miraculously, she somehow managed to mouth the word *water* between all of the heaving and coughing. He quickly grabbed her glass of champagne and poured the bubbly into the sink and filled the flute with water, rushing it back to her. She was still coughing explosively.

"Drink this!"

Dee quickly grabbed the glass and guzzled the water down as Chris pulled it gently to slow her pace down.

"Wooo! Desiree, not so fast, you will make it worse!"

She took his advice. Gradually, her throat passageway cleared. "What a relief!" Dee panted. "My goodness, that is a scary feeling," she said, placing her hand over her throat.

Chris wiped away small droplets of perspiration that had formed a necklace on his brow. "You're telling me. I thought I was going to have to dive in there after you and call 911."

"Well, I hope you would have at least gotten a towel wrapped around me before some strange men came in here to whisk me away," Dee said, trying to make light of the issue and not ruin the romantic vibe that they had earlier.

"That would have been the least of your concerns, believe, me. Are you sure you're okay?"

"Yes, I'm fine." She scooted down further into the luxurious bubble bath. "Your question just caught me a little off guard."

"Really?" His eyes pleaded with hers to not give him another scare like that anytime soon. She nodded and smiled reassuringly as he gently massaged the spot on her head where she'd hit it.

"I really don't want to talk about work just now." She closed her eyes and enjoyed the soothing feel of his touch.

He threw his hands up, surrendering. "You will get no argument from me on that subject tonight."

"Good, then. Now that that's settled, tell me the name of the restaurant again where you were going to order our food?" Dee asked.

"*Fran . . . cais . . . Élé . . . gant,*" he said trying his best to pronounce the name correctly.

"*Francais Élégant . . . Francais Élégant . . . Francais Élégant.* You are a champion of the French this evening, aren't you?" she said with an alluring grin.

"*Oui, oui,* Madam!" Chris teased. "And for the appetizer, how about we start off with a sample of the French kiss," he quipped again in his unrefined French accent. Dee giggled as he bent his head to lower his lips toward hers, tenderly tugging on her bottom lip. Effortlessly, he slipped his tongue into her mouth and made an unremitting slow circular motion that intensified each time their tongues touched. She gently pulled back and opened her mouth wider as he obliged her with light thrusts of pleasures that left her longing for more of him.

"Oh, how I love French food," she purred as he caressed her back with a supple sponge and slowly reached down toward her buttocks, rubbing gently as he made his way up toward her back again.

"Feel good, baby?"

"Ummm . . . hmmm . . . you know it does. Don't you want to join me?" Dee said, clearing the bubbles away from her breasts and exposing her hardened nipples.

"No," he said unconvincingly as his manhood slowly began to stretch through his silk boxers.

"Well, it looks like someone else is in disagreement with you," Dee commented as she looked over at his bulging crotch and licked her lips.

Chris laughed. "Can you blame him?"

"Here, let me see if I can make him change *your* mind." She got on her knees and turned toward him, gently rubbing his inner thighs. "Come on now, Chris, at least put your feet in and let the jets work their magic on those linebacker legs of yours," she teased.

"It's tempting, very tempting, but tonight I'm going to let you enjoy this all by yourself, and then when you're finished playing bubbles, the two of us plan on joining you on that king-size bed," Chris said, pointing to his groin.

"All right, have it your way, baby."

"Oh, I plan on it," he said with a devilish smirk. "Don't you worry about that."

Dee lounged back in the tub and closed her eyes as he knelt down on the floor next to the tub. His large hands continued to bathe and massage her slowly. Chris caressed her breasts with the soft sponge and then with his fingertips, lightly rubbing her nipples until they stood at attention. He carefully covered each one with soft wet kisses and tenderly led the sponge down her stomach and down her inner thighs. He gently pried them open and twirled it between her legs.

"Ohhh . . . don't stop," she moaned.

"Just relax, baby, and enjoy the bath."

Chris turned the jets toward the center of her legs and gently ran his fingers on the outside of her lips, sending her to an underwater pleasure palace.

"Oh, Chris, you can't do me like this, baby! Get in here with me! Please!" she moaned unashamedly as the jets ran swiftly inside her. He caressed her face with his hands as she gently removed his left hand toward her lips and placed his middle finger in her mouth. She delicately moved it in and out, making his erection grow.

"Desiree, you are a naughty girl tonight aren't you?" Chris joked as he slowly removed his finger from her mouth. He took hold of her and lifted her up out of the tub. He proceeded to send her into another end zone by gently gliding the same finger inside her that she had just placed inside her mouth.

"Ummmm . . . what are you trying to do to me?"

"Do you like it?"

"OOOOO!" was all Dee could say as he released his finger from inside her thigh's vise-like grip and grabbed a towel, covering her like she was a rare gem.

He carried her out of the bathroom, all the while sucking her earlobes and running his tongue sensuously down her neck.

"Don't stop, baby, don't you *ever* stop," she pleaded weakly.

Chris laid her lovingly on the bed, spread eagle, and continued to dry her off with every inch of his tongue. He climbed onto her as he kissed the top her forehead and worked his insatiable tongue like he was running interference on the field. He moved in faster, then a little slower, staying in tune with her body's desires. Her body begged him to travel downward to her center core where he stopped just in time to taste her warm honey as it spilled over into his mouth.

"You ready for me baby? You ready for some lovin'?"

Dee was barely able to speak as she felt his penis grow even larger through the opening in his boxers as it rubbed against her inner thigh searching for her opening. She screamed in soprano as he lifted himself up to maneuver his boxers off, all the while steadily sucking, licking, tasting, and caressing her center until his penis replaced his tongue and penetrated her.

"Oh Chris, you make me feel so good!" Dee arched her back to receive him even more. As he moved in deeper she cried, "Harder . . . harder . . . I'm almost there!"

"Not to worry, baby, that's why I'm here to take you over the goal," he chuckled.

He sucked her hardened nipples while massaging her lips between her thighs, which made her even more out of control. She wrapped her legs tightly around his waist in preparation for taking their passion to the next level. He obliged with vengeance as their bodies clung together like surfers on a surfboard, bracing themselves for an enormous tidal wave. Swiftly and steadily moving through the current, they picked up speed as they rode the tide with each passing wave of pleasure. Each became larger and louder than the one before, until they finally reached their shore cradled in each other's salt, and drifted off to sleep.

On-Time Arrival

It was 6:00 p.m., and Amanda had made it home exactly two hours before the first guest would arrive. With enormous anticipation, she scurried downstairs and found what had to be the most beautiful finished product of a basement that she had ever seen.

The craftsmanship was meticulous. The custom cabinetry was tucked neatly underneath the wet bar. The crown molding was stained oak and the recessed lighting added a soothing touch to the room. Amanda took off her shoes and dug her toes into the soft Berber carpet. The padding underneath seemed to mold to her feet like a good pair of broken-in bedroom slippers.

The tall columns that divided the basement were decked with green and gold balloons, Tracey's high school colors. Hanging from the ceiling were matching streamers and a glittered sign that read: "Congratulations, Tracey! We are so proud of you!"

She walked over to the other side of the columns and saw Tracey sitting in the corner with her head buried in her arms.

"Hey there, you!" Amanda called as she bent down and lifted Tracey's narrow face with her hands. Tracey's tears flowed into her palms.

"Mama!" Tracey's gray eyes danced with joy when she saw her mother standing in front of her. "I didn't think you were going to make it. I'm so glad you're here," she gushed, hugging her mother's neck.

"I told you, I wouldn't miss this party for anything in the world," Amanda said as she choked back her own tears. "I'm so glad you made it back home safely. I missed you." She took a step back to look at her daughter in full view and then hugged her. "Is everything all right, baby?" She hoped that Tracey would finally open up to her.

"I'm good. Now that you're here, everything *is* fine Mama," she said as she thought about how she had just made it back in time to change clothes and not arouse her mother's suspicions.

Why are you lying to me, Tracey? What are you keeping inside of you? "Well, good, then. I guess getting out into that fresh air did you some good, huh?"

There she goes again, trying to pump me for information. I wish I could tell you where I went Mama, but you would lose it . . . I just know you would. "Yeah, I guess it did!" she said, trying to sound upbeat. *More than you want to ever know.*

"So come on, girl, let's go get this party started! Where's the outfit we bought? While you're getting dressed, I want you to tell me all about your trip to Salt Lake City. "

"My clothes are upstairs," Tracey said as she took her sleeve and wiped her runny nose and her tears from her face. "And the trip was a lot of fun. I can't wait to tell you all about it."

"Well, let's go on upstairs so you can get out of those raggedy jeans and baggy sweatshirt before your guests arrive!"

Melvin got out of his red pickup truck and grabbed three bags of groceries and carried them into the house. He steadily kept bringing in more bags as he saw the guests arrive. There was still one hour left before the party.

"Hey there, young man."

"Hi, Mr. Landers. Let me help you with those, sir," Tony said as he placed a freshly cut bouquet of flowers on top of one of the bags Melvin was holding.

"Thanks," Melvin said, handing him both bags.

Tony hoisted the bags in front of him and followed Melvin, who opened the storm door partway with his foot and held it open for Tony to walk in.

"Thank you sir," Tony said, placing the bags on the kitchen counter.

"No problem. Hey, Tony, let me talk to you for a second," Melvin said, walking toward the living room.

Tony was nervous as he turned to follow Melvin. Melvin was not Tracey's daddy, but he could be worse than some biological fathers.

"Tracey's mama and me have been a little worried about her. Is everything all right?" Melvin looked at him suspiciously.

Tony felt like this was a trick question. If everything *wasn't* all right, then Melvin would probably blame *him* for it and kick his ass. If everything *was* all right, then he would want to know why Tracey was acting so different. And whatever the reason was, it had to be *his* fault! Tony could feel Melvin look straight through him as if he already knew what he was about to say.

"Listen, Mr. Landers, everything is cool with us. Really. She's been acting a little strange with me, too." *Maybe if he knows she's acting different with me also, then he won't blame me totally for Tracey's odd behavior.*

"Different how?"

Okay, here come the 50 questions . . . "Well, sometimes, her mind seems to be somewhere else."

"Yeah," Melvin said, stroking his chin as he thought about what Tony was saying.

One . . . two . . . three . . . four . . .

"So, what do you think it could be?"

Question number two . . . under five seconds . . . not bad. "Uh, I don't know, really. She says she's just anxious about going off to college. So I attribute it to stress, maybe." Melvin's eyebrows rose as Tony's voice trailed off. Tony could tell he didn't like the last part of his sentence. He cleared his throat. "Not that she has anything to worry about, being on a full scholarship and all."

Melvin patted him on the shoulder. "Yeah, I guess you're right."

"I am? I mean . . . yes, I am," Tony said, shocked that Mr. Landers wasn't going to continue with the third degree.

"Hey, let's keep this conversation just between us, okay?"

"No problem, Mr. Landers." *Whew! No problem at all!*

As they walked back to the kitchen, the aroma of a full smorgasbord of delicacies tickled their noses. Amanda was still putting the finishing touches on the feast of hot wings and three different pastas, each cooked in their own sauces of tomato basil, Alfredo, and a secret sauce that Amanda had conjured up herself. There was potato salad, seven-layer salad, seafood salad, meatballs, fresh fruit, and vegetable egg rolls. Fortunately, to save herself some stress, she'd planned enough in advance and did the cooking throughout the week. *No thanks to Pam*, she thought bitterly.

"Good evening, Ms. Shipman. Somethin' sure smells good."

"Well hello Tony and thank you. Don't you look dapper this evening?"

"Thank you, ma'am," he said as he moved the grocery bags to the table and put the flowers behind his back.

Tony was 6'3" and wore demure stainless-steel wire-frame glasses. It was a "barely there" look that accentuated his chiseled handsome features. His thick curly hair was the same mocha color as his eyes, and he was dressed in a well-coordinated ensemble of a cognac-colored sports jacket, matching pants, and a crew neck sweater that complemented his rich almond skin color. Amanda liked his good manners. And the fact that he had just received a four-year scholarship to Harvard University didn't hurt either.

"Hmmm. It smells like you tryin' to put a hurtin' on someone up in here!" Melvin blurted out.

"I was thinking the same thing when I walked in." Tony closed his eyes to take in the sweet smells of lemon bars, brownies, and a "Sock-It-To-Me" cake that was being pulled out of the oven.

Amanda laughed. "Oh, you and Melvin are too much for my ego! I just want everything to be perfect for this party this evening. I just feel so guilty that Melvin and Tracey had to do all of the decorating without me. I can at least make sure the food is done right!" She wiped her hands on her apron and set the desserts down on the hot pads on the counter. Melvin could see her guilt-ridden face and walked over toward her and kissed her on the cheek.

"You always do a fine job, baby," he said as he made his way back over to the table and started putting up the groceries. Amanda smiled, catching a glimpse of something that Tony was trying to hide behind his back.

"What's that you've got hidden behind your back?"

He placed his fingers across his lips. "Shh . . . it's a surprise for Tracey," he said, winking devilishly as he showed the array of white and red roses.

"Those are beautiful. Here, let me place them on top of the cabinet until you are ready to give them to her."

"Mama!" Tracey yelled in a panic from upstairs.

"Yes, baby? What is it?" Amanda rushed up the stairs to Tracey's room.

"I saw Tony's car pull up, and I can't zip the back of this dress," she said frantically.

"Honey, Tony is fine. He's in the kitchen helping Melvin with the groceries."

Tracey rolled her eyes. "Oh, Mama. Why is he doing that?"

"Because he's a gentleman and knows that if he's going to date you for very long, he better at least act like he doesn't mind helping out if your mother needs it." She firmly patted Tracey on the bottom and then zipped the dress.

"Turn around now. Let me look at you." Tracey turned around slowly like an angel on a music box. The silky gold fabric dress was form fitting with a simple and straight neckline in the front and back. It tastefully accentuated her shapely hips and well-formed breasts. She wore a pair of sling backs the same shade as her dress.

Tracey reminded Amanda so much of herself that it left her breathless. Although, unlike Amanda, Tracey was tall and model thin. She had Amanda's eyes and wavy hair, but her face was definitely the spitting image of her father's. Her skin was a rich brown coffee with a just a hint of cream.

"You look beautiful, Tracey."

"Thank you, Mama," Tracey said.

Amanda noticed she was suddenly drifting miles away. *There she goes again. What is going on with you, Tracey?* "Baby, is everything all right?"

Tracey smoothed out her dress and took a long look in her full-length mirror behind her door wishing she were back with *him*. He was so charming and she loved how their conversations made her feel so good about herself.

"Tracey!"

"I'm sorry, Mama. Did you say something?"

"You're so far away. Where were you just now?"

"Oh, Mama," Tracey said, trying to smile thoughtfully. She hoped that her evening was not going to be ruined with a lengthy discussion about her feelings. "Do you think Tony will like me in this dress?"

"If he's not blind!"

"Thank you, Mama." *Thank you for not grilling me, and thank you for saying Tony will be pleased with me in this dress.*

"You're welcome, baby." *But just know you're only off the hook for tonight. I will find out what is going on with you. One way or another.*

Tracey kissed her on the cheek and glided down the staircase. She peeked in the kitchen and saw Tony helping Melvin with the groceries.

"Wow, you look great!" Tony said as he opened his arms and gave her a big hug. Melvin decided it was a good time for him to start carrying the food to the basement and give them a few minutes alone.

"Oh, I almost forgot. I've got something for you." Tony pulled the roses off the cabinet and handed them to her.

"Tony, they're beautiful!" she gasped, looking into his eyes. Then he pulled her toward him, pressed his lips against hers, and gave her a slow, passionate kiss.

"I better get these into some water before they wilt," she said, moving backwards in slow motion as they continued staring into each other's eyes.

Tony watched her leave the room. Her heart-shaped behind moved like a pendulum while her dress swayed then molded to her every curve. His arousal was hard to conceal.

"Tony, I have to say it again. Those roses are beautiful," Amanda said as she entered the kitchen.

"Thank you, Ms. Shipman," he said, quickly grabbing another bag and strategically placing it in front of his bulging crotch. He walked toward the other side of the kitchen to continue placing the canned goods in the cabinets.

"Hey, Tony, I'll finish the rest up," Melvin called out as he came back into the kitchen grabbing the bag from Tony and at the same time noticing his erection. Tony's face said it all; he wanted to become invisible.

Melvin's eyes motioned him toward the bathroom down the hallway. "Why don't you go on and get yourself together before the rest of the party arrives? I can handle things from here."

"Thank you, sir, I will."

Melvin pulled on Tony's shoulder for him to bend down. "All right now, watch ya' self! Don't do nothin' that you'll be sorry about later!"

"I *will,* sir."

"What'd you just say?"

"I mean . . . I *won't,* sir," Tony said trying to get the bass back in his voice as he made his way to the bathroom.

Amanda came back in the kitchen. "Melvin, thank you so much for pulling this together for me while I was at work."

"You don't have to thank me." He kissed her on the forehead and saw a tear well up in her eye. "Hey, *this is* going to be a wonderful party. I know what you're thinking. She'll be fine."

Amanda wiped her eyes with the bottom of her apron. "But she won't even talk to me, Melvin. She tries to evade me every time I ask her what's going on. You know that's not like our Tracey!"

"Amanda, don't spoil this evening by letting Tracey see you like this."

"You're right," she said dabbing at her eyes again.

"I'm going upstairs to take a quick shower," she said as she glanced at the kitchen clock. "We only have about thirty more minutes before the kids start coming."

"Amanda, those kids are not going to show up on time. The party doesn't even start until 8:00 and they won't be steppin' up in here until way after 9:00 or even 10:00."

"You're probably right. Maybe I put the food out too early," Amanda said anxiously.

"Amanda, the food is fine. Everything is fine, and more importantly, Tracey will be fine," he said as he kissed her on the lips and gave her a hug. "Just go on upstairs and get dressed, okay?"

"Okay, okay, I'm going!"

Melvin was wrong. A stream of Tracey's friends began arriving around 8:30 p.m. They were all dressed like they were going to a modeling competition. *These kids are wearing labels ranging from Dereon to Gucci to Prada. I didn't realize teenagers were so brand-name conscious,* Amanda thought. Even though she had a teenager of her own, she didn't raise Tracey to be infatuated with name-brand clothing. As long as it was good quality, that was the important thing. Sure, Tracey had a few designer clothes that she had purchased from the local Ross or Marshall's. But, some of the name brands the teens were wearing had her dumbfounded.

The DJ played all of the latest R&B and hip-hop music from 50 Cent to Alicia Keys. About thirty-five of Tracey's friends showed up with presents.

"Tracey, this party is fly, girl! I can't believe your mama let you throw down like this," her friend Anita said.

"Yeah, who made all of this food? It's off the chain," Deandre laughed while licking chicken grease from his fingers.

"Thanks. My mom and her boyfriend, Melvin, did everything."

"This food is dope! And the music is on point!" Deandre said between chews.

"I don't know how Tisa's party is going to come up against this one," Judy interrupted. "Hers is tomorrow night and I see she's ova' there in the corner taking notes with Cynthia," Judy laughed.

"Girl, please, I'm not even worried. I'm sure hers will be nice, too," Tracey said, waving her hand nonchalantly in the air while holding a plate full of food in the other.

"Yeah, right," Anita sneered. Both she and Judy looked at each other and laughed again.

"I bet your girl is going to be a serious copycat! She always has been envious of you, Tracey. And now that you are dating her man!"

"Who, Tony?"

"Who? Tony?" Judy mocked her. "Yes, Tony. You know she's had her eye on him since freshman year."

"No, I didn't know that. But oh, snap! Cause he's mine now," Tracey laughed. The grin on her face could be seen all the way from across the room, and it seemed to draw Tony toward her effortlessly.

"I hate to interrupt you ladies, but may I dance with my baby?" Tony said, reaching for Tracey's hand as Maxwell's sultry "Pretty Wings" bellowed through the speakers. Amanda and Melvin were both keeping a distant eye on them while taking turns refreshing the punch bowl and replenishing the food.

"Goooone, Miss Tracey," Anita said, teasing loudly in her ear.

"Yeah, do your thang with that *hot* Mr. Tony," Cynthia whispered in the other ear.

"Well, of course you can," Tracey told Tony. He took her by the hand and walked her to the dance floor. He gently wrapped his arms around her waist and slowly pressed his body against hers, taking in the scent of sweet flowers and mint. It was almost as if she had bathed in peppermint leaves. Suddenly he remembered Melvin's earlier warning and stepped back a few inches.

"What's wrong?"

"Nothing, why?"

"You usually don't dance this way, that's why!"

"Oh, that," he said coolly, trying to play off his little repositioning. "Well, uh, let's just say, I don't need to be getting my friend too excited right now," he said, eyeing his groin.

"Oh, I see," Tracey giggled. "I'm sorry," she said, following his lead.

Tony leaned in toward her ear and whispered just loud enough for her to understand him over the blaring music. "Listen, Tracey, I don't know how much longer I'm going to be able to keep this up!"

"What happened?" she whispered back.

"It's Melvin."

"Melvin? What about him?"

He's suspicious."

"Melvin is always suspicious," Tracey said, as she tried to whisper and nibble at his ear at the same time.

"Tracey, stop that!" Tony looked around for Melvin's shadow.

"What is with you? Ease up, will ya'? I'm just playin'!"

"Well, this is not the time or place to be doing that kind of thing! Trust me. Tracey, I'm serious." His voice lowered. "I don't want to be in the middle of this when it comes crashing down, and baby, believe me, it's going to come down hard!"

"Tony, just a little while longer, please!" she begged, as she pulled him closer to her and buried her head in his chest.

"Tracey . . ."

"Shhh . . . just dance with me, Tony. I don't want to do anything but be in your arms."

After two more slow songs, the DJ blended the second one into the upbeat lyrics of Mary J. Blige.

"Go, Tracey, it's yo' party! Go, Tracey, it's yo' party!" The chant went on for twenty minutes.

"Tracey, hey, that's your song. Now c'mon, let's get this party started!" Tony said, as he joined in the chant, relieved that Tracey was out from under him and decreasing his chances of worrying about another hard-on.

The last song ended right at 12:30 a.m. as Amanda had requested. By the time the last parent picked up their non-licensed teen, it was 1:15 a.m. and Amanda and Melvin were exhausted. Together they piled the last two bowls into the dishwasher and peeked out the window. They saw Tracey standing in the driveway waving goodbye to her last guest, Tony. When she walked back into the house to thank her mom and Melvin, they saw the lost and dreamy look on her face. She gave them each a hug.

"Thank you so much, Mama and Melvin."

"You're welcome, baby," Amanda said.

"It sure was a really nice party, Tracey. I know you will always remember it," Melvin said, followed by a peck on the cheek.

"Yes, I will. Well, I'm going to bed now." Tracey stretched her arms out and headed up the stairs. "Good night," she said with a yawn.

"Good night, baby," Amanda answered back.

Melvin stretched his arms. "Well, Miss Amanda, I guess I'll be heading home, now."

"Oh, I'm sorry you have to leave at such a late hour. I know you're tired."

"I am. But, I'll be fine."

"Melvin, you can stay here on the sofa bed if you want to," Amanda said hesitantly.

"No, thank you," he chuckled, surrendering his hands in the air. "The last time I slept on that thing, I had to go to my chiropractor for a month."

"All right, then. Call me when you get home, okay?"

"I will, baby," he said, then kissed her and walked to his truck.

Tracey slipped out of her dress and stuffed it under her comforter so it looked like she was in the bed. She pulled out her favorite pair of skinny jeans and her Hampton T-shirt and looked through the window, waiting patiently for Melvin's truck to pull away. She eased open the window and slid out onto the balcony, then crept down each rung of the white trellis until she reached the ground floor. She walked for two blocks and then jumped into Tony's car and took a deep breath as Tony drove off. "Is everything okay? Did anyone see you?" Tony asked nervously.

Tracey shook her head as she slowly dug down into her purse for her phone and began decisively pressing the buttons.

"Who could you possibly be texting at this time of night?"

"My Aunt Dee."

"Who is Aunt Dee?"

"She and my mom used to be really good friends."

"Used to be?"

"Yeah, they still care about each other. It's just complicated."

"Tracey, this is crazy! I thought you didn't want anyone else to know about this. Now, you're bringing in a third party? *This* Aunt Dee—who by the way—I never heard of until now!"

"I know this sounds crazy, but Aunt Dee has always been great about giving me advice and I really *need* some right now."

"No, what you *need* is your head examined! And after the doc is finished examining you, it will be my turn!"

Cabin Pressure

Pam looked in the mirror at her bloodshot eyes. The clock on her nightstand flashed 8:00 p.m., but her body's clock felt like it was closer to midnight. While bubbles filled the tub, she slipped off her suit and dropped it and her undergarments on the bathroom floor.

She grabbed her cup of herbal tea near the sink and set it on the side of the tub next to her sponge and potpourri-scented candles. Pam lit the candles and watched the bubbles grow larger until they eventually rose to the edge of the tub.

"All I want to do is soak my tired ass in this tub and go to bed," she said as she stepped into the tub, immersing herself in the warm bubbles and laying her head back on the foam pillow. She closed her eyes and drifted off to sleep until the phone shattered her peace.

Damn, Murphy's Law! She looked at the caller ID panel next to the tub but didn't recognize the phone number. Her curiosity got the best of her as she picked up the phone to see if the person left a message. The phone indicated she had a message, and she dialed in her code.

"Hello, Pam. It's me, Greg."

Pam's heart felt like it had been blasted with a defibrillator. She caught her breath and held the phone tightly to her ear as she listened in disbelief to Greg's message. She fumbled for her tea and wished she had poured something stronger in her cup.

"I've been calling you at work and at home, but you are not returning my calls. I really need to see you. I'm leaving the country in a week, and I'd like to see you before I leave . . . for good. This will be my final call, Pam. So, if you're listening, I just want you to know that if I don't hear from you, then I'll assume that you want to leave things as they are. But, if you do want to talk, I'll be at Piedmont Park tomorrow morning at 8:00 where we used to meet. If you can't be there, please call or text me. My cell number is 312-555-6878. Good bye, Pam."

Pam sat straight up in her bed. She stared at the clock on her nightstand for what seemed like the umpteenth time and watched the lit numbers slowly change to 5:00 a.m. She thought her *worst* nightmare was Amanda quitting right before her major trial. She was wrong. Greg had managed to top that.

"I can't believe I've let that bitch and that son-of-a-bitch get me so worked up like this," she swore, punching her pillow in a futile attempt to make herself comfortable as she struggled to fall asleep. The phone rang and she looked at the clock through one eye and saw it was only fifteen minutes from the last time she looked.

Shit, let me guess. She pulled on the phone cord and maneuvered the receiver to her ear and answered groggily. "Greg?"

"Is this Pamela?"

Pam stared at the receiver. *Who in the hell is calling me at this ungodly hour and calling me Pamela?* "Pam speaking," she said rudely to the unfamiliar voice.

"Oh, I do apologize, Pam. It sounds like I awoke you from your beauty rest." The Italian accent on the other end of the receiver hummed through the phone like a soothing wake-up call.

"Marco?"

"Yes, it's me."

"I'm sorry. I thought you were someone else." She looked at the clock again and rubbed her eyes. "What are you doing calling me at this hour? And better yet, how did you get my home phone number?"

"Well, to answer your first question, my flight just got in, so I'm in town. And to answer your second question, as you were so evasive about giving me your phone number yourself, I did some detective work and found it on my own."

"I see. Detective work, huh? I thought I told you not to call me."

"No, you said you would probably give me your number if I met you at another time or place."

Pam was silent. She could not help but be a little flattered by Marco's assertiveness. A tiny smile began to form on her lips. "Well, *I'm* impressed. You get an 'E' for the effort you've made, considering we just met last week at a party."

"You are quite impressionable."

"And you are quite incorrigible!"

"Am I, now?" he said, trying to feign innocence. "When can I see you?"

Her smile grew larger as she gazed up at her ceiling. This guy just didn't know how to take no for an answer. "You can't," she said coolly.

"Why not?"

"I have a lot of things I have to do at work today."

"Well, I'm sure whatever it is, *you* will make sure that it is taken care of."

"True, very true." There was a dead silence between them. She was a sucker for an accent.

"Pam? Are you still there?"

"Yes, I'm here."

"Well, what about tomorrow?'

"Tomorrow's no good either."

"Hey, I just thought of a crazy idea. Are you . . . how . . . you say . . . game?"

"Game for what?"

"Game for a quick breakfast?"

She laughed. "A quick what?"

"You know, breakfast. The most important meal of the day for you Americans."

"Oh, and it's not for the Italians?"

"Not really, for me, anyway. But, aside from that, come meet me for breakfast."

"You're serious?" Pam was taken aback by his persistence.

"Of course I'm serious."

"Didn't I just say that today is not good for me, either?"

"Don't you normally eat breakfast?"

"Yes, but . . ."

"Then it's settled."

"Settled?"

"Yes, I'm staying at the Ritz Carlton, which is right down the street from your office. So you can come here for a quick bite and make it to work in plenty of time."

The sound of the alarm clock blared 6:00 a.m., giving Pam a jolt as she hit the snooze button and reset her clock for 7:00 a.m.

"Pam? Will you meet me for breakfast?"

"No, Marco. Perhaps another time."

"All right, then, another time," he said, sounding both surprised and disappointed. "Call me if you change your mind. My flight doesn't leave until the day after tomorrow at 8:00 that night."

"Okay, but I won't be changing my mind."

"I hope you get everything done at work before I leave."

"Thank you, Marco. I hope so, too. Goodbye."

Pam and Marco had a most unusual first meeting. She received an invitation to attend a victory party at one of her client's homes, Memorial Hospital's chief surgeon, Dr. Gerald Collins. As his estate was only fifteen minutes from her firm, her intent was to make a brief appearance on behalf of the firm and leave to return to her office and review the Tyfish case.

Gerald Collins was as debonair as he was handsome, and women flocked to him. Pam guessed he was about fifty-five years old, but he looked forty-five. She wasn't sure if it was just good genes or several plastic surgeries that made the good doctor able to hang onto his youth. There was no trace of gray to be found in his charcoal mane, and his body looked like he had been a long-time triathlete. Dr. Collins had been voted one of Atlanta's most eligible bachelors until his third wife nabbed him, barely before the ink had time to dry on his cover story in *Southern Prestige*, a new upscale social magazine targeting the elite of the South.

Pam was Collins's defense attorney for a case where he was being sued for authorizing the surgery that ended a football player's career. Ironically, the football player was nicknamed Highway Hathaway for his phenomenal speed. He was driving 180 miles an hour on a dirt road when he hit a bump sending his 2009 Porsche 911 Turbo into an uncontrollable tailspin. The car flipped over several times with Highway still strapped in the seat belt, trapped between the dashboard and the steering wheel. The impact was so forceful that the front of the dashboard bolted through his leg and partially severed it. The rescue team had to use the Jaws of Life to pull Highway from the mangled vehicle, and an emergency helicopter rushed him to Memorial Hospital.

Under Dr. Collins's instructions, the surgical team had to make a quick decision to amputate his leg because Highway was losing a lot of blood and was about to go into shock. The irony was that it saved his life and ended his career at the same time. The football player was suing the doctor for loss of wages and for amputating his leg without his consent.

Pam proved that Collins acted on behalf of Highway's best interest because he was unconscious at the time that the emergency unit brought him to the hospital. Without the doctor's quick and compassionate thinking, not only would Highway *not* have a career, but he also wouldn't have a *life* to live either. The jury acquitted Collins and the hospital of any wrongdoing. Pam was now his lifelong hero and one of the highest revenue generators at her firm.

As Pam pulled up to the iron gates of the estate that day, the security guard checked her name off the list, and she proceeded up the winding driveway. She couldn't help but notice the lush gardens strategically planted around the periphery of the estate. Reminiscent of an Italian villa, the property boasted cypress trees, deep red rose bushes, and fragrant rosemary and lavender bushes that curved along the walkways and the sloping grounds.

A stunning Tuscan mansion stood at the top of the long winding driveway, drenched in a soft marble yellow tone accentuated with a burnt amber Tuscan tiled roof. Guests were greeted by a lovely water fountain that displayed a grandfather reading the Old Testament to his grandson.

"Dr. Gerald Collins is livin' large. This place is unbelievable," Pam said as she parked her car underneath the stone detailed portico and was greeted by a valet.

"Good evening, Ms. Madison. Welcome to Collins *tagliare di Italia,*" said the very attractive young man. He opened her door and took her hand to assist her out of the car.

"So, Gerald has a name for his place, too?" The valet smiled and nodded. "That figures," Pam said quietly under her breath. "So, what does that mean in English?"

"Collins's slice of Italy," the valet politely answered.

Gerald would be the one to give his estate a name and no less after him. He was truly in love with his success and worshipped the ground he walked on. No wonder she admired him so much; she laughed to herself as she handed the valet a ten-dollar bill.

"Thank you, madam, but we are not taking tips this evening."

"My, my, my. He is truly celebrating," Pam said, impressed, as she kindly took back her tip. She walked across the cobblestone driveway to two twelve-foot mahogany doors. Before she could pull the cord doorbell, a very meticulously dressed butler appeared and opened the door to the most stunning grand foyer Pam had ever seen. The entire area was punctuated with imported marble flooring, Venetian columns, and a stunning domed ceiling that featured hand-painted angels seated on top of clouds.

"Welcome, Ms. Madison. Dr. Collins will be so happy that you were able to come," he said stiffly.

"Why, thank you," Pam said, somewhat caught off guard by the butler's familiarity with her, especially because they had never met.

"Let's hear it for the best attorney in the world," shouted a loud voice from the top of the banister. The voice was Dr. Collins's, and Pam couldn't tell if he was inebriated or just truly excited to see her at his party.

"Dr. Collins! Hello, there!" she shouted back.

"Please, you know I hate that formal title coming from you," he said, feigning annoyance.

"Gerald," Pam quickly corrected herself as he made his way down the winding staircase. His usual air of sophistication was complemented tonight by a black smoking jacket and charcoal gray ascot. His lips formed tightly around an unlit imported cigar, his trademark whenever he threw lavish parties. Champagne glasses raised, and the crowd cheered, "Hear, hear!"

The butler arrived with a glass of champagne for Pam. She politely took it and raised her glass to her audience and took a sip. A drink was what she needed right about now, to take the edge off of her startling welcome. She had no idea that Dr. Collins was going to make *her* the focus of his party.

Every doctor, lawyer, and political constituent had flown into Atlanta for this party, which seemed like more of a congratulatory party for Pam instead of her client. Pam decided she would rise to the occasion and take advantage of the accolades that people were bestowing upon her.

Dr. Collins motioned to his wife, Adrienne, to join him in the middle of the foyer. She tried her best to maneuver her way gracefully through the large crowd that was beginning to huddle around Pam. The hostess's exotic bluish-green eyes surveyed Pam from across the room, her large belly leading the way as she waddled toward her. Adrienne was seven months pregnant and was wearing a lovely tea-length white linen maternity dress with a pearl neckline that revealed a small portion of her cleavage. Ruffles skirting the dress swayed elegantly as she walked. Her dark chestnut hair was pulled back taut and neatly twisted into a bun that was adorned with a pearl barrette, matching the beads on the bodice of her dress and her pearl-studded earrings.

For a moment Pam felt her hand instinctively rub her own stomach as her thoughts drifted to another place.

"Are you okay, Miss?" The gentle voice appeared out of nowhere as she immediately shoved her hand down and stood at attention.

"Oh, yes, I'm fine. Thanks," she said as she glanced up at the dark-haired man who was looking at her with intrigue. Pam looked back over at Adrienne and thought she was the quintessential doctor's wife: refined, beautiful, loved to entertain lavishly, chaired on major social and civic organizations, managed the household, and enjoyed all the comforts of her husband's money. At the ripe young age of thirty-three, she managed to do what many women only dreamed. She became Mrs. Gerald Collins, and had no intentions of being the *former* Mrs. Collins . . . *ever.*

"Wow, my friend truly has it all," the Italian accent spoke again.

"Yes, they seem perfect for each other."

"And that's a rarity these days," the handsome Italian quipped. "To find someone compatible enough to want to spend the rest of your life with—that says it all."

Pam was surprised by his comment and could only smile. "A lawyer at a loss for words, now that's unusual," he joked.

"I'm sorry but *who* are you?" Pam asked, trying hard not to sound put off by his candid remark. For all she knew, he could be Gerald's brother and that would be the last person she wanted to insult. But, when she turned around for him to respond, he was gone.

Adrienne made her way over to Pam and extended her hand. "Pam, it's so good of you to join us. This absolutely could not have been a celebration without you." She winced slightly and placed her hand on the side of her stomach.

Gerald was walking toward her. "Honey, are you all right?"

"Oh, the baby just kicked, that's all. It just caught me a little off guard."

"Well, I think I've got a little slugger in there who might just be ready to come out and hit some balls with Da-Da," he said, talking to her stomach.

"Oh, Gerald! You are such a . . ." She grabbed hold of the side of her stomach again and used the other hand to hold onto Gerald's arm. "Wow, now, that was a big kick!" Adrienne bent over, still holding onto her side. "You may have something there, dear."

"See, I told you. Please excuse us for one second Pam, while I take Adrienne over to the keeping room to have a seat. I think you'll be more comfortable with your feet propped up, and you can still be in the midst of mingling with our guests."

"Oh, Gerald, you don't have to make such a fuss," Adrienne said coyly, pretending to protest.

That's right, work it, girlfriend. Enjoy being pampered now, because once that baby gets here, you will be too tired to try and look that gorgeous, and Gerald's eyes will start wandering elsewhere just like they've always done. Pam sipped her glass of champagne and watched the butler walk toward Adrienne and pour her a cup of herbal tea as Gerald massaged her shoulders.

"Gerald, I'll be fine," Adrienne said, tapping him on the hands. "I'm not the first woman on earth to get kicked by a baby! Ow!" she said, grabbing her stomach again. "Please go on back over to Pam. She has worked hard on your case and deserves a little attention. Edward will take good care of me, won't you?"

"Of course, madam," Edward answered.

"See, Gerald . . . now, scoot!"

Gerald kissed her delicately on the hand and held it close to his chest before placing it gently in her lap. He grabbed another champagne flute off the silver tray on the table and returned to his guests.

"Ladies and gentleman, let me just say that if you are ever in need of an excellent attorney, then Pam Madison of Sterling, Mathis, and Silverman is the one to get the job done. I can't tell you how relieved I am to have had such a fine attorney and to have won!" Gerald said, shaking his head in relief. "I've spent a ton on legal fees with this great firm," Gerald chuckled as he lifted his glass in the air. He firmly shook Pam's hand and gave her a congratulatory hug. "Believe me, to see justice work on your side—it is all definitely worth it!"

A few guests had gathered in the living room while the others were looking over the loft at Pam. This was Pam's finest hour, and she knew she'd better take advantage of all the praise the good doctor was giving her.

"It has been both an honor and a pleasure to represent such a fine physician as Dr. Collins," she said looking into his grateful eyes. "You represent honor and integrity and always put your patients first. This was a difficult case to try, but not a difficult client to represent." Pam lifted her champagne glass toward him. "Congratulations again, and thank you for entrusting Sterling, Mathis, and Silverman with your case," she remarked, cleverly making sure that people would make a mental note of the name.

The applause echoed throughout the mansion as Pam walked confidently back to the living room. She sat down on the rose-hued silk chaise next to the mahogany baby grand piano. A line had started to form in front of her with guests asking for her business cards. And just as before, out of nowhere, toward the end of the line, stood that same tall, attractive man who'd spoken with her earlier. He appeared to be in his early '40s and was wearing a classic navy two-button Prada suit that fit like a custom-made glove on his 6'2" deeply tanned, sculptured frame. He wore his hair a little long for her taste, but she thought the way his wispy curls tucked neatly behind his ear lobes was sexy. She felt his deep blue eyes staring at her as he moved in closer. His cologne smelled of a fresh mix of mandarin oranges, berries, and sweet ginger.

"You are a *very* beautiful and a very talented lady. I would love to talk with you if you could spare a few minutes," he said with an irresistible Italian accent.

Mmmm . . . that was the sexiest dimpled chin she'd ever seen on a man. *All right, Pam, stop it! You cannot afford to do this to yourself.* Her thoughts were interrupted by his succulent lips that seemed to pronounce each word in a deliberate and steady rhythm. She gained her composure and looked at her watch.

She folded her hands across her chest and crossed her legs. "You have *one*," she said, trying to keep her professionalism.

He smiled and that irresistible dimple appeared again. "Only one minute?"

"Yes. *One*."

"Okay, I'm Marco. It's a pleasure meeting you," he said, as he extended his hands to shake hers.

Pam nodded with approval as she felt him grip her fingers tightly and then tenderly release them, almost as if he were surreptitiously seducing her. Pam felt a slow tingling build up inside of her.

"So, how do you know Dr. Collins?" Pam asked.

"He and I are good friends."

"Hmmm . . . that's nice," she responded casually. As she looked him over, their eyes locked for the first time. His pensive look started to make her feel uncomfortable.

Marco felt her uneasiness, but it was difficult for him to focus his eyes anywhere but on her.

"Well, it was nice meeting you," she stood up and turned to walk away.

"Hey, wait a minute. Is *that* it?"

Pam turned to look back at him. "I said *one* minute." She glanced at her watch. "And it's over." He was a very good-looking Italian man, but she wasn't interested in him or anyone else right now.

"Can I get at least another sixty seconds?"

"For what?"

"Well, we could talk a little more, or perhaps you would be so kind as to give me your home telephone number."

This man must be smokin' something real good. "*My* home phone number?"

"Yes . . ."

"Oh, come, now. What makes you think I'm going to give my phone number to a stranger?"

"But I'm not a stranger. You know my name." His smile was broadening.

Pam laughed. "You're good, but not that good. Do you live in Atlanta?"

"No, I'm here visiting from out west for a few days. But I do travel to Atlanta quite a bit."

Pam looked at her watch again.

"My sixty seconds are up again?"

"Sorry, yes. I've got another big case coming up and I really need to be getting back to the office."

"I understand, duty calls." He took her hand and kissed it. The touch of his moist lips made her heart race. "What about what I asked you earlier?"

"What was that?" she said, pretending not to remember.

"Your phone number?"

"Oh, that? No, I don't think so."

"But why not?"

"It's just not my thing, Marco—to give my home number out."

"Your *thing* is not to give your number out *period*, or just not to *me*?"

"Hey, listen. You seem like a really nice man, but right now is just not a good time for me. So let's just leave it at that, okay?"

"So if I had met you at another time and place, you would let me call you?"

"Another time and place, yes, I think so," Pam said, surprised at herself for even pondering his question.

"Ooh! You hurt my heart!" he said, with a mock stab to his heart. "Until next time. *Arrivederci*."

"Goodbye, Marco," Pam said, as she made her way to Dr. Collins and his guests to say her farewells.

After Pam replayed the meeting with Marco in her head, she immediately got up, jumped out of bed, and sprinted down the hallway to the one place she felt at peace when everything around her had gone awry. She sat down in the middle of the floor of her home office on her Persian rug and imagined herself drifting away on a cloud. She began to breathe deeply and was just about to get into her private zone when she heard her alarm clock blaring from her bedroom. She looked up at the crystal clock on her wall and saw that it was now 7:00 a.m.

"This will just have to wait until later," she said as she headed hastily toward the bathroom. She took off her purple satin floor-length nightgown and let it drop to the floor before she got into the glass shower. She turned the water on full blast, working up a soapy lather and washing her body briskly, then let the water flow forcefully onto her tense muscles. She went through her schedule in her head as she shampooed her hair.

Okay, first things first. She needed to tell Pete that she'd have to get another paralegal to assist her with this case or she was screwed. After that, she needed to take a second look at the files that Amanda put together. Damn that woman!

Pam got out of the shower, dried off, and strolled over to her walk-in closet, which was the size of a small guest bedroom. She chose a black pair of satin panties, a matching lace bra, and a sheer pair of stockings, and then dressed in front of her full-length mirror.

After sifting through six racks of summer and winter suits, she haphazardly threw the summer clothes in a pile on the floor until she got to her collection of fall Saint John suits.

"I'll wear you to plead my case today to Pete," she said, pulling out a sheik navy two-piece skirt suit and a black pair of sky high Manolo Blahniks.

She sauntered over to her crowded makeup table and brushed on just enough bronze eye shadow to emphasize her infamous eyes. Next, she put on a light red lip liner, complemented by ruby red lipstick, and carefully lined her eyes with a light brown pencil. She gave her cheeks a hint of rose blush and finger-combed her short curly brown hair to let it dry naturally. Her look was completed with a pair of small gold-hoop earrings and her favorite custom leather briefcase with her initials embossed on the front.

Pam handed her keys over to the concierge when she got down to the elevator lobby. Within minutes, her silver Mercedes-Benz SLK 350 Roadster appeared in the circular driveway. She slid behind the wheel before remembering she had to make a stop before heading to her office.

May Day . . . May Day

It had been only an hour since his brief telephone conversation with Pam, and Marco could not get this intoxicating woman out of his thoughts. He still couldn't believe how she had just blown him off.

"Damn," he said to himself as his fingers tapped the base of the phone. There was something about Pam that further piqued his interest. Before he knew it, his fingers were dialing again.

"Hello, Collins residence," a stiff and decorous voice answered.

"Gerald, please."

"May I ask whose calling, sir?"

"It's Marco."

"Marco, who?"

"Marco who do you think?" he said impatiently as he rolled his eyes. He had forgotten just how arrogant Gerald's butler could be sometimes. The butler knew exactly who Marco was. He just enjoyed acting important.

"Hold on, sir. I'll see if Dr. Collins is available." A couple of minutes passed. Marco was about to hang up when Gerald finally answered.

"Hello, Marco?"

"Yeah, it's me."

"Is everything all right?" he inquired as he stared at the clock.

"I thought you'd be up and out by now, my friend. It's 7:30 in the morning."

"Normally I would be. But I'm off today."

"And his majesty, Edward, woke up his master to speak with me? Oh, my, I must tip Edward an extra quarter the next time I'm there!"

"Very funny," he said "It must be important because you're calling me at the crack of dawn. But, as usual, you don't want anything, so I'm hanging up and going back to sleep with my beautiful wife. Goodbye."

"Hey! Hold on a second." Marco thought he heard Adrienne's whispering in the background. It was obvious he had picked a bad time to call his friend. He heard giggling.

"Good morning, Marco," Adrienne said.

"How is the mother-to-be?"

"We're fine," she responded in a cooing manner. "So, Marco, why are you *really* calling?"

"Adrienne, give me the phone," Gerald hissed. Marco could hear Adrienne gigling again, and he could imagine the two of them wrestling for the cordless phone. Adrienne loved to tease, especially when it came to his best friend.

Marco heard more giggling as Gerald and Adrienne fought over the phone. He waited patiently for their childish behavior to end.

"It's about Pam," Marco said, though he wasn't sure if either of them had heard him.

Finally, Gerald spoke, "I don't know about her personal affairs other than she's single," he said, pacing back forth. "Why don't you just ask her out?"

Marco sighed heavily. "I tried that."

Gerald took the phone from his ear and covered his mouth so Marco would not hear his laughter. "She refused *you*?"

"Let's just say she's got a really big case coming up and . . ."

"She blew *you* off for a case. Now it's becoming a lot clearer. This is priceless."

"Ha!" Adrienne shouted loud enough for Marco to hear her. "*She* blew *him* off. Now that's a first!"

"Calling *you* was a big mistake! What was *I* thinking?"

"Okay . . . okay . . . if you can't support a best friend when a woman rejects him, then what kind of friend would I be, huh, buddy?"

"Very funny," Marco mumbled. He knew Gerald loved every minute of this. "Listen, I called because you worked with the woman for several months, so I figured you of all people could give me some advice on how to get . . ."

"Laid?" Gerald retorted.

Adrienne laughed hysterically in the background. "She's going to be a hard nut to crack even for the irresistible Marco Grimaldi!" she yelled.

"Tell Adrienne when I want her opinion, I'll be sure to call when she's in labor," Marco jabbed back.

"Now, there's no need to be nasty," Gerald said, protectively.

"I just need to know what kind of vibe you got from her when she was working on your case." Marco sounded so helpless.

"She is strictly business. Perhaps too much. That's why we won. I don't know how she does it, but she made me feel as if I was her number one priority. I know she had several other big cases she was handling. She's so driven. But, she moves very slowly, very carefully and then BAM! She has a surprise waiting for you. She's talented. Man, she's mesmerizing, but intimidating as hell in that courtroom! But, like I said, I didn't get one glimpse of her personal side. Pam kept that all to herself."

"Hmmm. So that's what she likes—catching people totally by surprise?" Marco quipped.

"She does the surprise element thing in the courtroom well. I mean, she must have had some compelling evidence about Highway Hathaway's ass. Before the case was over, she had the guy thinking about suing *Porsche* instead of suing *me* for his accident," Gerald answered reflectively.

Marco laughed. Pam looked as if she could bite the head right off of a cobra without batting an eye, but his instincts told him there was more to her than just a high-priced suit and a keen legal mind. Marco intended to uncover her stoic persona and get to know every inch of the real woman.

"Well, Marco, my friend, if there was a man who could open up a heart of stone and make it bleed, it's you. The question is: why her?"

"Why not?"

"It's obvious she's not going to give you the time of day or else you wouldn't be calling me. With all of the women I've seen you bring through here, I don't understand why you would go through the hassle when you've had someone like Sha—"

"Don't say her name, please!" Marco begged.

"All right," Gerald said.

"I was lucky to escape that one. She was crazy and only interested in my money anyway—you know that!"

"No, you like to think that, but she really loved you. Adrienne and I both saw how she felt when she caught you with that long-legged bimbo. Marco, what was her name?"

"It was Clarissa. And she's not a bimbo!"

"She is in comparison to Sha—"

"I warned you, Gerald! Don't say that woman's name or I'm hanging up!"

"Well, *she* was devastated when she caught you with Clarissa," Gerald scolded.

"And still *is*!" Adrienne chimed in again.

"Listen, I didn't call you to dredge up my past relationship with my ex-fiancée. I've moved on. Let's just say that it's been a while since I met a woman who's as spirited as Pam."

"And who's independent, makes shitloads of money, and doesn't want to give you the time of day. Hey, that's it! She's the equivalent of a female Marco!" Gerald shouted. "That's it, isn't it? She reminds you of *you*! And who do you love more than anyone else in this world?"

"HIMSELF!" Adrienne joined in.

"All right . . . all right, who made *you* a psychiatrist?"

"Well, I've learned from the best," Gerald chided.

"Whatever, Gerald. As always, it's been a pleasure talking with you and Adrienne. When can I come by for more insults?"

Gerald laughed. "Hey Adrienne, Marco wants to know when he can come by for some more insults?"

"Tell him to be here for dinner tonight at 8:00 sharp. I'll have Edward whip up his favorite ziti and meatballs with a delicious sorbet for dessert."

"May I bring a guest?"

"You're not thinking about bringing Pam, are you?"

"Why not?"

"Now *that* could turn out to be an interesting evening," Gerald said.

"Glad you think so. So call her and invite her. You owe me anyway! I'll see you at 8:00." He hung up the phone and chuckled at the thought of Gerald listening to a dial tone.

Close Connection

Dee opened her eyes with care, looking and remembering her night. She stretched her arms, pulling the blanket and causing Chris to stir. His long eyelashes fluttered against the nape of her neck. One of his legs was draped across hers while his large, hardened penis rested insistently on the back of her buttocks as she lay on her side.

"Good morning," Dee whispered into Chris's ear. Her stomach rumbled faintly.

"You hungry for more, baby?" Chris teased, poking her with his erection.

Dee turned to face him, firmly grabbing his cock as she nibbled on his ear lobe. "Actually, I'm *still* hungry for that French food you were supposed to order us last night."

He thrust his growing organ into her hand and moved back and forth. "All right, now, don't start something you can't finish." Dee's stomach growled louder as she laughed at him. "I can't believe you're waking up this early—hungry—especially as I filled you up with enough lovin' that should have tied you over at least until breakfast!"

"Oh, you've filled me up, all right," she mused. "But I'd feel a lot better if I could order up some eggs and sausage with a side of pancakes."

"Aight, aight, a brotha can take a hint. I'll call room service." Chris turned to pick up the phone. "Oh, hell, naw!" Please don't tell me . . ." he groaned as he glanced at the clock on top of the nightstand.

"What's wrong?"

"Where's my watch?" Chris asked brusquely.

"Over there, on the dresser, but . . ." She watched Chris run in panic to the dresser and glance at the clock.

"Shit! It's 10:00!" Chris yelled.

"It's 10:00!" Dee dashed out of bed and grabbed her robe. Her crew pick-up was in thirty minutes, and she had to get this man out of her room, put on her flight attendant uniform, and get her behind in that lobby so she could catch her flight. How was she going to do all of that without blowing her cover?

"How in the world did this happen?"

"It's called not setting your alarm clock *before* you get your sex on," Chris scoffed as he hastily buttoned his shirt and zipped his pants. "Now where are my socks and shoes?"

"You didn't wear socks, and your loafers are over there by the fireplace," Dee said rushing over to retrieve them and tossing them to him while he hurried to fastened his belt and put his shoes on.

"Thanks, baby. Listen, I hate to run out like this, but I've got a meeting with my coach at eleven, and he will have my ass if I'm late again!"

She grabbed his hand and rushed him to the door. "Hey, don't worry about it. I've got to get out of here myself."

He looked at her apologetically. "When will you be back in Miami?"

"In two weeks. For the National Conference of Black Lawyers," she responded, knowing that her schedule would bring her back to Miami at least four times that month.

"I'll see you in two weeks, then." Chris pulled her into his arms and gave her a quick thrust of his tongue.

Yes, you most definitely will!

Chris grabbed his keys from the fireplace mantel and ran out the door as Dee scrambled to get ready for her flight. Fifteen minutes had passed when Dee's cell phone rang.

"Auntie Dee? It's me, Tracey!"

"Hey, darlin'! How are you?" Dee said, detecting a little anxiety in Tracey's voice.

"I'm cool. Did you get my text last night?"

"Ah . . . no. I've had my cell phone off. Is everything all right? "

"I really nee—"

"Tracey," Dee interrupted. "Hold on a sec, I've got another call coming in." It was Chris. She hoped he didn't forget something. Dee seemed to be doing a bizarre dance as she tried to dress and juggle calls.

"Desiree, sorry to bother you, baby, I know you're probably on your way out. But I forgot to ask you something. I need a favor."

"I'm getting ready to walk out now. I hope you didn't forget something."

"No, I didn't. I'm not calling for me; it's for one of my team members. He needs a lawyer."

Dee almost dropped the phone. "What does he need a lawyer for?"

"I think one of his one-night stands is trying to pin him on a paternity suit."

"Oh, I see. Yes, he would need an attorney but . . ."

"Desiree, can you just talk to him? I didn't make him any promises, but I told him about you."

"Ah . . . yeah . . . okay. I'll talk with him." She suddenly felt the need to take the phone and hit herself upside the head with it.

"Okay, I'll bring him to meet you in the next couple of weeks."

"Okay, see you then—gotta run! Bye, Chris!" Dee hurriedly clicked back over to Tracey.

"Tracey, are you still there?"

"Yes, I'm here. Is this a good time? You sound a little rushed."

Dee looked at the clock as she closed her suitcase and gave herself a once over in the mirror. She knew she needed to rush to the lobby, but Tracey sounded like she really needed to talk.

"I'm going to put you on speaker, okay? I don't have my earpiece, and I still need to brush my hair and teeth. But, I'm listening. Go ahead."

"This is kind of personal, Aunt Dee. Is anyone in the room with you where they can hear me?"

"Nope, just me," Dee answered as she took a comb to her hair and then grabbed a toothbrush. While they were still on the phone, Dee gathered her suitcase and room key, then scurried out of the door while still trying to maneuver the phone to her ear. "Tracey, I'm about to get on an elevator, so I may loo . . . Tracey, hello?" she said while stepping into the elevator. The doors opened before she could dial Tracey back.

"Hey Dee, we're headed to the van," Birdie announced with a wave.

"Okay, I'll be right there," Dee waved back as she walked over to the checkout desk to turn in her key. Her phone rang.

"Hi Tracey, I'm sorry about that. I figured we would get cut off as soon as that elevator door closed."

Tracey laughed. "Can you talk now?"

"I feel terrible about this because I can tell by your tone that this is a conversation that we need to have in private."

Tracey sighed deeply. "And you can't talk now, either, right?"

Dee shook her head and looked at her watch. She could see the crew loading their bags on the van as she neared the glass doorway. "I'm so sorry, darlin', but I'm headed to the crew van, and I won't be able to talk now."

"When will you be back in Atlanta?"

"I'm actually on my way back now, and I'll call you when I get there."

"Promise?"

"Yes, I promise."

Stand By

Surprised to find Tracey at his front door, he said, "Hey, what are you doing here?"

"I *had* to see you."

"Does your mama know you're out this late?" He knew Tracey's answer immediately when he saw her staring at the floorboards. "C'mon, Tracey, you know better than to be out this late at night. Your mama will be worried sick about you."

"Please, just a few minutes. I just had to see you."

"No, Tracey, you've got to go home," he said, escorting her to the door.

"Please? You said on the phone you had something you wanted to show me."

"I know, but I didn't mean tonight! Besides, it can wait. I'll show you some other ti—"

"No! I don't want to wait!"

"Tracey, I'm not going to stand here and argue with you. You can get into a lot of trouble for sneaking out like this. Shoot! We both can! How'd you get here, anyway?"

"A friend of mine dropped me off."

"Who?"

Tracey shook her head, and her eyes pleaded with him not to make her tell. "Listen, I'm going to get this for you and then I want you to go back home. Or I'll take you myself." He quickly went in the bedroom and returned with a beautifully wrapped green and gold box.

"Oh, this is wrapped so pretty! How did you know my school colors?"

He smiled at her enthusiasm. "A green and yellow bird told me. Go ahead and open it."

Tracey carefully unwrapped the gift then took out the black velvet box inside and caressed it. She finally opened it. She gasped.

"You like it?"

"I don't know what to say," she whispered. "It's gorgeous, such a beautiful necklace."

"Now, that's your birthstone in the middle," he said, pointing to the large stone. "Your mama's is on the right, and mine is on the left. Now you can keep the two of us close to you when you go away to college."

Tracey's eyes began to fill with tears. "Here, put it on me," she said, pulling up her hair.

"Tracey, I just can't tell you enough how proud I am of you—I know your mama is too," he said, working his hands to fasten the gold chain around her neck.

Tracey was silent for a moment as she twirled the precious stones in her hands. She hated that she had to sneak out like this. But that was how it had to be for now.

"Hey, there. Earth to Tracey," he whispered in her ear. His gentle voice made her smile.

"I'm sorry. I just was a million miles from here."

"I see that," he said as he touched the side of her cheek.

She placed her hand on top of his and held it. "It's just hard to believe I'm sitting here with you and we are finally together."

He looked at Tracey, lifted her hand and clasped it in his. "I already told you that it hasn't been because I didn't want to be with you. Or even try for that matter."

"And you can't explain all of the returned letters?"

"I already told you. I never got them. Now, sweetheart, you've got to get back home before your mama finds out you're gone. That's if she hasn't already."

Tracey had so many questions. Now was just not the time to ask. She squeezed his hand, and then placed it close to her heart.

In less than two hours she would be celebrating the end of her high school era. Now she was starting a new one: going away to college and getting to know her father.

Excess Baggage

Greg buttoned his leather trench coat and checked the time on his cell phone for the second time in ten minutes. He was early as usual. Here he was, sitting on a park bench while a crisp and cool September breeze blew through his hair. If Pam came, she would show up on time . . . as usual. He looked at his watch again, and it was 8:00 a.m. on the nose.

Pam's heart pounded double-time the closer she got to him. Her instincts told her to run in the opposite direction.

"Hey, there. Thanks for showing up," he said as he stood up.

Pam nodded and gave him a brief smile.

"It's a little nippy today for this time of year." Greg raised his coat collar. "You want to walk or sit?"

Pam shrugged her shoulders and tightened the belt around her all-weather coat.

"Okay, let's walk then," he said.

Pam kept her distance between them. She looked like a miniature doll next to his 6'4" frame. His fair skin looked a little pale, considering. And he still kept his dark brown curls cut close enough that she could hardly tell that he had them.

His dreamy light gray eyes pierced through her, invoking an uncomfortable familiarity. She felt herself purposefully ignoring his gaze.

"It's *really* good to see you," he said, trying to make eye contact. Pam gave a weak smile as she continued walking.

"Man, nature is so beautiful, you know? Wow! Look at those deer over there running!" He pointed and inhaled deeply as if it was the first time he had smelled fresh air.

"Everything just looks so different to me, now," he said as he looked at her sadly. Pam nodded and her heart softened for a moment as they stood in silence and watched the deer.

"I never thought I'd see this again. Or you for that matter." Greg turned to her, touching her hair, then stammered, "I messed up."

Pam thought she could handle meeting with him, but she suddenly felt weak in the knees. She walked toward the duck pond and sat on the bench. Greg followed her and sat down next to her.

"When I was locked up, all I could do was think about you and what happened," he said, barely able to look Pam in the eyes.

Pam took deep breaths, praying her tears would not come. She tried to refocus by shaking her head slowly and massaging her temples.

"Hey, I know that look. You're in that zone again, aren't you? Do you still keep that home office of yours like a temple to meditate in, like you did when we were back in Chicago?"

Pam found it sobering that he even remembered her idiosyncrasy. Nevertheless, she was not here to talk to him about Atlanta versus Chicago. She tried to speak as calmly as she could. "Greg, what do you want? Why in the hell did you call me?"

"Baby . . ."

Pam raised her hand to Greg's face and her voice became louder. "Please . . . don't call me that. I never want to hear that word come from you again. Do you hear me?"

"Pam, I'm so sorry."

"Yes, *you* are and so am I! I don't know what on earth I was thinking about agreeing to meet with you! I can't take this—I just can't!" Tears formed and she could no longer stand it; she got up abruptly and walked away.

Greg jumped up. "Please, Pammy, don't go," he said pulling her hand.

Pam wiped her eyes with her other hand. A small smile formed on her lips because Greg was the only person who called her Pammy.

"Good, I can still make you smile. I always said you look tough on the outside, but on the inside you are just as soft and sweet like jam. And as I can't call you Jammy, I'll always call you Pammy," he whispered in her ear.

She followed him reluctantly back over to the park bench.

"Thank you for coming to hear me out," Greg said. "I couldn't think of anything but you and what happened to our—"

"You can't even say it! Our baby!"

"I know," he said as he balled his fists. "I've been avoiding it. I just had to. It killed me not to be with you when it happened."

Pam stared at the pond as if she could draw strength from it. She did not want to bring up the past. She placed her hand gently over Greg's mouth. "It's behind me now. I don't want to talk about her."

"I know—but I do! I never heard from you again! Dee would come by, but . . ."

"Dee? What in the hell was Dee coming by to see *you* for? She *never* told me that!"

"Well, that doesn't surprise me at all. She was like a surrogate mother for you when you lost . . . I mean, she didn't want you to know," Greg said as he dropped his head and peered down at his hands. "She felt like I needed to know the update on your progress because I was on suicide watch at the time. And she helped me *not* to kill myself!"

"I never knew . . ."

"I didn't want you to know. I had put you through so much already."

"I can't believe Dee never told me this."

"I begged Dee not to tell you. She was a good friend to me. Something I didn't have in anyone else after I lost you. You know, Pammy, it's been three long years, and I needed to see how you've been doing."

Pam batted her eyes to hold back the tears, then made eye contact with him. "It's been difficult for me—very difficult. I'm not the same woman that I used to be."

"What do you mean?"

Pam was silent again. "What I mean is that I'm very bitter, Greg. I try not to be, but I am. I'm afraid to even get close again with another man. I still harbor so much bitterness and hate for what happened between us. It's hard to believe that's what drives me through the caseloads and the ungodly hours. Not to mention, I just lost one of my best friends that I've known for years because she says I've treated her so badly."

"Who?"

"Amanda Shipman."

"Amanda? Your girl from Spelman?"

"Yes, I helped her get into SMS on *one* condition—that she never take advantage of our friendship or ask for special treatment. And then she up and quit on me, just like that!" she said snapping her fingers.

"Well, unless she's changed dramatically, I can't imagine Amanda acting like that without good reason."

"Oh, so what are you saying? I'm lying?" Pam lashed out and snatched her hand from his reach.

"No, I—"

"Listen, I'm not here to discuss that woman," Pam said, seething at the thought that she was sharing anything personal with Greg.

Greg held up his hands and started playfully backing away. "Whoa, hey, I'm not here to judge you." His tone was empathetic. "I didn't come to talk about Amanda, either. I just wanted to see you and tell you that I want you to be happy."

Pam rolled her eyes at his ridiculous suggestion. He inched himself closer and reached out to touch her hand. "Pam, you deserve happiness. True love. Don't allow what happened to us ruin your life."

"Greg, it already has," she said removing her hand from his reach. "But you know what the irony in all of this is?"

"No," he said, twisting his hands together.

"This horrible experience has made me one of the most successful attorneys in our firm. All I have to do is think about June 16 and . . ."

"No, Pammy, don't . . ."

"When I waited in my wedding dress in a chapel filled with people!"

"Please don't do this—"

"And you never showed up!"

"I didn't mean for it to happen that way. You know I wanted to be there!"

"You never showed up because you were being handcuffed on our wedding day!"

Greg grabbed her and tried to hold her close. "Pammy, please, let's not . . ."

"Let's not what?" Pam yelled as she yanked away from him. "Discuss the fact that you were arrested for being a CPA who was on the take at his own accounting firm!"

Greg was quiet. Pam needed to let this out. He had served his time in federal prison, and now it was his turn to face the moral prison sentence with her.

"All I can remember was feeling like it was my darkest nightmare coming to life as Dee drove me to the jail. She was in her bridesmaid dress, and I was still wearing my wedding gown—veil and all—hoping that this was some terrible mistake." Pam laughed and tried to choke back her tears. "I actually thought that they had the wrong guy, and that I would just clear this minor error up and we would go on and get married! Ha! What a fool I was!"

Greg put his hand on her back to comfort her, but Pam was on a roll. She sharply pulled away from him. It was as if she was the defendant giving her testimony to a jury, as if he were still on trial. "My God, Greg, you lied to me! You lied to our family. Everybody!"

"I know, Pammy. I know," Greg whispered.

His self-restraint only fueled her anger more. "And not to mention the fact that I worked my ass off trying to defend you. Then I find out that all of the evidence the Feds had against you was overwhelming!" Pam's hands were trembling. "And that was the day I lost her." The tears that Pam had been holding back now flooded her eyes. "I had to sell the $600,000 house we bought together! I had to get my name off of all our bills! Damn you, Greg! You made my life a fucking financial mess!"

Greg had more self-control than Pam could take. He had learned to be that way biding his time in prison. The quieter he got, the angrier she became. Her words spewed out of her mouth like a scorpion's venom.

"Here I am thinking that I was marrying someone who loved me for me, and you were running a scam on me just like the rest of these brothas out here on the take! I was four months pregnant and poof! Our baby girl was gone in an instant! Just like you! I hate you! I hate you!" Pam started pounding at his chest with her fists. He managed to pull her arms down and hold her as she sobbed against his chest.

"I'm so sorry. I didn't mean for it to be this way. I love you, Pam. I always have."

Pam pulled back as he wiped the tears from her face. "Greg, I don't want to continue to feel this way. I have so much hate inside of me, and the thought that Dee stayed in contact with you . . ." She shook her head angrily as her words trailed off.

"Oh, Pam, please let me set the record straight with your girl, Dee. She was not sympathizing with me—no way. And not under any terms was I to contact you while I was still in prison. She wanted you to have a fresh start. Hell, I had even thought you might be married by now."

"You're kidding, right? I can't go through that walking down the aisle thing again. You drove me out of town, Greg! The news hit the paper like an uncontrollable fire. *Successful Attorney and Wealthy CPA Wedding Ends up behind Bars*," she said, pointing in the air to an imaginary headline. "I couldn't take the rumors."

"So, that's why I kept getting a disconnected number when I tried to call you. You had already left Chicago and moved to Atlanta," Greg said.

"If it hadn't been for Dee checking on me, flying in and out of Atlanta while I was in the hospital in Chicago, I don't think I would have survived. My mother had to be hospitalized for our entire trauma. My siblings blamed me for getting caught up with someone I didn't know—again. Nothing's been right since."

Greg's words were stuck in his throat. He could only look at Pam with tear-filled eyes as he felt them run down his face.

Pam threw her hands up in the air with exasperation. "Well, you asked how I've been. And now you know."

"Pam, I know nothing is going to change what happened between us. But I need to at least admit to myself and to you that I just got caught up in the life. It just seemed so easy to take a little bit here and there. I had seen other CPAs do it before without getting caught. And . . ."

"I know you thought *you* could get away with it. But at what cost? How could you think you could get away with stealing over half a million dollars?"

"I was stupid."

"Yes, you were. And I was *stupid* for agreeing to marry you."

"You didn't know . . ."

"You're right. I didn't know. And that was my fault. I got so caught up in your handsome looks, your wining and dining me, and I fell for you—all of you—and way too hard from the first day I met you. Now look at us," she said as she hung her head down and felt an ache in the pit of her stomach. He took his hand and stroked her tear-stained cheek. The warmth of his touch made her tremble. She shoved his hand away. "Just leave me the *hell* alone!"

Greg ignored her remark and lifted her face with his other hand. He moved in closer and kissed her lips tenderly. His tongue felt so good inside her mouth.

"Greg, I gotta go," Pam said, almost out of breath.

"Pam, I'm sorry," he whispered. "Can you ever forgive me?"

"Forgive you?"

"Yes, I've changed Pam. I found the Lord."

"You *found* the Lord in prison?" She managed to laugh. "I didn't know He was ever *lost*!"

"Okay, you're being sarcastic, but I'm serious."

"And what did the Lord tell you, Greg, when you found Him in prison, huh?" She paused still stunned about his newfound spirituality. *Where was his faith when he was stealing that money three years ago?*

"He told me to—"

Pam held her hand up to stop him. "You know what? Don't even bother answering that." Her voice started to quiver as she buttoned the top button of her coat. "Just save your testimony, Greg. Save *all* of it for your probation officer."

Briefing

While buckling into her jump seat, Birdie asked, "So, Dee, did you get a good night's rest?"

"Yeah, I did, actually," Dee grinned. "How about you ladies?"

"Oh, yes, we were quite comfortable. I love that hotel. We missed you at dinner."

"I know. I was so tired Birdie, that I slept right through it," she said, smiling again at the thought of Chris keeping her *busy* through dinner.

"Well, you missed out on some good Mexican."

Yes, but I bet what I had was a whole lot better than what you had. "Yeah, I'm sure. What's on your mind, Birdie? You look like the cat that just swallowed the canary."

"Oh, nothing." Birdie started to giggle.

The plane began its roll for take-off and they both got into the "ready" position—palms up underneath their thighs, and their heads resting firmly on the back of their jump seats. The engines grew louder.

"Am I missing something here?" Dee said.

"I just heard someone talking this morning." Birdie started laughing so hard that tears were running down her face.

"All right, Birdie, what's up? I'd like to get a laugh also."

Birdie took out a tissue from her smock and wiped the tears from her eyes. The plane had finally reached the cruising altitude and the captain had turned off the seat belt sign. They both unbuckled their seatbelts to start preparing the carts for the beverage service.

"Well, when I was coming down the elevator this morning, I happened to be in the same one as Chris Dickerson—my, he is handsome," Birdie said as she fanned herself playfully. "Anyway, he was talking to someone on his cell phone about an attorney friend of his named Desiree. Dee was her nickname and she was from Atlanta. Supposedly, she works for this big firm, and he was going to ask if she would help his friend out with some type of legal problem." Birdie burst into laughter again. "Is that not the most hysterical thing you've ever heard? I mean how many people would you think had the same first name as yours? Not to mention you both live in Atlanta!"

"That is ironic," Dee said with a hollow laugh. "What else did he say?"

"Oh, he was talking about how he stayed in this woman's hotel room that kept him up so late that he was now running late for a meeting." Birdie started to whisper. "He kept going on and on about how sexy she was." Birdie was beginning to look embarrassed as Dee's face flushed.

"Geez, these men have no shame these days," Dee said, trying to balance bags of pretzels, but dropping them on the floor instead.

"Here, let me get those," Birdie said, looking at Dee suspiciously.

"Thanks. I guess I'm all thumbs today."

"Hey, it happens to all of us."

"You know, these jocks really have the life."

"It seems that way," Dee said, trying to sound unconcerned.

"I mean, they run around with all different kinds of women—probably have one for each day of the week—get a big ol' fat paycheck for getting a ball across a goal line. In the meantime, these silly women believe anything and everything they tell them just so they can be a part of their own fantasy. The truth is, the women that date these men need to take a cold hard look at themselves."

"Well, you sure seem to know about the life of an NFL player. Have you had first-hand experience?"

"No, but when you've been flying as long as I have, you've seen it all. These women have no lives. Usually they're insecure about themselves and are dating them so that they can have some identity through them."

"Really, now? So, you don't think a woman can have her own career and date a jock?"

"They can, but it's rare." Birdie laughed.

Dee couldn't tell if Birdie was trying to see if *she* was really the woman that Chris was talking about.

"Hey, are you ladies ready for the beverage service?" Jodie said as she walked into the galley.

Dee filled the buckets with ice. "Yes, I'm ready."

"Hey, Birdie, did you tell Dee who you saw in the elevator this morning?"

"Uh, huh, she told me," Dee said, anxiously, before Birdie could answer.

"Hey, you have a law degree, don't you, Dee?"

"Yep, sure do," Dee said as she unlatched the brake on the cart.

"I didn't know you had a law degree," Birdie chimed in.

"Yeah, she's big time. She got it from Columbia. I remembered when we flew a line together shortly after you had gotten it," Jodie said.

Dee was hoping that the uneasiness she was feeling wasn't showing in her face. She could feel the depths of Birdie's eyes penetrating through her.

"So you *are* an attorney!"

"Nope, still need to take and pass the bar," Dee said as calmly as she could.

"So, the plot thickens," Birdie laughed.

"What plot?" Dee asked, trying to sound naïve.

"Oh, Birdie's just trying to be the private investigator that she's always wanted to be," Jodie chuckled. "It's such a coincidence, though, that the person Chris Dickerson was talking about had the same name as you."

"Yes, it is. Well, it's obvious that I'm not the only Dee in the world." Dee pulled out the beverage cart from the galley. "C'mon, let's get this service over with."

Back at Base

S she poked her head in the doorway, Dee shouted, "I'm home! Is anyone here? Pam?" Legal papers were scattered across the kitchen table and a sink load of dirty dishes greeted Dee.

"Man, this place is a mess! Why she picks this spot to do her business, I'll never know." Shaking her head, she locked the door behind her. With luggage in tow, she walked briskly through Pam's clutter cave and retreated to the cleanest part of the condominium—her bedroom.

Dee's room was her own private getaway. It exuded tranquility, something she definitely needed in order for her to return to her *real* world. The room's décor was influenced by her many trips to the Mediterranean. Soft yellow faux painted marbled walls served as a backdrop to the king-size bed, which was upholstered in antique gold silk. Crackle-finished bed chests with marble tops flanked the sides of the bed. The bed coverings were a combination of luxurious silks in gold, coral, and blue hues punctuated by solid and striped pillows with the same color scheme.

Across from the bed was a small sitting area with an elongated window lavishly draped in gold and blue drapes that hung to the hardwood floors. The nook consisted of a neoclassic round wooden table and an overstuffed cane-backed chair where Dee would often unwind with a good book.

"Ahhhhh, there's no place like home," Dee giggled, mimicking Dorothy in *The Wizard of Oz.* She clicked the back of her heels three times before kicking off her shoes and collapsing backwards onto her bed.

She lay there for a while and briefly contemplated taking a nap, but decided instead to unpack from this trip and repack for her next one. Afterwards, she changed into some gray sweatpants and a red tank top and decided to call Tracey before she proceeded back into Pam's mess hall. Before she could press the last number, her phone rang.

"Hello."

"Auntie Dee!"

"You beat me! I was just about to finish dialing your number."

"Oh good. So, this is a good time to talk?"

"It's a perfect time," Dee said as she sat down on her bed.

"Okay, let me first catch my breath. There's so much going on that I don't know where to start."

"OOOOOkay," Dee said sounding a little apprehensive.

Dee could hear Tracey breathing laboriously as she began to speak. "Well, I don't know how to say this, but when was the last time that you and Mama have spoken?"

"Hmmm . . . it's been a while."

"That's what I thought. Well, Mama has been really having a hard time at work lately with *Ms.* Pam."

Dee shook her head. She always did think it was a bad idea for Pam and Amanda to be working together. And of course, Pam kept her business issues to herself, especially if it was dealing with Amanda.

"What happened?"

"I'm not really sure, but I know she is not working there anymore."

"What? She quit or Pam fired her?"

"Like I said, I'm not sure. But, the two of them really have some issues, and I can tell that it's really been bothering Mama. Can you talk to them, Auntie Dee?"

"I can try, but you know Pam and your mother's history. It will take a hurricane and a monsoon to get them to see eye to eye."

"I know, but . . ."

"I'll see what I can do."

"I know, you can't make any promises," Tracey chimed in.

"Is that what has been so important for you to tell me?"

"No! There's more. It's about mama and my dad." Tracey's voice sounded apprehensive and excited at the same time. Dee paused long enough not to sound totally caught off guard. Last she heard, Tracey father's had no contact with Amanda. Melvin was the only man that had been in Amanda's life for some time now.

"So what about them?"

"Well, I don't quite know how to say this, but we've been communicating for a while now—and long story short, he wants me to tell mama."

"You mean Amanda doesn't know?" Dee went from a seated position on the bed to standing at attention on the floor.

"Uh huh."

Dee paced the floor, imagining Amanda's reaction once she got wind of what her daughter was doing behind her back. "Oh, Tracey!"

"Auntie Dee, Mama would have a baby cow if she knew I was seeing my dad!"

No! Twin baby cows, Dee thought. *And I definitely don't want to be a witness to that birth.*

Pam's M.O. was always the same. Whenever she had a crisis at work, she came home and made it a crisis as well. Dee glanced over at the sofa and saw Pam's robe and slippers lying on the floor next to a half-empty cup of stale coffee.

"She must have pulled an all-nighter," Dee said seeing files tossed about on the floor. There were handwritten notes scattered around the kitchen table lying next to a mountain of pens and pencils. She sorted through Pam's paperwork and placed it in neat little stacks on the table, making sure to keep them in order. Next, she dutifully picked up the rest of Pam's belongings and returned everything to Pam's office where she felt like she had just stepped onto the set of a remake of *The Twilight Zone.*

Pam kept her office as immaculate as a shrine. Beautiful African art and expensive oriental rugs flanked the hardwood floors. In the middle of the room sat a custom designed mahogany desk, given to her by one of her thankful clients who'd purchased it while on one of his many jaunts to Egypt. Two plum ultrasuede chairs sat in front of it, adding to the room's elegance. A breathtaking view of Buckhead, the premiere section of town for Atlanta's elite and *wannabe* elite, topped it off.

The bookshelves were filled with enough legal books to put Harvard's Law School bookstore out of business. Dee and Pam had shared some of the books in college. Back then, she, Pam, and Amanda swore that when they became lawyers they would open up a firm together. Pam had kept her end of the bargain. Amanda came in a close second as a paralegal. For Dee, that dream seemed light years away. If Pam wanted to, she could run a small law practice right from the comforts of her own home. Why Pam opted for the kitchen table instead remained a complete mystery to Dee.

Their kitchen was entirely too pretty for Pam to leave it as a mess hall. The decor was a unique blend of colors of salmon pink and apple green. The white ceramic tile floors were accented with ivy etched on alternating squares. Their sorority color theme was the work of an interior designer who was also an AKA.

After Dee finished sweeping the kitchen, she vacuumed the crumbs from the living room floor, and then wiped the perspiration from her brow. When she heard the doorbell, she yelled, "Just a minute!"

"Don't leave me standing out here all day," the voice shouted back through the door.

Dee smiled at the sound of the familiar voice and jogged up the steps of the sunken living room and threw open the door. "Sedrick, hi!"

"Hi, stranger!" Sedrick gave her a bear hug. Dee stood on her toes to reach his 6'3" frame. She inhaled the refreshing aroma of his cologne as he released her from his grasp.

"When did you get back in town?"

"Just a couple of hours ago."

His hazel eyes scanned the apartment and he shook his head disapprovingly. "Don't tell me. The maid is off today, and Pam hired *you* to clean up her mess again," he teased.

"Sedrick, now, you promised."

"I know. I said I wouldn't tease you about your *compulsive* disorder for cleaning, but Dee, come on, Pam's a grown-ass woman, you shouldn't have to . . ."

She placed her hand over his mouth before he could finish his sentence, grabbed him by the hand, and walked him to the living room.

"Nice suit," Dee said as she tugged on his tie. He was wearing what looked like a custom-made suit. It was charcoal gray complemented by a crisp white French cuff shirt and gray silk tie.

"Thanks. I do look pretty good, don't I?" Sedrick laughed as he smoothed out his tie.

"So what's the occasion?"

"Meeting with my bank."

"I see, so you had to dress to impress, huh? Well you give the *appearance* that you're worthy of credit anyway," Dee laughed.

"So you got jokes, I see. Don't hate baby, you just jealous!" Sedrick's smile broadened as he thought about how much they used to tease each other in college about how the other one dressed.

"Hardly! Do you remember the time when you were walking around the campus thinking you were all that, and that girl came up to you—what was her name?" Dee asked.

"Desiree? Man, she was so fine!"

"Yes, her." Dee rolled her eyes at him. She was a little disgusted with herself that she used that same name to dupe Chris. "Yeah, Desiree tapped you on the shoulders and told you that your pants were nice, but you paid a little too much for them and snatched the price tag off your waist and handed it to you!" Holding her stomach, Dee doubled over with laughter.

"Yeah, that was pretty embarrassing."

Dee slapped him teasingly on his knee. "Mr. GQ, at least that's what you thought you were anyway."

"Was, and still am! And what about you, Miss Ebony Fashion Fair? You thought you were turning a couple of heads a few times as you walked over to math class at Morehouse. Seemed to me like every time you had a class at The House you had on a new outfit."

"Well, a girl had to look good going to class," she said, playfully smoothing her ponytail.

Sedrick laughed. "You didn't look like you were just going to class. You looked like you were getting *paid* to get dressed just to go to class!"

"Yes, we were both feeling ourselves back then, weren't we? Man, how time flies."

Sedrick looked at her in admiration and contemplated his thoughts before he spoke. "But on a serious note, I must say, Miss Dee, there was never a prettier campus queen than you. You made an already *handsome* brotha look extra good on that day," he said, pretending to smooth out his shirt.

"Yes, I did, didn't I? And you didn't make such a bad king, yourself, Mr. Meals on Wheels!" she said hitting him lightly on his chest.

"Aw, man, you just had to go there. Now, you're gettin' ready to dog out my frat."

"Oh, no, I can't dog out Mr. cool Kappa!"

"Okay, go on. I know you just can't wait to dig in."

"Oh, *au contraire* sir, but you were a trip in college. You would have those silly women eating right out of your hand. They would look at those big puppy dog eyes of yours and melt like butter. Geez! I couldn't believe how they let you charm the pants right off of them," Dee said, smacking herself on the forehead in disbelief.

Sedrick looked a little embarrassed that she still remembered his wild ways from so many years ago. "Dee, now you know it wasn't like that at all."

"*Puh-leeze*, who are you trying to fool? Boy, I know you better than you know yourself."

Sedrick could only laugh because he knew she was telling the truth. He was known as the most charming man on campus, with charisma that drew the ladies right in like moths to a flame. He took advantage of his boyish good looks that gave him an innocence that made women feel like he could never do any wrong.

Sedrick never spent money on groceries. His Kappa brothers nicknamed him "Mr. Meals on Wheels" because some woman was always driving food over to his apartment at least five days a week. Everyone except Dee. She was the only woman who ever looked at him *only* as a friend, and unbeknownst to her, she was the only woman that didn't have a clue about his true feelings.

"All right, next topic," he said as he walked across the living room, marveling at the colorful painting on the whitewashed wall. "Cool, I see you got a piece of Fennell's work," he said, trying to change the subject. "That's a nice one."

"Thanks, I got it on one of my layovers in San Fran. The colors are so vibrant that it draws you right to it, doesn't it?"

Sedrick nodded. Dee could see that he was getting a little embarrassed about her teasing him. "Okay, I see I've beaten you down too hard going down Memory Lane. You're starting to sweat a little. Want a bottled water?"

"Very funny. Yes, that would be great," he said as he walked back toward the loveseat. He sat down and flipped through the *Ebony* magazine on the coffee table. After Dee pulled out two bottles of water from the refrigerator, she found herself staring out of the bay window at the glistening swimming pool ten stories below. Two gorgeous men had just gotten out of the pool. They were sitting in the lawn chairs and letting their chocolatey, drenched bodies dry off in the sunlight. *No wonder Pam always did her work in the kitchen. This view was much better than the one in her office any day.* She opened up her bottle to take a sip as her thoughts moved toward Chris.

"What, cha' doin' in there, woman? Digging a well for the water?"

Dee walked back in the living room and handed him his water. "Oh, don't get your briefs in a wad."

"Thanks. And I wear boxers, not briefs." He laughed as he watched Dee give him a disgusting look. "You brought up the underwear thing, not me." His hand reached for the glass, gingerly touching her fingers as she released it.

"You're welcome," Dee said, oblivious to Sedrick's mild attempt of flirtation. She stretched her arms, causing her tank top to rise slightly above her midsection. Sedrick's eyes were drawn immediately to her smooth stomach. It was a mystery to Sedrick as to how many crunches this woman did a day to keep such firm abs.

I know Dee takes kickboxing, too, but damn! I had no idea she had such definition. Unconsciously, he patted his own stomach to reaffirm *his* tautness. With such a hectic schedule, he had little time to go to a gym on a regular basis.

Dee sat back down on the sofa and crossed her legs Indian style. "So, how is the construction coming for your new building?"

"Great! We've run into a few snags, but nothing we couldn't work out."

"Sed, that's wonderful. You have worked really hard."

"Yeah, this last year has definitely been a killer for me and the other doctors, but I'm glad it's almost over."

"Well, you know Pam and I will be right there cheering you on when you cut the ribbon on that new building."

"Yeah, *my* two girls right there in my corner. A guy couldn't ask for much more," he said, raising his hand to give Dee a high five.

"I know that's right." Dee's top rose again as she jumped up to slap his hand. His eyes caught another flash of her stomach.

"Damn," he whispered.

"Did you say something?"

"I said *Sam.* I need to call and check in on Samantha, one of my patients." He moved in closer to her. "So, what's happenin' with you these days? How's the flying going?"

Dee shook her head and got up to straighten the coffee table and sofa pillows. Her drawn face reflected a sudden mood change.

"Hey," he said laughing, hoping Dee's mood would return to normal.

"What's so funny?"

He took a sip of his water and perused the *Ebony* article. "Have you had a chance to read this yet?"

"No, that's my mail pile, but I haven't looked at it yet."

"Well, it's pretty interesting. Women can do some wild stuff according to this article. It's called, 'The Five Mistakes Women Make With Men.'"

"Really, we can make that many, huh?" Dee stopped straightening the room and walked over toward him.

Sedrick's phone went off before he could respond. He looked at the text message. "All right, gotta go. Duty calls."

"You better get a move on then."

He stood up and hugged her for as long as he could without making her feel uncomfortable.

"It was great seeing you, Dee."

"You too. Here, let me walk you to the door."

"All right. Tell Pam I'm sorry I keep missing her."

"I will. Talk to you later."

Dee had just begun sorting through her three-day mail when the doorbell rang again. Who could that be? She knew Sedrick didn't forget anything.

"Delivery for Pamela Madison," the doorman said when she opened the door. He handed her a bouquet of exotic tropical foliage that included a delightful blend of ginger, protea, and orchids.

"These are absolutely breathtaking. Hold on a sec, Eugene, I'll run and get your tip," she said, running back to the change drawer in the kitchen.

"Thanks, Ms. Bridge. Tell Ms. Madison she sure is one lucky lady. Someone really thinks a lot of her."

They most certainly do, she thought as she closed the door and placed the vase on the end table in the living room. "Let's see who it is." Dee knew she was being nosy but opened the card anyway.

> *One of a kind flowers for a one of a kind lady.*
> *I hope to see you again soon.*
> *Sincerely,*
> *The man you're too busy to have breakfast with!*

Dee slipped the note back in the envelope. Well, whoever he was, good luck. He may starve to death if he was waiting to take Pam out to eat. Dee wished Pam would consider seeking some professional help. Her doctor would be great for her, but nobody knew Dee was seeing a psychiatrist.

Dee sat back down on the sofa and flipped though *Ebony* until she came across the article that Sedrick had mentioned earlier. "The Five Mistakes Women Make With Men." Number one: not being truthful. Dee slammed the magazine shut, walked over to the telephone, and immediately dialed her psychiatrist.

Nose Dive

When Pam pulled into the parking lot of Sterling, Mathis, and Silverman, thoughts of her meeting with Greg resurfaced. She felt the deluge of tears begin to fall. *Shit! I've got to get a handle on myself.* She took deep breaths and tried to refocus her thoughts. This case she was about to try was too important to let emotions rule over logic. She couldn't help but notice the dark oil stains on the spot where Amanda used to park her car. The empty spot seemed so barren without the champagne-colored Camry.

It was already 9:00 a.m., two hours later than when Pam usually arrived. Amanda was typically at work at least one hour before Pam walked in and would have case files already organized and waiting for her. Today was the first time in three years Pam's day would start off without Amanda. Damn Amanda and her ungrateful ass!

Pam walked toward her office. Pete Sterdivant, the hiring manager, was right on her heels. His charcoal trench coat swayed behind him as he followed Pam in dogged pursuit.

"Hey, Pam. Getting a late start today, are we?"

Pam looked at her watch without breaking her stride. "Yes, *you* are getting in rather later than usual. What's going on?"

"You tell me. I heard Amanda turned in her resignation on Friday." He tried to maneuver his folders to keep the papers from falling out while he held onto his briefcase.

Pam continued to walk briskly as she entered the building. "My, word travels fast."

"I got a call from the office at home late Friday night because I was off on Friday," he said as he clumsily readjusted his horn-rimmed glasses back up on his nose.

Pam nonchalantly pressed the elevator button. "So?"

"So what happened?" Pete finally caught up to her and looked at her sternly.

"I think it says it all in the letter, which, by the way, should still be on your desk where I left it," she said glaring back at him and cutting her eyes to stare at the numbers at the top of the elevator. The elevator doors opened and she stepped in, secretly hoping they would close on him.

Pete was as unrelenting as a pit bull. He pushed his way through the narrow closing of the elevator's doors. Pam rolled her eyes and let out a disappointed sigh. "By the way, how soon will I have a replacement? I need someone, as in yesterday, to assist me with the Tyfish case."

Pete didn't seem to hear her question. "I just don't get it. She was one of our best paralegals. I just didn't think she would quit."

"Yes, well we all didn't think, but she did. And now she's gone, and I say good riddance," Pam said firmly as the doors opened. She stepped brusquely off the elevator. "The replacement, Pete? When will I get one?"

"I'll have someone sent to you by lunch."

"I suppose I should be grateful," she mumbled as she turned down the corridor, leaving Pete taken aback by her response. He walked to his office and saw Amanda's resignation letter cloaked in an envelope on his desk. He opened it and was surprised at the letter's terse words.

> *Dear Mr. Sterdivant,*
> *Effective immediately, I am resigning from Sterling, Mathis, and Silverman.*
> *Sincerely,*
> *Amanda C. Shipman*

Pete folded the letter and tapped it against the top of his desk. He quickly picked up the phone to buzz his secretary.

"Yes, Mr. Sterdivant," Donna answered.

"Donna, get Amanda Shipman on the phone for me, will ya?"

"Right away, sir."

Pete waited a few seconds before Donna buzzed him back. "Mr. Sterdivant, no one is picking up the phone, and her voicemail did not pick up. I can call back later."

"Just give me her number, and I'll try her myself later today," he said with some irritation.

"404-555-6671." Pete scribbled the number on a yellow sticky note and stuck it on the front of the phone. "Is there anything else I can do for you, Mr. Sterdivant?"

"No, that will be it for now. Thanks Donna."

"You're welcome, sir."

Pete stared at the number, for a few seconds as he hung up the phone. He knew that he would have to start interviewing for another paralegal immediately because he didn't want to overload the others with Amanda's casework. Unfortunately, for now, they would have to make do with who they had for the *Johnson v. Tyfish Systems* case. *And of all cases, too*, Pete thought, dumbfounded. Amanda couldn't have left at a worse time. And the big question still remained unanswered—why did she leave?

Stephanie Walker, another paralegal, had been pulled from another attorney to work part-time on the *Johnson v. Tyfish Systems* case with Pam. Stephanie took a second glance in the full-length mirror and buttoned the top button of her grey wool suit. Her thin frame and poised walk resembled a ballerina about to take the stage on opening night. When she left the ladies' bathroom, a rush of adrenalin ran through her. Enthralled at the idea of assisting on one of the firm's largest cases made her both excited and tense. Her hands became clammy as she tapped firmly on Pam's office door.

"C'mon in," Pam called. She sat buried behind a mound of paperwork on her desk. She had just checked her messages and saw that Marco had called twice that morning. His persistence was flattering, but she did not have the time to respond to his overtures.

Stephanie slowly opened the door and was astounded at the amount of paperwork. "Miss Madison? Are you in there?" Stephanie joked.

Pam poked her head out from behind the stacks and gave a half smile. "Take a load off," she said, pointing to the chair across from her desk. "So, you've been assigned to me part-time, eh?"

"Yes, Ms. Madison, I have."

"Well now, tell me what you know about the *Johnson v. Tyfish Systems* case?" Pam demanded as she crossed her arms tightly across her chest anticipating her answer.

"Well, I just found out that I was assigned the case today, so . . ."

"So, what can you tell me?" Pam snapped.

"Well, not a whole lot. I mean, I know that our client is being sued for misappropriating $15 million dollars from his company."

"Why is that all you know about the case?"

"I beg your pardon?" Stephanie asked with a puzzled look on her face. "Well, I just found out about it, and I haven't had an opportunity to . . ."

"To find the time to pay attention to the details of the case?" Pam blared.

"Yes. I mean, no. That's not what I meant."

"What's your name again?"

"It's Stephanie. Stephanie Walker."

"Oh, yeah, that's right," Pam snapped her fingers as she remembered. "Well, Stephanie, I've heard about you and I'm not impressed."

"But I don't understand what you mean."

"From what I've heard, you *don't* understand a *lot* of things, and I don't have time to sit around and explain them to you."

"But I don't think . . ."

"No, I don't believe you *do that either!*" Pam scoffed.

Stephanie watched Pam roll her eyes and pick up a piece of paper with one hand and the phone with the other and began dialing.

"Pete, this is not working," Pam snapped.

"*What's* not working?"

"*Stephanie* is *not* working," she said accusingly.

Pam saw Stephanie's face turn a crimson red. "Ms. Madison, please," Stephanie interrupted. "I really want to work this case with you."

Pam raised her hand, gesturing her to silence herself. Stephanie slumped back in her chair, wanting to melt right out of sight.

"Listen, Pam," Pete yelled as he snatched his glasses off his nose. "This is a big case. And it's going to take work bringing someone up to speed on it. Give Stephanie a chance. She's a good paralegal."

"Pete, I don't want good. I want outstanding. I want impeccable. I want—"

"AMANDA!" he yelled into the phone like a wild man. "And unfortunately we don't have her to give to you, because in case you've forgotten, she quit!"

"I realize that. But, trust me, this case is too big for me to have to work at bringing someone like *her* up to speed." She eyed Stephanie disapprovingly. "Give me someone else. Find me someone who does not have to go through Basic Case Knowledge 101."

Stephanie squirmed and wanted to run out of the office and forget this day had ever happened. She was so devastated by Pam's belittling remarks that her legs grew as heavy as cast iron steel and her body felt paralyzed from the neck down.

"You're insufferable, Pam!" Pete said.

"I know I am."

"If you weren't such a damn good lawyer, and if this wasn't such a huge case for the firm, I'd tell you to work with who I gave you or go straight to—"

"You don't need to finish the sentence, Pete. I love you too!" Pam hung up the phone and continued reading through her files without looking up from her desk. "Sorry, but this is just not going to work out."

Stephanie sat there looking stunned, dejected, and ready to be cast aside.

Pam nodded at the door. "You may leave now. As you can see, I've got a ton of paperwork to sort through."

First-Class Meal

Pam wheeled into the Collins's estate. She thought how strange it was that Gerald had invited her to his home tonight. She wondered why he was so insistent that she meet a friend of his who was selling a business and wanted some legal advice.

"Sure, let's schedule to meet at my office sometime next week," Pam said.

"No, he really wants to meet as soon as possible."

"How soon is soon?"

"How about tonight? My house for dinner?" Pam laughed before catching herself.

"What's so funny?" Gerald said.

"Oh, nothing. I'm truly sorry. I just didn't expect you to say that."

"Well, will you be available?"

"Yes, of course I'm free. I'd love to come." After all, Gerald Collins was one of the firm's biggest and richest clients. Who in their right mind would refuse an invitation from him? "Well, it may be a good idea to bring in Bill as well. He's known for drafting and negotiating some of the best contracts."

"No, I'm sure you can give him whatever he needs. It's not a huge deal."

Then why the big urgency? Pam wondered. "Okay, Gerald, what time?"

"How's 7:30 sound?"

"Okay, I'll see you then."

And now here she was, standing in front of Gerald Collins's mansion and ringing his doorbell.

"Good evening, Counselor Madison."

"Good evening, Edward." Pam walked in, and he helped her out of her jacket.

"Come right this way," he said, escorting her to the living room. This was the same place where she'd met Gerald's handsome friend, Marco.

"Pam, I'm so glad you could make it." Adrienne tried her best to waddle gracefully down the stairs. Her stomach had gotten a lot bigger since the last time Pam had seen her, but she looked just as radiant. Her pale blue silk dress hung loosely below her bodice and flowed like a gentle sea breeze. Pam's mind wandered for a few seconds, remembering her own brief pregnancy.

Gerald walked into the room and disrupted her moment of reflection. He was holding a silver tray of martini glasses. "All right, listen up, everyone. Edward made martinis, and they are lethal!" He set the tray down and removed one of the martinis. "Cheers!" he said, laughing, as he raised his glass and gulped down two sips." He shook his head as if he were getting a sudden rush of adrenalin. "Pam, are you having one?"

"Sure, why not?" She took one off the tray and took a long sip. "Wow, this *is* really good!"

"It's an apple martini. Gerald here forgot to mention that," Adrienne added proudly.

"Well, I'm the one who gave Edward the recipe, and you failed to mention that," Marco added while making his surprise entrance into the room. He smiled at Adrienne.

"Sure you did, Marco!" Adrienne said, rolling her eyes at him.

Pam glanced up quickly and almost spilled her drink. There was the mystery man again. He always just seemed to pop up when she least expected it.

"Marco?"

"The one and only!" He grinned.

"Wait a minute, don't tell me you're . . ."

"*I'm* the prospective client," he said before she could finish her sentence.

"But Gerald, you said . . ."

"Pam, I hope you're not upset with me, but I did bring you here under a little bit of a false pretense."

"But not totally," Adrienne chimed. "Marco does have some business that he wants to discuss with you."

Pam looked at Marco right through the core of his eyes. "Why didn't you just tell me this over the phone when you called?"

"I tried to get you to meet with me but you refused," he said, trying to sound victimized. "And since Mohammed couldn't come to the mountain . . ."

"You arranged for the mountain," she said, pointing to herself, "to come to you." Pam took a long, hard sip of her martini, emptying the glass.

First Greg. And now this guy. These past two days of unexpected meetings had been more difficult than having back-to-back cases. Pam looked over at Gerald and Adrienne. "I don't know, guys, I'm not getting a good feeling here."

"Well, let's discuss this more over dinner. Come on now, you are hungry, aren't you?" Marco interrupted before Gerald or Adrienne could intervene.

Pam smiled slightly. "Oh, so there really *is* a dinner? I was beginning to wonder about that as well."

"No, we love to eat around here," Gerald joined in.

"Yes, especially Adrienne," Marco quipped.

"Very funny. Ha! Ha! Ha! Well, I'm eating for two! What do you expect?"

"Are you sure there's only one in there?" Adrienne pinched him on the arm.

"Ow! Did you see that counselor? She attacked me. Can I sue her for pain and suffering?"

Pam smiled. The three of them together could put on a stage show, she thought. Marco did have kind of a fun sense of humor even though it was a little warped at times.

"All right, let's go eat," Gerald said. They all followed him down the winding hallway that led to the dining room. The oversized table for eight had been downsized to an intimate table for four. The place settings were the most beautiful bone china and Waterford crystal Pam had ever seen. The palladium window in front of the table offered a generous view of the rich gardens. A lovely white gazebo served as a gorgeous backdrop to the sparkling in-ground swimming pool.

"Hey, Adrienne, where's my ziti and meatballs you promised?" Marco said as he watched Edward enter with lamb chops, roasted garlic potatoes, and spinach soufflé.

Edward looked at him tiredly. *Really, Marco, you are so crass at times.* "Sir, it will be out shortly, along with your sorbet that Madame Collins requested. Counselor Madison, may I get you anything else?"

"Get her a side order of the ziti, too," Marco answered back.

Edward looked at Marco hopelessly. "Will that be all right, with you, Counselor Madison?"

"Yes, that will be fine, Edward," Pam said, trying to contain her laughter.

"Very well, madam. It will be here very shortly." Edward eyed Marco, annoyed, and returned to the kitchen.

Marco looked at Pam and smiled. He loved the way her eyes lit up when she thought something was funny. Pam felt his stare and looked back at him and caught him off guard.

"So, Pam, how is that case you've been working on?" Marco said, clearing his throat.

Pam cut into a small piece of lamb. "Not as well as this lamp chop is doing," she chuckled as she placed it in her mouth and chewed it delicately. "But I'll survive."

Marco looked at her again with a small twinkle in his eye. Pam's silk blouse was buttoned just above her cleavage, accented by a double strand of cultured pearls. Her silver-gray skirt outlined her hips like a mold to a sculpture. Marco couldn't take his eyes off her. "I'm sure you will, Counselor."

"So tell me, Marco, where are these papers you need for me to look over?"

"They're in the living room. I thought you could look them over after dessert." His mouth curved upward and opened slightly as he displayed the most perfect set of teeth Pam had ever seen on a man. Marco caught a glimpse of her fixation on his mouth and was pleased there was something about him that she did find attractive. Even if it was *only* his pearly whites.

Pam looked away from him, directing her attention to Gerald and Adrienne, who had gotten caught up in a seductive game of feeding each other. "Ahem, Adrienne and Gerald."

"Ah, yes. Pam," Adrienne said a little embarrassed at her and her husband's table manners.

"Sorry, I guess we got a little carried away, huh, dear?" Gerald said, as he kissed his wife on the mouth.

"You two are something else," Pam said, shaking her head and laughing. It had to be a white thing, cause black folks just didn't act like that at the dinner table. "I just wanted to say that the food is simply delicious. My compliments to the chef."

Gerald wiped his wife's lipstick from his mouth. "Glad you were able to make it, Pam. So, how are things back at work for you now that your trial is over?"

"Couldn't be better. What can I say? You saved my career, and I'm eternally grateful."

"We both are." Adrienne squeezed his hand.

Marco looked at Pam with a devilish grin. "And *I* want to feel grateful, too. Come. Let me show you the papers. Perhaps we can have dessert in here while you look them over. Adrienne and Gerald won't mind if we take our dessert in the living room."

"Go right ahead," Adrienne and Gerald sang in unison.

"I'll tell Edward to serve dessert to you there," Adrienne said as she watched the couple walk into the living room.

"So what do you think?" Adrienne whispered in Gerald's ear.

"Too soon to tell. I mean, she's not giving him any signals, you know?"

"Well, I think Marco is in for a run for his money."

"Maybe. But in this case, for the first time, he's in the race all by himself."

Edward entered the living room and handed Pam and Marco strawberry sorbets.

"Thank you Edward. They look delicious," Pam said.

"I can handle it from here, Edward," Marco said, taking both of their dishes and placing them on the table.

He dipped Pam's spoon into her sorbet and turned to feed her. "Here, try some," he said.

Pam shook her head. Marco was unbelievable, relentless. Just wouldn't take no for an answer. He reminded her of someone, but she couldn't think who. She politely took the spoon out his hand and fed herself.

Marco smiled at her as if her reaction was no surprise. He shrugged his shoulders and picked up his own sorbet and began to savor it.

They were both silent. It was almost as if they were waiting to see who was going to say something first. Pam looked up at Marco and smiled. She admired his self-assurance. She could see that he was definitely the kind of man who went after what he wanted. And right now he wanted her. A startled look cast across Pam's face, and she stopped eating. She had just figured out who Marco reminded her of. She dropped her spoon in shock.

"Pam, are you okay?" Marco asked, walking to his briefcase to get the paperwork.

"Yeah, I'm fine," Pam said. *Relentless, won't take no for an answer, and self-assured; all of that rang a bell.* Astounded, she looked up at Marco, knowing right away that she was meeting a male version of herself.

Pam quickly took the papers from him and started to look them over. "You know what? On second thought, I'm going to skip dessert. I will take your papers back to my office and have a look at them there. I'll return them to you with my comments via express mail."

"But, I thought . . ."

"Marco, I appreciate your efforts, I really do, but I have to say your timing right now is not good. I'm just not interested in men. Period."

Marco was stunned. "Oh, I'm sorry. Gerald *did* tell me you kept your personal affairs personal, but I had no idea that you were a lesbian," he whispered.

Pam laughed heartily for the first time all evening. Her eyes lit up like a firecracker. "Oh my, I guess that didn't come out right. I love men, really I do." *Used to anyway,* she thought. "What I'm trying to say is that I'm not a lesbian. I'm straight—*very, very* much so," she giggled.

He blew air into his cheeks and then released it. "Well, that's a relief!"

"But, I'm not interested in a relationship at this time."

"Who said anything about a relationship? I just want to be friends. Everyone needs those, right?"

"Listen, after I look over your business papers, you will technically be a client, and I make it my policy not to *befriend* or *date* clients."

"Then give me back my papers," he said, reaching for them. "Charge me for the time you've spent this evening. I'll pay you and then we'll call it even. Our business will then be over, and we can become friends."

A smile tickled her lips. Part of her wanted to keep it inside, but there was something about him that just made her want to let it go. "You're relentless, you know that? You should have been an attorney. Which begs the question, what do you do for a living, anyway?"

"Ah . . . ah . . . ah . . . first things first. Do we have a deal or not?"

Pam raised her eyebrow at him. She found herself slowly handing Marco back his papers as he pinned her with his eyes. She extended her hand and gave him a firm handshake.

"It's a deal," Pam said reluctantly. Marco relaxed his gaze and winked.

"Now, tell me *your* occupation," Pam demanded.

"Oh, I will. But not tonight. Now, don't give me that look," he said, referring to the frown on her face. "It will give us something to talk about as *friends* the next time we meet. Until then . . . *Arrivederci."* Marco bowed, kissed the back of Pam's hand, and then disappeared out the front door.

Descending

Dee's eyes shifted to her feet as she admitted, "I was always comfortable with who I was. I wasn't always messed up like this, you know, I mean the lying . . . My parents taught me that if you worked really hard, the end rewards would be great." Her eyes grew moist remembering.

The doctor listened intently as she continued, giving her a reassuring nod now and then whenever she paused with her story.

"I would meet people every day and talk on different topics, but inevitably the same question would pop up."

The doctor looked at her mouth, careful not to miss any detail of what she was going to say next. She intrigued him. Dee was rambling today, but he listened very closely. "So what was the question that bothered you so much?"

"It was always the lead-in question, ya know? 'So what's your background?' And I would tell them. But once they find out that I'm a college graduate and have a law degree, that questioning look always crosses their faces. And next comes the lead-in question." Dee widened her eyes dramatically for effect. "'But *why* do *you* do *this* for a living when you obviously have so much going for you?'" she said, throwing her hands in the air.

"And what is your response?"

"I'm silent for a few seconds, and then I let out a loud theatrical sigh and explain that it's a lot less stressful and the pay isn't bad either."

The doctor laughed out loud. "I wasn't expecting that one." Dee's problems paled in comparison to other patients he treated. Dee, on the other hand, just needed someone to listen to her. Low self-esteem was her biggest problem.

"It's been so long since I dreamed of becoming a lawyer like my roommate," Dee confided, changing the subject as her voice trailed off.

"I didn't realize you had a roommate. You've never spoken about her. I'm assuming your roommate is female."

"Are you sure I've never mentioned her?"

"No, I don't recall that," he said as he perused his notes.

"Hmmm, well, we both graduated from Spelman and then attended Columbia Law School. Together, we graduated in the top ten percent of the class."

The doctor nodded. "Very impressive, the two of you. Very impressive."

"Well, *she's* impressive anyway. She went on to become a lawyer, and a darn good one."

"So, how come she's a lawyer and you're not?"

Dee looked down again and thought about his question. It was so hard to admit the truth. This conversation was becoming very draining. Having to talk about the demons that haunted her was a lot more difficult than she had thought. She paused, reflecting on how she would answer his question. "I just became very disillusioned."

"Why is that?"

She grinned slightly. "I should have known that you were not going to just let me get away with that answer."

He smiled back. "You were right."

"Well, I just decided *not* to become what I *thought* I always wanted to be and instead chose a totally different path." Dee quit talking for a moment as if she was having difficulty completing her next sentence.

The doctor could sense her uneasiness. "It's okay, just take your time, okay?" he said as he stopped taking notes. He rested his elbows on his knees and leaned in toward her.

Dee nodded and slowly took a deep breath. "When I took on this new path, I became disillusioned again. I felt that I was being questioned and that my real reason for choosing an alternate path was because I was so insecure with who I had become."

"And your roommate?"

"What about her?"

"How did *she* feel about this sudden change in direction? I mean, you two obviously made a lot of plans together, right?"

Dee didn't want to talk about Pam anymore or even mention her name to him. If Pam knew about the secrets she was keeping, she would be devastated. And Lord only knew that Pam couldn't stand anyone talking about her business, even if it was only Dee.

"Dee, did you hear me?"

"Yes, I did. I don't want to talk about that."

"I think we should. There is obviously something there that you haven't dealt with, and maybe this will help us understand why you feel like you need to lie."

Dee exhaled and wiped the perspiration that was streaming down her forehead. She thought about how strained it had been between her and Pam since she'd first told her. She hadn't talked about it since their big blowout almost ten years ago.

Dee's voice started out in almost a whisper. "This is just between you and me, right?"

"Of course it is. It's completely confidential. I can assure you of that," he said, making a scout's honor sign.

Dee smiled at his sense of humor and felt a little less apprehensive. After all, this was her psychiatrist, and she should be able to discuss whatever she wanted with him. Besides, it wasn't like Pam was going to find out.

"Well, at first she was really angry with me, and then she got really furious."

"Go on."

"Well, I'm not the only person that she was outraged with. You see, there were *three* of us who had planned to open a law firm one day."

"Who is the third person?"

"Her name is Amanda."

"What happened to Amanda? Why didn't she keep her end of the deal?"

"Amanda got pregnant in her senior year in high school."

"I see."

"She really struggled through Spelman and tried to hang in there with law school, but raising a child and keeping up with the courses became too much for her."

"What is Amanda doing now?"

"I'm not sure, but the other day, oddly enough, her daughter was on one of my flights. It has been a while since I've seen Tracey."

"Why is that?"

"You would have to ask, wouldn't you?" Dee smiled weakly. "Well, when Tracey was born, Amanda asked me to be her godmother. She was always closer to me than my roommate."

"Oh? Why was that?"

"Because we just got each other, I guess. You know, back then my roommate was soooo intense. Even now I sometimes don't know how she does it. Amanda and I on the other hand, we're a lot more laid back. We wanted to be lawyers, but *she* ate, drank, and slept it. We didn't."

"I see, so what happened to the relationship between you and Amanda?"

"I moved in with my roommate." Dee chuckled.

"Huh?"

"I know it sounds crazy. I used to have my own place, and I was trying to save some money to buy a condo. But, with my travel schedule, I wasn't sure if it was the right move for me. So, she and I were talking one day and she said I could move in with her. That way I could save some money and she'd have some company."

"Okay, so what does this have to do with your relationship and Amanda's?" The doctor was well aware that she was intentionally omitting her roommate's name. But he would get around to that at a later date. Dee was opening up to him, and he didn't want to break the momentum.

"Things just got complicated. My roommate had gotten Amanda a job at her law firm. At first it was great because she was working with one of the firm's top partners. And then BOOM! CRASH! My roommate is the attorney she was working for!"

"I take it that was a bad move."

"The worst! Amanda did not want to come by and visit when my roommate was there because she was giving her a hard time at work. Ultimately, things just got too complicated. I just heard from her daughter recently that Amanda no longer works with the firm, and I haven't spoken with her to confirm anything."

"So, you and Tracey lost contact because of this?"

"Believe me, it was not my plan, but Amanda started pulling away. She would always have some excuse why we couldn't meet for lunch, or she was too busy to talk when I would call. Then she started making excuses for Tracey as to why we couldn't get together. She had a dance recital, or she was out with friends, etc. It was ridiculous! I just gave her some space and hoped that she would eventually see that just because I was living with her, it wasn't going to change the dynamics of our friendship."

"But, it did?"

"Yeah, unfortunately." Dee took a deep breath. "But, at least Tracey and I are in contact again."

"How do you think Amanda will feel about that once she finds out?"

Dee shrugged her shoulders and barely looked in the doctor's direction. "I hope she's okay with it. After all, I have always loved Tracey. She knows that. I just think that my roommate and Amanda had issues, and for some reason Amanda thought that I was going to side with my roommate. So, she just took the high road without discussing it with me."

"It sounds like your roommate has a very strong hold on the two of you. You and Amanda both have allowed her to put a wedge between you two. Do you and Amanda feel like you have failed her and feel guilty about it?"

Dee looked down at the floor and nervously started tapping her foot. "Yes," Dee said softly. "But in her case, she took a heavier blow. She has had three people who were very close to her fail her."

"Three?"

"I was the first, Amanda was the second, and her fiancé was the third."

"Okay, let's leave the fiancé and Amanda out of the picture for now and discuss you. Have you thought about how you are going to work out the next part that solely has to do with you?"

Dee tensed up at his words. "What are you talking about?"

"Well, let's start with *this*," he said, spreading his hands apart to refer to her situation. "Does your roommate know that you've been pretending to lead the life of someone you're not?"

"Goodness, no! She'd freak! I mean, she's barely able to trust again after her breakup with Greg. She's gotten over me not becoming a lawyer, but if she knew I was doing *this!*" Dee was embarrassed at the thought and hid her face in her hands. "Oh my, I don't even want to think about it," she whispered.

The doctor looked at her empathetically and stopped taking notes for a minute. "Would it really be that bad?"

Dee took her hands from her face. She was astounded by his question. "Obviously, you don't *know* my roommate . . ." She could barely finish her sentence. It had been almost three years since she'd had to speak about Pam's ordeal. She was so deep in it that she felt like she had lost a part of herself on that day that Pam's baby died.

"I was with her, you know. It was just a few days after the wedding was called off. Greg had just been indicted for tax fraud and embezzlement. I just remember her screaming like someone was stabbing her. And when I ran into the bathroom to see what was wrong, the baby was lying there between her legs. I called 911, and they took her to the hospital. The doctor called it a spontaneous miscarriage caused by the hazards of emotional stress. After about two days they wanted to send her back home. I told them she had to stay. She was almost comatose. I didn't know what to do with her," Dee said, shaking her head sadly.

"What about her family?"

"One of her sisters came by to check on her, but the incident between her and Greg was so overwhelming that it sent her mother into the hospital. Her family didn't even know she was pregnant."

The doctor listened at the anguish in Dee's voice. He could see that this was an agonizing discussion for her, but it was important that he encourage her to get it out.

"So now do you see why I can't tell her? The lies she went through with Greg almost killed her. He lied to her about everything. Money, his business, himself—everything! Finding *this* out about me would kill our friendship forever. I just know it."

The doctor resumed jotting down a few more notes, then folded his hands before speaking. "I can see how you might think that. And I'm inclined to agree with you for now. But, Dee, once you get this monkey off your back, what do you plan on doing? Lies have a way of coming back to haunt all of us, and no matter how hard we try to bury them, the truth always has a way of making it back to the surface."

"You're right. I do know what I'm doing is not normal."

"Then why do you think you do it?"

"I think it makes me feel better about myself. I mean, it's almost like I'm living someone else's life, and I want to get out of this person and say 'Hey, I'm a really intelligent woman who can do better for herself financially and career-wise, but I'm trapped in this flight attendant body and can't get out!'" She laughed bitterly.

"Can't get out? Or afraid to get out?" he asked.

Dee thought about what he was asking. The words froze in midair. She remained silent. She walked to the window, placed her hand on the sill and stared out blankly. "I don't know if *afraid* is the right word," she whispered. She took her time to think about what she was going to say next. "If I were afraid, then I probably wouldn't have agreed to assist this guy with a lawsuit that he has pending."

"What guy and what lawsuit?" The doctor's eyes widened when he heard this.

"He's a friend of Chris's. You know—the football player."

"Yes, I remember you talking about him before. He's the one who thinks you're an attorney, right?"

Dee nodded and her embarrassment was reflected on her face. "Yes, he's the one."

"And tell me more about this lawsuit."

"I don't know all of the details, but it sounds like some woman's out to make him her baby's daddy," Dee laughed.

"And he asked if you could represent him?"

"I already know what you're thinking."

"Good, then I hope you figured out the answer as well."

Dee stared at the carpet in silence. He knew from her body language that she was not going to give him the answer he wanted.

"I'm just going to talk with him. I do have a law degree, you know."

The doctor looked at her with a raised eyebrow. "Yes, you do."

Dee paced in front of the window then stopped—confused and annoyed. "What have I gotten myself into?"

"Is that a rhetorical question, or do you really want me to answer it?"

Dee blew air from her mouth then shrugged her shoulders. She turned to the window again and stared out blankly. She was silent at first as she pondered his question carefully. "I don't know what I want. Isn't that why I'm seeing you? But I'm pretty sure that I can do this," she mumbled.

"I'm sorry, did I hear you correctly? You *think* you can do it?"

Dee gave him a slow deliberate nod.

"How far do you plan on going with this?"

"I haven't thought that far yet, ya know?"

"Deirdre, as your therapist, it is my obligation to warn you about the ramifications this can have."

"I'm fully aware of them."

The doctor resumed his note taking. "And you still intend on doing it? Interesting."

"Look!" Dee said defensively. "I'm just talking to him. It's not like the guy wants me to take his case to trial or something. I already told you I graduated in the top percent of my class in law school. I think that says something."

"Are you trying to convince me or yourself? I mean, your plan is to what? Apply what you learned in textbooks to someone's real-life case? How would you feel if I were pretending to be a psychiatrist?"

Dee felt her face grow hot. Confused and upset, she couldn't answer him. She hadn't thought everything out, and he knew it.

"You need to be sure that what you're doing is in your best interest. I would certainly hate for this to blow apart in your face and you end up behind bars for something as negligent and criminal as this."

Out of nowhere, the doctor's attitude seemed to change. A smile formed on his lips as he looked at her thoughtfully. "Dee, you are remarkable, you know that?"

Dee rolled her eyes toward the ceiling, feeling as if she was on a roller coaster with him. "What are you talking about? First you have me going away to prison for being a criminal and now I'm remarkable? What gives, Doc?"

The doctor nodded. He knew she didn't understand the direction in which he was taking her, but *he* certainly did. "Listen to me. The positive is that *you* already know what your capabilities are. You've just admitted it. That's a good start, but there's one thing that's missing."

"What do you mean?"

"What do *you* think it means?"

"I have no idea! Why don't *you* tell *me*? You're the psychiatrist."

"I'm disappointed in your sarcasm."

Dee shrugged her shoulders and spoke reluctantly. "It means that I know that I have other abilities—I probably need to legitimize them."

"By doing what?"

"I'm not ready for that."

"Ready for what?"

Dee's face avoided his. She knew he was talking about her legitimizing herself by taking the bar. "You know, you're right. Maybe I'll just refer him to my roommate. She may be able to assist him."

He smiled widely. "That would be a smarter idea, Deirdre. You catch on fast."

She looked at the large clock on the wall and stretched her arms out. "Thank you, Doctor. I can see that my fifty minutes are just about over," she said hastily.

"Ah . . . ah . . . ah . . . not so fast, Ms. Bridge."

Dee turned around in surprise. "What?"

"You can't leave without your assignment," he reminded her with a childlike grin.

With a confused look on her face, Dee asked, "What assignment?"

"It's an ethics assignment. You definitely have them," he laughed. "We've just got to raise the bar on them. No pun intended," he laughed.

Dee stared questioningly.

"When you feel like you're about to be dishonest, I want you to think about your ethics, or in your case, why you haven't become a legitimate attorney. That should be your focal point to help you get on track. After all, even lawyers have ethics, right?"

It depends on who the lawyer is, Dee thought smugly, nodding in agreement.

He could tell that she was still not convinced that this was a feasible idea for her. "I'm not saying this is a quick fix, Dee. It's just part of the process. The decision to stop lying is totally your call."

Dee looked up at him briefly. She needed time for all of this to soak in. "Thanks for your advice."

"So, are you going to take it or not?"

Dee smiled. "I'll let you know next week," she said as she winked and walked out of the office.

Dee walked down the hallway from her doctor's office, feeling a vibration on her hip from the inside of her purse. She quickly sifted through the bottom of it, found her cell phone, and glanced at her caller ID.

"This is Dee."

"Hi, Desiree, it's me."

"Hey, Chris!" *What perfect timing,* she thought. Dee was somewhat stupefied at the irony. She sneaked a peek at the doctor's door, hoping he wouldn't walk out and hear her conversation.

"I was just checking with you. My boy is getting a little antsy about his situation, and I was wondering when you would be able to meet with him. We play in the ATL on Friday. Will you be available to meet then? Maybe we can discuss it over dinner and drinks?"

Dee was silent for a moment. She thought of the session she'd just had with her psychiatrist. Doc was right. She needed to face up to the fact that she wasn't a lawyer. And to pose as one would be criminal. However, it wouldn't hurt just to talk with him. No harm done. Right?

"Dee, are you still there?"

"Hey, yeah, I'm here. I was just taking a look at my appointment book. I'm free all weekend. Check with him and let me know what time is good for him to meet."

"You're a life saver, baby! Thank you."

"It's my pleasure. You know I'll do anything for you, Chris."

Smooth Air

As he playfully knocked hard on Amanda's bedroom door, Melvin joked, "All right now. Rise and shine, sleeping beauty!" He was carrying a silver tray heaped with a plate of eggs Benedict, turkey sausage, waffles, and fresh-squeezed orange juice. Melvin accompanied the feast with a single red rose nestled next to her silverware and the morning paper.

Amanda jumped as she caught herself gazing again at the old photo that she kept in her wallet. Not wanting Melvin to see her with it, she quickly shoved it back in its compartment and placed the wallet in her nightstand. "Melvin, you spoil me too much," Amanda said, scooting out from under the down comforter. She sat up, smoothed her hair, and smelled the fresh coffee brewing from the kitchen.

Melvin sat the tray down on her lap, took off his black leather slippers, then tightened the belt of his maroon and black terry cloth robe around his bulging middle, which was starting to take on the shape of a full-sized football.

"Well, you gonna need some spoiling, especially as you're gonna have a lot of time on your hands now that you quit that big fancy law firm last week," he said before leaving the room. When he returned he was carrying two cups of coffee and a tray for himself.

"Please don't give me indigestion *before* I've even had my breakfast."

Melvin took a swig of his juice and sat down on the edge of the bed next to her. "Woman, who you kiddin'?"

"I loved that job before I had to start working with that beast of a woman."

"Baby, you shouldn't have let her chase you out of something you loved."

"She didn't chase me out, I got fed up and quit. You should see her. I don't think even she knows who she is anymore. She still holds a grudge against *me.* I can't believe after all these years she's still mad that I didn't keep my promise. I had to tell her things change, lives change, people change!"

"I know baby, and I'm proud that you stood up to her, but now what are you gonna do? Hmmm? Sit around here by yourself all day and watch soap operas?"

"You know I hate soap operas," Amanda said, slapping his arm.

"Ow! You don't have to get abusive on me, Suga'!" Melvin said, playfully rubbing his arm.

"I've got plenty to do!" Amanda said defensively. "Tracey is going off to college, so I'll be getting her ready for that. Next, I'm going to redo her room." Amanda chuckled and pointed to his stomach as she sipped her coffee. "Or if I get really bored, I can sit around and watch that belly of yours get ready to hatch."

Melvin looked down at his stomach and started to laugh. "You right, and this ol' breakfast I'm eating sure ain't helpin' none, either," he said, shaking his head as he ate a forkful of eggs. He laughed again at himself and smacked his lips. "But, damn, it sho' taste good!"

"All right, now. You know you better watch it. The doctor already told you that you needed to watch that cholesterol."

"You right. I'm gonna get back to the gym this week. I was looking kind of buff there for a while, ya know?" He flexed the large muscles in his arms. "Have you made any headway with Tracey yet about what's going on with her?"

"No, I'm just trying to give her some space and hope she will come to me when she feels the time is right."

Melvin took a large bite of his sausage and closed his eyes as he chewed. "That's probably the best thing."

"You sure are enjoying that piece of meat, aren't you?" Amanda laughed. "I like how you tried to change the subject to Tracey. You're still buff, but honey, you need to get a handle on that mid-section."

"Oh, so you think I'm trying to bring it back to Tracey?" He rubbed her hand and smiled. "I will get a handle on it. I've just been gettin' so many referrals that I've got more business than I can handle. I had to turn down two jobs last week. I had five guys working on one job. Two others called in sick, and I couldn't do it all by myself. As much as I would have liked to have made that extra fifty grand, I got too much stuff goin' on at the same time, ya know? Just haven't been able to find the time to work out."

"Yes, and part of that was my fault because you were here finishing out my basement before Tracey's party," Amanda said, feeling a little guilty.

Melvin playfully tapped her on the tip of her nose with his forefinger. "Hey, Tracey is my girl too, ya know. And I would do anything for her and her mama. No contract is more important than the two of you."

"Oh, and the basement looks so wonderful, Melvin. And that party . . ."

"As the young folks say: it was *tight*!"

Amanda smacked him playfully on the arm. "Oh, so you know the lingo too now, huh?"

"Yes, I guess you could say I know a little something," he said, holding onto his tray as he kissed her on the neck.

Amanda smiled. "Well, Tracey was something else, wasn't she?"

"She stood out in the crowd, as they say."

"I think I like that young man she's dating. He at least seems to take her out of her mood swings that she's been having lately."

"Yeah, what's his name?" Melvin said, snapping his fingers.

"Anthony."

"Yeah, he goes by Tony, though. Smart kid, real smart kid. Got a scholarship to one of them Ivy League schools on the East Coast."

"Harvard."

"Yeah, that's right. I talked to him about Tracey. I don't think it's anything to worry about."

"Well, I sure hope you're right."

"Yeah, they seem pretty tight. I don't know how he and Tracey are going to stay together, being in different cities."

"Tracey won't have time to be thinking about anything except those books. She's got to keep her scholarship, you know."

"Don't fool yo'self, Amanda. Tracey's an attractive young woman." He smiled lovingly at her. "Takes right after her mama. Boys are going to be on her like flies to a trashcan."

"Oh, Melvin, couldn't you think of another way to say that? Flies to a trashcan—yuck!"

"You know what I mean. She's pretty. Men are going to be falling at her feet, and Tracey is gonna have to decide who she's goin' step over and who she's goin' allow to get up off that ground and be good enough to walk with her."

"Melvin, you and your crazy sayings!" Amanda giggled. "Well, all I have to say is that she's there for one reason and one reason only, and that's to get an education. All of that other stuff is secondary."

"Well, you keep leavin' those blinders on when it comes to Tracey. I've seen how she looks at Tony, and I've seen how he looks at her. And believe me, she ain't gonna be just *studyin'* those books at Hampton. You wait and see," Melvin said, pointing his finger warningly at her.

He took a bite of his waffles and shook his head in delight as Amanda got quiet and drank her juice. "All right, all right. I know when to move on to the next subject. Okay, that's enough about Tracey *and* my bulging gut," he laughed. "Let's get back to your decision on quitting your job."

"Well, I'm fine with my decision," she said, relieved that they had gotten off the subject of Tracey. She paused for a few seconds as Melvin looked at her questioningly.

"Really?"

"Yes, really. I think I'm well overdue to take some time off and do some soul-searching, maybe even take a couple of weeks and do some traveling."

"Wooo! Did you come into some money that you forgot to tell me about?"

"No, silly, I've got a little money saved up, and I've been waiting to use it for a special occasion. And this is occasion enough for me," she said as she polished off the last of her waffles. "As a matter of fact, I think I'm going to be joining you in that gym. I could take some pounds off myself," she pointed to her own middle spread. She knew she was about twenty-five to thirty pounds too heavy for her five-foot-four-inch height.

"Not too many, Suga'. You know I like my women healthy," Melvin said as he reached under the cover and pinched her on the thigh.

"I know," she said, leaning to kiss him on the cheek. "Now, let me get out of this bed and get in that kitchen and wash these dishes."

"What time is Tracey coming home?"

"Oh, it won't be until later this evening. Wanda's mother called last night and said that when Tracey and Wanda got up today, she was going to take them shopping."

"Hmmm . . . so, now that you don't have to rush off this morning to work like you usually do, and Tracey will be out for most of the day, do you think we have a little time for . . ."

Amanda blushed at the thought. She couldn't remember the last weekend she was able to wake up leisurely next to Melvin without rushing out to work on something for Pam. They had so few intimate moments because she never let him spend the night while Tracey was at home. And she didn't spend the night with him because she didn't want to set a poor example for her daughter.

"Oh, Melvin, that sounds *really* good to me!"

"Maybe we can even take in a matinee later today," he said as he untied his robe and slipped his nude body under the covers.

Amanda walked back in from the kitchen and joined him underneath the warm blankets, snuggling close to him. His brawny, caramel arms held her tightly and stroked the lace of the bodice on her negligee. He buried his face between her breasts and teased their curves with the light touch of his mustache. Amanda giggled at the sensation and ran her fingers through his coarse dark hair. She kissed him zealously on his full lips.

Amanda felt so protected in his arms. Melvin was her constant when the world around her seemed to be unsteady. With the ease of a trapeze artist, he lifted the straps of her gown with his fingertips, guiding them down slowly to her middle section. With his teeth, he slid the remainder of the negligee down to her inner thighs. Amanda moaned in anticipation as he moved up her body like a sleek panther, his tongue circling swiftly between her thighs and purposely bypassing her center. He worked his tongue back into her mouth and glided back down to her stomach.

She gasped as she felt his manhood work his way slowly and stealthily inside her as she raised her legs even wider to receive his full thrust. It had been so long since Melvin had made love to her that she wondered how she could have allowed herself to get so caught up in her work and deprive herself from this ecstasy. Melvin's moves became harder and stronger as he delicately moved her nipples in and out of his mouth and whispered long-awaited passions in her ears. "Don't you ever make me wait this long! You hear me, woman?"

"Yes, I hear you," she repeated over and over again in his ear. Her nipples stood straight up at the command of his voice. He pushed himself farther inside her and maneuvered her hips on top of him as she rode him wildly. Not wanting to lose their rhythm, he grabbed her hips and held on tightly until their bodies fused together and their sweet juices merged and flowed out in between them.

Amanda lay on top of him, breathless and panting until she looked toward the phone's caller ID screen. "Melvin," she whispered, "you are not going to believe who's calling me."

"I didn't hear the phone ring," he said, kissing her on the neck.

"I know. I had the ringer on silent and forgot to turn it back on, but look at the caller ID." Melvin leaned over to look at the screen. "Well, are you going to answer it or should I?"

"Melvin!" Amanda whispered loudly. She thumped him playfully on his behind. The phone continued to ring silently. Melvin looked disapprovingly at her with his dark brown eyes.

With a sigh she flipped open the phone. "Hello."

"Amanda? This is Pete Sterdivant."

"Hello, Mr. Sterdivant, how are you?" Amanda said, sitting straight up and covering her breasts with the sheets as if he were standing in the room.

"Well, I'm glad to have finally caught up with you."

"You're at work on a Sunday?"

"I've had to play a lot of catch-up this week. You know, we had someone very important leave us quite abruptly. I've been trying to reach you for a few days now, and haven't been able to leave a message."

Amanda was stumped by what to say. "Uh, my ringer's been off." She glanced over at her answering system attached to the phone. "And I guess I accidentally unplugged my phone's system."

"I see, well, I've got you now, and that's all that matters. Amanda, let me get right to the point. You left here so abruptly that we never got an opportunity to talk about it or to follow the proper procedures for your exit interview. And quite frankly, the firm has been up in arms since your departure. Bill McKesson has been adamant about us getting to the bottom line of why you left."

Amanda smiled at the thought that Mr. McKesson still thought so highly of her, even after her leaving the firm on such short notice. "I do apologize about that. It was under extenuating circumstances."

"Would you mind coming by the office sometime this week so we can talk? Bill will be in on the meeting. You were one of our best paralegals, and we don't take losing someone of your caliber lightly."

"I don't think me coming in there is such a good idea, Mr. Sterdivant," Amanda said, looking at Melvin, who was mouthing at her to go and see what the man wanted.

"But why not? We were hoping that we could work out whatever it was that caused you to leave."

"I'm just not sure if that's going to be possible." Melvin frowned at her.

"Amanda, please reconsider."

"Okay," Amanda answered hesitantly. "I'll come in, that's the least I could do as I didn't give you a proper two week's notice."

"How does this Wednesday morning at 9:00 sound?"

"I'll see you then, Mr. Sterdivant."

Amanda hung up the phone and waited for Melvin's response. His silent approval said it all. He opened his arms for her to climb back in so they could pick up where they'd left off.

Oversold

When Dee walked into the private dining area, she immediately felt like drowning herself inside the room's blue flooring, which reminded her of a vast ocean about to turn a tide. She felt the briefcase handle begin to slip from her sweaty palms.

"Hey Desiree, good to see you!" Chris said kissing her on the cheek. "You okay? You look a little pale."

Dee smoothed her hair into place with one hand, as she held on tight to her briefcase. "Oh, I'm fine. You look *good.*" She gave him a sexy-once over, trying to divert attention from herself. She admired his Prada leather boots and his toffee-colored shirt and matching trousers.

"Thanks. I'm glad you approve," Chris grinned and gave her a peck on the lips. "You're lookin' pretty good yourself there. That skirt has got the kind of grip that I'd like to have on those hips myself," he whispered.

Dee blushed. "Thanks. Who are all of those people sitting with you?" Concerned, she counted about nine people seated at his table. "I thought it was going to be just the three of us."

"T decided he would talk business later, so he invited some of his boys to come down to the Blue Pointe for some drinks and appetizers. That's him at the head of the table."

"I see. So his name is T?"

"That's his nickname. He's real name is Theodore. He goes by T or Teddy."

"T is a good choice. He doesn't look like a Theodore."

Chris laughed. "Nor does he act like one. You'll see. My boy is *bananas*!"

Great, can't wait. Dee grew nervous with each minute. It was one thing to pull this off with Chris and his friend, but it was a whole different story to do it in front of nine other people. Dee felt her knees begin to buckle.

"Hey, I got you. Are you sure you're okay?" Chris said, holding her around her waist. Dee was so out of her league right now that the last thing she needed was for her knees to prevent her from moving the way she knew she needed to go.

"I'm so embarrassed," Dee said, hanging onto his shoulder. "It's the shoes. I just bought them a few days ago, and I'm not quite used to walking in them yet. Why don't I just come back a little later? My office is not too far, and I can grab another pair of pumps and get some work done while you and the posse hang out."

"Well, do you want to take them off?"

"Take what off?"

"Those sexy stilettos, silly. There's no reason for you to just drive back for another pair of shoes. It's cool. Just take 'em off."

Okay, that excuse will not work, and I definitely don't do barefoot in public. "Ah no, Chris. Just let me sit down for a moment over there in the corner. Over there by the *door*."

Chris's arms were still around her waist as he escorted her to the chaise in the corner. "Hey, I'll be right back, okay?"

Frantically, Dee started planning her escape. *Chris, I'm not feeling well, all of sudden. Maybe I need to go home and just lie down. Or maybe I'll say, "You know? This might take a little longer than I expected and as you've got all of these people here, let's just reschedule it for another—"*

"Yo, yo listen up everyone!" Chris said at the top of his voice as he pointed to Dee in the corner. "Over there is the one and only Counselor Desiree Bradshaw!"

What in God's name is he doing? No. I was just about to sneak out of here! All eyes were on her as she clutched her briefcase even tighter. She felt like her heart was about to leap out of her chest and onto the floor.

Dee managed to get the strength back in her knees to walk back to the table.

She extended her hand politely and briefly surveyed the room, the same way she did on an airplane when she was trying to locate her nearest exit. Unfortunately, there was only *one* and she had walked away from it.

She glanced over at the three women seated next to T. They looked like last month's pin-up girls. Their breasts were oversized and overexposed in tight-fitting microfiber material that looked like knockoffs from Barbie's Closet.

"Hi," said the streaked blonde haired woman putting her hand out to Dee.

Dee shook her hand. "Hi there."

The young woman threw her hair back over her shoulder and eyed Dee up and down again. Dee smiled at the other two ladies who were both wearing too much weave that they'd paid too much for. They reminded her of the characters in her favorite children's book, *The Cat in the Hat*. Thing 1 and Thing 2.

"How ya doing, Counselor Bradshaw," T said. All thoughts of Thing 1 and Thing 2 vanished from her mind when T came toward her. He was finer than Chris. *How could that be possible?* Dee thought.

"Please just call me Dee. I mean Desiree," she said as she extended her hand, trying not to stare at his firm chest and full biceps that were enhanced by his silk shirt. He shook her hand firmly, smiled, and teasingly gave it back to her. Dee glanced toward the floor trying to avoid the obvious, but her eyes couldn't help wandering back up the leg of his trousers that fit his firm thighs perfectly. She cleared her throat and blinked her eyes, trying to maintain some type of self-control. But it was obvious to him that she was feeling him and that the sensation was mutual.

T couldn't stop staring and was glad to know no one could hear what he was really thinking. His thoughts were running rampant. *Chris told me she was fine. But damn, she's got me on fire,* he thought, eyeing Dee seductively from every angle and pulling out the chair next to him. "All right, then. Dee would you like to order a drink?" Before T could get the chair out from underneath the table, Chris tapped him on the shoulder.

"I got this. Down, boy. Let's not forget why she's here, man, okay?" Chris joked, knowing full well where T's intentions were going.

"Oh, my bad, man. I was only trying to be a gentleman." He grinned and raised his hands in surrender. "You know me."

"Yeah, I *know* you, aight!" he said, slapping T's back. Dee laughed while she watched Thing 1 and Thing 2 look at each other as they watched the other men seated at the table eye her like she was *their* last supper.

As Dee composed herself, a tall, thin, fair-skinned black man walked into the room. He looked to be in his early thirties and was neatly dressed in a dark double-breasted custom-tailored suit. Dee sucked in her breath when she saw him make his way to the table. She recognized him as a passenger on her flight from just a few weeks ago. He had ordered two rum and cokes with a twist of lime and lemon. She had overheard his conversation and found out that he was a sports agent, traveling to see a prospective jock. She closed her eyes briefly and prayed. *Lord, please don't let this guy have as good a memory as I do.*

"Hey, what's up, T?" he said, leaning in to give him a pat on the back and a quick handshake.

"Hey, Quint! Man, glad you could make it!"

"How's it goin,' Chris?" Quint said, giving him a high five.

"Can't complain, can't complain. I hear you're about to sign the twenty million dollar rookie right out of high school."

"We'll see, we'll see. His mom's not feeling me. She wants him to go on to college."

"What? He's got a guaranteed twenty mil, and she wants him to go get a piece of paper?"

"Hey, some people are just like that, ya know? And it's my job to show them otherwise," he said with a sinister laugh.

"Well, if anybody can do it, you da man!" T laughed and punched him lightly in his shoulder.

Quint turned and saw Dee. "Hey, *you* look familiar."

Dee's nerves were coming unraveled. If Quint figured out where he knew her from then she was finished before she could even get started.

"I know this is going to sound corny, but don't I know you from somewhere?"

"It's quite possible. I do get around," Dee joked, trying to shrug off her inner fear. He kept looking at her face, snapping his fingers like he was trying to jog his memory.

"Hey, this is going to be my attorney, Counselor Desiree Bradshaw," T jumped in proudly. "Counselor, meet the one and only Quinton Richardson. We call him Quint."

"Nice meeting you," Quinton said shaking her hand.

"Same here." Dee nodded.

"Counselor Bradshaw here is goin' to get me straight with this skank who is tryin' to make me her baby's daddy and take my fuckin' money!" T interrupted.

"My heart goes out to ya,' brotha. Desiree, what's the name of your firm?"

"Sterling, Mathis, and Silverman," Dee announced before she could stop herself.

"Really. SMS, huh?"

Dee did her best to look self-assured as she nodded affirmatively.

"I didn't know they hired another sista'. When did you start working there?"

"It hasn't been that long."

Quinton kept shaking his head and giving her a puzzled look. "It will come to me sooner or later, 'cause I never forget a face. Especially someone who looks like you."

Dee could tell that his brain was working overtime to figure out who she was. Her only saving grace was that she was dressed in business attire and not in her uniform. That was the only reason he was having difficulty making the connection.

"Hey, tell Counselor Madison I said hello."

Great, he knew Pam. What in heaven's name was she thinking when she said she worked at her firm? Smart move, Dee, real smart move.

"Now, Pam Madison, that's a heavy sista' right there," Quinton said as if he knew her style all too well.

Feeling her throat starting to close up, Dee sipped on her glass of water. She had to remain calm. "I will," she nodded.

Quinton turned toward T. "Hey, T! Stay strong man, I'm out."

"You leavin' already? You just got here."

"I know, I just stopped by to say hello. I've got some business I need to handle on the home front."

"You mean the Kelly front, don't you?" A boyish grin spread across Quinton's lips. "She's still got you whipped, I see," T teased.

"Hey, don't hate me, playa'. Just 'cause you wish you had somebody at home waitin' on you!"

T laughed. "Yeah, now you know that's a *damn* lie!"

"Listen, hang in there, man. You've got a sista' workin' from SMS. You gon' be aight!" He gave him a high-five and a fist bump. "Besides, you need someone to whip yo' wannabe playa' ass into shape!" He laughed.

T grabbed his shoulders and pretended to escort him out of the door. "Now *it is time* for you to go. Talk to you later, man."

"You do that," Quinton said walking over to Chris. "Hey, Chris, talk to you later. Give me a call when you guys are ready to have me come and see you get beat by the Falcons."

"Aight. Man, we gon' have to call security up in here!" Chris yelled.

"I'm out . . . I'm out!"

"Yeah, you betta' be! In here talkin' trash like that!" T joked as he and Chris watched him skillfully work the room with his usual grace and charm.

As the posse thinned, Quinton lingered. He worked the room, hugging and kissing every single woman in the dining area, and exchanging high-fives with the guys like he was the host of the party. He kept eyeing Dee from across the room. The more he looked at her, the calmer she tried to appear. She felt like a pawn in a chess game waiting for the inevitable capture.

Quinton finally said his last goodbye and left from the private dining room. As he turned the corner, he noticed two familiar faces seated at a corner table feeding each other bread sticks.

"Amanda and Melvin!"

"Quinton?"

"Hey, how are you, Amanda?" He bent down to give her a hug.

"How you enjoying that sauna, man?" Melvin said, wiping his hands on his napkin as he stood up to shake his hand.

"Me and the old lady are lovin' it. I'm about to get home right now and get in it after I take a few laps around that pool you put in for us. Man, you sure know how to do some home improvements," Quinton laughed.

"He is really good. I keep tellin' him that. You ought to see my basement he finished," Amanda chimed in.

Melvin felt himself blush. He tried to hide his embarrassment by wiping his face with his napkin. "All right, ya'll stop it now. You gon' make my head bigger than what it already is."

Quinton laughed as he pointed to Melvin's head. "Well, I'm sure it can't get no bigger than that fat wallet you makin' off of all us *po'* people."

"You hardly *po',* man. I heard about that twenty million dollar man you 'bout to sign up."

"Man, I need somethin' to pay for all of them bills I accumulated with you," he said, laughing again as Melvin nodded in agreement. "So, what are you two doing on this side of town?"

"We're celebrating," they both said in unison.

"Hey, you two are finally getting hitched, huh?"

Amanda blushed. "No, not this go round."

"It ain't cuz I don't want to, either," Melvin chuckled.

"Stop it, Melvin," Amanda said lightly tapping Melvin on the thighs. "We're celebrating me quitting my job."

"And *then* them calling her back again to *rehire* her!" Melvin laughed.

"What? *You* quit SMS?" Quinton sat down in the vacant chair at their table. His eyes bulged in disbelief.

"Yeah, I did," Amanda said proudly.

"But why? I mean, they're one of the top law firms in the country, if not THE top one. And rumor had it that you were the number one paralegal."

"Let's just say that Amanda got tired of a little someone running a power trip on her all the time," Melvin said defensively.

Quinton laughed. "You've got to be talking about Pam Madison."

"Yep, the one and only," Amanda sighed at the thought of her.

"I remember when she represented our firm two years ago. She was somethin' else then."

"Yes, I remember that case. I worked on it. And I never will forget it. Pam had me there to almost one o'clock in the morning many times."

"Daaamn! She's a kick-ass, huh?"

"That's an understatement. But your firm did win, didn't it?"

"Oh, yeah, and we had a wind fall." Quinton laughed. "One of our clients was in breach of contract and let's just say, Pam got it *all* worked out and then some."

Amanda shook her head at the thought of her. "You know, she was beyond herself back then. But now . . . wooo weeee! She really thinks she's *Miss Thang,* as my daughter would say!"

"So you just got fed up and up and quit?"

"Yep, my baby just got tired of the bullshit," Melvin chimed in. "She and Pam go way back, man. Amanda and Pam went to Spelman and some of law school together."

"Damn, I never knew that."

"A lot of people don't. Amanda and Pam wanted to keep it like that too, right baby?"

Amanda took a long sip of her water. "It doesn't matter anymore," Amanda said, patting Melvin on his knee.

"'Sides, it ain't like she needs that job anyway," Melvin said as he gently squeezed her hand and kissed her on the cheek.

"So, what do you think about the other sista they hired?" Quinton asked.

"What other sister? Pam's the only black attorney there, unless somebody got hired between last week and now when I quit."

Confused, Quinton stroked his chin and thought about Dee. "Well, I just met this young woman over in the private dining area who said she works for SMS."

"Really? What's her name?"

"Desiree or something like that. I can't remember," he said, snapping his fingers.

Melvin looked at Amanda curiously. "That name don't sound familiar," he interjected. "I don't ever remember you mentioning a Desiree before."

"That's because I don't know anyone by that name that works at SMS, unless of course she was just recently hired."

"Well, she's over there in the private dining room helping out one of my buddies with a case. Why don't you go over there and take a peek at her?"

"Well, I *am* a little curious."

"Go on baby, do your detective work. I'll order for you," Melvin teased. Amanda playfully rolled her eyes at him as she followed Quinton back to the private dining area.

"Hey, Quint's back!" T yelled. "I thought you had to get back and report to Kelly."

"Aight, man, I done told you before, stay OUT my business! I want you to meet a personal friend of mine. Amanda, this is T. T, this is Amanda."

"Nice meeting you, Amanda."

"Same here."

"Amanda used to work at SMS as a paralegal, and I wanted her to meet your friend." Quinton looked around the room, "Where is she?"

"Hey Chris, where's your girl?" T yelled across the room.

"I think she went to the ladies' room."

"You want to wait on her, Amanda?" Quinton asked.

"No, that's okay. Maybe I'll catch her coming out of the ladies' room. What does she look like?"

"She's about 5'10". Long brown hair. She's really attractive."

"So are a lot of women in here. What's she wearing?"

"Now, you know me, I ain't too good with women's clothing," Quinton said, trying to remember Dee's attire. "I think it's a skirt and blouse, maybe silver or gray. Yeah, that's it."

"Hey, that's pretty good. I've got to go in there, anyway. I'll introduce myself. It was good seeing you, Quint. Tell Kelly that Melvin and I said hello."

"I will."

Amanda entered the blue marble restroom, admiring the circular stepped basins that adorned the bathroom when she noticed a woman, who, from the back, bore a striking resemblance to Quinton's description.

"Hi. Are you—oh my God! Deirdre?"

Dee's mouth dropped open and she felt her breath stuck in her throat. "Amanda!"

Amanda and Dee stood frozen for a moment. Neither of them knew what to say at first, but instinctively they raised their arms and embraced each other.

"How have you been?" they both asked at the same time.

"It's been such a long time. I just can't believe this!" Amanda said, still giggling.

Dee raised her eyebrows. "Well, you stopped taking my calls, remember?"

"I know. I feel really bad about that, too. I've wanted to call to apologize, but I just couldn't find the words. Tracey's been asking about you, too."

"I had her recently on a flight. She's growing up too fast!"

"She is, and she told me. Melvin and I are both really proud of her."

"I bet your parents are proud, too," she said trying not to slip and mention Tracey's father.

"They are ecstatic! Before I forget, I ran into Quinton Richardson in the restaurant and he told me you were working for Sterling, Mathis, and Silverman. I mean, I'm sure Pam told you that I quit the firm. When did all of this happen? Pam didn't hire you as my replacement, did she?" Amanda laughed sarcastically.

Dee suddenly broke out in a cold sweat. She felt like she was about to drown in it. This was not happening. She needed to think fast. "Really? Quinton must have misunderstood me. People were kind of loud in there. He probably just didn't hear me when I said Steinman, Madison, and Estervan," Dee said quickly.

Amanda looked at her suspiciously. "I'm not familiar with them. Where are they located?"

"In New York."

"Really? Wow! So, you passed the bar and now you're moving to New York? "

"I haven't decided yet."

"So, what about your job with the airline?"

"Like I said, I haven't thought this all through, but I'm thinking I'll work during the week and fly out on weekends."

"Hmmm. What does Queen Madison think of your plans?"

What in the world am I doing? Amanda is one of my dearest friends and I'm lying to her. I don't know what to do. If I tell her the truth, she'll go back and tell Quint, and then he'll tell Chris and then I'm really screwed. "You know. I haven't really had time to discuss it with her. As a matter of fact, I didn't know you quit the firm until I spoke to Tracey recently."

"Pam didn't tell you?"

"No."

Amanda looked hurt. "Obviously, it wasn't a priority for her."

"Hey, Amanda. This thing between you and Pam, I just think you need to really . . ."

"Just don't." Amanda raised her hand.

"Don't what?"

"Don't defend her."

"I'm not def—"

"Yes, you are—you always have."

"Amanda, c'mon you know that's not . . ."

Amanda glanced around the bathroom and took a breath from deep within. "Listen Dee. This is not the time and definitely not the place for us to have this discussion in the ladies' room. Let's do this," she said taking out a piece of paper and pen from her purse. "Here is my new phone number. Is yours still the same?"

"Yes."

"Please call me. I promise I will answer this time!" Amanda smiled. "Or better yet, I'll call you. Let's set up some time to go out and talk. Agreed?"

"Agreed."

"I'm looking forward to catching up," Amanda said, winking.

"Same here."

Dee smiled and waited for her to go into the stall, then hurried from the room and hid behind the pillar wall. She felt like a fugitive as she snuck a quick peek around the corner to see if Quinton was anywhere nearby. She scanned the room until she spotted Quinton standing and talking to Melvin.

She remained behind the pillars until she saw him disappear. She heaved a sigh of relief. Her silk blouse was sticking to her like honey on a warm biscuit.

"Hey, Dee," Amanda called out.

When Dee turned around and saw Amanda, she all but leapt out of her heels. She barely caught herself before she lost her balance, almost spraining her ankle in the process.

"Hey, I didn't mean to startle you," she said, catching Dee by the arm before she fell to the ground.

"Oh, I'm so embarrassed. Thanks," Dee said, as she smoothed her hair out of her face.

"Are you okay? You don't look too well."

"I'm not feeling too well, either, ya know? I think I'm going to call it an evening. Hey, thanks—thanks again, for ah . . ." Dee tried to use her hands to indicate what she was trying to say, since her words had vanished.

"Catching you!" Amanda said, finishing the sentence for her. "No problem. Are you sure you're going to be all right? Do you need some assistance?"

Dee finally let go of the wall and almost toppled over again from nervousness. "No, I'm fine. I'm sure. Thank you, again."

Amanda was concerned about her friend. "Hey, Melvin is right over there," she pointed out from the corner. "We can give you a ride home, if you need one."

"Oh, no, please. I'll be fine." She fumbled around in her briefcase for her keys. She was having difficulty catching her breath.

"Dee, I'm concerned. Are you here with someone?"

"There's this guy named Chris Dickerson."

"The Miami *Dolphins,* Chris?"

"Yeah, that's him. Please just tell him that Desiree suddenly became ill and that I will call him later."

"Who is Desiree?"

"That's just a nickname he calls me," Dee answered and was ticked off at herself for accidently revealing some of her charade to Amanda.

"All right, Desiree," Amanda looked at her oddly. "I don't want to be presumptuous, but I think he should come get you and walk you to your car."

Dee lifted her shaking hands that held the keys. "No, please. I'll be fine. Just give him my message, okay?"

"Okay, then. Be careful."

"I will," Dee said, managing to limp her way through the doorway and back to her car. "I'll call you."

Fueled to Fly

Silent chill filled the courtroom. Pam and the prosecuting attorney, Linda Garret, took to the *Johnson v. Tyfish Systems* case like two piranhas battling for the last piece of human flesh. This was the final day of deliberations, and the jury had already been on duty for two weeks. They looked as if they had just as much animosity for Pam and Linda as they had for each other. Since the onset of the trial, the highly publicized case played out like a courtroom scene from a Hollywood movie. And both women were competing for the starring role.

For every piece of evidence Linda had against Pam's client, Pam had just as much evidence to prove his innocence. Each witness from both sides had a strong alibi, and both Pam and Linda made excellent attempts at discrediting each other's witnesses. But the witnesses were steadfast and answered each question thoughtfully and honestly—or appeared to, anyway.

Linda, like Pam, was at the pinnacle of her career. She, too, reveled in the idea of being able to be a part of such a high-profile case. She had also attended Columbia Law School, and they worked together on cases in the past. But no other case had been this big, and no other had ever pushed their careers so far into the spotlight.

Linda was Pam's exact opposite. She was soft-spoken, yet extremely persuasive in the courtroom. Linda was not nearly as attractive as Pam, but what she lacked in physical beauty she made up for in legal expertise and charm. She was known for her cropped afro and conservative outfits of classically designed suits and low-heeled Aigner pumps.

Pam's client's stomach churned. If Titus Johnson was found guilty, he could face a maximum penalty of twenty years for embezzlement. His face was emotionless. Pam had used this as strategy since the beginning of the trial.

"Guilty or innocent, Mr. Johnson, our motto here is, never, *ever* let them see you sweat!" Pam's voice ranted in his ear throughout the day, reminding him that, in her opinion, any hint of emotion could tip the verdict either way. So, to play it safe, they took the middle road and let the jury decide his innocence based only on the evidence that was presented.

Mr. Johnson leaned toward Pam, clutching his stomach. "I think I'm going to be sick."

"Believe me, the last thing you want to do is hurl in this courtroom. Here, take this," she said, pulling a Tums out of her purse. "Take a deep breath and focus on that window over there."

He looked up at the jury, his eyes searching for answers. Nothing was there. Next, he turned to look at his wife and three children, who were holding hands and praying silently. Their faith gave him some semblance of hope.

Meanwhile, Linda's client, Tyfish's executive team, sat stiffly, passing notes back and forth. While their strategy was causing Mr. Johnson to unravel, it was only fueling Pam's confidence.

Judge Terry Ferguson entered through the wooden doors. The courtroom stood in her honor. The lines in her face showed the stress of her job. Gray roots always seemed to pop up no matter how many times she dyed them.

"Who is the spokesperson for this jury?" Judge Ferguson asked.

A short, soft-spoken woman stood and raised her hand. "I am, Your Honor."

"Has the jury come to a verdict?"

"Yes, we have, Your Honor," the woman said confidently.

Mr. Johnson's head fell to his shoulders. This was the first time that he had shown emotion throughout the trial. The spokesperson didn't know if he would make it through the verdict. She thought he looked weak and nauseated as she watched him clutch the base of his stomach. Pam saw the queasy look on her client's face as Linda flashed a premature victory smile. If Pam won, she wanted to permanently delete that smug look on Linda's face.

"Would the defendant please rise?" Judge Ferguson asked.

"Breathe. Breathe and focus on the window. It's going to be all right. Just breathe," Pam whispered. Pam saw Mr. Johnson close his eyes and take a deep breath as though he was lifting pressure from his stomach. He held onto the table as he braced himself to stand.

"Madame Foreperson, have you reached a verdict?" the judge asked.

"Yes, we have Your Honor."

"What say you?"

"As to the single count of embezzlement, we, the jury, find the defendant, Mr. Titus Johnson not guilty." The stout woman looked over at Mr. Johnson and made eye contact with him for the first time.

"Yes! We won!" Pam said. Mr. Johnson grabbed her and buried his head in her shoulders as the tears flooded down his cheeks.

"Thank you, God! Thank you, Pam," he wailed as he raised his fists high above his head.

The courtroom was in an uproar as Mr. Johnson's family screamed and ran to embrace him while Tyfish Systems's vice president screamed, "We'll appeal! You won't get away with this, Titus!"

Titus looked at him with a hateful sting in his eyes. He lunged toward him as Pam grabbed him by the shoulders. "Appeal all you want, it will only be the same outcome. I'm innocent!"

"Order! Order in this courtroom!" Judge Ferguson yelled as she slammed down the gavel. "Counselor Madison, get a hold of your client!" The courtroom fell silent. "This courtroom is still in session. I have not dismissed anyone!" She looked toward the jury box. "Thank you, jurors. You have done a good job in doing your civic duty. You are free to go, Mr. Johnson. This courtroom is now dismissed." Judge Ferguson authoritatively slammed down her gavel for the last time.

Linda was notably disappointed by the verdict. She put her pride aside for a moment as she walked toward Pam. "Congratulations, Pam," she said through pursed lips. "Mr. Johnson . . ."

Mr. Johnson nodded. He was still hugging his family, who had formed a small ring around him. Pam was not fooled by her façade of professional courtesy. Linda was enraged and harbored strong feelings of envy and injustice in her heart, and Pam knew it.

"Well, you know what they say," Pam said arrogantly.

"No, I don't. But something tells me you're going to inform me."

Pam looked at her with all of the indignation she had been assembling for this very moment and paused before she spoke. "They say in court *someone* always loses."

"That's true, Pam. Someone does have to lose," Linda said.

"It's just that in my case, it has not, and it never will be me." Pam gave her a dismissive look and snapped up her briefcase. "Excuse me while I go out to give a statement to the deluge of reporters that are waiting to hear about *me* and my *client's triumph.*"

Near Miss

As Dee walked through the revolving door, a man bumped into her, causing her packages to fall to the floor.

"Here, let me help you with those," a nearby man said as he raced over to help. His voice was as smooth as brass and caught Dee's attention right away. She looked up into the bluest eyes she'd ever seen.

"Thanks, I guess chivalry is *not* gone."

"Not for me, anyway. Did you see that guy? He didn't even look up," he said as he bent down to retrieve the books from the floor.

"I don't think he even realized he bumped into me. He was pretty preoccupied with his conversation."

"I don't know how someone could miss bumping into you," the stranger said admiringly, looking at Dee's flawless skin. He looked at her as though she was a fine work of art and was immediately taken in by her natural beauty. Her straight hair flowed around her shoulders, giving her a regal aura.

"I don't mean to be nosy, but where'd you get these books?"

"At this little bookstore not too far away from here, actually. They sell all types of old books," she said, finding herself lured in by his powerful gaze. His skin was lightly tanned, highlighting his straight, russet brown hair. He was every bit of a blue-eyed George Clooney look-alike, and Dee loved her some Clooney.

"These are some interesting topics," he said, perusing through the titles before placing them back in her bag. "*Osteopathic Medicine in the 1800s*,

Naturopathic Medicine, 1900s. If I'm not being too presumptuous, are you in the medical field?"

Dee looked down at the books. She'd bought them for Sedrick. Even before Sed became a doctor, he loved to read about anything that had to do with medicine, especially books dating back to the 1800s. The hold this stranger's eyes had on her allowed her to come up with only one answer.

"Yes. I'm a medical student at Morehouse Medical School in Atlanta."

"Morehouse, yes, I'm very familiar with Atlanta. I have a client there. We just did some PR for him at his hospital. So, what are you doing in San Diego?"

"Oh, I'm here attending some workshops in pediatrics, and we had a little break in our schedule so I did a little shopping," Dee sounded so convincing that she almost believed it herself.

"I see. If you don't mind, I'd really like to talk with you again."

"That's funny. I was thinking the same thing."

"Really? How long will you be in town?"

"This is the last day for the workshops, so I'll be leaving tomorrow afternoon."

"That's too bad."

"Oh. And why's that bad?"

"I was hoping we could hang out a bit. How about dinner tonight? Unless, of course, you already have plans."

Only with my crew. "No, I was going to do some studying and order up room service."

"Okay, then, let me give you my card. Here is the hotel where I'm staying," he said as he scribbled his information on the back. He immediately stopped writing on his card. "I can't believe this!"

"What?"

"We didn't even introduce ourselves."

Dee laughed. "Well, I'm Debra Mitchell. You can call me Deb," she responded.

"And I'm Steven Cushman. And you can call me Steve, or Steven," he joked. "Why don't we meet here in the lobby this evening at 7:00? Just give me a call if anything changes. If not, I'll see you down here tonight."

"All right, thank you," she said, taking the card from him. He stared at her one more time, still holding onto the card and gently squeezed her hand. "Well, I'm here on business, and I see some of my cohorts signaling for me to get back into the luncheon," he said, nodding at three white businessmen waving. He finally let go of her hand and walked back toward the group. "Looking forward to seeing you later."

Dee stared at the card and wondered what she had just gotten herself into. She couldn't understand why her lies flowed so smoothly. It was one thing to be an attorney; she had that down pat because of her background. But now she had to pull off being in medical school, too. Maybe listening to all of Sedrick's stories about his patients would finally pay off. At least she hoped so.

Turnaround

Amanda walked slowly through the double doors of Sterling, Mathis, and Silverman. All of the familiar faces welcomed her, anticipating her homecoming.

"Well, Miss Amanda, I sure am glad to see you. So, are you back for good?" Carol Ann asked as she leaned in toward her.

"No, I'm here to meet with Mr. McKesson and Mr. Sterdivent."

Carol Ann raised her eyebrow as if to say, *What is the big meeting about? And why didn't I know about it?* "Have a seat and I'll tell them you're here." She strutted back behind her desk to buzz them. "Mr. McKesson, Amanda is here, sir."

"Good! Send her on back."

She stood again and walked back toward Amanda. "Well, you heard him. You know the way," she said pleasantly, extending her arms toward the corridor.

Sounds of papers shuffling and the clerical staff buzzing made the firm such a vital place. Amanda remembered how much she used to enjoy the energy that filled the firm.

She stood in the entryway and softly tapped on Pete's wide open door. Pete looked up and his eyes greeted her cordially. "Hey, Amanda. Thanks for coming in," he said, as he stood to shake her hand, gesturing for her to take a seat.

"Hello, Amanda, it's good to see you," Bill McKesson said, gently placing both hands on top of hers and shaking them warmly.

The room was filled with an inexplicable positive energy she couldn't ignore. She had a hard time digesting the fact that they felt she was important enough for them to *call her*. And, based on the sound of Pete's voice from previous conversations, they were anxious to get her back.

Pete sat back in his chair and folded his hands as if he were contemplating his next sentence. "Amanda, as I mentioned, we called you in here to discuss the reason you left us so abruptly, and without the proper two-week notice."

"Yes, we can't afford for our employees to leave the firm all of a sudden and never know why," Bill chimed in, almost as if they had been rehearsing each other's lines.

Amanda thought pensively about their questions before she spoke. She fidgeted with the string on the sleeve of her sweater and exhaled as she made eye contact with them both.

"I've had some personal matters that I've been neglecting, and my job was interfering with them," she said, trying to sound convincing.

"So you couldn't take vacation time to be off?" Pete interjected.

Bill scratched the side of his toupee. "You must have several weeks built up because I can't remember when you *weren't* in the office."

Amanda looked down at the floor. She knew they knew she was lying. Should she tell them the truth? That one of the only black females, a soon-to-be partner and former friend was an overbearing, insensitive, callous-hearted bitch of a person? She thought about all of the long hours of labor she'd spent with Pam. And suddenly Melvin's voice bolted through her head like a freight train. Why should she allow Pam to intimidate her to quit something she loved? Maybe it was time for her to tell Pete and Bill about their past and what type of demon they had really hired. If nothing else, perhaps it would help them be on the lookout for the next poor victim who had to work underneath Pam's vise-like grip.

"You're both right," she said feeling a little more confident. The string on her sweater had gotten longer. She twirled it until she snapped it out from underneath her sleeve and slowly began to speak. "I've felt like my back was up against the wall. It felt as if there was a tight grip around my throat, and I was being squeezed harder and harder until finally I had to let go. I had no other choice. I couldn't breathe."

Bill and Pete looked troubled. Bill spoke first. "The grip you are speaking of—was it the workload?"

"Or someone?" Pete interrupted.

Amanda paused, thinking about the words that were about to come from her lips. Yes, she would speak the truth. After all, she had nothing to lose. "It was *someone.*" Amanda suddenly felt a burst of relief erupting from so many years of holding those words inside.

"Can you tell us who this *someone* is?" Bill asked in a concerned tone. "We don't want this person to think they can continue to taunt people this way. This firm was built on integrity and if we can't treat our own right, then God help us when we expect the system to do *us* justice."

Amanda slowly filled her lungs with air and then released it. Her words were deliberate. "Pam. Madison."

Bill and Pete looked at each other and nodded as if they had known the name before she spoke it. She proceeded to tell them everything about her relationship with Pam and how Pam had treated her.

"Thank you, Amanda. This information you have given us is very serious. We will investigate this matter. As you know, Pam is one of the best attorneys we have in this firm," Bill said, looking at her pensively. "I had no idea that you and Pam were classmates. This is so uncanny."

"I realize that, sir, and that is why I didn't feel comfortable telling you the truth when I quit."

"But we're glad you did," Pete chimed in as he and Bill nodded in agreement.

"Amanda, we're going to work diligently in our efforts to get this resolved. And when we do, would you consider coming back to work?"

"Yes. Yes, I would. Thank you." Amanda was caught off guard by his question. She spoke before she could think about what he was asking.

"Good, then. We'll be in touch."

They both rose from their chairs in unison. "Thank you for stopping by Amanda," Bill said.

"Yes, it was good to see you," said Pete.

Bill opened the door and walked out with her to the elevator. "How's Tracey doing?"

"She's fine. She's headed off to school in a few weeks, so I'm getting ready for one less space at the dinner table."

"I know how that is. When our last one left for college, my wife and I didn't know if we should cry or celebrate," Bill laughed. "Here's your elevator. You'll be hearing from us in a few days. But in the meantime, enjoy the extra plate on the table while you still can. No matter how old they get, they always manage to come back to it."

Amanda laughed as she stepped into the elevator. "Thank you, sir. Goodbye."

Special Meal

Dee's flight arrived at LaGuardia Airport right on time at 2:03 p.m. Steve, her latest boyfriend victim, had asked her if she could spend some time with him in New York while she had a break between her *medical* classes. And just as Steve had promised, a blue Lincoln Town Car was there to pick her up. The driver was holding a sign that said "Dr. Debra Mitchell."

"Good afternoon, Dr. Mitchell. Welcome to New York. I'm Charles," a portly, distinguished-looking man remarked as he took her luggage and placed it in the trunk. He was wearing dark blue trousers, a stark white shirt with a red tie, and a matching single-breasted jacket. His attire reminded her of a pilot without the cap and wings.

"Doctor?" *Oh, yes . . . I almost forgot.* "Why, thank you," she said, shaking his hand. "But I'm not a doctor yet. I'm still in medical school. I take the boards in a few months. And then I'll be Dr. Mitchell." She smiled. Dee watched his hands open the car door for her and thought he had the most neatly manicured nails for someone with such stubby fingers. She got in the car and slid into the supple blue leather of the backseat.

Charles smiled at her through his rearview mirror. "Mr. Cushman asked that I take you directly to his office. He was not able to get off as planned to meet you, but he said that he would make up for that inconvenience later."

"That's fine." Dee was preoccupied with the sight of all the cars that were starting to fill up the freeway. She thought about how she had cleverly maneuvered her way into an all-expense paid trip to New York thanks to the PR guru Steve Cushman. Since they'd met that afternoon in San Diego three months ago, their relationship had been an escapade that seemed to continue on autopilot. Her mind reeled back to their first meeting in her hotel lobby and their unforgettable first date. And today she was in New York, still seeing him under false pretenses.

Dee remembered her first date in San Diego with Steve as if it were yesterday. She felt a tinge of guilt as she reflected back in time.

She had already manipulated the first part of the evening in her head as she removed a newly purchased cell phone from her shopping bag. She carefully took the cell phone out of its packaging and programmed the number on speed dial into her old cell phone.

"Just a little added protection, Mr. Cushman," she said, as she discreetly clipped the new phone underneath her jacket. She glanced once more in the full-length mirror and was glad she'd decided to pack her cream-colored pants and matching lace blouse. She wore an elegant single strand of pearls. Her ears were double-pierced with a diamond stud and a pearl earring. She unpacked a small matching handbag and a pair of cream-colored mules. Feeling well dressed for just about anything in California, she headed out the door and into the elevator.

"Well, he-e-el-lo!" Steve said as the elevator door opened. Then he handed her a bouquet of white roses. He looked quite dapper and comfortable in his casual crew neck shirt and black jeans that fit his derriere quite nicely. His sweater was a nice complement to his beckoning azure eyes. Dee was elated by his thoughtfulness as she took the flowers and enjoyed the aroma of each one.

"The flowers match your outfit perfectly," he said, impressed with himself at the coincidence.

"Yes, they do. You PR people don't have hidden cameras placed in the rooms, do you?"

"No, but I like the thought." Steve put his arm around her waist and escorted her to the concierge, who stood at attention like the Royal Guard in England.

"Yes, sir. May I help you?"

"Can we get a vase for these flowers? We're having dinner this evening in the hotel restaurant. We'll be back to pick them up later this evening."

"I'd be delighted, sir. Would you like for us to just deliver them back to the room?" he asked moving his eyes toward Dee.

"Oh, yes. That is very nice of you. Is it possible to get them wrapped again so I can take them back on the plane with me?"

Steve slipped him a fifty-dollar bill and winked. "Of course," the concierge agreed. "Ma'am what's your room number?"

"675. Thank you."

"You are very welcome. Enjoy your dinner," he said as he placed the crisp new bill in his uniform vest.

Steve opened the double doors for Dee to walk into the restaurant, where the maitre d' greeted them.

"Good evening, Mr. Cushman."

"Hello, Shelly. This is my friend Debra."

Shelly shook her hand and turned to smile at Steve. "Nice meeting you, Debra. We have your table waiting for you, Mr. Cushman."

"Thank you."

Dee felt like a celebrity walking the red carpet. All eyes focused on them, and it was obvious Steve knew many of the people who nodded and smiled at him as they made their way over to a secluded corner table overlooking the ocean.

"So, Mr. Cushman, are you some type of VIP? I don't know many people who walk into a restaurant and get a private table while the whole room is watching."

Steve grinned. "Are you sure it's *me* they're watching and not *you*?" he said, raising his eyes at her alluringly. His eyes were so glued on her that she felt as if he were trying to put her into a cataleptic state.

Dee winked. "Well, you know, I hadn't thought about that. It probably *is* me," she teased back as the waitress came over and filled their water glasses.

"Would you and your guest like to hear about our specials this evening, Mr. Cushman?"

"I'll pass and have my usual, but Debra would probably like to hear them. Right?"

"But of course," Dee said, nodding for the waitress to begin her descriptions.

"Tonight we have a delicious salmon almandine, fresh asparagus, and delectable new potatoes. Or we have a succulent duck served with a vegetable medley and creamed potatoes."

"Mmmm, they both sound delicious! What does Mr. Cushman usually get?" she asked, eyeing Steve.

"I'm a lobster man. And, believe me, it's the biggest and tastiest you've ever seen on this side of the ocean."

"Well, that's what I'm having, then," Dee affirmed as she handed the waitress the menu.

"Okay, then, two Maine lobsters coming right up," the waitress said.

Dee looked out of the window at the vast body of water massaging the sandy shore. The moon had just touched down, its light serving as a backdrop against the Pacific Ocean's turquoise canvas.

"The view is breathtaking," Dee said as she kept her eyes focused out the window.

"Do you want to walk out there a little later and get a closer glance?"

"That would be nice. I think I'd like that."

He smiled and rubbed her hand gently. "You know, Debra, I like your spirit. You seem like a very intriguing woman."

"Not as intriguing as you, I'm sure," Dee teased as she gazed around the room at his entourage of associates.

Steve squeezed her hand, then brought it up to his lips and kissed it tenderly. His flirtation was subtle, but Dee felt his fiery heat through her body as he gently squeezed her fingers and stroked each one separately.

"I travel quite a bit to California. We have quite a few clients across the country, but I find myself in San Diego more often."

"Well, that makes sense." She watched his hands move from hers to the inside of his jacket pocket. His hand fumbled around until he pulled out a pack of Marlboro cigarettes. He took one out and prepared to light it.

"Oh, I'm sorry, Debra. Do you mind?"

Dee looked at him with astonishment and revulsion. "I'm afraid I do."

Steve immediately put the cigarette back in the box and pushed it over to the far end of the table. "Oh, I *am* really sorry. I need to give up this nasty habit anyway," he laughed. "And of course you're becoming a doctor. I can see how that would be quite a contradiction and insult to your field if you did *not* mind me smoking."

"Yes, it would," Dee said quietly, momentarily forgetting that she was sitting there with him under false pretenses.

"So, that brings me to the obvious question. What made you go into medicine?"

There it was. The $64,000 question. *Okay, Dee what made you decide to go into medicine? You haven't thought that quite far yet, now, have you?* As she thought about her answer, she turned to look out the window that faced the hotel lobby. Two members from her crew were getting off the escalator. She pried her purse open carefully, just wide enough to press the automatic program on her cell phone. And just as she had planned, her other cell phone started buzzing.

"I'm sorry," she said, looking at the phone's screen.

"Is everything all right?"

"I'm so embarrassed, but it looks like I have to return this call."

"Okay, I'll tell the waitress to hold your food until you get back so it won't get cold."

"Thank you," she said as she walked briskly out of the restaurant and caught up with her crew, Shaun and Lorraine, before they entered the restaurant.

"Hey, Dee. Wow, you look stunning. Where are you off to?" Lorraine asked.

"Thanks. I was meeting a friend in the restaurant, but the service is so slow. I was just coming out to call my girlfriend and tell her not to even bother coming here. We're going to find someplace else to eat."

"Really?" Shaun said, surprised as she looked at Lorraine. "I heard their service was the best in town."

"I'm sure that it usually is, but they have a new chef in training and things got unusually behind," Dee insisted.

Lorraine glanced at her watch. "Well, I'm glad you told us. We were just about to go in there and grab what we thought would be a quick bite. But we still have time to walk over to that little café down the block."

"The movie doesn't start for another hour, so we should be okay," Shaun interjected. "Glad we ran into you, Dee. I hope you catch your girlfriend in time."

"Thanks. I'm sure I will. She's never on time anyway," Dee laughed. She took out her cell phone and pretended to dial the number. She waited until Shaun and Lorraine were clearly out of sight before returning to the restaurant where a lobster feast was awaiting her.

"I saw you walking back, so I told the waitress to go ahead and bring it out. Doesn't it look *too good* to eat?"

"No," Dee laughed as she dug in with her fork. She cut a small morsel and chewed.

Steve laughed. "You are merciless!"

"And hungry!" Dee said as she placed another portion in her mouth.

"*Bon appetit*!"

"Yes, it is," Dee said, delving into her baked potatoes and carefully wiping her mouth with her linen napkin. She looked up, and Steve was smiling at her adoringly.

"What?"

"Nothing," Steve said, shaking his head in delight as he continued to chew. He was enjoying watching her enjoy her food. He loved women who were not caught up in getting small portions because they were watching their figure. Debra had a gorgeous figure, and *he* could watch it all night.

"Did you take care of that call?"

"Uh huh," she said, nodding between swallows. "Where were we before I had to leave?"

"I was asking you about how you decided to—"

"Oh, yeah, get into medicine." Her brief encounter with her crew had given her some buying time to think about that question. "I've got a really good friend who kind of talked me into it when we were in undergrad. I took a few biology courses and have always been pretty good with math and science. I did some summer internships in the medical field when I was in college, and I just liked the field and wanted to pursue it." *Now, that was pretty smooth girl, if I have to say so, myself!*

"Where'd you go for undergrad?"

"Spelman."

"Ahhh . . ." Steve nodded approvingly. "Excellent school."

Dee smiled. "So what about you? Did you major in public relations when you were in college?"

"No, ironically I started off as a premed-slash-biology major also. And then I got really bored with college altogether. I started working part-time in the summer with my dad's friend who had an event planning company. I really enjoyed the variety and mix of putting on events and talking to people. When I returned back to school in the fall, I would assist with putting campus parties together. I wrote a few articles for the campus paper and then eventually moved up to writing press releases for the local city paper and then BOOM! Just like that, before I knew it, I dropped out of Yale my junior year and took a chance on starting my own company. Now, 15 years later, I'm a PR icon," he chuckled, as he squeezed some lemon onto his lobster.

Only a white boy could pull that off with no degree, Dee thought, reflecting on how she was sitting across from him with *two* degrees, and a career path that was leading nowhere fast!

"That's a great story," Dee said, barely above a whisper.

"Hey, it's no big deal—really," he said, sensing Dee's uneasiness. "Hey, let's finish up here and take a walk on that beach. I want to see that pretty face of yours in the moonlight." Steve motioned for the waitress to bring the check.

As they headed toward the beach, Dee took off her mules and rolled her pants up to her thighs. Steve watched each curve of her leg as she slowly worked her pants up the other thigh. A breeze wisped through her hair so she pulled it off of her face and braided it.

Steve had already taken his shoes off and rolled his pants to just above the ankles where Dee could see the curly strands of hair wrapped around his legs. The same locks of curls could be seen through his partially unbuttoned shirt.

"All set?" he said, waiting for Dee's nod of approval. "So, let's run!" He grabbed her purse and pulled her hand like a little boy on his first day at the beach. The wind felt good blowing across her face. She laughed at how playful he was as he jumped through the small waves and lifted her up and down, swinging her until the waves were large enough to fall over them and drench them completely.

"Oh, no!" Dee screamed and laughed. She was enjoying the cool wetness more than she thought she would. The salty water trickled into her mouth as a sudden gush of rain droplets broke from the sky, rinsing the ocean's salt from her lips.

Steve stood back and looked at her like she was a rainbow that had just appeared. He stroked the wet locks out of her face. Her face looked as if it had just been sketched by an angel. Dee watched his eyes focus intensely on her wet clothes that were now showing a silhouette of her lace undergarments. She looked so sexy and radiant that he reached toward her and sealed her moist lips with a fateful kiss.

"So, what field of medicine are you studying?" Charles, the driver, said, breaking Dee's reverie. She immediately brought her thoughts back to her present day in New York while she uncomfortably witnessed Charles maneuver and loop his way through the sluggish traffic. The Midtown Tunnel looked like a cabby's convention with the yellow cabs lined tightly up against the walls with everyone moving nowhere.

"I'm sorry, what did you say?"

"I said what field of medicine are you studying?"

"Oh, pediatrics." The sound of her voice was so assertive that she amazed herself.

"That's great. We need more doctors to care for children."

"Do you have kids?"

"Four kids and twelve grandchildren," he said proudly, flipping open the visor on the passenger's side and pulling out a steady stream of pictures.

"Wow!" Dee squealed in amazement. "You sure have a big family."

"Yes, and every single one of them are in and out of the pediatrician's office on a regular basis," he mused. Charles picked up his cellular phone and voice-activated Steven's number. "Mr. Cushman, I'm stuck in the tunnel. It may be another thirty minutes before we get out of here—sure thing, sir, I will."

"So, what did he say?" Dee asked, wondering why it was so urgent that he contact Steven because he was in traffic.

"He said that if it was more than a half hour, then just to take you straight down to The River Café in Brooklyn."

She stroked her camel hair sweater and black jeans and looked down at her casual boots and brown suede fringed jacket. "I'm not dressed for dinner."

"You don't have to be dressed up to go in there. This is New York. People wear a little bit of everything. You'll see. You look fine."

Dee glanced down at her watch. "Did he say why he wanted to go there so early?"

He politely shook his head. "I'm just the driver, Ms. Mitchell."

Dee stared out her window and was happy that she did not have to get out in traffic every day. The traffic in Atlanta was bad, but at least she felt confident enough to drive in it. She could never drive in New York. It was just too packed.

All of a sudden there was a break in the traffic and Charles took off like a sprinter just out of the blocks. "Finally!" Charles said, honking his horn in relief. The utility vehicle that had stalled had been moved over to the side of the street. "Well, it looks like you'll make it on time to Mr. Cushman's office after all," he said as he continued uptown.

Steven's fiftieth floor office was well appointed and had a panoramic view of Manhattan. The office was filled with wall-to-wall mahogany paneling. No expense had been spared on the parquet floors, plush carpet, or elaborate chandeliers that sparkled from the domed ceilings, Dee decided. Steve was truly at the top of his game. He owned and ran one of the largest public relations firms in the country, Cummings and Associates.

When Dee got off the elevator, the double glass doors opened to the grand marble foyer and the perky receptionist greeted her politely. "Good afternoon. May I help you?"

"Yes, I'm Deir—I mean, Debra Mitchell, I'm here to see . . ."

Before Dee could finish her sentence, the receptionist stood up and shook her hand. "Oh, hi! Let me take you back to his office." She wore a black and white couture dress and matching leather pumps. Dee felt a little self-conscious as she looked down at her casual attire. "I'm Mildred, by the way. He's been anticipating your arrival. How was your flight?"

"On time," Dee joked. She could count the times on one hand when her flights landed on time at LaGuardia.

"That always helps," Mildred interjected in a lively voice. "Come on, Steve's office is right this way." All eyes were on Dee as she followed Mildred past the cubicles. The office consisted primarily of women straining their necks to see who Steve's new lucky lady was this time.

Steve's name was stenciled in gold on a black lacquered nameplate centered in the middle of his door. Mildred tapped on the door lightly, easing it wide enough to poke her head in. "Knock, knock."

"Hold on just a minute, Bruce. Mildred just walked in," he said muting the phone.

"Ms. Mitchell is here to see you, sir."

"Great! Mildred thanks for showing her back here," he said raising his forefinger for her to give him a minute. "Hey, Bruce, we'll see you later; that special guest I was talking about has just arrived." He quickly hung up the phone, brushed his fingers through his hair, buttoned the top button of his shirt, and adjusted his silk tie. He stood up in front of the large picture window, gave himself a quick once-over in the reflection, and then motioned for Mildred to let Dee in.

"Come here!" Steve said, grabbing Dee around the waist and hoisting her in the air.

"Steve! Put me down!" Dee giggled.

He gently placed her back on the floor and turned around to lock the door. Dee looked suspiciously into his bright blue eyes. He stared at her for a few seconds before pulling her face close to his. He planted a kiss on her lips that left her feeling light-headed.

"Wow! That is certainly a warm welcome!"

"Sorry about coming on so strong, but a guy can't help it when you're so irresistible. Here, have a seat next to me." He pointed to the padded chairs in front of his desk gesturing for her to sit down. "So tell me. How are things going?"

"Busy, very busy," she answered vaguely, knowing where the conversation was headed.

Steve heard the trace of trepidation in her voice. "You're still going to graduate on time, right?"

Dee's eyes shifted toward the awards lining his shelves. "Yes, and I'm still interviewing with various hospitals. My, my, my, these are impressive." She hopped off her chair and walked over to the awards, trying to change the subject. "Most Distinguished Public Relations Professional of the Year, Highest Ranking Revenue Achiever! You are the *man*, aren't you, Mr. Cushman?"

"It's nothing," he said, pulling a cigarette from his pocket.

Dee turned her nose up in disgust.

"Steve, I thought you gave up those nasty things!"

"Oh, yeah, I forgot," he winked teasingly, placing them back in his jacket pocket. "I've got a surprise for you later today. I'm glad you were able to stop by here first."

"Me, too. Although if I knew that I was meeting you at your job instead of your place, I would have spiffed up more," she said, holding her hands out to display her clothing.

"You look good to me." He pulled her toward him again and placed his arms around her waist. "But you may want to spruce up a bit before the surprise that I have for you at The River Café."

"What's going on there? Charles mentioned it to me on the way over here."

"Well now, if I tell you, it won't be a surprise, now will it?"

Dee looked at him suspiciously. "Okay. Do you want me to change here or are we going back to your place?"

"Right *here* is fine with me," he said, pointing to where she was standing and eyeing her as if she were a Cheshire cat.

"Very funny, Steven. I think I'd rather get dressed in the ladies room down the hall."

"C'mon, I'll walk you there," he said, pretending to be disappointed. He took her hand and escorted her down the hallway. All eyes rose again above their cubes, and Dee could hear faint whispers.

"Damn, she's gorgeous."

"Yeah, Steve certainly knows how to pick 'em."

Dee smiled and shook her head, trying not to show her embarrassment as she walked past the men and into the bathroom. Steve entered one of the cubicles and politely interjected. "Next time could you guys at least wait until she's passed before you start gossiping?"

"I'm so sorry, Mr. Cushman. It won't happen again, sir," said David, one of his favorite junior account executives. His face red from embarrassment, he rushed to get busy with the paperwork that was stacked on his desk. Steve knew he'd meant no harm and turned his back to him so he wouldn't see him grin.

When Dee came out of the bathroom, she looked both stunning and chic. She'd pulled her hair back into a tight French braid and wore a fitted black knit dress with a low back and neckline. As she sauntered back down the hallway to Steve's office, she glanced over at the two men who'd been talking about her earlier and decided to have a little fun with them.

"Hi, I'm Debra."

David and Matthew seemed startled by her presence.

"Hello, Debra, nice meeting you. I'm David and this is my coworker, Matthew," he said, feeling a little awkward.

"Hi," Matthew replied with a sheepish grin.

"So, what's that I heard you say earlier about Steve knowing how to pick 'em?"

David's face blushed red as a trick deck of hearts. "Um, that wasn't Matthew. It was me. I just meant that all the other . . ."

Dee raised an eyebrow. "Oh, please continue."

"I mean that he has some really nice ladies that come through . . . and . . ." At that moment it appeared to Dee that David wanted the floor to rise up and swallow him. He started fumbling with his bow tie, still trying to figure out what to do with his hands after he took them away from his mouth.

"Hey, guys, how's the research going on the Brooklyn account?" asked a young woman who seemed to appear from nowhere. She was sharp, poised, and very focused. She extended her hand to Dee. "Hi, there, I don't believe we've met. I'm Nancy."

"I'm Debra."

Nancy scrutinized Dee's appearance. Surely, *she* wasn't the new account executive, coming dressed like she was going to an after-hours party. David and Matthew were waving frantically for her *not* to ask a smart-ass question. But they were too late. "Are *you* the new account executive?" Nancy said, as she eyed her up and down.

"No. I'm dating Steve," Dee said politely, waiting on her next remark while David and Matthew decided this was their cue to leave. It was all Dee could do to keep from bursting into laughter at the look on Nancy's face.

"Oh, I see. Great dress," she said, trying to recover.

"Thank you. Well, it was nice meeting you," Dee said, turning to walk back to Steve's office. She lightly knocked and waited for him to answer.

"Come on in."

"Ahem," Dee said as she folded her arms across her breasts and watched him intently.

"Oh, hold on just a second, Bruce," he said. He quickly turned around his chair and held his hand over the receiver while his eyes traveled around her body. "You look delicious."

"And you need to tell Bruce goodbye." Dee reached over his desk and walked her fingers over toward the phone's button to hang up on his caller. He grabbed her hand before she could press it, sliding her index finger into his mouth and gently sucking it. Dee grinned and slid her finger out of his mouth.

"Bruce, I gotta run. I need to put out a fire here. Okay, we'll see you then," he said as he held onto her hand, taking the finger he'd had in his mouth and pressing it on the phone's button.

Dee looked innocently around the office. "Fire? I don't see any fire."

"That's just an industry term we use here when things are getting a little heated." He walked around his desk and pulled Dee toward him. He kissed her tenderly on the forehead, making his way down to her lips before stepping back to take in her beauty. "C'mon, we better go."

Dee kissed him with her mouth open and pressed her body hard against his. "What's the big hurry?" she said as she pulled his tie, forcing his face to come back toward hers.

"Dr. Briscoe hates it when people are late," he said between kisses.

Dee kissed him some more. "Who's Dr. Briscoe?"

"Damn, I wasn't supposed to tell you," he said, pulling back again from her.

Dee gently tugged on his tie again as he resisted. "Tell me what?"

"No, that was my surprise! I can't believe I let you use your feminine wiles to get it out of me," he said jokingly. "C'mon, I'll tell you more about it on our way to the restaurant." He grabbed his suit jacket off the coat rack along with her luggage as they breezed down the corridor toward the front desk.

"Have a good evening, Mr. Cushman, Ms. Mitchell," Mildred said. Dee looked at her and smiled.

"You have a nice one, too," Steve said, bending down to look in his message box. He still had about fifteen messages that he had to return. "Anything urgent?"

"Nothing that can't wait until Monday. Now, go on and have a nice time!"

"Okay, as you're twisting my arm. C'mon, Debra, let's go get us a couple of martinis," he said as he placed his arm around her shoulders.

"Drink one for me, too!" Mildred yelled back as they headed out the door.

❧

"Geez, Steve, slow down!" Dee grabbed her head as they went over a large pothole, thinking it would go through the fabric-covered roof of his BMW Z4 Roadster.

"Ahhh, Deb, you'll be fine. I'm sorry. That's what I love about this car; it lets me zip in and out of traffic while everyone else just sits there."

"I see the thrill," Dee snarled. Her nails gripped the dashboard until they came to a stoplight.

"All right . . . all right. I'll take her down a notch or two. I don't want you to be all frazzled when we get there."

"Well, thank you." Dee felt relieved when the car slowed to thirty miles an hour until they entered the restaurant's parking lot.

"Good evening. Welcome to The River Café," the well-groomed valet said, as he walked over to the passenger side to open Dee's door.

"Thank you," Dee said accepting his hand as she got out of the car. Dusk made the city lights sparkle. Her eyes danced at the sweeping views of the New York skyline. "This is so pretty."

"I know. It's hard to believe that we are nestled right under the Brooklyn Bridge," Steve chuckled as he looked down at his watch. "We're a little early. Do you want to go to the bar and have a cocktail before dinner?"

"Sure, why not?" Dee followed the hostess to the Terrace Room. The bar area was filled, and conversations flowed around the room. There was a mix of business attire and evening clothes. *Yes, it's true; anything goes in New York,* Dee thought as she listened to the soft piano music playing in the background while they ordered their drinks.

"I'll have a glass of chardonnay," Dee said to the bartender.

"And you, sir?"

"I'll take a martini, served very chilled with no olive, please."

"What's a martini without an olive?"

"I hate olives. I thought I told you that," he said pulling his chair closer and leaning in to whisper in her ear. "I'm so glad you were able to take some time off and come and visit me." He brushed a few strands of wind-blown hair out of her eyes and kissed her forehead. "Now I can see you better my dear."

"Me too," she giggled as the bartender placed their drinks down in front of them. Steve slipped her a one hundred-dollar bill.

"Keep the change. We'll each have one more after these," Steve said, not looking at the bartender but keeping his eyes focused on Dee.

"Thank you, sir." The bartender rang up their order and placed her hefty tip in her pocket.

Dee circled her finger around the brim of her wine glass and looked at him thoughtfully. "So, tell me about this important Dr. Briscoe, Miscoe," she laughed. "Why am *I* meeting him?"

Steve took a long sip of his martini and slid his arm delicately around her shoulder. "Okay, I guess I'm just going to have to tell you as you obviously don't want me to surprise you, judging from all of your questions. Dr. Bruce Briscoe is who I was talking to earlier when you tried to hang up on him," he said, playfully scolding her. "He, my gorgeous lady, is the chief of pediatrics for one of the most prominent hospitals in Atlanta. He also happens to be one of my clients, and he was very impressed with how we publicized the opening of his new children's wing at the hospital. And he said if I ever needed anything to give him a call. And as you're studying to be a pediatrician, I thought I would introduce you to him in the hopes that he would assist you in choosing a residency program." Steve lifted his glass and clinked it against hers, glancing toward the doorway. "As a matter of fact, speaking of the good doctor, here he is now," Steve said, waving him over.

Dee's face looked as if she had been smacked hard by a block of ice. It lost all of its coloring, and her hands shook uncontrollably. Before she knew it, Dr. Briscoe had made his way to the table, and Dee was trapped like an unarmed soldier in an ambush.

Decompression
(The Next Day)

The living room was dark except for the illumination of the streetlights filtering in through the Venetian blinds. A pint of Haagen-Dazs chocolate ice cream sat on the coffee table, and a lumpy blanket rocked back and forth. Dee was underneath it, sobbing uncontrollably, while pulling its frayed edges up over her head. The front door opened and a flash of light hovered above her head as she continued to cry harder.

"Dee! Are you here? Girl, I've got some great news! I wo—" Pam stopped before Dee could answer. She dropped her purse at the top of stairs and rushed toward her. "Dee, what the . . . Dee, is that you? Are you all right?" She forced the covers out of Dee's hand and saw her best friend looking as if she had been diagnosed with a terminal illness. Her tear marks were black from streaks of mascara that had been running down her cheeks, and her hair was so matted to her face that traces of her lipstick were stuck between strands of hair.

Dee looked up at Pam and immediately turned away and began wiping her tears. "Hey, girl," she said quietly. "Excuse me for a minute, will you? I'll be right back," she said as she grabbed the container of ice cream. She choked back her tears.

Pam followed Dee to her room and stood in the doorway. "What's going on?"

Dee shook her head silently as Pam hugged her and stared down at Dee's hands. "Dee, what happened to your fingers?"

"It's nothing," Dee said barely above a whisper as she sat on the bed. She looked down at her hands and folded them between her legs. Embarrassed, she turned her head and moved away from Pam.

"What do you mean nothing? Look at your hand!"

"I was at a restaurant last night in New York and accidentally broke a wine glass that I held too tightly, okay? A friend of mine took me to the hospital and the doctor bandaged my fingers."

Pam peered down at her hand. "Geez, Dee, did you have to get stitches?"

"No, fortunately. I can't talk about this anymore, okay?"

"Why not? You talk to me about everything."

"Trust me. Let's just leave it at that."

"How can you say that? I don't understand."

"Listen Pam, you and I haven't had a real heart-to-heart since . . ."

Pam got up from the bed and began to pace back and forth. It was still difficult for her to breathe when she thought about him. "I know."

"You told me to never mention his name in this house. Remember?"

Pam nodded as she walked over to the small sitting area and sat down in Dee's oversized chair. She placed her head in her hands. Her voice fell silent as she thought about her recent brief encounter with him. "It still hurts. I can't seem to get rid of the pain. I met him at Piedmont Park recently."

"What? When did he get out of prison?"

"Just recently."

"But how? I mean, why was he in Atlanta?" Dee was stumbling all over her words. She couldn't get them out fast enough.

Pam laughed softly. "I know. I felt the same way. I guess to see me. But, he's fine. He's moving to Europe."

"Why Europe?"

Pam shrugged her shoulders. "I didn't ask—just didn't want to know." She could feel herself getting emotional again. She walked back to the window and stared at the Friday night traffic piling up on Peachtree Street.

Dee didn't know what to say. The last time she'd seen Greg, she had told him in no uncertain terms to stay away from Pam. Pam was so vulnerable after the loss of the baby and her marriage that she thought just seeing him would only push her over the edge.

Pam managed to look over at Dee. "He told me that you had been seeing him while he was in prison. Oh, and he's saved too," she said casually.

Dee bowed her head. "I wanted to tell you but I couldn't. I'm sorry, but there just never seemed to be a good time. I'm not surprised he found some religion. He needed to do something to save his sorry soul."

Pam smiled at her comment and felt the tears fall gently down her cheeks. "I understand, Dee," she said as she wiped them away. "At first I was so mad at you for seeing him behind my back, but then he explained what you were trying to do and I appreciate that. I just thought I should let you know that. But your words hurt me earlier. Your situation has nothing to do with what happened to me and *him!* I can't believe you feel like you can't talk to me."

"It has *everything* to do with you. Just look at how emotional you are. Still."

"Dee, I've made my peace with him now. I'm fine, really."

"No, you're not! You haven't been able to deal with anything that's not work-related since he went to prison! You can't even say his name out loud!"

"Dee, I'm fine."

Who do you think you're fooling? She watched Pam pull a tissue from the tissue box on the dresser and blow her nose. Dee said her words cautiously. But, they came out quicker than she planned. "What about Amanda?"

Pam turned around briskly still holding the tissue to her nose. "What did you say?"

"I said . . . what . . . about . . . Amanda?"

"So, you know?"

"Yeah, I know."

"When did you talk with her?"

"I ran into her last week."

"And you didn't tell me?"

"I was hoping you would tell me! I'm sick of being caught in the middle of you two!"

"You feel caught in the middle? Why?"

"Because I have always been the one to try and keep the peace."

"Peace?" Pam laughed. "There has never been any peace with the three of us. That was the reason why we worked so well together. All of us had our own way of making noise!"

"Pam, you just can't let it go can you?"

"Sure, I've let it go. You and Amanda are the ones who seem to be clinging on."

"You're joking right?"

"Dee, you brought this on, so let's finish it. Look me in the eyes and tell me that you love what you do."

Dee immediately got up and started walking away.

"Where are you going? I asked you a question."

"This isn't about me, Pam."

"Sure it is. It's about you and Amanda still clinging on. You want to be a lawyer but are too damned scared to take the bar. Amanda wants to be a lawyer, and she's let her excuse of being a single mom not allow her to do what she's good at."

"She's a good paralegal."

"No, she is a great paralegal! But, she would make a helluva attorney! And it still pisses me off that both of you have taken the easy way out. That's why I gave her such a hard time at work. I wanted her to quit and go back and get her law degree. She knew those cases just as well as I did. I kept her there night after night, trying to get her to see that she could be just as good, if not better than I am. She hated me for it. But, I knew exactly what I was doing."

"But, it backfired on you."

"Yes, it did. And just like you, she just didn't have the confidence. She let her excuses of being a mother or not being married take over her passion. And you, geez, I just don't know what happened to you. You can't possibly enjoy flying around being a servant in the sky!" Pam placed her hand over her mouth, but it was too late. "I'm sorry Dee. I didn't mean—"

"Yes, you did. You meant every word of it."

"Okay. You're right. I did mean every word of it. But, I didn't intend for it to come out that way."

"Well, that's why you are the successful one, Pam. You say what you mean and break people down until you get what you want, right?"

"Okay, let's call a truce here and end this discussion before it turns into something that we'll both regret. I've already lost one friendship, and I don't want to lose another."

"So, you do regret that Amanda quit?"

Pam looked at Dee piercingly. "I'm done talking about Amanda. I'm changing the subject. So, are you going to be able to work like this?" she asked, turning the attention back to Dee's hand.

Dee was glad to see that Amanda's departure did strike a chord with Pam. Now, the only thing she had to do was hope that the two of them would mend their friendship. For now she would play along.

"Okay, okay truce! If I tell you about it, will you stop bothering me?"

Pam laughed. "Yes, I will." She lifted Dee's hand again and examined it. "What happened to make you hold the glass so tight?"

"I don't know. I guess it was just cheap glass, okay? The doctor said it would heal in about a week. I'm off for a few days anyway, so I'll be okay to go back to work. Now, you know all about me and my drama, so since you won't let me bring up Amanda, are you ready to tell me how you're really doing since you saw—"

"No! Please let's just leave him in the past. I've worked out my feelings. Really."

Dee looked apprehensive. "Pam, you really need to talk with someone."

Pam burst into laughter. "Oh now, that's rich. You think *I* need a shrink?"

"I mean, look at you."

"Dee, I'm warning you. I came in here tonight because I care about you. This was not supposed to be about me, remember?"

"I'm sorry, Pam. I didn't mean to come down on you like that."

Pam saw the drained look in Dee's eyes. There was more to this than broken glass, and she knew it. Pam didn't want to argue anymore. She was tired and had done enough arguing in the courtroom these last few weeks, and didn't want to start over again at home, especially about Amanda or Greg.

"Hey, listen, it's been a long day for me, too. I'm going to take a bath. Will you be all right?"

Dee nodded, ate the last spoonful of melted ice cream, and went to her bedroom and closed the door. Pam's earlier exhilaration about winning her case seemed ho-hum right now. She would tell Dee at another time.

The doorbell rang just as Pam was about to retreat into her own room. She walked up the stairs and checked the peephole and opened the door. "Sedrick! Your timing couldn't be more perfect!" Her smile widened as she stood on her toes to reach up and hug him.

He squeezed her hard, almost lifting her up off the floor. "Hey, I just stopped by to say hi and congratulations!"

"You heard?"

"Your face is plastered across all the television screens. My nurses were glued to the television in the breakroom watching you. Here, look for yourself," he said, walking over to the television and pressing the remote control. Pam was wide-eyed as she watched herself with what looked like hundreds of microphones in her face, a crowd of television reporters, and her client and his family standing behind her like she was their guardian.

"Yes, it was a tough trial, but truth and justice was on our side today. I'm proud to be an integral part of the legal system, and I'm glad that the jury saw who the *real* victim was in this case. Thank you," Pam said as she turned away from the cameras and walked off with her client and his family.

"Well, all righty now, Attorney Madison!" Sedrick joked giving her a high five. Pam jumped up to reach his outstretched hand.

"Well, thank you, thank you very much," she said imitating Elvis Presley. They both laughed. "I still can't believe the news is still running that story."

"I can! So, when do you make partner?"

"I don't know exactly, but it should be very soon."

Sedrick turned to look at the pile of rumpled blankets that had taken on a life of their own on the sofa. "What's all this? Did you feel like you needed a nap after your big trial, Counselor?" He grinned.

Pam put her head down and shook it slowly as she thought sadly about Dee hiding something from her. "No, Dee was."

"Oh, she's back?" Sedrick sounded surprised. "So, what'd she say about your win?"

"I haven't had a chance to tell her yet. She's kind of down, so I didn't think it was such a good time right now. But, hey, since you're here, maybe you can bring her out of her dark mood. I was going to take a bath."

Sedrick shrugged his shoulders. "That's cool."

"I'll tell her you're here."

Sedrick nodded at her as he took a seat in the kitchen and stared at the starry sky. His career was going great. Could things have been different between him and Dee if they hadn't been such good friends for so many years?

"Hey, Sed." The sound of a familiar voice interrupted Sed's thoughts.

Dee was standing over him, wearing a pink floor-length terry cloth robe with matching slippers when she bent to kiss him on the cheek.

"My! Aren't *we* a lovely vision of Pepto-Bismol this evening?" He stood to give Dee a hug and held her longingly, breathing in the scent of her hair that smelled of fresh strawberries.

Dee laughed and gently pushed his chest. "Careful, I might just barf up all of my ice cream on you."

"Are you feeling okay?" he asked, touching her face with the back of his hand. "What happened to your hand?"

"I'm fine, doctor. Just a little cut. It looks much worse than it is, believe me," she said impressed, by his warm bedside manner.

Sedrick looked deep into her eyes. He could tell that something was weighing heavily on Dee and he couldn't stand to see her in so much pain. "You want to sit down in the living room and talk?"

Dee sat down next to him with a blank look on her face. "In here is fine."

"Okay, so why the doom and gloom?"

Dee was silent as her bottom lip began to quiver. Sedrick pulled her toward him and held her close.

"Oh, Sedrick, you're so fortunate," she said looking at him reflectively as tears again surfaced in her eyes.

"Hey, why the tears if I'm so fortunate?" Sedrick said lightheartedly, trying to make her smile.

"Just like Pam, you go after what you want."

"Dee, where is all of this coming from?"

"Oh, never mind," Dee whispered as she got up and walked to the other side of the room. Sedrick followed, stood behind her, and touched the back of her head.

"I just don't know when my life became so darn complicated. Sometimes I just want to crawl up into a dark cave and never come out."

"Dee, whatever is bothering you, you know we can talk, right?"

"I know." Dee turned to look into his eyes. "Sedrick, can I ask you something?"

"Yes, you can ask me anything."

"Okay, what if you met a woman you really liked and she was everything that you could ever imagine. Then you dated her for six months and all the time you were thinking she was a nurse?"

"All right . . ." Sedrick said thoughtfully, wondering where Dee was taking this conversation.

"Then you find out that she's a waitress at IHOP."

Sedrick held out his hands and waved them in the air. "Okay, back up and rewind."

"What?"

"It's just what you're saying would never happen!"

"Why? Because you wouldn't date a waitress, right?"

"No, because I would know where she worked. At some point, I would have either called her at work or been by to see her on her job."

"But what if she always had an excuse that prevented you from finding out what she really did?"

"Look, Dee. I'm not some simple-minded brotha."

"Of course not, but—"

"There's no but. I would know, especially if I really liked her. I'm just not the type of man to be dating someone who would try and play me for a fool. And if I found out what she was trying to do, then I'd tell her to go play another brotha' 'cause this one ain't having it."

"And that would be it, huh? You would just forget about her just like that?" Dee said, snapping her fingers.

"No, I wouldn't just forget about her like that." He snapped his fingers back at her. "Especially if I cared about her. But I wouldn't try to get back with her either."

"Because she lied to you?"

"Not only did she lie, but she didn't trust me enough to let me make up my own mind about if I wanted to have dealings with her. It's not the occupation, baby, it's the *person* in the occupation."

"So, you would have dated her knowing that she was a waitress at IHOP even though you're a doctor?"

"It wouldn't matter to me if she picked up garbage."

"C'mon, Sedrick! Garbage?"

"Well, maybe not garbage. That could get a little smelly at times," he said, laughing at the thought. "Anyway, my point is this: If I like you, I like you. Just 'cause I'm a doctor doesn't make me a better person. As a matter of fact, it's not the occupation that makes you a better person, it's the good that you do for others *with* your occupation that makes you a better person." Suddenly, his cell phone went off. He looked down and saw that his girlfriend, Miranda, was texting him for an afternoon booty call.

"Duty calls, I see."

"Yeah, I guess it does," he said, turning the sound off, a little embarrassed by Miranda's timeliness.

Dee leaned over and kissed him on the cheek, momentarily taking his mind off Miranda's text. He felt a strong desire to take fate in his hands, but his better judgment told him to leave her lips alone for the time being.

"Thanks for dropping by, Sed. I'm feeling better already."

"Well, good. I'd better go. I'll call you later and check on you. I can let myself out," he said as he walked up the stairs and closed the door behind him.

Pam was moisturizing her face when her telephone rang. She wiped the cream from her hands on the towel and picked up the receiver.

"Congratulations, Counselor." A smooth Italian voice flowed through the receiver, and a huge grin spread across Pam's lips.

"Marco?"

"I can't believe I actually caught *you* and not your voicemail or your secretary."

"I know, I've been pretty busy. You did get my message thanking you for the flowers, though?"

"Yes, and I got your stiff bill, too. Five hundred dollars!"

"Be happy. You got a discount. It should have been a thousand."

"Wow, you're expensive," he laughed. "But, I understand now, especially after seeing you on the news today."

"You saw it too, huh?'

"Yes, but television does not do justice to your beauty. You are so much lovelier in person."

There he went again with his smooth-talking self. She thought that maybe after he got her bill he would leave well enough alone. But she had to give it to him. He didn't scare easily. "Well, thank you, Marco."

"You're quite welcome. Hey, did you get any of the messages that I left with your secretary?"

"I did. I know you've been trying to get in touch with me."

"Yeah, for a couple of weeks now."

"I know, I've just been swamped with the case, and then by the time I was done at work, I was just too wiped out to call once I got home."

"I won't take it personally," he said pleasantly. "So, how does it feel to be the most popular attorney in the state of Georgia?"

"I'll let you know more when I get the offer of partnership. Other than that, I think it's pretty exhilarating."

"Well, do you think as this case is over with now, you'll have a little down time? Or have you already started defending your next client?"

Pam paused for a moment and thought about what Dee said. She *didn't* have a life. "Actually, I do have a little down time."

"I can't believe I heard you right. Did Counselor say she had some down time?"

"Very funny," Pam said as she dabbed some more cream on her face.

"Well, I'll be in Atlanta this weekend. Would you be available on Friday for me to take you to dinner to celebrate your victory and for me to give you your check?"

"Hmmm . . . I suppose so. Did I hear the word *check*?"

"Okay, I'll take that as a yes," he said assuredly. "How about I pick you up at your home at 7:00?"

"I'll meet you at the restaurant."

"Somehow I thought you would say that," he said, sounding somewhat disappointed.

"And you're right. I'm not getting in the car with someone I hardly know."

"Well, I thought it would be nice to pick you up so that you could get to know me better as we go on our first date."

"Ahem . . ."

"Oh, yes, forgive me. I forgot. We're not dating."

Pam was amused. "I'm glad you remembered."

"Hopefully that will change soon."

Pam shook her head and remained silent. "I'll call you around 5:00 on Friday and let you know where to meet me," Marco said fondly.

"Sounds good, Marco. Until Friday."

"*Arrivederci.*"

"*Arrivederci,*" Pam said as she hung up the phone and looked in the mirror. She was amused at how funny she looked. She went over to the sink and rinsed the cold cream off of her face, wishing her internal scars could vanish as easily.

Bumpy Ride

It was 7:00 p.m. and Marco Grimaldi was seated at a corner table, looking very debonair. He was dressed in a black suede sports jacket, taupe crew neck shirt, and a pair of black, pleated wool pants. A gold candle twinkled in the dark room, flickering against his handsome face. He took a sip of his cognac and looked up as a striking woman walked toward him.

Pam glided around the tables like a swan. She wore a cranberry knit dress that cradled her hips. It was slit at the shoulders with a low neckline that revealed just enough of her bust to make Marco envision the rest.

"Good evening."

"Wow!" he said, as he stood up. Pam extended her hand. He gave her a light kiss on her fingers that sent an unexpected flutter throughout the pit of his stomach. He pulled her chair out and motioned for her to sit down.

She had a small smirk on her face. "Should I take that as a compliment?"

"I'm sorry. I'm just a little stunned. Of course it's a compliment, I just had no idea you could . . ."

"Could what?" she said egging him on.

"Oh, nothing. You look radiant."

"Oh, come on, now. Surely you were about to say something else."

Marco grinned, flashing his dimple again. He was smart enough to change the subject and Pam decided to let it go . . . *this time.*

"I took the liberty of ordering us a bottle of champagne," he said as he lifted the bottle from its chrome bucket, turning the label toward him. "I hope you like Dom Perignon."

"I love that champagne. How did you know?"

"I didn't. I just assumed that for a woman of your elegance it would only be fitting," he said as he signaled the waiter to pour the champagne into their glasses.

Corny, corny, corny, Pam thought as she smiled slightly. As the waiter poured the champagne, they watched the bubbles rise to the tops of their glasses. A jazz trio featuring a singer, a keyboard player, and a bass player took the stage.

Pam laid her head back into the warmth of her black velour chair. She closed her eyes as she listened to the band's smooth melody. "This place is so relaxing."

"Good choice. I love jazz, too," he said as he leaned forward to clink her glass with his. "It's good to see you so relaxed."

Pam smiled. "I'm usually not. My work leaves very little time for me to unwind, but when I do, I love to listen to David Sanborn, Grover Washington, Miles Davis, and just about any other jazz artist. I come by here every now and then and check out who's playing," she said, lightly tapping her fingers on the table to the rhythm of the soulful sounds.

The tall, lanky waiter made his way through the crowd again. His long curly blond hair was pulled back in a ponytail, and his face was covered with acne. "Good evening, I'm Mitch. Hey, aren't you that lawyer that just won that huge lawsuit?" Pam nodded politely as Marco looked at her proudly.

"Man, if I'm ever in trouble, I'd sure give you a call," he said admiringly.

"You and me both," Marco joined in.

He nodded, acknowledging Marco's comment and turning back to Pam. "Do you have a card on you?"

"Sorry, not tonight. I'm just here to have a good time," she said, trying not to sound impolite. "But the firm is Sterling, Mathis, and Silverman. Feel free to give me a call if you need a lawyer."

"All right, I'll do that. Thank you," he said as he handed them their menus. "Your name is Pam Mathis, right?"

"No, it's Madison."

"The one and only," Marco interjected as he raised his glass in the air.

"All right, guys. Enough already," she said, trying to deflect the praise.

"Well, I'll give you a minute or two and come back and take your orders," Mitch said, turning away.

Pam browsed the menu. "Hmm, let's see here. I'm going to have the prime rib tonight."

"So, you're a carnivore?" Marco said, sounding somewhat pleasantly surprised.

"Big time carnivore."

"I wouldn't think that just by looking at you."

"I know many people make assumptions about me because of my size, but I'm a meat-and-potatoes woman. I can eat all day long and not gain a pound," she laughed.

"Here's to good genes," Marco said, playfully raising his glass.

"Here! Here!" Pam joined in while touching his glass with hers. "What about you? Are you a vegetarian?"

"No, I wish," he said as he looked at her like he wanted to drink her up like an expensive glass of champagne. "I'm a meat eater, too."

"I think we're both having the prime rib tonight," Marc told Mitch when he came back over to their table.

"How would you like it cooked?"

"Medium," they answered in unison, laughing.

"Excellent choice," he said as he jotted down the orders. "I'll be right back with some warm bread."

"So, Marco, how long will you be in Atlanta?"

"Call me Marc. It sounds more American," he laughed.

"Okay, Marc. You didn't answer my question."

"How long would you like for me to be here?" he asked flirtatiously.

"You're too funny."

"Would you like to dance?"

Pam looked at him suspiciously and a little apprehensively. After all, Greg was the last man she had danced with up close and personal. "Sure. I'll give it a try," she said guardedly as they walked to the dance floor.

Marc slowly moved his hands around her waist and cautiously pulled her toward him. His smell was intoxicating. It felt so good to be held, Pam thought as he pulled her closer. Too afraid to let herself feel again, she suddenly pulled back.

Marco looked at her intensely "Is everything okay?"

"Yes, I'm fine."

"Are you sure? Because you seem a little tense all of a sudden. I don't bite, ya know? Well, actually, I do a little bit, but not on the first date," he grinned.

Pam smiled as she looked at his cute dimple that appeared each time he smiled. She wanted nothing more than to let go of the pain she felt every time a man looked into her eyes. *Damn you, Greg.*

Marco could feel her body continue to stiffen. He slowly removed his hands from her waist. "Pam, why don't we just go back to our table?"

"No, please. Let's continue." *Dee's right. I have to let go.* "I'll be all right," she said as she let her body relax again, allowing herself to flow with the music.

"You're a pretty good dancer for a lawyer," he said playfully.

"Is *that* supposed to be a compliment?"

"Of course. What else would it be?" Marco teased.

"A girl can't be too sure with you. I'm still sensitive from the first *questionable* compliment that you gave me when I first got here," Pam jibed as he suddenly spun her around and pulled her back into his arms.

"Wow! I haven't done that move since I was a little girl."

Marco twirled her around again. "Really? That long ago?" She laughed as he unexpectedly pulled her so close that she could feel the firmness of his chest and his inner thighs. His touch was making her weak.

"So, tell me more about when you were a little girl."

"My sisters and I used to take turns with my father dancing to some of his favorites, like Miles Davis and the good ol' sounds of Duke Ellington. That was a long time ago, though."

"Is your father still alive?"

"No, he died when I was in college."

"Oh, I'm sorry."

Pam placed her finger over her lip, signaling for him to stop. She lowered her head, attempting to hide the hurt look on her face. She couldn't believe that Marco brought these types of feelings out of her. It had been years since she'd danced like that with her dad and a long while since she had felt like crying about it.

"It's okay. I'm fine," she said as she got her rhythm back.

"Hey, it looks like our food has arrived," he said, hoping to get her out of her somber state.

"So, tell me about you, Marc," she said.

"My life's an open book." He pulled out her chair and felt Pam's dubious stare. Pam was apprehensive, and he didn't know whether she was always this intense or just cautious because it was their first date.

"Thanks."

"You are very welcome. Seriously, now, what is it that you would like to know?"

Pam laid her napkin in her lap and waited for Marco to sit down. "Okay, for starters, how did you end up in America? I'm assuming you're Italian?"

"Your assumption is correct. I moved to America as a young man in my late teens, early twenties. I can remember my brother and me sneaking in the back doors of clubs to watch the band set up. I always thought I'd be a musician," he said, looking over at the band reflectively.

Pam began to cut her prime rib, listening intently to his story. "So, what *do* you do?"

"Aha! She's interested enough to ask me about my occupation," he laughed. "That's a good start."

Pam grinned. "So, what's the big secret?"

"It's not a secret. I usually like to get to know someone first before I discuss what I do for a living."

Pam turned up her eyebrow and looked at him pensively. "Well, is it legal?"

"Extremely."

"Hmm . . . interesting," she said, contemplating her next thought. "So, if you won't tell me what you do, can you at least tell me what school you went to? Or is that something that I have to find out later?"

Marco smiled at her inquisitiveness. He could see what Gerald was talking about. Pam was definitely a force to be reckoned with. She was determined to get him to tell her what he did one way or another, and he was enjoying her twenty questions.

"Harvard."

"What a coincidence. My twin sisters went to Harvard," Pam said, delicately nibbling on another piece of meat.

"You have a twin?"

"*They're* twins."

"I was about to say, there's no way there could be two of you running around," he said as he wiped a piece of food from the corner of her mouth.

"Well, I don't know what to make of *that* comment."

"It's a compliment, I assure you. So what are your sisters doing now?"

"Pauline is married to a pro-basketball player over in Europe and doesn't work," she laughed. "And Priscilla teaches third grade." Pam shook her head at the thought.

"You seem disappointed at their career choices."

"No, I'm actually very proud of them. They're both just like my mom."

"Really? In what way?"

"They both have families and place them above anything else. They just do what makes them happy."

"The three P's, huh? Pamela, Priscilla, Pauline."

"Yes, start saying *those* three times fast," she laughed.

Marco loved to watch her lips move. He had an insatiable desire to touch them with his own. "I bet your mother got tongue twisted all of the time, heh?"

Pam became silent as she thought about how much she missed her family. Their relationship had been strained since she and Greg had broken up.

"Are you okay?"

"Oh, I apologize. I was just thinking about what I said. My mother would just expect all three of us to come running when she called one of us, because she would always get our names mixed up," she laughed fondly.

"And who are you like?" he asked as he poured some more champagne into their glasses.

"Most definitely my dad," Pam smiled again as she thought about her father. "Chief Madison," she said, raising her glass toward the ceiling.

"What was he chief of?"

"Chief of Police for Chicago. He always stood strong no matter what the odds were. My brothers Gerald and Michael both followed in his footsteps."

Marco sipped another glass of champagne. He wanted to know everything about her. "So, your brothers are police officers?"

"Gerald is a firefighter, and Michael is a police officer."

"So, one brother fights fire, the other fights criminals, and you fight for justice."

"Now, that's an interesting way of putting it. No one's ever quite said it like that," she said as she gazed into his eyes, feeling his warmth run through her body.

Marco laughed. "It's just pretty amazing when you think about it. You've got a big family. Let's see," he said as he started counting on her fingers, kissing each one at a time. "Two sisters and two brothers. Five of you. I never would have thought," he said, ending with a final kiss to the back of her hand and folding it into his warm palm. Aroused by his touch, Pam gently pulled her hand back.

"I'm sorry. I'm making you feel awkward. Look at me kissing your hand in public. I apologize. I got a little carried away."

A statuesque blonde woman, wearing a fitted three-quarter length black sequined dress, appeared out of nowhere and walked behind Marco's chair. The look on her face made Pam feel very uncomfortable.

"Yes, look *at you* getting carried away. Until it suits you, and then look out! He'll drop you, girlfriend, *after* he gets what he wants."

Still holding his steak knife, Marco turned around quickly to find his worst nightmare standing in front of him. "Sharon?"

"Yeah, it's me. In the flesh. Bet you thought you'd never see this body again, huh?" Sharon mocked. She looked like she wanted to jerk the steak knife out of his hand and stab him. Her face grew red, and her hands shook as she pointed her finger directly in Marco's eyes.

"Sharon, you are way out of line. I'm sorry Pam." He turned toward her. "Would you excuse us for a minute?"

"Don't try and use some of your psychobabble psychology on me!" she screamed before Pam could answer him. Everyone in the restaurant turned to look at her. "You are such an act. I'm telling you, watch him, girlfriend, or you'll end up miserable like me. He's a chameleon clad in a $4,000 suit!" She threw his glass of champagne in his face and hauled off and smacked him.

Marco was stunned. He jumped up and grabbed Sharon by the arm and escorted her from the restaurant. The young waiter immediately came over when he saw Marco leave the restaurant.

"What the heck just happened?"

Pam had a blank stare on her face. "I don't know. We were having a nice conversation and then suddenly out of nowhere this crazed woman appeared and starting shouting at him. I don't know whether to leave or wait for him to explain himself."

"I was just coming by to see if I could get you some dessert, but considering what just happened, I guess dessert is not such a good idea."

Pam chuckled. "You know, Mitch, I think I will be skipping dessert as well as this whole scene. But I'm leaving the *bill* for him," she said, placing her napkin on her plate and walking swiftly toward the door.

"I heard that, Counselor!" Mitch chimed in.

As Pam set out to open the door, a young couple walked in. She looked at the young man as he turned around to hold the door open for Pam.

"Why, thank you."

"You're welcome, ma'am."

The girl he was with stopped in her tracks, and she and Pam recognized each other immediately.

"Tracey?"

"Ms. Pam?"

Pam felt a little uncomfortable with the surprise encounter from Tracey, but nevertheless she didn't show it. She gave Tracey a half hug.

Tracey stepped back. "Ms. Pam, please. I don't mean to be disrespectful, but please don't put your hands on me."

"Excuse me?"

"Tony, *this* is Ms. Pam Madison." Tony extended his hand, and Pam shook it cordially.

"Hi," Tony said with a clueless look on his face.

"Nice meeting you, Tony."

"This is the woman I told you about that had it in for Mama."

"Oooh, *that* Ms. Pam." Tony tried to stop the flow of his words before they came rolling out.

"Tracey, it's obvious that you are upset. And it is also obvious that you don't know the entire story."

Tracey's voice began to rise, "I don't. But, I know enough. You and my mother were good friends at one time, and you tormented her until she had to quit her job."

Tony placed his hand firmly on her shoulder to quiet Tracey, who obliged by lowering her voice. "If it weren't for you coming down on her so hard every day, she would still be there. What kind of person does that to someone who is supposed to be their friend?"

Pam raised her hands in a surrendering gesture. "I'm not going to stand in this restaurant lobby and argue with you, Tracey. I'm going to save you and your friend here from embarrassment and be on my way."

"I see, so you think I'll be embarrassed, huh? Or is it that *you'll* be embarrassed?"

Tony pulled Tracey's arm. "C'mon baby, not here. Let it go."

Pam turned to Tracey. "Listen Tracey, you are too young to understand the history between your mother and me, but I can tell you this—if you raise your voice to me one more time, then I will give you one embarrassing moment that I promise you will never forget. Now, take your boyfriend's advice and let it go! And take some of mine, too. Go and have a *real* chat with your mother and get the *entire* story, okay? Have a nice evening," she said, as she sashayed out of the door.

Marco paced back and forth outside the restaurant and shook his head deliberately at Sharon. He wiped the champagne off his face with his sleeve. "What is the matter with you, embarrassing yourself like that?"

Sharon was crying hysterically, and her mascara was running down her face. "I still love you, Marco. I told Gerald and Adrienne that I can't live without you," she said between sobs, pulling at him like a first grader. "Didn't he tell you?"

"Get off of me! See, this is exactly what I'm talking about. I told Gerald that you have no self-control!"

Sharon screamed right in his face. "How can you get over me so quickly? And with a *black* girl at that! How do you think that makes me feel? Huh?"

Marco stopped cold and then moved back quickly in case she was thinking about slapping him again. It was just like Sharon to make such an ignorant remark. She knew she had hit a nerve with him and was waiting for his reaction. "Listen, Sharon. Pam's color has nothing to do with it. I like her for who she is, not for her race."

"Yeah. Sure. How many times have you slept with her, huh?"

"Sharon!" Marco caught himself before he decided to even address her probing. "You have issues! And a lot of them. That's why I couldn't marry you. You know that!"

"What issues? That I've been there for you at your every whim? I cooked for you, cleaned for you, and helped you manage your household affairs. Slept with you . . . hell, I even sucked your—"

"Hey, stop it," he whispered loudly and looked around, embarrassed. "I can't do this anymore, all right," he said, waving his arms wildly. "You've got to get hold of yourself. You can't come out in public making these types of outbursts. We just didn't work out. Honest to God, Sharon, as a psychiatrist, I really feel like you should seek some professional help!"

"You arrogant son of a bitch! I'm screwed up because *you* made me that way!"

"No, you're screwed up because you *chose* to be that way. You want a man to complete you. You want me to make up for all of the things your father never gave you. You want someone to take care of you because you don't want to do it yourself. I can't do that, and I won't do it. I can't live my life for someone else, and I can't be with a woman who expects that of me, either. I'm sorry, Sharon. Please, let me recommend you to one of my colleagues. You know I have a huge practice. I can recommend one of the best—"

"Hell, no! I don't want anything from you. Do you hear me? I wish I never met you!" she sobbed as she ran across the street.

"Sharon!' Marco shouted, as he watched her run to her car and speed away. He sat on the curb and buried his hands in his head.

"Shit! Pam!" he said, suddenly remembering he'd left her inside the restaurant. As he turned around to go back inside, he saw Pam standing in front of the door. He dropped his head down and spoke just above a whisper. "I'm so sorry about all of this. How much did you hear?" He felt so humiliated.

"Well, I now know what you do for a living," she said softly, not wanting him to know that she had heard the majority of the blowout.

Marco could not look at Pam. He resented that Sharon had spoiled his first opportunity to make a good impression with her. And just when Pam was finally letting him in, too. Why in the hell of all restaurants did she have to pick this one? And tonight of all nights? He wanted to kick his own ass.

Marco looked at her remorsefully and cleared his throat before he spoke.

"Well, I'm sure this is the last I'll be seeing of you. I bet you're really glad that you drove your *own* car," he said almost incoherently. There was a brief silence before he spoke again. "Will you at least allow me to walk you to your car? I still owe you your check from reviewing the contracts."

Pam looked at him and suddenly saw him in a different light. They both had people in their lives that they were once close to, and somewhere down the line things just got out of hand. Marco was no longer the cocky and carefree man she'd seen in the restaurant earlier. She felt connected to him through his pain and humility, and understood all too well what he was feeling right now—and especially after the browbeating she received from Amanda's daughter.

She nodded. "How about I just put it on your tab?" she said, smiling warmly.

Marco breathed out, relieved she'd offered him a second chance.

Clipped Wings

As the passengers boarded the plane, Lorraine said, "Hi. Welcome aboard, sir."

"Thank you. Can I just go ahead and give you my jacket now?" The tall gentleman asked while juggling the *Wall Street Journal*, two *Sports Illustrated* magazines, and a laptop. "I'm already feeling a little warm in here."

"I'd be glad to," Lorraine said, taking his jacket while he took his seat in first class. "Here, Dee," Lorraine said, handing her the man's jacket. "Would you mind hanging this up for the gentleman in 7D?"

"No problem," Dee said taking the coat, then continued to fill glasses with ice for the on-ground beverage service. After she finished with the last glass, she grabbed the seating chart. She enjoyed checking out the names of the privileged few who could afford a first-class ticket on such a short flight from Atlanta to Orlando. Today was going to be an easy day and a welcome break. She was on a brief hiatus from her three-day trips and was doing a quick turnaround to Orlando and back. While glancing at the seating chart, she recognized one of the names, but couldn't remember why.

"Quinton Richardson, 7D," she said. She began taking her passengers drink orders starting with the first row and then working her way back to 7D. "Mr. Richardson, may I get you something to . . ." Her words vanished as she felt a slow sinking feeling rising from the base of her stomach.

Quinton looked up from his *Sports Illustrated* and was just as stupefied. He dropped his magazine on the floor. "Counselor Bradshaw?" His thunderous voice seemed to echo through the entire first-class cabin. The passengers turned to look at her. Dee's face was scarlet.

"Oh, hi," Dee said meekly. She felt like digging a hole and crawling in it. "Would you care for something to drink, sir?"

Quinton stared straight through her. "A rum and coke with a twist of lime and lemon." Now he remembered how he knew her. She was the same woman he had seen on his last flight out to LA. The nerve of this woman pretending to help his buddy out. And all the while she was lying to him. Unbelievable.

He watched her rush back to the galley and return with his drink. Her hands shook as she set the glass on his tray table, praying that the drink would not spill in his lap. There was nothing left for her to say. She was busted.

"Flight attendants, prepare the cabin for departure," the pilot announced over the PA system.

"Lorraine, can I please work the back of the cabin?" Dee pleaded. "There aren't that many passengers up front, and I really would like to switch positions."

"Okay, let's do it on the next leg of the trip. Shaun's boyfriend is flying on a pass in the back, and I promised her she could stay back there with him."

Lucky Shaun, Dee thought. *At least she dates somebody that works for the company and can fly for free like she does.* Dee let out a disappointed sigh and placed both hands over her face, wiping the perspiration from her forehead.

"Hey Dee, are you feeling okay?"

"Yeah, Lorraine. I just need some water."

"Why don't you just go in the galley and take a minute. I'll pick up the rest of the glasses up here." Lorraine proceeded to pick up the remaining glasses in the cabin as promised, but when she got to 7D, Quinton handed her a note along with his glass.

"Would you please give this to Desiree," he said, looking toward the galley. Her name had finally come to him.

"Do you mean, Deirdre, the flight attendant in the galley? We call her Dee."

"Ah yes, I'm sorry. *That's* her name," he said with a smile so warm that Lorraine flushed. *She lied about her name, too, huh?* He gently took back the note and scribbled something else on it and handed it back to Lorraine.

"Sure thing," she said, taking the note out of his hand. The captain made the final announcement for takeoff; and Dee and Lorraine strapped themselves in their jump seats.

"Hey, Dee, I think you have a secret admirer," Lorraine whispered in Dee's ear. Dee's face showed no emotion. She was just trying to hold it together through takeoff.

"Yeah? And who might that be?"

"Mr. Richardson in 7D told me to give this to you."

Dee's stomach sank. Lorraine smiled back at him and handed her the note. Dee exchanged a quick glance with Quinton as he watched her reaction. Completely rattled, her hands trembled like an earthquake, but she finally managed to read the letter. *To: Desiree/Deirdre. You either tell Chris the truth or I will. I'll be back in Miami one week from today. The JIG is up! Quinton.*

Crash Landing

It had been two weeks since the *Johnson v. Tyfish Systems* case had ended, and Pam had heard no mention of a partnership. She had received so many congratulatory cards and flowers from business associates that her office was beginning to look like a flower shop.

She was reflecting on the morning after the case when she walked into the kitchen and saw Dee perusing through a stack of old newspapers waiting to be recycled.

"Pam! Oh, my God! Why didn't you tell me?"

Caught off guard by her outburst, Pam quickly rushed toward her to see what was wrong. And there it was. Her face was plastered across the bottom half of the newspaper along with a two-page article on how she'd pummeled the prosecution in the *Johnson v. Tyfish Systems* case.

"Girl, that's *old* news," Pam chuckled, leaning over Dee's shoulders.

"Old news, huh? Why on earth didn't you tell me that you won this huge case? It's been almost two weeks. C'mon, Pam, you talk about me. Now look who's the one keeping secrets." Dee looked hurt as she waited for Pam's response.

"The truth is that I was going to tell you right away, but that was the evening you hurt your hand. It was not a good time for you. Surely, you remember how that last night went with us . . ."

Dee got up and gave her a hug and whispered, "I do remember, and I can respect that. Thank you, and congratulations!" Suddenly Dee's voice raised to a high octave pitch of excitement. "Hey, since we are on the subject of you and SMS . . ."

Pam raised her eyebrows. "Yes?"

"Have you heard anything about Amanda since she quit the firm?"

"No," Pam said dryly. "But, I did run into Tracey and her male friend the other night."

"Really? That's a coincidence," Dee said sounding a little suspicious. "How'd that go?"

"Well, let's just say that she is definitely her mother's child when it comes to speaking her mind."

"What did she say?"

"She was pissed off and blamed me for Amanda's departure."

"Well, she is very protective of Amanda. That *is* her mother."

"Yep, she sure is," Pam answered with an allusive tone.

"Well what happened?"

"All I'm going to say is that she's lucky she got off easy because she's a child," Pam laughed sinisterly.

Dee could see that this conversation would not end on a positive note, so she didn't even bother to respond. She just walked over to the phone and began punching in numbers.

"Who are you calling?"

"Sedrick."

"Sedrick?"

"Heck, yeah! We've got to take you out on the town and celebrate, girl!" she said, changing Pam's mood instantly. "So clear your calendar tonight, because I'm off and I hope Sed's not on call because we are goin' to have a good time."

Pam laughed as she grabbed her thermos of coffee. "Just call me at work and give me the details. I'll be there if you all can make it work."

"See you later." Pam headed out the door chuckling.

Dee waved to Pam and then closed the door when she heard a buzzing sound coming from the other side of the room. She looked at her cell phone and saw that she had a text message that said, *CM.*

"Oh now, what?" Dee pressed in her auto dial to call Tracey.

"Hi, Auntie Dee. I see you finally got my text," she giggled.

"When did you send it?"

"Ummm, don't worry about it. I remember you told me that text messaging was not your forte. You are still a little old school, but it's okay." Tracey giggled again.

"Funny, Funny! Ha ha. I'm okay with texting. I just prefer the voicemail sometimes. So, what's up?"

"So you haven't spoken to Ms. Pam?"

"Yes, she just left, why?"

"Did she tell you that I saw her the other night?"

Dee became silent. She didn't know if she wanted to hear the details or not. "She didn't go into details," Dee's voice trailed off.

"Yeah, I bet," Tracey mumbled. "Well, I told her exactly what I thought of her."

"What does that mean, Tracey?"

"It means that I don't like how she treated Mama, and I let her know it."

Dee could only imagine how the entire scene played out without Tracey telling her. And the fact that Pam didn't want to discuss it either had her a little concerned. But she knew that she shouldn't be totally surprised.

"Tracey, you need to stay out of your mother's business, especially when it comes to Pam," Dee warned.

"I'm not afraid of her, Aunt Dee. What is it with you and Mama?"

"What do you mean?"

"The two of you seem like you can't stand up to her." Tracey laughed loudly. "What is she like four-feet tall and 90 pounds?"

"Now, Tracey . . ."

"Okay, five-feet tall. She's gotta lot of bark going on, too."

Dee could tell that Tracey was having a grand time making fun of Pam, and even though it was comical, Dee was not going to partake in it. "Trust me when I say that she has a bite, too—a very large one."

"I say bring it on."

"Tracey, believe me, you don't want to go there. *Please* believe that."

"But . . ."

"Listen," Dee abruptly changed the subject. "I'm done with that conversation, and you know I would not steer you wrong."

"But, Auntie Dee, you don't under—"

"Yes, I do. I understand that I'm moving onto another topic. How are things going with you and your father *and* mother?"

Tracey was quiet, and Dee knew it was not because she cut the conversation short on the topic of Pam. "Tracey, you still haven't told your mother?"

Tracey whispered, "No."

"When do you plan on telling her?"

"I don't know if I can."

"Oh, Tracey, this is not good at all."

"I know. It's wrong, but I just don't know *how* to tell her."

"Tracey, you've got to do it. You're putting me in the middle of this by keeping secrets from your mom and—"

"I know. I don't want her to fall out with you, too, like she has with Ms. Pam."

Dee let out a sigh of relief. At least Tracey understood the ramifications. Tracey's voice became still as though thinking very carefully about her next sentence.

"Can you be there when I talk to her?"

Dee dropped the phone.

"Hello, Auntie Dee. Hello? Are you there?"

Dee had a puzzled look on her face as she stared at the phone and listened to Tracey's muffled voice calling out to her. Why did she keep getting herself tangled up in all of this drama? First, it was Chris. Next it was Quinton, and now it was Amanda and her daughter.

Pam was in her office facing the picturesque skyscrapers in front of her window. She reflected again on her victory from just two weeks ago. But the entitlement that she greatly anticipated had not yet arrived. Until today.

She had received an email from Bill McKesson asking if she was available to meet first thing this morning with him and Pete. The time had finally come, her *entrée* into the big league. Her telephone buzzed. She looked at the caller ID. It was Pete.

"Hey, Pam. I've got Bill over here in my office now. We're ready to meet with you."

Pam's fingers froze on the mute button. This was finally it; Bill McKesson meeting with her could only mean partnership. The other senior partners were probably going to meet with her later. She laughed hysterically and clapped her hands as she released the mute button.

"I'll be right over."

"Good, we'll see you in a few minutes."

Pam swung her chair around like a kid who had been warned on several occasions not to do so. She raised her hands in the air and softly yelled, "Yes!" She pulled a compact mirror from her purse and took a long look at herself. Then she stroked her short curls and carefully brushed on a light lip gloss.

Pete and Bill were standing stiffly against the desk when she entered. They both looked at her pensively, and then walked over to the conference table in the corner of Pete's office. She saw two small stacks of papers lying neatly on top of the table.

"C'mon in, Pam, please have a seat," Pete said awkwardly, extending his arm to the cushioned cherry wood chair that sat between both of them. Something was strange about their behavior. They were so elusive, almost sinister. Was this how they treated someone who was about to be made partner?

"Thank you," Pam answered as diplomatically as she could, feeling a frost forming around her.

"Pam, we were very proud of your work on the *Johnson v. Tyfish Systems* case. Titus Johnson can't stop calling this office and singing your praises," Bill said, breaking the ice a bit.

"Thank you."

"Yes, you've won a lot of cases for this firm and have brought in significant revenue, especially for someone so young." Pam nodded, waiting anxiously for what they would say next.

"And although you have obviously learned your way around the courtroom very quickly, there are some issues that have been brought to our attention that we feel need to have some further clarification before we offer you a partnership," Pete interjected.

Pam swallowed a lump in her throat. *Did he just say before a partnership was offered? What the hell did he mean by further clarification? What was going on? Were these two white boys smokin' crack? And why was Pete even in here? He wasn't even a damn lawyer, let alone a partner.*

Pam could feel her temperature rising. She began to unbutton her jacket. No matter what, she would not lose her composure. She had built her reputation on being a professional who remained, irrefutably, one of the best lawyers in the firm. She would not let them take her down. Not now, not ever.

"Gentlemen, I'm a little confused here. Exactly what are you saying to me?" Pam said with her signature courtroom voice. "Bill, am I going to make partner?" She looked them both square in the eyes, daring him to say otherwise.

"Not at this time, Pam," Bill said, avoiding her eyes.

Pam's breathing became heavy. Her eyes looked as if they were about to roll out of their sockets. Now she fully understood how Titus Johnson felt in the courtroom *before* his verdict had been read.

"Why not?"

"Because of these," he said as he pushed the two small stacks of papers in front of her. She saw Amanda's name at the top, along with those of seven other paralegals in the firm. All were statements of mistreatment and harassment under distressing work conditions.

"Do you have anything to say, Pam?" Bill asked.

So, this is the thanks I get, huh? I brought in Amanda when she needed a job and this was how it ended up? Ain't this a bitch. Pam looked Bill straight between the eyes. "Well, does it really make a difference what I have to say? I mean, after all, it's obvious that you have gone behind my back without my knowledge and gotten statements from every whining paralegal in this firm to discount my credibility."

"Pam, that is not what has happened at all," Pete said.

"Well, based on the evidence that I'm looking at, it sure looks like that to me," she said coolly, quickly thumbing through the papers. "Did it ever occur to you to come to me first?"

"Yes, as a matter of fact. But to be honest with you, it snowballed before we could get to you," Pete said defensively.

"We asked Amanda to come in here to discuss her abrupt resignation," Bill said, trying to diffuse the tension.

"Oh, so it's clear to me where all of this is coming from. Oh, the poor dejected, self-righteous paralegal, which I'm sure she was all too eager to tell you."

"No, that wasn't how it happened at all. As a matter of fact, she was hesitant to disclose any of it," Pete retorted. "But she finally admitted that she found working for you to be quite stressful, and she saw that it was affecting her personally, which was the reason for her abrupt departure."

"Then, as we were discussing how to handle this with you, a few statements from other paralegals started trickling in, with confirmed witnesses verifying their statements," Bill interjected.

"She's lying! And I want a meeting with the four of us and damn it, I want it now!" She pounded her fist on Pete's desk.

Pete kept a watchful eye on her. Rising slowly, he chose his words very carefully. "Pam, I don't think that would be the best thing to do right now, especially with you being so volatile."

"Volatile? Is that what you think this is? No, I'm not volatile. I'm mad as hell! How dare she go behind my back and meet with you and Pete about me, and I'm not even given the courtesy to tell my side of the story!"

"Pam—"

"Pete! I've worked too damn hard to let Amanda ruin my chances at a partnership. You guys knew how I was when you hired me. As a matter of fact, that was the one thing you liked about me. I got the job done and at *that* time you didn't care about *how* I did it as long as it was legal."

"Pam, we've—"

"Bill, you guys are unbelievable!"

"Listen, Pam," Pete said. "We need to discuss this further with you. Perhaps you need some time to cool down."

Pam looked at Pete with all the restraint she could muster. He could see that what she really wanted to do was take his neck in her hands and slowly squeeze it until his head popped off. She took a deep breath and calmly spoke.

"Pete, I'm going to tell you this one more time. If you turn me down, I'll talk to Amanda on my own. Set up the meeting and call me. Bill, Pete, I'm giving you fair warning now. If you don't do what I'm requesting, then I promise you, this firm will need an attorney whose tactics are far worse than mine."

"C'mon, Pam. You can't be serious. That's your anger talking," Bill said, trying to smooth things over.

Pam quickly gathered up the documents. "I'm assuming you've made copies, so I will be taking these with me, thank you." She waved the stack of papers in their faces as she left the room.

This Way To The Exit

With only two visits under Dee's belt, the place was already taking an unwelcome familiarity. As she waited, Dee thumbed through an *Architectural Digest*. Then glancing around to ensure no one else was in the waiting room, she removed her sunglasses that masked her dark and puffy eyes.

"Good afternoon, Deirdre." The doctor's voice resonated through the waiting room as she walkd into his office.

"Hello," Dee answered as she sat down in the leather chair across from the psychiatrist's sofa. She walked into his office. She could never figure out why someone would want to lay down in a doctor's office and talk about themselves. The only office she ever laid down in was the gynecologist's office. Period. And that was only because she had no choice. The doctor detected a twinge of nervousness in her voice as he tried to ease into their discussion. "Dee, I'm in no hurry. You can start when you are ready," he said as he folded his hands in his lap.

Dee hadn't noticed the doctor's suaveness before. His normally relaxed manner seemed even more laid back than usual. She wondered what type of deep secrets he had in his past.

She stared out again at her favorite view of the snow-capped mountains. She wished she could ski her way right out of her troubles. She visualized herself racing rapidly down one of the massive peaks that would twist and turn down every slope. With each stroke of her ski poles, she'd move at a swifter pace until she skied her way right out onto a cliff, then jump spread-eagle into the endless white powdery crystals below.

"So, how did your ethics homework go with Chris and his friend?"

Dee stared down at her usual visual spot on the carpet. He knew the answer to his question before she opened her mouth. "I failed the assignment. Miserably."

"What happened?"

"I ran into someone on the plane that recognized me from my association with Chris. I'm not sure how far he's going to take it, but either way, I need to get to Chris before he does. He already gave me fair warning. Here, look at this." She pulled Quinton's note out of her purse. Dee slumped in her chair as the doctor read it.

He set it down on the table next to him and shook his head. "So, what's your plan?"

Dee felt tears brimming in her eyes and then falling down her face and shrugged her shoulders. "Oh, and that's not the worst of it."

"Explain, please."

"I ran into Amanda."

"Your friend from Spelman, right?"

"Yes, my roommate's paralegal, or former one I should say."

"What about her?"

Dee was so nervous that her words starting spewing out like water from a fire hose. "Her daughter, Tracey, is now confiding in me about stuff that she doesn't want her mother to know and it has me caught in the middle."

"Slow down, and let's stop right there. *No one has you* caught in anything, but *you*. You are the one who draws these situations to yourself." Dee looked at the doctor puzzled. "What I mean is that you get yourself in these predicaments and act surprised when everything starts to blow up in your face. This issue with your friend's daughter—it is you who is allowing it to grow into a larger problem by trying to talk to Tracey without her mother knowing about what is transpiring."

Dee's head dropped in guilt and exhaustion. She was almost afraid to tell him about her next plight. "You're right," she said, solemnly. "The issue with Tracey is something that I can probably work out, but there's something else I haven't told you."

The doctor looked at Dee sympathetically and sucked his bottom lip to try to keep from interjecting. "Does it have something to do with this?" He pointed to the note she had handed him earlier. Tears started cascading down her face again, and he got up to hand her a tissue.

"Yes, I pretended to be a lawyer to Chris's friend even after I told you I wouldn't. Then there was this incident that happened in New York with Steve." Dee blew her nose and then recounted her evening in New York at The River Café when she purposefully broke her glass with her hand in order to avoid the meeting Steve planned with Dr. Briscoe.

"Dee, you're getting more twisted up in lies each time I see you."

"I know," she said between sobs as she blew her nose again. "I just don't know what I'm going to do. I know I need to be honest, doctor. But I don't want to . . ."

"Don't want to what, Dee?"

"I don't want to . . . to lose them," she said barely above a whisper.

"There are no guarantees, Dee. Does your fear of losing them mean you are considering telling them the truth?"

Dee cried harder. She had to clear her head. She got up from her chair and paced back and forth, still picturing herself on a pair of skis racing down the mountains.

"Let's talk about that for a moment."

"What?"

"Thinking about how you might go about telling these men the truth."

Dee pondered his question before she spoke. "Well, I suppose I would invite Chris over to my hotel room and just try to ask for his forgiveness. That's if Quinton hasn't gotten to him first." Dee's voice trailed off as her tears welled up again.

"And what about Steve?"

Dee was overwhelmed at the thought of having to be truthful to both of them at the same time. "He's a little different. He's white, you know," she said as she wiped the corner of her eye.

"Is that significant?"

"Well, I just don't want to fall into a stereotypical role," she said as she sat back down in her chair and rocked back and forth.

"What stereotypical role?"

"A gold digging black woman. Oh never mind, you wouldn't understand."

She sighed and placed her hand on her forehead in frustration. "You've probably never even dated a black woman."

"Do you think that's how he would look at you?" he asked ignoring her comment.

"I don't know. I believe I'm the first black woman he's ever dated."

"Really? Why do you think that?"

"It's just a feeling I have—the way he looks at me."

"I see. How do you feel about him?"

"I think he's sexy."

"Is that all?"

"I like his company. I'm not trying to marry the man or anything."

"Do you think he would want to marry you?"

"Probably not."

"Why is that?"

"We've never discussed it, but I just can't see him hooking up long-term with a black woman, you know?"

"So, basically you're just seeing him for what?"

"For fun, and we have great sex."

"So, if it's just for fun and great sex, why do you care if he stays with you or not once you tell him the truth?"

"I don't know. You're the doctor. Why don't you tell me?" Dee was a little irritated by all of his probing questions.

"Let me understand this. Chris, the black guy, is the one with whom you're going to let the chips fall where they may, and Steve, the white guy, the one you don't intend to have a future with, is the one you're most afraid to tell?"

"Yes. I mean, no . . . I'm afraid to tell both of them. I just don't know." Dee hung her head and wrung her hands. She knew she was being shallow about these two guys. But she was smart enough to know what *her* bottom line belief was. When it came right down to it, she would take the black man over the white one any day. When times got tough, she felt that Chris would stay by her side. If the road got too rough, she felt that Steve would take the high road.

"Well, do you want my professional opinion?"

"Sure, that's what I'm here for, right?" Dee said, knowing she was being a smart aleck.

"I think you do know, but you may not want to admit it to me. But deep down inside you know the answer." Dee looked at him blankly. She didn't know how to react to this answer. He had her figured out.

"Listen, I have another assignment for you. And this time you better pass." He grinned. "I want you to go home tonight and think about when the lying started and then ask yourself what it's going to take to make you stop. I want to discuss this at our next session."

"In the meantime, what am I supposed to do?"

"What do *you* think you should do?"

"Tell Chris and Steve the truth," she mumbled.

"And what about the situation with Tracey and her mother?" the doctor added.

Dee gave a slow sigh. "Get her to talk with her mother before I get too deep in it. I don't want to lose her friendship, either."

"Well, I'm glad to see we are getting closer to you seeing what is best for you," he said as he glanced at the clock. "Unfortunately, our fifty minutes are up, and I can see that we have a lot more that you want to discuss. Please, Dee, call me if you need to schedule a phone session before we meet again," he said as he got up from the chair and walked toward the door.

"Doctor, may I ask you something personal?"

"You can ask. And I'll let you know if I can answer it," he smiled.

"What would you do if you dated someone like me and found out that she was not who you thought she was?"

"Dee, every person is different. And what I would do would not be what you would do. How do you think *you* would handle it?"

"I don't know. I'll let you know next week when I've done the rest of my assignment."

"I look forward to it."

Unexpected ETA

"Okay, baby, so do you have everything you need?"

"Yes, Mama. For the zillionth time."

"All right, now, your Aunt Dora and Uncle Jack will be waiting on you when you get there, okay?"

"I know, Mama."

"And Melvin and I are going to fly down there on Saturday to come to the orientation."

"Mama, I know. I'm glad you're going back to the firm. And with a raise, too. And now that you won't be dealing with the *Queen of Evil* again, you'll be able to really enjoy your job," Tracey said as she hugged her mother for the third time.

"Thanks, baby. It's not quite that smooth yet, though. Pete called again. He wants me to have another meeting with them this morning. I just feel so guilty that I can't take you to the airport."

"Mama, I'm a big girl. It's no big deal, really." She playfully nudged Tony in the ribs. "Tony will make sure I get there. Right, Tony?"

"Yes, ma'am. She'll be fine. I'll make sure she gets on that flight."

Amanda looked at Tracey sadly and grabbed and hugged her a fourth time. "Oh, all right."

Tracey rolled her eyes at Tony as she smiled. She hugged her mother again while she took a step back to look straight into her eyes. "Now, Mama. Don't start your first day back at work worrying about me."

"Hey, who's the daughter and who's the mother here?" Amanda pulled her in again and gave her a lingering hug that was even longer than the previous one. It was one too many hugs for Tracey, and she was glad when her mother finally stopped and hugged Tony.

"Thank you, Tony," Amanda said as she patted him on the back.

Tony started the car and drove out of the driveway. "Okay, so what time does your flight *really* leave?"

"Not for at least three hours. So, I've got plenty of time to check in, get settled . . ."

"And meet *him*." He pressed his foot down hard on the accelerator as they merged onto the freeway.

"Don't say it like that!"

Tony looked over at her and gave her a quick glance. "Like what?"

"*HIM!* Like he's some type of scum."

Tony looked at the oncoming traffic through his rearview mirror before changing lanes. "I guess if you're cool with it, then I should be, too."

Tracey playfully slapped him on his knee and then put in an Alicia Keys CD, *Fallin*. "Good, then. I can't wait for you to meet him. You know he used to play football with—"

"The Tampa Bay Buccaneers. Yes, I know. You told me, remember?" *Like a trillion and one times.* "He was the number one draft pick, right?"

"Yeah," she giggled.

"I guess he and your mom's relationship was something like this song, huh? 'Fallin' in and out of love, over the years?"

"Shut up, Tony. See, now, that wasn't even necessary."

"Yeah, you're right. I apologize. But, I don't like lying to your mom and *especially* Melvin. He just looks like he can put a hurtin' on a brotha.'"

Tracey laughed, "I know, he can be pretty intense, but he's just being protective."

"Why does this have to be such a big secret?" Tony looked over at Tracey and pinched her playfully.

"Ow! Boy, what's wrong with you? That hurt." She pinched him back harder in his shoulder.

"So are you going to answer my question?"

"What question?"

"Why haven't you told your mother about your father?"

Tracey flung her hair out of her eyes and sighed.

Tony sensed her frustration as he grabbed her hand. "I'm sorry. I didn't mean to get you upset."

"It's not you, Tony."

"Then what is it? I don't understand. It's like, all of these years, your father has not made any contact with you, and now all of a sudden he pops back into your life these last few months before you're off to college and then POOF! He's gone from this guy named Rickey Mavers to Daddy. And in the meantime, you're lying to your mom about where you're going. You're sneaking out to see him, and now you've gotten me wrapped up in this all the way up to my eyeballs."

Tracey squeezed his hand and stared out the window. Everything he was saying was true, but there was so much more to the story. She looked back at Tony, whose eyes kept darting from the road to her.

"Tony, it's very complicated, and I can't tell you everything right now. But I promise that eventually I will. Right now, I just want you to meet him and judge him for yourself."

"Cool," Tony said, as he thought about Tracey's dishonesty. If she could do this behind her mother's back, what was she capable of doing to him?

"Cool," Tracey repeated as she squeezed his hand.

"Just so you know, I'm not *cool* with having to share you the last couple of hours we have together."

"Tony, come on. My father's not going to come between us."

"He already has," Tony mumbled.

"Listen Tony, please don't go there. Not now," she said.

Tony could tell that he had stepped over the line. If he really wanted to be supportive, he would have to change his attitude and just trust that she was doing the right thing.

As Tony unloaded the luggage at the ticket counter, he felt a firm hand grab the handle at the same time.

"Here, let me help you with that, son."

Tracey heard the familiar voice and immediately stopped breathing. She broke off her conversation with the ticket agent and ran. "Daddy!"

"Hey, sweetheart! Looks like you're packed for the next four years."

"Miss, you're holding up the line," the ticket agent said.

"Oh, I'm sorry. I'll be right there. Daddy, this is my boyfriend Tony I told you about. Tony, this is my father, Rickey Mavers."

Tony looked at Rickey, surprised that a man of his age was in such good shape. He still looked as if he could run some yardage. "The pleasure is mine, sir."

Rickey eyed Tony carefully. Tony looked like a ladies' man—just like him when he was his age. He looked real clean cut and polite too, or so he seemed. What were Tony's *real* intentions with Tracey?

"It's my pleasure, also," Rickey responded.

Tracey watched them shake hands. She was so relieved that Tony agreed to meet him.

"Miss!" the ticket agent called out again.

"Sorry, guys, I'll be right back," she said as she ran back to the ticket counter. "I really do apologize. That's my dad," she said giddily, handing the agent her identification and looking back at them over her shoulder.

"Yes, I can see the resemblance," the agent said coolly.

"Really?"

"Uh huh," she said without looking up as she entered Tracey's information into the computer. "Here you go," she said as she handed back her ID. Have a nice flight."

"Thank you."

"Okay, guys. I'm all set." Tracey placed one arm around Tony and one around her father and gave them a squeeze. "I've still got two hours before my flight, so let's find someplace to sit down," she said as they headed over to the seating area in front of the security checkpoint. She looked at her father and didn't know what to say first.

"Daddy, I was telling Tony about how you were the number one draft pick for the Tampa Bay Buccaneers." Rickey looked at Tony and grinned.

Tony knew exactly what he was thinking. So, the former Buccaneer Mavers was really impressed with himself. But, he didn't care if he was the first draft choice. All Tony wanted to know was how a man could abandon his child. Period. His parents had been married for twenty years and never once would his father ever consider abandoning his family. What kind of man was he beneath that charming smile? His shirt looked like it was tailor made by Versace himself, and his shoes looked like he paid about five hundred dollars just for the buckle alone. And that Rolex watch on his wrist had to put him out several grand. But he was still cheap in Tony's book.

"So how long did you play for Tampa?" Tony said, trying to sound interested for Tracey's sake.

"I played for four and a half years. Until I got cut because of a knee injury."

"So what have you been doing for the last 18 years?" Tony felt Tracey's eyes cut him to the quick. "I mean, what are you doing now?"

Rickey glared at Tony. He better not try and play him like that in front of his daughter. The next time he pulled something like that, he was going to have to set him straight and embarrass his young ass. "I've been involved in a lot of business deals," he said.

Yeah, I bet, Tony thought. "Really? What kind of business? I mean, if you don't mind my asking." He eyed both Tracey and Rickey.

"No, I don't mind at all. I'm looking at some franchise opportunities in different cities, including here in the Atlanta area."

"So does that mean that you'll be moving down here?" Tracey interjected.

Rickey smiled at Tracey. She was looking at him like he was her hero. "Temporarily. If the deal works out, then maybe I will consider moving to Atlanta permanently. I'm flying out a little later myself to see about some of these businesses."

"So, Tracey, what do you know? Your mom and pop will be sharing the same city." Tony could only hope there was enough room in Atlanta for Rickey's ego to match the tornado that was about to come through once Amanda found out that Tracey had been secretly seeing him.

Tracey looked at Tony questioningly. Where did that statement come from? She wished Tony would keep his flippant remarks to himself.

"Well, I'm sure there's enough room in Atlanta for both of us."

"Yes, of course there is." Tracey smiled nervously and glanced at the time on her cell phone. "Man, look at the time."

"I can't believe we've talked this long," Rickey said.

I can't believe I've stomached you this long. Tony managed to put on a smile. "Me neither, Mr. Mavers, it's been ah right."

Rickey looked down at his watch. "Hey, sweetheart, it looks like you have only about ninety minutes until your flight leaves."

"I know. I guess I better head on through security. You never know how long these lines will get." She looked at Tony sadly. "I hate to leave the two of you, especially since you are getting along so well. I knew it would be like this."

Rickey cleared his throat. "Ah, baby girl," he said as he gave Tracey a long hug and kissed her on the cheek.

Tony turned his back for a minute and pretended to cough. He didn't want Tracey to see that he was really feeling a little anxious and that he had to say goodbye to her in front of her father—and having to pretend that he was *fine* with everything.

Just as Tracey opened her eyes and stepped back from her final embrace with her father, she saw Dee walking past the ticket counter holding a little boy's hand. The little boy looked to be about five years old. He was wearing khaki shorts and a white Mickey Mouse t-shirt, and he was hugging a stuffed dog.

"Is that your mommy and daddy over there?" Dee asked. The little boy nodded as Dee walked him over to the Asian couple who was running toward him.

"Thank you! Thank you!" they said as they grabbed and hugged him and checked him over and over to make sure he was okay. Tears ran down the little boy's face as he nodded.

"This airport is so big, and he got away from us when we boarded the train," the father said in his best English speaking voice.

Dee smiled and patted the boy's dog. "He's okay. I'm just glad I saw him and had time between flights to help him." As Dee turned to go back through security, she saw Tracey waving her arms and beckoning her to come over. "What in the—?"

"Auntie Dee, Auntie Dee, come over here!"

Dee made her way over to the threesome and was speechless when she saw Rickey.

"Auntie Dee, this is my boyfriend, Tony. Tony, THIS is my Aunt Dee who I have been telling you about."

"Hi," Tony said extending his hand. "Tracey has told me a lot about you."

"It's ALL good I hope."

Tony nodded. "Yes, ma'am."

"Well, well, well, Mr. Rickey Mavers, how are you these days?" Dee said in a chilling tone.

"I've been good," Rickey retorted.

"Wow! The two of you know each other?" Tony was stunned.

"Yes," they both answered regrettably.

"But, it's been a while since we've seen each other," Rickey snarled.

"Not long enough," Dee snarled back and eyed him up and down.

As Tracey watched their bantering in disbelief, she decided to intervene and hopefully smooth things over. "I told Auntie Dee that we had found each other," Tracey said nervously.

"So, where have you been Rickey, all these 17 years?" Dee asked firmly.

Tony grinned as he watched the flares between them start to ignite. He caught himself before he laughed out loud. Tracey's Aunt Dee was not holding anything back. She was saying everything he wished he could say, and he loved every minute of it.

"I've been handling my business," Rickey answered back in a brash tone. "I can see that I can't say the same thing about you though 'cuz you *still* up in everybody else's business," he mumbled. He immediately went over to Tracey and kissed and hugged her one more time as Dee tried to gain her composure.

"Did you say something?" Dee quipped.

"It was nothing."

"Yeah, that's just like *you*, nothing," Dee scoffed.

Rickey disdainfully eyeballed Dee from head to toe. "Don't you have a flight or something you should be trying to catch?"

Dee glanced at her watch and then looked at him piercingly between the eyes. "No."

"Ahem . . ." Tracey interrupted. "Well, I do," she announced as she pulled Dee toward her. "Hey, go easy on him, Auntie Dee. He's not who you think he is, okay?"

"Hmph! Since when?"

Tracey's tone became firm. She pulled Dee a couple of steps away from her father so he couldn't hear. "Aunt Dee, he's my dad. I know you know about my dad and mama's history, but I promise you that there is more to the story."

"R-e-a-l-l-y? And I suppose he told you that, huh?"

Tracey inhaled deeply and rolled her eyes. "Yes, Aunt Dee, and I believe him. Listen, you've got to stop treating him like he's got some type of disease. I'm spending more time trying to keep you two from going off on each other than spending time with Tony—who, by the way, is just sitting over there waiting this drama out. Look at him."

"Yes, I see him, but I'm not concerned with Tony's feelings right now. I'm concerned about you. You know your mother used to believe your father's words, too, and you see where that got her, right?"

"Aunt Dee! Please, just stop it!"

Dee threw her hands up. "I'm sorry. I really didn't mean for that to come out like that. It's just that I remember when you were born. I know your parents were kids themselves. But your father was not there for you or Amanda when he should have been. Your mother has done an excellent job in raising you, and I don't want him to come into your life and *undo* any of it."

"He won't. You'll see."

"Well, I'm not holding my breath."

Tracey looked up at Dee with sad eyes. "This is exactly why I didn't want to tell Mama. But, I didn't expect you—of all people—to react like this."

"Tracey, you haven't even told me the whole story about you and your father. How did you find him? Why has he been MIA all of these years?"

"Well, I've tried to but . . ."

Dee folded her arms and tapped her foot impatiently. "Okay, tell me now, then."

Tracey peeked at her cell phone's clock and knew there was not enough time before her flight to tell Dee everything.

"I see, now you've gotta go, right?"

"I'm afraid so. Oh, Aunt Dee," she said as she grabbed her neck and hugged her. "I'm so sorry things have turned out this way."

Dee started feeling a little ashamed of her reaction toward Rickey. "I promise to be on my best behavior," she said, as she placed her arm around Tracey's shoulder and walked toward Tony and Rickey. They were both seated at separate ends of a bench with their backs to each other. Neither one of them shared a word between them. As Dee and Tracey got closer, they both stood up.

"Hey, Tony, I'm going to leave the two of you alone to say your goodbyes, man. You don't need me hanging around here," Rickey said, waiting for Dee to make one of her smart comments.

Dee remained silent, and Tony was caught off guard by his gesture and Dee's unexpected surrender.

"Thanks, Mr. Mavers," Tony said.

"Oh, Daddy." Tracey smiled as she hugged him. He released her and backed away to give the two of them some privacy.

"Be good, and call me when you land, okay?"

"I will. Bye, Auntie Dee."

"Bye, darlin'. Tony, it was good to meet you. Take care of yourself, okay?"

"It was nice to meet you, too. I will and thank you," he said, as he watched Dee and Rickey part in different directions.

"Well, I guess this is it. It's just you and me now, finally." He breathed in a sigh of relief. "You know I love you, Tracey."

"I love you too, Tony. And no matter what, I'm going to work to keep this relationship."

"Me too," he said as he bent down and kissed her on the mouth. He held her close as if he could stop her from slipping away. He was still thinking about Rickey's sudden appearance in her life and was tempted to ask her about it again, but decided this was not the right time. All that mattered was that Tracey was in his arms at this moment. He kissed her again before she walked through security.

Suddenly, a loud voice bolted through the crowd. "Tracey! Wait!"

"Mama?"

"Yes, baby, here, you forgot your carry-on."

"Oh, my, I must have left it on the kitchen table."

"You did," Amanda said breathlessly.

"Oh, Mama, you're so out of breath."

"I know," she said, panting harder. "I just wanted to make sure you got it. I figured you would still be out here talking to Tony."

"I was just about to go through security. I'm glad you caught me. Aren't you supposed to be at work?"

"I called and told Bill what happened. I'm on my way after I leave here." Tracey looked up at Tony with a concerned look on her face. Her mother was in no condition to run through the airport like that.

"Listen, Tracey, go on. You don't want to miss your flight. I'll sit here with your mother while she catches her breath."

Amanda patted his back. "Thank you, Tony. Bye, baby." Amanda kissed her on the forehead.

Tracey's eyes pleaded with Tony not to let her mother in on her secret. He winked to let her know that her secret was safe. He and Amanda watched her finally make her way through the security checkpoint.

Twenty minutes had passed before Amanda finally caught her breath. "I'm okay, Tony. Really."

"How about I buy you a bottle of water?"

"That's okay. I'll be fine. You can go on now. Thank you."

"Okay, well, at least let me walk you back to your car."

Amanda smiled at Tony. He was such an honest and respectful young man. She was relieved that she could trust him with her daughter. "Your parents did a good job in raising you, Tony."

"I'll be sure and tell them you said that. They'll appreciate the compliment."

As they headed toward the exit, the crowd in the airport thickened. The security lines were now backed up creating snake lines outside of the airport.

"It looks like Tracey made it here right before the security meltdown."

"Thank God for that. I would have been a nervous wreck if this had happened to her. I'm sure this will be on the news tonight."

Dee checked the flight departures and saw that her flight was going to be delayed. She spotted Rickey and decided it was time for her to speak with him face-to-face without flinging insults.

"Hey, Rickey."

"Oh, no, not you again. What do you want to accuse me of this time? Besides, I thought you had a flight to catch."

"It's been delayed."

"Just my luck."

"If you have some time, I'd like to speak with you."

Rickey looked at his watch. "I don't know if that is such a good idea. You know, airport security has been heightened around here, and I'm not interested in being assaulted today."

"Funny, Rickey."

"Excuse me, Dee, but I've just spotted Tracey's boyfriend, and I need to have a quick word with him."

"I'll go with you."

"Suit yourself. Hey, Tony! Over here!" he called as he made his way through the thickening crowd.

"Mr. Mavers, hey, I thought you were gone." Tony tried to remain as calm as possible as he watched Amanda nearing the exit.

As Amanda came closer to the door, she turned around to look for Tony. When she spotted him, she blinked hard. Her eyes were playing tricks on her. When she realized she wasn't hallucinating, her face felt like it was on fire and her feet became paralyzed. The crowd kept moving until it pushed Tony, Rickey, and Dee right in front of her. Everyone's worst nightmare had come to pass, and Tracey had escaped it all.

Not Just Peanuts

As Pam pulled her car into the parking lot, she couldn't help but notice that Amanda's old parking spot was occupied. She slowed down and wheeled in closer.

"Well, I'll just be damned," she said as she eyed the personalized tag, Shipman 1. "Well, well, well. Look who's here." Pam pressed down hard on the accelerator and sped into a parking spot four spaces down from Amanda's. Sitting behind the steering wheel, she took a few deep breaths before grabbing her briefcase and stepping out of the car. She talked to herself as she walked briskly toward her office building and into the elevator. "Pam, no matter what happens, you've got to be the one to maintain control." Just before the elevator reached the fiftieth floor, Pam pulled back her shoulders, smoothed out her tailored pantsuit, and stepped out of the elevator doors.

"Good morning, Carol Ann," Pam said as she breezed by, barely giving her an opportunity to respond.

Pam's first stop was her office, where she turned on her computer and checked her emails. Next, she proceeded to Bill's office and knocked sternly.

"It's open."

Pam walked in on what looked like a cozy rendezvous between Bill and Pete. They were seated at his conference table, drinking coffee, and there was a third cup across from them.

Pete spoke first. "Pam, hello."

"Hello," Pam said dryly. "Where is she?"

"Who?" Bill asked.

"Amanda." *As if you didn't know.*

"She's not here," Pete answered back.

"I just saw her car in the parking lot."

"Her boyfriend, Melvin, stopped by briefly to drop some of her things off. You must have just missed each another."

"Why is Melvin dropping some of her things off?"

"She had an emergency this morning," Bill replied.

"That's not what I'm talking about, and I think you know that. Why is she having her things dropped off if she is no longer employed here? Additionally, I have already expressed to both of you that I wanted to speak with her."

"And we've arranged that," Pete added.

"Really? So, when am *I* going to be able to meet with her?"

"She'll be working as Bill's chief paralegal starting next week. She'll be in at 8:00 a.m., and you can set up a meeting with her then."

"Oh, I see. So you hired her back with a promotion, and you've refused to make me a partner?"

"Listen, Pam, let's not end up like we did last time, all right? We can discuss your issues calmly and rationally. With all of us in here as you requested."

"I think we've discussed it enough." Her tone was strangely mysterious and obviously made the men uncomfortable—and she was enjoying every minute of it. "If I wasn't clear before, then I definitely am now." She grinned then walked over to the door. "This isn't over, gentlemen. Not by a long shot!"

Grab Your Oxygen Mask

Amanda felt like her air was cut off. "Amanda?" The sexy, silky voice echoed as Amanda looked up at him, feeling an eerie sense of *déjà vu.*

"Rickey?" She looked into his raisin-colored eyes and at his smooth mocha skin, which looked as flawless and youthful as the day she'd first met him in high school. She looked at Dee and Tony in bewilderment.

"Dee? Tony? I don't understand."

Shit! Tony thought as he looked up and saw that he was caught right in the middle of the crossfire between Tracey's mama, new daddy, and now the auntie.

"Yeah, it's me," he said, almost as blown away as Amanda. "How have you been?" Rickey laughed nervously.

"Why are the three of you here? And together?" she said, pointing her finger at them.

Tony was stunned. He wanted to say something, but nothing would come out of his mouth. Meanwhile, Rickey was trying to figure out what to say to her. Dee was speechless, too.

"Are any of you going to answer me? Dee?"

"I just ran into everyone on my way to work, Amanda. Go ahead. Ask them."

Without blinking, Amanda stared straight at Dee. "Why do I get the feeling that there is more to this than you are telling me?"

Dee shrugged her shoulders and started staring at the floor, and Amanda immediately knew there was more to this story. "Tony, let's start with you."

"Hey, let's leave Tony out of this, okay?" Dee insisted. "Why don't you just go on home, son? Ms. Shipman and I—"

"Tony, you're not leaving until I get an explanation," Amanda demanded.

"Amanda, I'll handle it," Rickey intervened.

Tony's head was bouncing back and forth between the two of them like a ping-pong ball. He didn't know who to answer first.

"What in God's name is there for you to handle, Rickey?" Amanda said, doing her best to avoid making a scene at the airport.

"Amanda, please. Just let the boy go."

"He's right," Dee chimed in, surprising herself that she was siding with Rickey.

Amanda nodded and looked at Tony shamefully.

He felt like Judas, the disciple, who betrayed Jesus. He knew she would never feel the same way about him again. She threw her hand up for him to leave.

"Ms. Shipman," Tony spoke cautiously. "I hope when you find out what happened you'll see that I really wanted you know the *truth.* I'm sorry."

"What in the world is going on here? How come everybody seems to know what's going on except me?" she shouted.

"Go on, Tony, please. I'll handle it from here," Rickey said.

Tony looked at Amanda one last time, hoping to see some sign of forgiveness in her eyes before he left. Unfortunately, there was none.

"Well?" Amanda looked at Rickey, impatiently tapping her foot. "And you, Dee! Are you flying in or flying out? When I last saw you, you told me you practiced law during the week."

Dee had to think fast. She had already forgotten that she had told Amanda that lie at the restaurant. "Ah, this is my off week, so I'm flying."

"I can see that." Amanda answered mockingly.

Dee knew by the sound of her tone that she was not convinced.

Rickey placed his hand on Amanda's shoulder. "Hey, if you would just calm down a moment, I can explain."

Amanda pulled her sweater taut around her breasts and jerked away from him. She didn't know if she felt more anger or nervousness. "I'm waiting." She paused. "How do you and Tony know each other?

"And how are you involved in all of this, Dee?"

Rickey knew that he had to come clean with Amanda. He didn't like the fact that she looked at him like she was waiting for a lie to come out his mouth, but under the circumstances, he understood her position.

"The long and short of it is that Tony brought Tracey to the airport and

I met her here. Dee was here already. She just happened to run into us." He exhaled as he waited for her reaction.

Amanda thought that her ears were playing tricks on her. She shook her head swiftly to make sure she heard him right. "You've been here to see who?" Amanda looked straight at him, daring him to repeat his sentence.

"This is really awkward, Amanda."

"I'll say it is! You've never been in contact with Tracey before. So why now?"

"That's the same thing I've been asking Tracey ever since she told me," Dee blurted out.

"That's because you've never allowed me to be a part of her life!" Rickey spat.

"Oh, no! Hold it just one minute, here, Dee. Do you mean to tell me that Tracey told YOU and not ME that she has been seeing him?" Dee looked nervously at her watch. "Are you going to find the answer in that watch of yours? Dee, what do you have to say for yourself?"

Dee started breathing heavily. "I didn't want to be the one to tell you this. I had hoped that Tracey would. She's been calling me lately, and she told me that she's been seeing Rickey, but we never got around to the details."

Rickey threw his hands up innocently as Amanda's eyes suspiciously followed him. Her eyes then moved to settle on Dee's mouth. It was moving, but she couldn't believe what was coming out of it.

"I still don't know the entire story," Dee said innocently. "But, I did insist that she tell you because I did not want what happened with you and Pam to happen to us."

Amanda thought quietly to herself for a moment. Dee was probably telling the truth. Tracey had been acting so distant lately that it made sense that she would reach out to Dee. Dee had always been there for Tracey and for her, too, even before all of these *Pam Shenanigans* started.

"Okay," Amanda said slowly. "I believe you."

"Good, because right now I was going to have to make a decision if I was going to have to stand here and argue to defend myself, or leave you mad so I can make my flight."

Amanda laughed to herself. "Go to work."

"Thank you. I will."

"But you ain't goin' nowhere, Mister!" she said, pointing her finger in Rickey's face.

It had been years since Dee had heard Amanda talk like that. She didn't know she still had it in her to go off on him. She looked at Rickey and whispered, "That's my cue to go. Good luck cuz you are certainly in for the beat down of your life," she warned as she rushed toward the security checkpoint.

"Bye," Rickey mumbled. His hands were shoved in his pockets, and his head was down like a schoolboy who was waiting for a disciplinary meeting in the principal's office.

Amanda was so close to slapping Rickey that she had to step away from him. "You are really something."

"C'mon, Amanda, what do you want me to say?"

"How can you stand there in front of Dee and say that I didn't want you to be a part of Tracey's life when year after year, month after month, I've written you letters, and you sent them all back to me."

"What the hell are you talking about? I never once got any letter from you."

"Don't you curse at me, Rickey Mavers. I'm not one of your groupies you can disrespect."

"Is there a problem here, folks?" An undercover police officer dressed in street clothing came up to them. He pulled out his badge and showed it to them. Rickey spotted his large gun and immediately lowered his voice.

"Good morning, officer," Rickey said, a little embarrassed.

"Mornin'," he nodded. "You two don't seem like you're having such a good one today. I've been watching you for the past fifteen minutes, and your discussion is looking like it's getting pretty intense, so I'm going to have to ask you to take this outside of the airport grounds."

"Yes, sir. I'm sorry for the outburst. We're about to wrap this up, because I do have a flight to catch in about two hours, if that's okay."

The officer nodded and gave him a warning look.

"I apologize, too, officer. Thank you," Amanda said as she looked up at Rickey and rolled her eyes. She thought about how she had kept every single letter that she had ever written to him in a box on the top shelf of her closet. She didn't know why she kept sending him more letters since he'd returned all of them. And the even bigger unanswered question was why she still had them.

The officer kept a close eye on the two of them as Rickey pulled Amanda by her arm and led her through the doorway. "This conversation is not over. You do know that, don't you?" he said firmly.

"Let go of me," she whispered loudly in his ear.

"I will, when we get outside, okay? I don't feel like getting arrested today by Bubba." He smiled at the officer as he escorted her out.

"Don't you have a flight to catch?"

"I'll cancel it, Amanda."

"Now, that's a switch. You'd cancel something for me?"

"Listen, there's obviously a seventeen-year disconnect here, and we need to get it straightened out. Can we go somewhere for coffee?'

"No, I have to go into the office today for a meeting."

"So how about you meet me for dinner later this evening?"

Amanda looked at him with contempt. She was so incensed at his pretense of innocence in all this. She didn't understand why he felt like he had to lie about not responding to her letters.

"Dinner after seventeen years? You've got to be joking."

"Why? Would Melvin mind?"

"Melvin? How did you know about—"

Rickey was silent as he watched her get more worked up by the minute. He still knew how to throw a bone at her and watch her chew on it and spit it back at him. She had not changed since they were in high school, and even though she was mad as hell at him, she was still appealing.

"Don't you dare bring him into this mess. You're not good enough to even say his name out loud."

"Okay, okay. I'm sorry. Look, you got me going here, okay? That wasn't fair. I know it. But you said it yourself. It's been seventeen years. I've changed a lot in those years, and I think we need to discuss this, especially because I'm going to continue to have a relationship with our daughter."

Amanda couldn't take any more of his arrogance. She pulled her hand back as far as she could and slapped him hard across his face. "You obviously have had too many passes hit you in your head. The answer is no!"

Rickey rubbed the side of his face and tightly grabbed hold of Amanda's wrist. She looked in his eyes, but the display of anger she'd expected was nonexistent. What she saw was the high school sweetheart she'd fallen in love with so many years ago. She saw the hurt look on his face and tried to gain her composure while he spoke to her in a low voice.

"All right, I probably deserved that. But Amanda, if you won't do it for me, do it for Tracey. In a few more months she will be eighteen, and she will legally be able to make her own decisions."

Amanda thought for a moment about what Rickey was saying. Her mind raced with a series of questions. She felt her composure eroding as she began to think about what a conceited jerk he was. He was planning on having a relationship with Tracey with or without her permission. The nerve of him to try and take away her baby. She wouldn't let it happen.

"You know, Rickey, you're right. On second thought, I will have dinner with you."

"Really, that's great," Rickey said with a great amount of relief in his voice. "We can settle all of this then."

She faked a sincere smile. She wasn't going to settle anything.

"How about that Italian restaurant, Veni Vidi Vici, in Midtown?"

"Okay, that's fine," she said, trying her best to sound believable. "I'll meet you there around 6:30."

"Thanks, Amanda. I'll see you then."

Preparing for Touchdown

Dee said playfully into the phone's receiver, "Hey baby, I'm baaaack!"

"I see that. When did you get in?" Chris asked groggily.

"Just a few hours ago. Did I wake you?"

"I was just getting up. I had a hard practice today, and I was kind of beat, but I knew that I had to get my energy up because my girl was coming to town."

Dee loved to hear him refer to her as *his* girl. She wished that he would always feel that way about her. But after tonight, those words might soon be only a memory.

"So, do you want to come over here tonight, or I come there?" The frog slowly left his throat, and his voice returned to a normal baritone.

Dee thought for a moment about his oasis with a backyard beach. After her almost disastrous encounter with Amanda and Quinton, she would love to take a dip in the warm ocean, and then soak her worries away in his oversized Jacuzzi. Later, they could take a sauna together and make love until their bodies were too hot to touch. Their evening would end with a tepid shower that cooled their bodies just long enough to give them the energy they needed to rekindle their desires again in his oversized king bed.

Her thoughts stopped short when she remembered what tonight was really about—her lies. The airport scene was minor in comparison to the assignment that she had agreed to complete for her psychiatrist. She was scheduled to meet him again next week, and she had to do this or else she would be a failure in her own eyes as well as in his.

"I think I'd rather you come over here. I've got to leave midmorning, so it would be easier for me to leave from here to the airport."

"All right, no problem."

"I'll see you in a half hour, baby."

After she hung up the phone she went over to the full-length mirror and unbuttoned her long satin black blouse down to her navel. She smoothed out her thigh-fitted black leggings and briefly considered changing into one of her usual "come hither" negligees, but she knew that if she was going to move forward, she needed to do it fully clothed. Fifteen minutes had passed since she spoke with Chris, and there was a knock at the door.

"Room service."

"Yes, I'll be right there," she said, relieved that it was not Chris. She had almost forgotten she had ordered up Chris's favorite foods. She clutched the opening of her blouse as she opened the door. The waiter walked in with a white linen table and a single red rose. He rolled the tray over to the sitting area and lifted each silver tray for her to inspect.

"Here you are, Miss Bridge: two lobsters, baked potatoes, chef salad, and two bottles of Chablis that you requested. Over here, we have two cheese pies and regular and decaf coffee."

"Everything looks fine, thank you," she said, barely glancing over at the entrée as she pulled out a twenty from her shirt pocket and handed it to him.

"Thank you, Miss Bridge, but the tip is already included in your check."

"Oh, yes, that's right. I hadn't even looked at the ticket," she said despondently. "Thanks." She placed the money back into her pocket and walked him to the door. She nervously checked her watch again and decided to go into the bathroom and freshen up one last time before Chris's arrival.

She brushed her hair and touched up her makeup as she thought long and hard about how she had gotten herself into this predicament. Things had begun to change for Dee on the day she graduated from law school. Everyone she knew seemed to know what they wanted to do with their lives, except Dee. Even her little brother, Michael, was a successful doctor. She remembered her family standing up and clapping when they called her name. "Deirdre Bridge," her law professor called out, but Dee didn't hear her. "Deirdre Bridge," she called out again, while Dee stared at the professor standing at the dais. She could read her professor's lips forming her name. Dee slowly stood up, walked toward her, shook her hand, and finally took her diploma. She took a quick glance at her family, gave them a wave, and returned to her seat.

She watched the other graduates get their diplomas, smiles on their faces. Her head pounded. Was that really how she wanted to spend the rest of her life? Countless hours, depositions, law books, and listening to people she'd have to defend that were really guilty? It would probably take years before she could make partner at any of the firms. Who was she kidding? She had been studying all of her life. She wanted to have some downtime for herself. Oh my God, she couldn't do it. She didn't want to be a lawyer.

And that was the day she made her life-altering decision. Her family was so devastated, and her relationship with her father had been strained ever since.

"You want to be a what?" Her father looked at her like she had two heads.

"A flight attendant," Dee whispered.

Dee's father looked at her mother. "Wanda, you better talk to this girl. I didn't spend over a hundred thousand dollars for her to go and be something that doesn't even require a degree. You better talk to her, Wanda, 'cause I can't even look at her right now," he said as he walked out of the room, holding his head down.

Dee's mother looked at her as if someone close to her had just died. She spoke just above a whisper. "Why, honey? I don't understand." She raised her hands to touch Dee's face and brought them back down. Her hands were trembling, badly.

"I'm sorry, Mama. I don't know what's come over me. But I can't do this right now. I just don't have the energy."

"I thought you and Pam were going to do this together. All you have to do is pass the bar, baby. Can't you at least do that?"

Dee shook her head. "I'm scared, Mama. Pam is not afraid of anything. She'll ace it the first time. I know she will."

Dee's mother embraced her, holding her like she was three years old. "Tell Mama what you're afraid of."

"Michael is a successful doctor. Daddy and you have both done well as educators. You both have doctorates."

"And you have a law degree, baby. So what's the problem here? There's something you're not telling me."

"I'm afraid that I won't pass it the first time, Mama. I don't think I can. I couldn't bear to look at Pam or myself if I failed. So many wannabe lawyers have to take the test over and over again. No reputable law firm wants someone who can't even pass the test after so many tries."

"That's not true, Dee. Besides, why would you think you would be one of those people? You made it through law school and graduated at the top of your class."

"Mama, I've been under a lot of pressure. Pressure you would not believe. I made it, yes, but not without a lot of struggling, lots of caffeine, and sleepless nights. Don't get me wrong; I really do want to do this one day. Just not now, okay?"

Dee's mother couldn't believe what was coming out of her daughter's mouth. "Dee, your father is going to have a stroke and a heart attack over this. I can't be the one to tell him."

"Mama, please. I can't talk to him like you."

"I'm sorry, baby. I won't do it."

"Mama."

"No, Dee, it's your decision. You tell him."

A loud knock at the door and the ring of her cell phone broke her thoughts. Dee looked at her phone and saw that it was Tracey. The knock at the door grew louder.

"Hey, baby, you in there?"

Dee nervously squeezed the phone and waited for the call to go to voicemail. She couldn't deal with Tracey's issues when she had her own to deal with.

"Be right there, Chris!" Her lips quivered.

She immediately gulped down her second glass of wine and gave herself one last quick glance in the mirror. Quinton was right. Her jig was up.

Reroute

Amanda had mulled over her wardrobe for at least an hour. It had been seventeen years since she had seen Rickey. For the first time in a long time, she found herself concerned about fashion. She decided on a pink chiffon dress with ruffles around the bodice that flared a little bit at the hem. She held her breath as she turned around slowly and sucked in her stomach, picturing herself thirty pounds lighter and seventeen years younger. She had managed to make time for a hair appointment, which was a surprise both to her and her hairdresser, who saw Amanda only when she was taking Tracey to get her hair done.

Her long hair flowed to her shoulders. She'd removed her naturally tight curls with a relaxer, compliments of JE Sensation, the upscale hair salon that Tracey had been pleading with her to go to for years. She still couldn't believe that she'd paid $80 to do what a straightening comb would have done. But she had to admit her tamed curls and the sheen in her hair made her look at least five years younger.

She hesitated for a moment as she slipped on her black patent leather dress sandals with the two-inch heels. What was she doing? Rickey ignored Tracey her whole life and now he wanted to be a part of it? She was only fooling herself—the dress, the hair. She should just call him up and cancel. Better yet, she should just not show up.

The sound of the phone interrupted her thoughts. "Hello." Amanda answered.

"Hi, Mama." Tracey's voice sounded like something was bothering her. Amanda momentarily forgot about Rickey.

"What's the matter, baby?"

"Tony called me and told me about what happened at the airport."

Amanda was silent for a moment. "I see. Tracey, why didn't you just tell me about Rickey?" Tracey was silent. "Tracey? I know you hear me."

Tracey sighed. She was glad to be 600 miles away and not have to face her mother's wrath. "I just couldn't. Mama, I knew that you never would have let me see him if I told you."

"I don't understand. How long has this been going on, and how did you two get together in the first place? And what about Dee? You're confiding in her before even telling your own mother." Amanda felt a little woozy. How could she have not known? Her child was living right under the same roof, and she had no idea she was seeing him.

"Mama, just meet with him, and he'll tell you about it."

"How did you know that I was supposed to meet with him?"

"Tony overheard you two talking. He said that you thought he had left, but he stayed just in case something went down. He said that after Auntie Dee left, you and Daddy got stopped by an undercover police officer."

"He saw that?" Amanda felt so ashamed. And now, she was calling Rickey Daddy.

"Uh, huh. Mama, please, I know you. You are probably getting dressed right now and thinking about not showing up, aren't you?" Amanda nodded but didn't say anything. "Please, Mama, just go for me okay?"

"I don't think I like this Tracey. You lied to me. Everyone knew except me. You, Tony, Rickey, and Dee. If Melvin knew about this he would—I don't even want to think about it." The thought of Melvin's name made her tremble. He would be beside himself if he knew that she was meeting Tracey's father for dinner.

"I know, Mama, and I'm so sorry. I'm begging you to just listen to him. You'll feel different once you've heard him out."

Amanda sat on the bed and stared at her dress. She knew that deep down inside her heart ached to know the truth. But her pride stood in the way.

"Mama? Are you still there?"

"Tracey, I can't promise you anything right now. I can only say that I'll think about it."

"All right, Mama. Let me know what you decide, okay?"

"Bye, Tracey."

Unavoidable Tailspin

Dee's head was in a whirl. She ordered two large bottles of wine and had already had three glasses before Chris arrived. She answered the door with a hint of seduction in her eyes, and grabbed him and kissed him forcefully before he could get the door closed.

"Hey, there. I'm glad to see you, too," Chris said between gasps of air. "Whoa, slow down, Dee, give me a chance to get in here, baby," he said, pulling off his windbreaker. He started kissing her back just as enthusiastically. Dee ran her tongue behind his ear, onto his neck, and back inside his mouth. She paused and took a deep breath and stared at him with hopeful eyes.

"I guess I didn't realize how much I've missed you," she said as the wine took over her body.

He hugged her tightly. "I can see that. I've missed you too." He slowly pulled back and brushed the hair out of her face. "You look beautiful, baby. Something smells good up in here. Whatcha' got cookin'?" Chris teased.

Dee had completely forgotten about the food she ordered and remembered that she planned to tell him the truth over dinner. "Oh, you know, a little wine, lobster, and potatoes."

"Well, I'm down for a little *snack*," he laughed as he rubbed his hands together in anticipation as he made his way over to the table. Dee carefully poured the wine in the crystal glasses and handed one to Chris.

"Here's to a wonderful evening, and with the most beautiful female attorney in the world." He clinked her glass with his. The words hung in the air like a sword, and she spilled the wine down her blouse as she brought it to her mouth.

Dee laughed nervously. "Ooops! I guess I'm a little off balance today."

"Hey, it seems like you started the party before I got here," he said referring to the half-empty bottle of wine.

"You're right, I did," Dee giggled as she took a napkin, wiped the wine from her mouth, and sat across from him.

"Baby, you seem a little out of sorts today," he said as he cut off a small piece of lobster and raised it to his mouth.

"You might say that." Dee poured another glass and gulped it down.

Chris put down his knife and fork, folded his hands in his lap, and leaned in toward her. "Well, whatever it is, it has certainly got you all worked up. My baby hasn't even touched her food. And we both know how you love to eat," he teased. He walked over to her and gently massaged her shoulders.

"Oh, that feels so good."

"You need to tell that firm of yours that they need to put me on retainer to be your personal masseuse," he said as he kissed the nape of her neck. "Man, I wish I could see you work in the courtroom. I know you work it, too."

Dee's thoughts left her as she listened to his false impressions of her. "Chris, you are so silly, stop it."

"Well, it brought you out of that black mood you were in, didn't it?"

She grabbed his hands and pulled them toward her lips and kissed them. "I've got something important that I want to tell you."

He looked at her with his deep-set eyes. "What is it?" he whispered, as he gently ran his fingers through her hair and kissed her on the lips.

"Oh, Chris . . ." she said, as she nervously pulled away and poured herself another glass of wine.

"All right, Desiree, you're startin' to freak a brotha' out here. What's goin' on?"

Dee sat down on the couch with her head hung and her glass in her hand. "I don't know how to begin."

"Desiree, hold up." He started pacing nervously back and forth and then stood in front of her. "Are you pregnant?"

"Heavens, no!" Dee said, amazed that the conversation had taken such a turn. She placed her hand across his cheek and felt his smooth skin. "Believe me, that would be easier to handle than this."

"I don't understand. You're not pregnant. And it's more serious than that?"

"It depends on how you look at it."

Chris was really beginning to worry at this point. If it wasn't pregnancy then could it be an STD or even AIDS or HIV? He got up and went over to the table and poured himself a glass of wine, chugged it down, and then opened up the other bottle and poured another one.

"Chris? Are you all right?"

"I don't know, baby, that depends. You tell me," Chris held the bottle tightly in his hands and eyed her like he could see straight through her.

"Tell you?"

"Am I *all right*?" Chris said anxiously. "I mean, what's up with you? You ain't pregnant. What's goin' on? Something you need to disclose that I need to know? What's the big secret?"

"I do need to disclose something to you, I just don't know how to."

"Well, let me make it easy for you," Chris said as he poured himself another glass. "Whatever you got to say, just say it, okay?"

Dee had never seen this side of Chris before. He was agitated and looked mean. Was telling him really the right decision? She was foggy from the wine, and she hadn't really thought about how she would begin to tell him.

"All right, Chris," she said, as she felt her stomach flip. "This is probably not going to sound too good, especially coming from me." She stretched her hands over her head and tried to stand but tripped back onto the sofa. "Well, I guess I need to sit then, don't I?" She laughed hoping he would say something, but he remained stoic.

"Okay, I'll just come out and say it. The truth is that you really don't know who I am. And neither do I, for that matter," she said under her breath.

Chris watched her every move for any clue that could help him figure where the conversation was going. He drank another glass of wine. He was getting a bad feeling about Dee.

Dee had lost count of how many glasses she had as she stumbled toward him. She fumbled with her words as she tried to explain herself. "You see, baby," she said as she grabbed his limp hand. "I'm not the woman you think I am." *Did that come out right?* Dee giggled. Her head kept twirling as she was trying to put the sentences together. "You see, a *real* woman wouldn't do the things I've done.

I mean, I'm just not the *right* kind of woman, you know . . . I've been pretending to be someone else all this time instead of being honest with you and letting you know who I really am. I mean, I guess it could be worse—I could have AIDS or something. But thank God that's not the case. But *this* is not a good thing. I mean, we can work it out—that's if you want."

"So, this has nothing to do with you giving me some type of STD or something?"

"Oh, my! You didn't think that?" Dee doubled over with laughter.

Chris's expression did not change. "So what the hell are you talking about?" *I can't understand a damn thing that just came out of this ho's drunken mouth. What the fuck?* Suddenly he realized what she was referring to—something that he never dreamed would ever happen to him as a man. But, the same thing had happened to one of his team members recently. Same story. Different circumstances.

"Desiree, you don't have to say another word," he said as he lunged toward her.

"What in God's name are you doing?" Dee's face was filled with horror.

"I'm going to start with kicking your ass, and if you're lucky you can leave on your flight tomorrow with your teeth still in your mouth!" Chris started to raise his fists in the air.

"What the . . . I can't believe you would hit a woman!"

"I don't hit *women*! But I do hit men who PRETEND to be women!" Chris started swinging at her jaw as she ducked underneath him. "This is just like that old ass movie *The Crying Game* . . . when the man is falling for this woman and later finds out that the woman he's been seeing . . . is really a man!" He came after her again and swung. Dee ducked as his fists missed her by only a few inches. "Damn you, Desiree! Or whatever the hell your name is!"

"Chris, stop it, you fool! I'm not a man."

"If you were a female, you wouldn't be able to duck like that," he said as he lunged toward her, and she managed to dart past him again.

She grabbed him forcefully by the arm and started to scream. "Are you some kind of crazy? Stop and listen to what I have to say!"

"Don't touch me, you faggot! I'll kill you!" Chris yelled. He reached for the empty wine bottle and broke it on the table as he raced toward Dee. "I bet you won't be able to duck this!" He pinned her up against the wall with his arm and began to choke her. He took his other hand and raised the bottle toward her head.

Dee gasped for air. "Chris, I AM A REAL WOMAN!"

"I don't believe you!" he screamed, as he brought the bottle closer to her head.

"Chris! Stop," Dee pleaded between gasps of air. She gave him a swift kick to his groin and broke away from his grasp. He unleashed her throat as she ran to the bed, holding her neck and coughing from lack of oxygen. "I'm not a man Chris, I swear to you I'm not a man," she said as she broke down on the bed and cried.

Chris was on the other side of the room, still in unrelenting pain from Dee's powerful kick. Tears were rolling down his cheek as he dropped to the floor and rolled around, moaning.

"Then who the hell are you?" Chris was barely able to speak.

"I'm a flight attendant and my real name is Deirdre Bridge not Desiree Bradshaw. My nickname is Dee," she said between sobs.

Chris was silent. He was in too much pain to ask her to repeat what she had just said. She could see the question in his face. "I'm a flight attendant, and I've been going by a false name," Dee repeated softly. "I'm Dee. The waitress in the sky," she said somberly.

Chris shook his head hard. The pain was still excruciating, but he needed to understand the words that were coming from her mouth. Dee understood clearly what his eyes were saying and his mouth could not speak. She looked at him pitifully and cried even harder. "I'm not an attorney. I've been ashamed of what I do for a living, and I wanted to be someone that I thought people would respect!"

Chris finally managed to speak again, despite the throbbing pain that was still jolting through his body. "You've been lying to me all of these months?"

"Yes."

"And T? That's why you never could come through for him, huh?"

Dee nodded.

"I didn't understand it at first, but now it's clear why you were so uncomfortable in the restaurant and had to have Quint's friend, Amanda, come and tell me you left because you were suddenly ill. Now, I get it! You weren't sick at all! I had called your bluff and you weren't ready for it." He looked at Dee and lowered his head. She hadn't seen that look since she'd told her father that she was not going to become an attorney.

"How do I know that you are telling me the truth now?"

"Go look in my purse."

"If I can get up after that kick, I'd be Superman," he said as he slowly tried to get up off the floor. An unexpected twinge pulled him back down to his knees. His head was also throbbing from the wine.

"I'm sorry, Chris. But I thought you were going to kill me," she said as she walked over to the dresser to get her purse.

"Oh, I was. Don't get me wrong." He thought about how he'd seen his entire career flash before his eyes right before Dee kicked him. He was so scared by the thought of how he'd lost his self-control that he forgot about his pain and managed to pick himself up from the floor. "Where in the hell did you ever learn to duck like that?"

"I take kickboxing."

"That figures," he said, as he finally caught his breath. "Something else that I don't know about you."

"Here," she said. She was still feeling a little light-headed from the wine, but managed to pull the contents she was looking for out of her purse. "Take a look at this."

"Is *this* what you wanted me to see? Your airline ID? So what does that prove?"

"Go look in the closet," she said walking him toward it.

"Flight attendant uniforms. So what?" Chris said as he sifted through them. "You could have purchased all of this stuff just to tell me another lie. And anyone could have a fake ID. Every time I looked in your closet before, you had a briefcase, double breasted suits—the works!"

"I thought you'd feel that way. That's why I want you to come downstairs with me when I check out so that you can meet the crew that I fly with."

"You've got to be joking."

"No, I'm not. I'm more serious than I have ever been in my life, Chris."

"Listen, Desiree . . . I mean Deir . . . Oh, hell! I'm not coming down to meet anybody. Especially not after a night like this."

"Look, Chris. I've been lying for a long time. All I want to do is be truthful for once. Even if you don't want to have anything else to do with me, at least we could end this relationship with the truth. *The real truth.*"

"I've had all the *truths* that I can take for one night."

"All right, then, if you don't want to meet my flight crew, then let me give this to you," she said, pulling an envelope from her purse.

"What's this?"

"It's an airline ticket."

"For what? You don't think that I'm about to fly some place with you do you?"

"Chris, it's an open ticket for you to see me work a flight. Maybe you'll forgive me eventually, and take advantage of it when your schedule permits."

"I don't think I can take any more of your *work*, Dee. Besides I don't need a *free* ticket from *you*."

"Won't you please let me try and make something right out of all of this?"

"No, I've got to get out of here," he said despondently. "The sight of you is making me physically ill. Here, take this back," he said handing her the ticket. "I certainly won't be needing it."

"Okay, maybe I'll see you later? I know you need some time to digest all of this." Her mouth quivered as she tried to hold back her tears.

Chris was tired of her performance and wanted to leave before the second act of her show. "Yeah, much *later*," he said as he grabbed his jacket and limped toward the doorway to let himself out.

Damaged Belongings

Dee felt as if she had been hit by an assembly line of cars. All she wanted to do was curl up with a good book and pretend that yesterday had never happened. She reveled in the fact that she and Pam's schedules were so opposite that they rarely were ever home at the same time. Today she was really looking forward to being home alone.

She slid the key into the doorknob, opened the door and pulled her luggage through. Without warning, her hopes of solitude were dashed. Still clad in her silk pajamas, Pam was sitting in the kitchen, reading the newspaper, and sipping a cup of coffee.

"Hey, what's up?" Dee walked in the kitchen and pretended to sound like she was happy to see her.

"Hey, girl," Pam said sluggishly. Her eyes stared out blankly at the bare branches that tapped softly against the kitchen windowpane.

Dee glanced down at her watch. "Pam, what are you doing at home in the middle of the morning?"

"Huh?" Pam answered, still preoccupied with the branch's images.

Dee sat down next to her. "I said, what are you doing home?"

"I'm taking a little time off, that's all."

"You?"

"Uh huh," Pam said, continuing to sip her coffee and stare outside.

Dee got up and placed her hand over Pam's forehead. "No fever. So what's really going on with you? Does this time off have anything to do with you and Amanda?"

"My answer remains the same. I'm taking some time off."

"You said that already, but why now?"

"I don't think I've taken a vacation in three years, and I deserve it." Pam sounded like she was trying to convince herself. She placed the cup carefully on the table and wandered toward the rays that were coming through the window, feeling the sun's warmth.

"Pam, I don't know what's going on, but I do know you well enough to know that this is not like you," she said thoughtfully. She looked down on the floor and saw a small stack of papers sitting next to her chair. Dee scanned the statements from each of the paralegals in the office. Amanda Shipman was typed on every document. She walked over and placed her arm around Pam, who stood erect, managing to hold back her tears.

"I was right. You are home because of this issue with Amanda. What is happening with the two of you? This is so out of control!"

Pam chuckled slightly as she walked over to the coffee maker and poured herself another cup.

"What does this mean?"

"Well, according to the firm, I won't be selected for partnership at this time." She choked on the words. "I mean, why would they make me partner if so many paralegals are afraid to work with me, right?" Pam turned her head back toward the window.

"Well, is any of it true? Any of it at all?"

Pam turned around and looked at Dee like she had just knifed her in the back. "Look, I work damn hard and have made that firm a helluva lot of money. And if you—or anyone else, for that matter—think that I'm going to let one whining bitch run through the firm and get all of these other whining-ass bitches to make besmirching and false accusations about me, then you're just as bad as they are! The only difference is that I'm not going to sue *you*!" Pam slammed down her coffee cup, spilling its contents onto the countertop before tearing out of the kitchen.

Dee followed Pam and stood in the doorway of her bedroom. It was hard to believe that she was talking about the same person that they went to Spelman with not so long ago. "Pam . . . I'm sorry . . . I didn't mean to imply that—"

"Leave me the fuck alone, Dee! It's bad enough that they won't even let me confront her to defend myself, and now I've got to defend myself to you, too! *All* of you can just go straight to hell!" Pam yelled, slamming the door in her face. Despite her better judgment, Dee opened Pam's door slightly and stood in the doorway.

"Pam, don't take this out on me. I was only trying to find out what was true and what wasn't."

Pam shot her an inquisitive look and all of a sudden she seemed miraculously calmer. "I know . . . I would have asked the same thing. I mean, it's what any good attorney would do, right?"

"Very funny, Pam. I'm not going to let you turn this into a discussion about me, okay? So, what are you going to do about this? I know you. I'm sure you've already got a plan."

"I really don't know yet."

"I find that really hard to believe, Pam. You? Listen, I don't know how all of this has spun so out of control, but I do know that Amanda is *one of us*. You can't allow this to happen. This relationship has to be salvaged."

"Why?"

"Because I can't come between you and her. I have a relationship with Tracey *and* Amanda, and I can't stand to see the two of you going at it like this."

Pam shook her head solemnly. "I'm just so damn mad right now that all I can do is picture myself placing my hands around the necks of Amanda and those pompous bastards!" She picked up a pillow from her bed and tossed it across the room, missing Dee's head by a few inches.

"Ooookay," Dee remarked, as she darted out of the way. "Maybe you *should* take a couple of weeks off and sort through this whole ordeal."

"I know. I really do need some time to think about it. I'm just so pissed off."

"I can see that, and I'll leave you to your thoughts, okay?" Dee started walking toward the den as Pam suddenly eased up.

"Hey listen, I shouldn't be taking my problems out on you. Please, come back. My bark is worse than my bite," Pam managed to crack a smile. "It's been a while since we've really talked. I've missed that."

Dee sat down next to her on the bed. "Are you sure?"

Pam glanced down and lifted Dee's hand. "It's good to see your hand is back to normal," she said as she eased it back down. "How are things going with *you*?"

Dee's eyes shifted away from Pam. She was surprised to see the conversation quickly turn toward her and Pam's sudden interest in her hand. "All right, I guess." *My hand is the only thing that is back to normal.*

"Just all right?"

Dee nodded hastily. She definitely didn't want Pam to know what had happened in Miami. "Hey, all is good over this way. I think you've got enough of your own problems at this point. You certainly don't need to hear mine."

"Hey, I guess we are both batting zeroes this week, huh?" Pam made the number with her thumb and middle finger as the phone rang. "Dee, hold on a sec. Hello?"

"Hello. May I speak to the most irresistible, smart, and beautiful woman in the room?"

"Hey there, Marc," Pam said. Her eyes suddenly lit up, and she managed to form a half-smile.

"I called you at the office and was surprised to hear you were on vacation."

"I know. I hadn't had the chance to tell anybody yet. It came up kind of suddenly."

"Is everything all right?"

"Yes, I'm fine. It's nothing I can't handle. Hey, can you call me back a little later?"

Dee shook her head no. "We'll talk later," Dee whispered, as she left the room.

"Okay, I'm back," Pam said into the receiver.

"Do you need to go?"

"No, it's okay . . ."

"Listen, I really want to see you again—kind of make up for the last time."

"Marc, I don't think so. I wouldn't be very good company right now."

"What do you mean? You should be on top of the world, lady! You have it all!" He was referring to the partnership he *thought* she had gotten by now. Pam could barely speak. Her throat felt like it was filled with cotton balls.

"Pam, are you there?"

Pam said nothing. She wanted to, but the words would not come out. She stared into the receiver and quietly hung it up. *I'm sorry.*

Cruising Altitude

The main lobby of Vini Vidi Vici was filled with people waiting for a table in the trendy restaurant. Amanda made her way back to the bar, sauntering through the smoke and extreme noise. There he was. He was seated and handsomely dressed in a tailored, charcoal gray three-button Italian suit, which he accessorized with a light gray shirt and tie.

Amanda's heart seemed to stop momentarily as old feelings surfaced. *What am I thinking? I'll get what I came here for, and then I'm gone,* Amanda thought defiantly.

"Hey Amanda, over here," Rickey said. His dark eyes penetrated the crowd as he walked toward her. The smell of his cologne was making Amanda weak. No matter how hard she tried to deny it, Rickey still looked good, even after all these years.

"Hi, Rickey." Her tone was cool as she suddenly remembered his arrogance at the airport.

"Wow! Look at you," he said hoping to warm the chill between them. She looked as stiff as the Mona Lisa. He touched her. "You look gorgeous, lady. I didn't realize your hair was so long."

How could you? You haven't seen me in seventeen years, Rickey. "Thank you." She patted her hair awkwardly. His hair looked as if it had just been freshly cut.

"It makes you look about five or six years younger," he said, as he found himself unconsciously reaching out to touch it. He loved women whose hairstyles looked natural. No extensions, no weaves.

Uncomfortable with his touch, Amanda pulled back slightly. "So, when will our table be ready?"

Rickey felt her uneasiness and pulled his hand back. "The waitress said in about ten more minutes. Do you want a drink?"

"Sure, why not?"

"Hmmmm . . . let me see, you look like an apple martini or cosmopolitan woman." He eyed her up and down as he signaled to the bartender to take their drink orders.

Amanda didn't know why, but she felt herself blushing. "Either will be fine," she said. She found it oddly coincidental that he knew her favorite drinks. *Did Tracey tell him that, too?*

"Is that a smile I see seeping out of those cheeks, Ms. Shipman?"

Her smile quickly faded. "Rickey, don't get carried away. I'm only here for Tracey."

"As am I," he said, taking the drinks from the bartender. He tapped his glass with hers. "To Tracey!"

"Sir, your table is ready," the waitress interjected.

Thank goodness, Amanda thought. *I don't know how much longer I can stand this.*

Rickey pulled Amanda's chair out, holding her drink while she took off her coat. "Here let me take that for you," he said, taking a quick look at her behind.

"Thank you."

Rickey nodded and gave Amanda a quick once-over. She had gotten a lot heavier since high school, but she was still a looker, and to him, she had the finest behind in Georgia. Amanda still had the same sweet personality that had made her so popular in high school even though she was hanging onto her poker face.

"I'll give you a few minutes to look over the menu and then I'll be right back," the waitress said.

"I already know what I want," Amanda said, quickly glancing over the menu and handing it back to her. "Let me get the salmon with a side salad."

"*Salmone with an insalta verde*. Good choice." The waitress scribbled down her order then turned to Rickey. "And you, sir?"

Rickey looked over the menu. "I'll have the veal cutlet and a garden salad, also."

"Great! *Scallopine al funghi and insalta verde.* I'll be back shortly with your dinner."

Amanda waited until the waitress left the table before she spoke. "Okay, Rickey, let's skip the formalities, all right? You got me here to talk about *my* daughter, so let's do that."

"You mean *our* daughter, don't you?"

Amanda shook her head somberly. "I said what I meant. Now, you tell me what is going on with you."

"Well, how about you start first."

"Me?"

"Why not *you*?"

Amanda could feel her tears waiting to fall. "Look, *I'm* not the one who wanted to meet after all of these years. You did! And as far as I'm concerned, you have been an MIA father since the day *my* child was born."

"And that's how you wanted it," Rickey flared. It took all of his strength to keep from raising his voice.

"Just stop it, Rickey." She caught herself before she lost control, just as another couple looked over at them. She immediately lowered her voice. "You never once answered any of my letters."

"All right, here we go again with that."

"Yes, here we go *again*," Amanda said, annoyed.

"Look, Amanda, the first time I had even *seen* your letters was when Tracey showed them to me." Rickey paused. "Damn it . . ." he mumbled under his breath.

"Tracey, what?"

Rickey looked like a little boy who had accidentally let out the big family secret. "Nothing."

"No. Please repeat what you just said."

The waitress came back with their food and set it down on the table. "Would either of you care for some freshly ground pepper?"

"No!" they both shouted at the same time. The waitress looked as if she might cry.

"Listen, we're sorry." Rickey's voice was sincere.

"He's right. We didn't mean to yell at you, really. Please accept our apologies," Amanda added.

"We'll let you know if we need anything else," Rickey chimed in. The waitress nodded and briskly walked away.

Rickey's voice grew calmer. "Listen, I wasn't supposed to say anything about it, but Tracey showed me some letters you had written and for some reason, I never got 'em."

Amanda clenched her teeth. "But how did she know where I kept them?"

"She said she happened to find them one day when she was cleaning out your closet."

Amanda nibbled on her salad, thinking back to when Tracey had last helped her with her closet. That was three months ago. Right when Tracey started acting distant.

"Amanda, I swear to you I never got those letters."

"Well, they were all returned unopened and in an envelope. Dummy me just kept sending and sending again, hoping you would open just one that had Tracey's picture in it. Just one!" she said, angrily stabbing her fish and shoving a tiny piece in her mouth.

"Amanda, this is mind boggling. I never got them. I swear. And it's not like I didn't try to reach you either."

"Rickey, stop it." She firmly placed the fork down on the side of her plate, restraining herself from stabbing him with it. "The only thing I've ever received from you is a transfer of funds from your account to mine for child support."

Rickey thought about what Amanda was saying. When Amanda had gotten pregnant, he was busy playing for Notre Dame. And with the NFL scouting him big time, his mother decided that she would be the one to handle his personal affairs. She had been the one to set up the bank account and wire the money. He didn't have time to do anything except play football. She opened his mail and—

"No, she wouldn't!" he said out loud to himself.

Amanda raised her eyebrow at him. "What did you say?"

Rickey sipped his drink. "Nothin'."

They were both silent. Amanda watched him as he slowly chewed his veal. His mustache didn't have a hair out of place, and his skin was as smooth as chocolate brown satin. Rickey's good looks remained true to him over the years. Too bad the rest of him was such a lie.

"Okay, Rickey, it's pretty evident that we are not going to be able to resolve the letter issue, but can you at least be truthful about how you found Tracey?"

Rickey's face showed his disappointment that she still did not believe him. "Fair enough. Well, if you don't believe me about the letters, I doubt if you'll believe me about how I met Tracey."

"You're probably right. But tell me anyway," Amanda sneered.

Rickey shook his head and looked at her intensely. "All right, Miss Smarty. But don't say I didn't warn you."

Amanda rolled her eyes and felt the urge to just get up and leave. What a waste of time it was coming down here to meet him. He wouldn't know the truth if it crawled out from under the table and set him on fire.

"Amanda, I'm telling you, it was so surreal. I was on the radio about the same time Tracey found those letters, I guess. It was Kiss FM, I think," he said, tapping his fingers on the table, trying to remember. "The interview was about young men who were getting drafted from their second year in college and going right into the NFL, like I did."

"Rickey, will you just get to the point, please? I didn't come here to listen to your stories about your radio interviews or your—"

"I know, but this has everything to do with Tracey," he pleaded.

Amanda sat back, impatiently folding her arms across her chest and nodding for him to go on with the story.

"Anyway, I swear they must have answered fifty calls, but it was that last one that blew everyone away. I'll never forget it. DJ Cal said, 'We only have a few minutes on the line here with Rickey Mavers. What's your question?' A young woman's voice blazed through the phone like a flare gun. She said, 'I'd like to ask Mr. Mavers why he has not seen his daughter in seventeen years?'"

Amanda opened her mouth to speak but managed only to gasp.

Rickey paused for a moment. "You asked me to tell you about how Tracey and I got together. I know you want to know, but do you think you can handle the truth?"

Amanda nodded slowly. She wasn't sure. If the rest of the story was going to be more dramatic than this, then maybe she needed another drink. She signaled the waitress with her glass to bring her another cosmopolitan. She couldn't remember the last time she'd had alcohol, and it had been even longer since she had two drinks back-to-back.

Rickey chuckled to himself, watching Amanda take another sip of her drink as soon as the waitress set it down. He knew how she felt. He'd felt the same way when he heard Tracey's voice for the first time.

"Anyway, Cal looked at me, and I must have been in total shock as he scribbled onto a piece of paper, 'You wanna answer this, man?' I was speechless. The lines on the phone lit up like a string of white Christmas lights. Then Cal picked up the line she was on and asked if she wanted to leave a contact name and number where I could call her. She said, matter-of-factly, 'He knows my name, and as for my number, it's 404-555-6189.' I couldn't take any more calls after that! They had to break right into a commercial."

Amanda stared into space. She didn't know if she was in shock from Rickey's story or if she was just tipsy. "Rickey, I don't know what to say. What did you do?"

"Well, Cal came over to me and said, 'Hey, man, you all right?' I could only shake my head slowly from side to side. I said, 'I can barely breathe, man.' He had one of his staff members go and get me some water and the phones were still lighting up like crazy and then he asked me, 'What you wanna do, man?' I couldn't do nothin'. Not a damn thing." He took another sip of his drink and closed his eyes. "The call just made me weak, you know? Like I had just been hit in the gut with a sledgehammer."

Amanda had rested her hand on the side of her face as she listened intently. She was still speechless and numb. Was this really Tracey he was talking about? It didn't sound like her.

"Anyway, Cal went back on the air, hoping—and I mean praying—that he would come up with something since I'd left him swimming in the deepest part of the ocean without a life jacket. I heard him say 'Yo! Listen up everybody, Rickey's gotta handle his business right now, but we gon' get him back here after he's straightened it out.' He looked me dead in the eyes. 'Right, man?' I was so weak; all I could say was 'Yeah.' His assistant had offered to give me some privacy in their reading area. I had to get out of there. I just asked for the number that Cal had written down on a piece of paper and then told her to tell Cal that I would holla at him later. I cursed your name all the way home that night," he said, looking at her with resentment for the first time that evening.

"Cursed me, why?"

"Cause I felt like you never told her about me. She hated me. She thought *I* was the reason why she never knew me."

"Rickey, have you forgotten? You *are* the reason."

"No, I'm not! I keep trying to tell you that, but you won't listen to me."

Amanda looked at him hopelessly. He had really convinced himself that he was not at fault. She relented for the moment as she carefully posed her next question. "So, did you end up calling her that evening?"

"Naw, you kiddin' me? I had to wait about a week before I could get up the nerve to call her." He paused again and took another sip of his drink. "When I finally *did* get up the nerve to call her, she answered the phone and my stomach just felt like it had just gone down a roller coaster slope. I told her that calling her up on the phone was a little awkward."

"Yeah, I bet," Amanda interrupted.

"I even told her that I wasn't sure if she was who she said she was."

"Oh, I'll bet she had something to say about that."

Rickey shook his head. "Man, that girl is somethin' else. You know what she said to me?" Amanda shook her head. She found herself hanging onto every word. "She said, 'Oh, I can show you all of Mama's bank receipts with your electronic transfers on it for my child support if you need proof that I'm really your daughter!'"

"And that's when you knew?" Amanda asked, still having a hard time believing that this was *her* daughter that they were talking about.

"I knew even before then. She sounds just like you, Amanda. And then she mentioned the little picture that you still keep hidden in your wallet of us at senior prom and asked if I would like her to bring that to me as well. Is that true? Do you still carry it around with you?" Amanda's silence answered his question. "May I see it?"

Amanda shook her head, her hands trembling around her glass. "Please, Amanda. I would love to see it. May I?"

Amanda couldn't believe that he knew her secret. She had always kept it in her wallet. It reminded her of the good times she used to have with him. Reluctantly, she reached for her purse and pulled out the picture.

"You had it laminated?" Rickey said surprised that she'd preserved it.

"Yeah, I guess I did," she said, feeling embarrassed. She had looked at it so often that it had become worn and tattered.

"Tracey really knows you, doesn't she?"

Amanda smiled. "Too well, I suppose. I've really underestimated her." She put the picture back in her wallet. She was afraid to ask her next question, but knew she had to. "So did you two start seeing each other shortly after that?"

Rickey nodded. "That same evening. And just about every evening after that when I was in Atlanta." He paused reflectively. "I was even in town the night of her graduation party."

Rickey looked up at Amanda and saw that tears were streaming down her cheeks. "Amanda, here, take this," he said, giving her his napkin. He raised his arm and called the waitress over. The waitress came over and gave them a strange look. "Is everything all right?"

"Yes, we're fine. May I just have the bill, please?"

"No dessert?" she said, handing him the check.

He handed her two hundred dollars. "No, we're leaving. Please keep the change."

"Gee, thanks," she said marveling at her 60 percent tip.

"No problem. Thanks for putting up with us." He looked over at Amanda, who was still wiping tears from her face. He took her by the hand, "C'mon, let me get you out of here."

"No, wait. I'll be okay."

"Listen, you're not okay. Just look at you. I was just as shocked as you were when Tracey contacted me."

Amanda cried again, and this time Rickey put his arm around her and escorted her out of the restaurant.

With their hands clasped together, they ran across 14th Street like two runaway kids darting between oncoming cars.

"Where are you taking me?"

"My suite at the Four Seasons," he said as the doorman opened the lobby door.

"No, Rickey."

"I just want us to talk in a more private setting," he pleaded.

Amanda looked at him suspiciously. Rickey did a scouts honor symbol and then pushed the elevator button. It opened immediately. "After you," he said, letting her get into the elevator first.

As they rode the elevator to the 40th floor, Amanda's ears popped a little. Rickey could sense her uneasiness as she kept her attention focused on the numbers lighting up at the top of the door. "We're here," he said as the doors pulled open as if in command of his voice.

They walked to his room, and he slid the key into the door. Amanda felt her body heat rise again as she caught herself staring at his physique. She watched his smooth hands push the door open and walk in first, signaling for her to follow him after he turned on the light.

"Rickey, this is really nice," Amanda said walking over to the black baby grand piano. She ran her fingers across the keys. It sat perched directly in front of the floor-to-ceiling windows. Across from it was a fifteen-foot sectional suede couch spread across the back of the wall. Across from that was a double fireplace that offered a sneak preview of the master bedroom.

"Thanks, I used to spend a lot of evenings here back when I played ball. C'mon, let me show you the rest of it."

Rickey took Amanda by the hand and led her on the tour of the two-bedroom suite, which ended with the most elegant bedroom she had ever seen. Imported tapestries hung from the walls, and a large chandelier was the focal point in the ceiling, bathing the room in a romantic glow. The bed sat high above the floor, accentuated with four ornate posts that looked to be at least two feet wide.

"This sure is a lot of hotel for one person."

"Well, I wasn't always single, Amanda."

Amanda knew he had gotten married. It had been in all of the papers and on television. *Nurse Leaves the Medical Field and Enters the Major League.* "Yes, I know. Whatever happened to you and your wife?'

"You mean my *ex-wife*, Delores," Rickey said sternly.

"Okay, I stand corrected. Your ex-wife."

Rickey was silent for a few moments and then started to move toward her and stopped. "It was a big mistake. You know, I didn't even see it coming."

"So, Delores gave you a shot of your own medicine, huh?"

Rickey laughed. "Yeah, I guess you could say that. Man, it seems like a lifetime ago. Women are just so forward now."

"You mean *some* women, don't you?"

"Oh, no offense to you, Amanda. But, nowadays, whew," he said as he took off his suit jacket and draped it across the sofa in the sitting area of the bedroom. Amanda saw his muscles through his onion-thin cotton shirt. He was still in great shape, she thought, catching herself again staring at his chiseled body.

Rickey sat down and rested his head on the back of the sofa, keeping his eye on Amanda who was still standing. "Sometimes every day was like Christmas for me. There was a time when I looked at women as beautifully wrapped packages and could open one up each day of the week."

"Hmm, so I heard." *What an asshole!*

"Hey, I didn't mean to offend you, really."

"No offense taken, Rickey. After all, I would only be lying to myself if I didn't say I was curious as to what you've been doing all of these years."

Rickey took off his tie and opened the top two buttons on his shirt. Amanda got a quick preview of the smooth skin. She quickly turned her head around, embarrassed that he'd caught her staring at him.

"When we lost contact—"

"You mean when you never made contact with me!"

"Amanda, I still stand firm on what I said. I mean, damn it. I loved you and even though a baby wasn't in my plans—"

"You wanted me to have an abortion!"

"Yes, at first I did, but I knew that wasn't what you wanted, so we agreed that you would have the baby."

"So, how come I never heard from you, huh? You accepted a scholarship to Notre Dame and then you were gone. I never heard from you again. The next thing I know, you're the number one draft pick and then you're off playing pro football."

"I tried to make contact with you, I swear."

"Here you go again with that lame excuse."

"Amanda, I did, I swear. It's just that Mama wouldn't—"

"Your mother wouldn't what?"

Rickey got up from the sofa and walked in the opposite direction of Amanda.

"Rickey, your mother wouldn't what?"

Rickey turned slowly toward her and looked at her with turned down eyes. He inhaled and then released his breath. "I think Mama is responsible for me not getting your letters and for you not getting mine."

"But why would she do that? I was about to enter my freshman year at Spelman. I was having your baby and her grandbaby!"

"Amanda, you've got to understand. When my father died, she had to be responsible for my younger brother and me. Daddy had a good pension, but she still had to work to provide for Kyle and me. She didn't want anything or anyone to stand in the way of us being successful. When I told her you were pregnant, she told me that she would handle it."

"Well, she handled it, all right."

Rickey nodded. "She did. And I would write letters to you and leave them for Mama to mail."

"And she never did . . ." Amanda's voice trailed off. "So, weeks turned into months, and months turned into several years, and all the while your mother was tampering with the mail. *She* was the one writing return to sender on all of my letters! She ruined our whole lives! She should be behind bars! Things could have been so different between us!"

"I know, Amanda. I just didn't realize it back then, you know?"

"I know," Amanda said sarcastically. "You were just too tied up with football."

Rickey dropped his head, humiliated as Amanda continued to chastise him. "But why didn't you just try and call me, Rickey? You could have at least called my parents."

"I did! Twice. I spoke with your father both times."

"He never told me."

"Well, he told me that you didn't want anything to do with me. And he talked about how disappointed he was with me and how I hurt you. He thought that it was in everyone's best interest that I leave you and the baby alone. Shoot, he even threatened me."

"Daddy?"

"Told me that if he ever saw my face, I wouldn't be capable of ever playing for another team again. He'd make sure of it! Shoot, that was enough to stop me tryin' to get in contact with you!"

Amanda's body shook, overcome with grief and pain. Rickey placed his arms around her as she felt herself dissolve into tears as Rickey spoke.

"That's when I decided to move on. I ran the women for a long time and then I got injured playing football."

"I remember reading about it," Amanda managed to say through her sniffles, feeling Rickey's fingers gently brushing her tears away.

"Delores was my nurse while I was in the hospital. We dated for a few months and, like a dummy, I thought she was in love with me. I found out she was in love with my money."

"That's too bad, Rickey."

"Yeah, for *her* it was. Fortunately for me, Mama was adamant about me getting a pre-nup. She hated Delores." Rickey laughed. "Old girl went out of the marriage with what she came in with. Nothing."

"Good 'ol Mama, huh?" Amanda said under her breath.

"Well, she was then. She's gotten old, feeble, and forgetful now," Rickey said sadly. "I had to place her in a nursing home when she started being a danger to herself. But she's in great hands."

Amanda felt her barriers wash away with her tears as Rickey spoke. He walked over to her and lifted her face, then kissed her on the mouth. "I've never stopped loving you, Amanda, and I never will."

Amanda could not think logically. She was so full of emotion that she allowed her passion to override her common sense. As she welcomed his kiss with an open mouth and a slip of her tongue, she suddenly felt her feet leave the ground. Amanda couldn't believe his strength. He lifted her up almost effortlessly, despite her weight, and laid her on the bed, stroking her long hair and caressing her breasts as he moved his fingers gingerly down the front of her dress and back up her thighs. Maneuvering his way to her backside, he gripped it and spread it open like ripe cantaloupe, hardly able to contain himself. He lifted her up with ease again, and removed her panty hose as his tongue found her sweet spot. She moved further down the bed, giving him permission for his fingers and his tongue to delve deeper.

Amanda moaned as she thought about how long she had dreamed of this moment. She still loved him. She still wanted him. And now she was alone with him in his bed, feeling the swell of his emotions rush inside of her. And, after seventeen years, she had finally forgiven him.

Lost and Found

"Oh c'mon, Pam. Stop turning the poor guy down!"

"Well, since you seem to care about his feelings so much, then why don't you go out with him instead?" Pam placed the exquisite bouquet of oriental white lilies that Marc had just sent her into a vase. She had been avoiding his calls for several days, and he obviously thought this would be a good way to get her attention.

"So, is this the same guy that sent you those other exotic flowers, too?" Dee asked.

"Exotic flowers?"

"Oh, come on, girl, don't play dumb."

Pam looked at her strangely until she remembered that Marc had sent her some flowers a while back. "Yes, he did send me some flowers. I had no idea what you were talking about."

"How could you forget something as beautiful as those flowers?"

"Yes, they were lovely, but to tell you the truth, I hadn't had much time to even think about them. I was in the middle of the Tyfish case."

"Yeah, obviously," Dee said, looking at Pam suspiciously.

"I'm serious, girl. It was no big deal, really."

"Well, the poor guy is obviously trying to make you think otherwise. What does he do for a living, anyway?

"He's a shrink, believe it or not."

"Really? You ever talk to him about anything personal?"

Pam stopped arranging the flowers and gave Dee a puzzled look. "You're kidding, right? No way! And if I did have some issues, he would not be the one that I would tell them to."

"Why not?" *You need to talk with somebody.*

"Dunno. Just not my thing, I guess."

"Well, I want to meet this man. Shoot! Ain't no need in both of us sitting around lonely. What's his name, anyway?"

"Marc something. It's so long, I can't really remember it. Listen, if you're interested in meeting him, I can set you up with him, okay?"

"Girl, I don't want to take *your* man!"

"He's not *mine* to take. Believe me. But if I did set you up with him, you know who will be upset."

"Who?"

"Sedrick!" She looked at Dee and laughed.

"Oh, yeah, right! Whatever, girl. Seriously, though, why don't you just give the guy a chance?"

"Why don't *you* just give Sedrick a chance?"

"C'mon, Pam. That's not fair and you know it. Besides, I hear that's he's seeing some new woman now."

Pam laughed. "Like she's competition for you?"

"Sedrick and I are good friends."

"Because that's how *you* want it. He's been wantin' you since freshman year and you know it."

"Here you go again . . ."

"Listen, I'll tell you what," Pam said, choosing her words carefully. "If you get more open-minded about Sedrick, I'll *think* about getting more open-minded with Marc what's his name." Pam giggled. "Is it a deal?"

"You know what, Pam? Just seeing you even entertain the thought of dating again makes me happy. I can't wait to meet this man."

"So, you're saying you'll be open minded about Sed?"

"I'm not making any promises I can't keep, okay? But, I do have a better deal."

"I'm afraid to ask. But, what is that?"

"If you agree to make amends with Amanda, I'll arrange the meeting and be there for the extra support."

"Leave it alone, Dee."

"But—"

"LET IT GO!"

Lost Baggage

Dee had managed to catch the first flight to Salt Lake City. She hadn't eaten much and was looking depressed when the doctor entered. He wore a dark chocolate double-breasted Armani suit and looked as if he could grace the cover of *GQ Magazine.*

"Dee, what's going on with you today?" He sensed Dee's uneasiness in her body language. He walked over to the chair and sat down to face her. Dee had decided to take a different position in the room and pulled her chair in front of his desk. Her hands were folded tightly across her breasts, and her legs looked as if they had been fused together.

"I did it."

"Did what?"

"I finally told Chris the truth."

"Well, congratulations, Dee. You passed your first assignment!"

Dee's lips quivered as she unsuccessfully attempted to close them together. She was barely able to hold back tears.

The doctor handed her a tissue and folded his hands across the top of his desk. Dee blew her nose, took another tissue, and wiped her eyes. "Then why aren't I happy, and why is it that all I do now is cry? I mean, I have nothing to look forward to anymore. I'm so tired and just want to be happy again," she said, feeling the tears slide down her cheeks as she buried her head in her hands. "See what I mean?" She looked at the doctor pitifully as her chest heaved with sobs.

"Now, now, Dee. It's all right—really. This is a good thing."

Dee had a puzzled look on her face. "I'm not sure I understand you, Doc."

"You are regaining your life again, Dee. Can't you see that?" he said.

"Oh, I can't keep doing *this,*" she said, her words sticking in her throat.

"You can't keep being truthful? Or you can't keep being dishonest?"

Dee understood what he was trying to get her to see. She knew that she had to come clean in order to start anew. But it was so hard. She just didn't realize the pain would be so raw. "I . . . I . . . just don't know what I mean anymore."

"Yes, you do, Dee. Tell me what happened in Miami when you tried our exercise with Chris."

"He tried to kill me!" Dee placed both hands over her face and wiped it dry. She burst into rolling laughter. "That low down, trifling woman-beater tried to kill me!"

The doctor flinched as Dee told him about her grisly encounter with Chris. He had no idea something like this would happen. Ever. "Dee, I'm sorry to hear that. You never made Chris out to be abusive."

"That's because he wasn't. I mean, geez, I didn't *think* he was, anyway. I guess that's what happens when you don't really know a person."

"How do you feel about what happened?"

Dee felt like the doctor was trying to give her a trick question. *How do you think I felt after that Miami ordeal?* "I'm crushed. Just crushed," she said, hanging her head down.

"No relief from losing all of that unnecessary baggage?"

"No, as a matter of fact, I now know what *lost* baggage feels like, and it doesn't feel good." She managed to smile.

"So what are your plans for Steve?"

"I may hold off on telling him until I recover from the Chris ordeal."

"I see. Dee, are there any men in your life that you are attracted to that know what you really do for a living?"

Dee thought long and hard about his question. Had she ever been truthful to any man she was attracted to? She shook her head in embarrassment as she looked at the patterns in the carpet.

"No one. Except for Sedrick."

"Are you attracted to him?"

"I've never looked at him like that. He and I have always been friends."

"In the true sense of the word?"

"What do you mean?"

"Platonic?"

"Oh, yes, totally. I mean, he's like my brother. I could tell him anything."

"Is Sedrick attracted to you?"

"Not in the context you're talking about. Why?"

"Well, sometimes men pretend to be an attractive woman's friend in hopes that eventually it will lead to something else."

"No way! Not Sedrick and me." Her tears turned to giggles. "He would never . . ."

"Why not? Is anything wrong with him?" The doctor raised his eyebrows questioningly.

"Sedrick? You mean as in gay?" Dee laughed out loud as she pictured Sedrick being attracted to a man. "Sedrick, gay? Now, that's a good one! Definitely not! But, on a serious note, I can't even imagine him being anything other than a . . ."

"Good friend?"

"Well, yes."

"Hmmm . . ."

"Where are you going with this?"

"I'm not going anywhere with this, *you* are."

"Huh?"

"Think about why Sedrick seems to be the only man you can be honest with."

"Okay, now you sound like my roommate," Dee said, rolling her eyes.

"What do you mean?"

"She's wanted the two of us to get together since college."

"She sees something you don't?"

"She always sees something I don't. That's just who she is," Dee said, reflecting on Pam's opinion about her and Sedrick.

"Sounds like she might be a little too intuitive for your taste."

Dee made a wry face at his statement. *Pam is intuitive. Way too much. Almost as intuitive as you are.* "My roommate and I are like sisters. Yes, sometimes she is a bit too intuitive for my taste, as you say, but I know she has my best interest at heart—she always has."

"Well good, then. Maybe you should listen more to your roommate. It would save you the trip from traveling all the way out here to see me." The doctor slightly grinned.

Dee smiled back. "She's not a psychiatrist, Doc."

"Well, in my opinion, you don't have to be to give sound advice," he answered.

"Well, believe me. She needs to use some of that intuition on herself."

"Why do you say that?"

"Well, I told you she hasn't trusted anyone since her breakup with her fiancé."

The doctor nodded. "Yes, I do remember. So what does that have to do with you?'

"Not me. Her."

"Dee, you're not making any sense."

"She's got this guy who calls her and sends her flowers, but she acts like she doesn't want to give him the time of day."

"I've been on that end before," the doctor chuckled. "So you think she's putting on an act, eh?"

"I know she is. I can tell you that he's been getting to her. But, she's so afraid to let him in."

"Well, sometimes it just takes people a lot longer to heal than others."

"It's been three years. She has to learn to give love a chance, and especially with someone who seems so crazy about her."

"Listen, take some time for yourself for a while and think about what direction you want to go in. The next time you come here, have a road map for me of your plan."

"A road map, huh?" Dee said suspiciously. She looked at the clock on the wall and saw that it was time for her session to end.

"Yes, let's see where you want to take your life. Nothing complicated. Just an outline for yourself. You still have one more trip to make to New York. When you are ready to go see Steve, I want you to be on the right path." He winked at her as he walked her out the door.

"All right, Doc," she said hesitantly.

"And in the meantime, ease up on that roommate of yours. She sounds like she really knows you and cares about you. I take it that you still haven't told her about you coming out here to see me."

"No, I'm not ready yet. Like I said, she has got a lot of stuff going on right now."

"Well, just think about it some more. Your roommate sounds like a very intelligent woman. I like her. Perhaps you should give her a little more credit."

Dee thought about his remark. *Maybe one day, Doc. But for now, this secret is going to stay between you and me.*

Hazardous Material

Steve's eyes widened when his intercom buzzed. "Yes, Mildred."

"Steve, I hate to interrupt you, but Bruce Briscoe is on the phone."

"Great, you can interrupt me anytime for ol' Bruce."

Mildred laughed. "That's exactly what he said."

Steve nodded, thinking about how arrogant Briscoe could be sometimes. "That figures."

"I'll put him through."

Steve tapped his pencil on top of a proposal while he waited for Bruce's call to come through.

"Hey, Steve."

"Bruce, what's going on, man?"

"Lots."

"So, tell me, are you going to be able to help my friend out or what?"

"That's why I'm calling."

"Okay, so are you going to be able to give her a recommendation?"

Bruce took a long pause before he spoke. Steve heard him exhale heavily through the receiver. "Steve, listen, man, I don't know how to tell you this."

"Tell me what?"

"How well do you know this . . . um . . . Debra Mitchell?"

A wide grin spread across his face as he thought of Dee. "I'd say I know her pretty well and getting to know her better every day. Why?"

Bruce paused again. "Damn, I just wish I didn't have to be the one to tell you this, Steve."

"You keep saying that, Bruce. Get to the point."

Bruce paused again. There was a long silence over the phone. Steve was starting to get agitated.

"Hey Bruce, I've got a hundred and one things to do today, man. Say what's on your mind."

"All right, you asked me. Your friend Debra, well . . . she's a fraud."

Fasten Your Seatbelt

Pam placed her last pair of silk pajamas in her Louis Vuitton luggage and snapped it shut. As she carried the luggage into the living room, she heard the knock at the door, looked at her watch, and smiled at Sedrick's customary timeliness.

"Hey, Sed, come on in," she said not looking up as he opened the door.

He bent down to hug her and saw the luggage. "I can't believe that *you* are actually going on a trip."

"And it's not business related, either," she answered before he could ask. Pam was stunned when an unfamiliar pair of eyes greeted her as she and Sedrick embraced.

"Ah, did you forget something?" she said playfully shooing Sedrick away from her.

"Oh, I'm sorry!" He took Miranda's hand and gently pulled her toward him and Pam. "This is Miranda. Miranda this is my good friend, Pam."

"Nice to meet you," Miranda said. Her accent appeared to be a cross between Venezuelan and Colombian.

"It's nice to meet you as well, Miranda," Pam said, trying not to reveal her shock that Sedrick hadn't introduced her before. *Was this who Dee had heard about?* Miranda was stunning. Her skin looked naturally tanned and was a nice contrast to her shoulder-length dark brown hair. She was slim and tall and appeared to have a special connection with Sedrick, but there was something else about her that Pam couldn't quite put her finger on. Maybe she misjudged Sed. Maybe he had moved on and Dee wasn't at the top of the list anymore.

"Coincidently, Miranda and I are headed on a getaway ourselves to the mountains, and since it's on the way from the airport, I figured this would be a good chance for you two to meet."

"Well, of course!" Pam extended her hand and gave her infamous corporate attorney handshake.

"I've heard so much about you and Dee!" Miranda said sounding a little too excited for Pam's ears.

Funny, I hadn't heard anything about you! Pam thought to herself. "Well, I hope it was all good."

"Oh, but of course. Sed had nothing but positive things to say about both of you." Miranda glanced around the room. "I absolutely love your place," she said admiring the paintings on the walls.

"Thank you. So, where do you live?"

"Funny, you should ask."

"Really, why?"

"Because Sed and I have been discussing finding a place together."

"Wow! I had no idea, Sedrick."

Sed coughed loudly, hearing the sarcasm in Pam's voice. He immediately changed the subject. "So you never told me where you are going in such a big haste."

"Vegas," she answered, giving him a playful smile.

"And with whooooom?"

"You're looking at her," she answered proudly while picking up her suitcases. Then she started playfully spinning herself around in a circle.

Sedrick burst into a thunderous laughter and tears started to roll down his cheeks. "That's a good one, Pam. You? Go to Vegas? Alone?"

Pam looked at him crossly, placed both suitcases back on the floor and put her hands on her hips. "What? A woman can't *take herself* on a vacation?"

"Yeah, but . . ."

"But *what* Sedrick?"

Sedrick tried to speak as tactfully as he could. "What made you decide to get out like this? I mean, it's so out of character for you."

"Oh Sed," Miranda interrupted. "Why would you say something like that to Pam?"

"Trust me, baby. This is not typical of Pam!"

"What made you decide to get out?" She lowered her voice to mimic him. "Sedrick, you make me sound like I'm some type of *cavewoman*. Miranda, doesn't he sound like a fool?" Miranda nodded and gave him a playful thump on his shoulder.

"I just call 'em as I see 'em!" He started beating his chest, trying to imitate a caveman while cracking up laughing.

"Oh, you got jokes today, I see. So, you're the caveman and I'm the cavewoman, heh? Maybe you should give up your medical career and do stand-up instead."

"No way. Doctors make much more money," he quipped. "Miranda's about to find out. She's in her last year of residency in obstetrics. Ain't that right, sweetie?" he said, winking at Miranda who responded with only a smile.

"So when is Dee due back in town?"

"Yes, I was looking forward to meeting her," Miranda chimed in.

"I thought she would have been back by now. But you know Dee, Sedrick."

"Yeah, always doing something unexpected," he fondly reflected.

Pam walked toward the bedroom and returned with one more suitcase. "All right, here's the last of it. Let me just leave a note for Dee, and I'm on my way," she said, scribbling a message on a piece of paper leaving it between the salt and pepper shakers on the kitchen table.

Sedrick threw the luggage over his shoulder and looked at her thoughtfully. "Well, I hope you loosen up a little while you're out there. Look at you, still wearing a business suit."

"It's a travel suit," she said, looking down at her taupe single-breasted jacket and matching pleated pants. I'm even wearing flats, see?" She pointed to her shoes.

"And a nice pair of flats, I must say," Miranda added. "They're Gucci, right?"

"Sed, this girl knows her designers!" Good thing that you both are making that big cheese," she winked.

"See, that's your problem. You're just buttoned up too tight."

"Sedrick, all I want is a little R and R."

"A little somethin' somethin' wouldn't hurt now either, would it?"

Pam laughed as she thought about just how long it had been since she had sex—she could barely remember what it had been like. "You're right about that, it wouldn't." Pam laughed again. "C'mon, let's go, I'm off to Vegas!" She unbuttoned her jacket, grabbed her purse, and followed Sedrick and Miranda to the door.

Missed Connection

The air was chilly, but the crisp breeze helped Dee to concentrate as she lowered the top on her vintage convertible Volkswagen before driving off. Steve was in Atlanta at a reception for one of his clients at the High Museum and was meeting Dee afterwards. Dee suggested that they meet outside on the balcony where the open air and crowd would lessen the chances of a scene just in case he wanted to do a rerun of her episode with Chris.

While parking her car, she had flashbacks of Chris wanting to beat her down to a pulp. The image frightened her. She decided to call Steve and cancel. She dug through her purse for her phone but couldn't find it. Suddenly she remembered unplugging it and leaving it on the kitchen counter. *All right, Dee, pull yourself together, girl. Now, you have no choice but to show up.* She parked the car. It was exactly 2:00 p.m. as she walked through the entrance of the museum.

"Hello, Ms. Mitchell." The voice had a serious tone.

"Hey there, you," she said, turning to give Steve a hug. He opened his arms coolly and hung them loosely around her waist.

"Well, what kind of welcome is that?"

He hugged her again, a little more tightly, but not much warmer.

"Hey, let's go over there so we can talk," he said, pulling her through the doors to the outdoor balcony.

"Steve, what's wrong? Did something happen at the gala?"

Steve grabbed her shoulders with both hands. His eyes pinned her to the corner of the balcony. "Is what I heard true, Debra?"

"Heard? Steve, what'd you hear?" *I can't tip my hand to him without first knowing what he is talking about. Maybe it has nothing to do with what I need to tell him.*

"Look, I just want to hear it from you that's all," he said, looking at her sadly.

"Hey, what's going on?" Dee said, placing her hands on top of his.

He looked down at her hands and briefly caressed them. "I'm glad to see your hand healed okay," he said thoughtfully before continuing with his inquisition. "Do you remember my client Dr. Briscoe?"

"Yes . . ." Dee answered nervously.

"Well, after you hurt your hand that evening, he and I talked about you a few days later. He said that he would check to see what type of med student you were and meet with your instructors and the other doctors to see what they felt were your strengths."

"Really?" Dee was stunned. *Oh God, he knows.* "That was generous of him." Dee felt the pit of her stomach began to turn summersaults.

"Yeah, I thought so too."

"Why'd he do that?"

"Well his plan was to meet with you after he met with them."

"Aha, I see," Dee said trying to figure out when she should just stop him and come clean.

"But guess what?"

Dee managed to form a small smile. "Steve, listen—"

Suddenly they both heard a loud scream come from inside the museum. Dee's flight attendant instincts kicked in, and she immediately ran toward the sound. Steve was just two steps behind her.

A woman was bending over a man's body and screaming as loudly as she could. "Someone call 911! Mr. Kinsey just collapsed! He needs a doctor, right away!"

Steve looked at Dee, and she froze. At that moment, she knew immediately that he knew she was not a doctor. However, Dee was trained well enough to check a person's pulse. The man's face was turning blue, and he looked unconscious. Dee bent down and put two of her fingers on the side of his neck and felt his weak pulse.

"What was he doing before he passed out?" Dee asked the lady.

"He was holding his throat."

"Can you remember anything else?"

"No, he just grabbed his throat and started turning blue," the woman started yelling at Dee. "What's with all the questions? Can you help him or not?"

"I'm going to do my best," Dee answered calmly. As he was not a very large man, it was easy for her to turn him on his back and place both of his arms by his sides so she could better assist him. "He has probably choked on something," she said as she slightly opened his mouth. "I see something back there."

The lady got more panicky. "Can you pull it out?"

"I can see if I can try and finger-sweep it out." She quickly pulled some latex gloves out of her purse that she kept with her at all times in the event that she ever had to do this on a flight. She slid her finger deeply inside the man's cheek and used a sweeping, hooking action across the interior of the mouth to the other cheek. When she didn't dislodge the substance, she proceeded to perform the Heimlich.

Steve rushed to her side and marveled at Dee's calmness.

Suddenly a bone flew out of the man's mouth and he started coughing profusely. Thank you, God, it actually worked. Dee's heart was pounding. "Sir, are you okay?"

The man nodded his head and managed to mouth a thank you to Dee between coughs.

"You're welcome sir." Dee turned to the lady who ran over to him and started hugging him so hard that it sent him into another coughing fit, except this time it was much longer and harder. "Ma'am, I think he'll be okay, but he needs to go to the hospital right away to get checked out."

"I'm on it, now," she said releasing him as she pulled her cell phone from her purse and began dialing.

Dee took a deep breath and looked up at Steve who was watching her every move. So many emotions were running through her, she didn't know if she should cry from sheer relief that her Heimlich worked, or laugh at how she got herself into this situation in the first place.

Steve gently patted her on the back. "You did good, Dee," he whispered. "You saved that man's life. I must admit, that was incredible."

Dee was quiet. She just nodded and waited on Steve's next move.

"Do you want to sit down?"

Dee shook her head. "No."

"Are you okay?"

"Uh . . . huh . . ."

"Let's go back outside." Steve walked Dee out to the balcony. This was not going at all as he had planned. He wanted to rail into her about what Bruce had told him, but he could tell that she was still shaken up.

Steve turned his back and leaned forward on the balcony and shook his head. He took a long deep breath then blew from his mouth. "Who the hell are you, *really*?"

"Huh?"

"Is your name *really* Debra Mitchell, because I already know you're not a real doctor. So what is your *real* occupation?"

Dee folded her hands in front of her, hoping they would stop shaking. She slowly whispered, "Deirdre Bridge is my real name." Dee inhaled. "My real occupation is . . . I'm a flight attendant."

"Why did you have to lie to me? And for so long? How long would you have kept up your charades if Bruce hadn't clued me in?" Steve reached in his pocket and pulled a cigarette from its holder. He laughed half-heartedly then lit the cigarette, taking a long drag, blowing smoke from his mouth.

"So why couldn't you just tell me what you did for a living from the beginning? You didn't think I would date you if I knew the truth?"

"No, I really didn't." She spoke softly as she squinted from the smoke.

Steve inhaled deeply and blew out several more short puffs of smoke. "Well, Deb . . . I mean, Deirdre, you were wrong. Dead wrong," he said as he put out his cigarette. "What you do doesn't matter to me." He pulled out another cigarette. "I've dated all kinds of women: exotic dancers, librarians, flight attendants, surgeons, models. You name them, I've dated them. I don't care what a woman does for a living. Just as long as it's legal!" He looked at her with such disapproving eyes that Dee could not continue to look at him.

"I'm so sorry." Dee was barely able to form her words.

He slowly started backing away from her. "Me too, Deirdre, me too . . ."

Dee called out to him. "So, is there any chance that I can redeem myself?" She blurted out before she realized people were starting to stare at her.

"I can't trust you, Deb, I mean Deirdre. There I go again! Hell, I can't even get used to calling you by your *real* name. It's like I never knew who you were. Put yourself in my shoes. I've been seeing someone who has been telling me she's one thing, and now I find out she's completely someone else."

"But, I made a mistake. Can't you forgive me?" Dee sounded so desperate.

"Yes, I can forgive you, but I can't be with you," he said sadly. "You need help, Deirdre, and the kind of help you need I'm not equipped to give you," he said turning and walking away.

"But, I can change Steve!" She broke down crying. "Please give me another chance. Please!" she loudly whispered. Her lips trembled as she watched him walk out of her life without even a second glance.

Surprise Landing

As Pam's cab pulled up to the Bellagio Hotel, she looked in awe at the enormous mountains and the bright lights of the Las Vegas city streets. The cabbie stopped and then opened the door for her. "I'll get your bags, Miss," he said, opening the trunk as Pam handed him a generous tip.

"Thanks a lot!"

She laughed at his enthusiasm. "You're welcome. This *is* Vegas, right? High rollers, right?"

"Ah, yes, that's right. Just be careful, though." He stared into Pam's eyes.

"What's that supposed to mean?"

"I've just seen a lot of people come out here looking just like you, that's all, then when they leave they can't afford to pay their hotel bills," he said as he rolled her bags through the opulent front lobby surrounded by a beautiful gold coiffure ceiling. "Just look at this place," he said as he pointed to the famous glass blower Dale Chihuly's 2,000 glass blossoms that adorned the ceiling. "This place even has money oozing out of its floors," he said laughing as he watched Pam gaze at the intricate designs of the beautiful marble floors.

"I see what you mean."

The cabby nodded. "Yep, so make sure you leave here lookin' just like you look today, or better." He winked at her as he placed her bags at the front desk.

"Welcome to Las Vegas's finest hotel, Bellagio," smiled the hotel attendant.

"So I hear," Pam quipped, handing him her driver's license and credit card.

"You will have a pleasant stay here, Ms. Madison. If there is anything you need, any member of the staff will be pleased to assist you. Your luggage will be in your room."

"Now, that's service!" Pam laughed.

"We do the best because *we are* the best," the hotel attendant smiled, extending his hand to shake Pam's hand. He handed her the room key. "Good day, Madam."

Pam turned and walked toward the elevator, noticing that there were many families staying at the hotel. For the first time since Greg, she started to wonder if she would ever have a family of her own.

A tall man wearing Ray-Ban sunglasses walked toward his room across from Pam's. Before opening his door, he took off his sunglasses, and Pam caught a quick glimpse of his face before he went into his room. She was stunned when she recognized her neighbor.

"Marc!"

"Pam!"

"What are you doing in Vegas?" They both laughed as they spoke at the same time.

"I come here just about every other weekend just to get away, and after a certain young lady wouldn't return any of my phone calls and then hung up on me, I felt dejected and needed to clear my head and get my ego back," he said, smiling at her. "So, here I am! What about you?"

Pam smiled back at him. "Well, right now, I'm just trying to get into my room, and it seems like this key has other ideas," she said, holding it up.

"Here, let me try."

"Be my guest." She handed him the key. Pam thought he looked handsome in his faded jeans and leather mules. His blue jean cotton shirt was partially unbuttoned, giving her a nice glimpse of the curly hair on his chest.

"Just a little turn to the right and *voilà*!" he said, opening the door.

"I've tried that key at least five times. Thanks, Marc." She looked up at him and felt a sudden twinge of guilt. "Hey, I apologize about not calling you back after I hung up on you. I meant to."

"But, you just forgot and flew to Vegas instead, huh?"

"Yes, I guess I did." Pam laughed.

Marc patted the top of her hands as he handed her key back. "Hey, why don't you come over and join me for a brandy? Maybe I'll accept your apology."

"I'm not a brandy girl, but if you have some chardonnay, I will take you up on that."

"C'mon over, I'll see what I can round up for you, Counselor."

"Okay, give me a few minutes to change, and I'll come on by. I suppose I could spare a *few* minutes for someone who saved me from sleeping in the hallway tonight."

"Good, then, the pleasure will be mine."

Once inside her room, Pam took off her shoes and dug her toes into the warm, thick carpet. She changed into a tan velour jogging suit, slipped on her tennis shoes, and headed across the hall. Marc opened the door before she could knock.

"C'mon in. Make yourself comfortable."

"Hey, no fair! Your room is bigger than mine," she said with a mock pout as she looked around his inviting suite.

Marc looked at her admiringly. "We can switch, if that would make you happy."

"I'm just kidding, Marc."

"Well, I'm glad that you are pleased, Counselor," he said as he handed her a glass of wine. "And I'm glad that you followed me out to Vegas. But what I don't understand is how you arranged to get a room right across from mine," he said giving her a devilish wink. Pam started to cough as she burst into laughter.

"I didn't think what I said was *that* funny!"

"Maybe not. But *you* certainly are." She set her glass on the table next to the sofa and laughed again. "This is just too weird!"

"I'd like to call it fate."

"Fate hasn't been too kind to me, lately," she said inching herself toward the window to take in the bright lights on the strip. Her look changed to that of sorrow.

"Really? How so?" he said. He got up and stood next to her, lifting her chin to look into her intense green eyes, feeling tears fall onto his fingertips. "Come here," he said, pulling her to him.

Pam's body was stiff at first, but just like a hardened piece of clay, she softened with each firm and gentle squeeze. She breathed in deeply, secretly hoping that her lack of oxygen would dry up her tears.

"I didn't make partner. That day when you called I had just had a big argument with one of the partners, and to add insult to injury, I treated someone very poorly that really didn't deserve it."

"Pam, I'm so sorry," he said pulling her closer to him. The healing warmth of his body spread over her like a down comforter. She still felt a little uncomfortable being in his arms and pulled back.

"I can't believe I'm letting myself go like this," she said wiping the tears from her eyes and straightening out her clothes. She walked back over to her wine and emptied her glass. "You know, I worked my tail off for that firm. I must have spent twelve- to fourteen-hour days every day there. And for what? I'm stressed out! I allowed my professional relationship to take precedence over a personal relationship that I had long before I was an attorney."

She grabbed the bottle of wine and poured herself another glass. "Hell! It's been three years since I've even had sex! Oh my!" She placed her hand over her mouth and giggled nervously. "I didn't mean to say *that.*"

"It's okay, really. We've all been there," he smiled.

"Oh, yeah, sure you have." Judging from the scene that she saw a few weeks ago, it sounded like he got it often, and pretty good, too.

"Well, if you're speaking about the unfortunate incident that you witnessed, you're right. But I'm not referring to her. I've been there, and I've lost a few friends along the way. I've been out of relationships and have not had sex." *Although the longest I can remember has been two weeks.* He smiled seductively at Pam.

"Here's to great sex!" she said holding her glass up. "Cheers!" She drank her chardonnay, enjoying the feel of the smooth liquid sliding down her throat.

"Well, I think you've done the right thing, you know, coming out here. It's important to take time out for yourself. I come here on a Friday and get the same suite, play a few slots, see some shows, and head on out on Sunday evening feeling refreshed for my day on Monday."

"You know, I'm beginning to think that I should have done this kind of stuff a long time ago."

"What? Vacation?"

"Yeah. I mean, everyone in the office seemed to take time off except me. And look where it got me." She took another sip of her wine.

"What you experienced was self-realization. Better known as a reality check."

"No. What *I* experienced was working my ass off and then getting cut off at the knees right before it was time for me to receive my *long* overdue partnership." She traced her finger around the rim of her glass as she reflected on what happened.

"As intuitive as you are, I find it hard to believe that you did not see that your partnership was in jeopardy."

"Marc, I tell you, I was totally blindsided by it."

Marc looked at her sympathetically. "I want to hear what happened."

"What good will it do?"

"You'd be surprised at how talking can help a situation. Have you talked to anyone about it yet?"

"I just told my roommate, briefly. But that was the night you . . ."

"I called? I guess my call put a big damper on your evening. Now I know why you never called me back."

Pam looked into his deep-set blue eyes and for the first time felt like she could get lost in them. "I was at a loss for words," she said, sitting down on the sofa and staring into her empty wine glass. "Just totally numb, ya know? I was all prepared to be told that I was going to be made partner, and then all of a sudden I'm hit with this stack of bullshit statements from paralegals that have accused me of harassment, cruelty, and unusual punishment—you name it!" Pam shook her head at the incredulity of it all.

"But why?"

"Let's just say that everyone at the firm finds me very intimidating."

"And what do you think?"

Pam was quiet for a moment. No one had ever asked her that question before. "Yes, it's true," she answered confidently. "But it's how I win all of my cases, and it's how I get people to respect me, except I really dug into someone who didn't deserve it."

"Who?"

"My paralegal and former college classmate and friend."

"How did you two end up working together?"

Pam blew out some air and started shaking her head. "Oh man, whew! When I think about how dumb that was, it makes me angry."

Marco reached for her hand and lightly stroked it. She felt a small quiver in her stomach and gently tried to pull out of his reach, but he gave her hand a small squeeze and it remained steady.

"It was supposed to be for a short-term assignment, and then it was three years later and we were still working together."

"What happened?"

"I didn't want our friendship to cloud our work, so I forced myself to become detached. I knew I needed her because she was the best paralegal in the firm, but my pride didn't want her to know how much I needed her. It wasn't my initial intent. But I made her feel inferior. When I think about how I treated her, I really feel terrible."

"Why do you think you feel the need to intimidate people so much to get what you want?"

"I don't know. I guess intimidation and fear have been the driving force behind all of my successes."

"Did someone intimidate *you* when you were growing up?"

"Not really. You know, I told you I was the third child of five siblings. It seemed like I always had to fight to get what I wanted."

"Hmmm . . . a case of middle child syndrome, heh?"

Pam managed to form a smile. "Yes, I guess you could say that. My two older brothers always got special treatment from my mother because she needed a lot of help when my father was at work. She looked at them like they were the center of the earth. Then, of course, that left me and my twin sisters. Those two got a lot of attention because they were the *twins*, and *together* they were quite a handful! My brothers were tight, the twins were each other's buddies, and I was kind of the odd one out, you could say. But as I got older, I got over it, and I didn't feel like I needed to continue to fight anymore with my middle child *drama* syndrome. I developed my own sense of self, went out into the world, became this great attorney, and just when everything was going the way I wanted, then . . ."

Marc squeezed her hand again and gently massaged her fingers. "And then what?"

Pam paused briefly feeling as if she was peeling off a layer of bruised skin that needed to be healed. "I can't believe I'm telling you this."

"Take your time."

"I was in a relationship that ended very badly." Her eyes watered again as she got up. "And when it ended, the loss was so great that it took a piece of me. I've managed to survive by just working really hard, you know?"

"And it helps to ease your pain when you hurt other people?"

"No, it just happens that way. Believe me when I say that staying focused on what I need to accomplish gets me through the day. Sometimes I guess my drive seems to step on other people's toes. What are you doing? Trying to psychoanalyze me or something?"

"No, I'm just trying to understand how that brain of yours works. I'm curious about something. You said your father was the chief of police, right?"

"Oh, you remembered? Yes, that is correct."

"Well, as your father was the chief of police, how did his subordinates view him?"

"They feared him, but they respected him," she said defensively.

"Hmmm . . . I see. Which was it more, fear or respect?"

Pam thought about that earnestly. "Good question. I used to think it was respect, but as I look back on it, I guess it might have been more fear than anything. My father was a gentle man, but he was very firm. He ran a tight ship, and if you weren't on the same deck then you had to jump off."

"Can you give me an example?"

At first Pam felt put off by the direction in which this conversation was going, but the more she listened to Marc, the more he made sense. Had she unconsciously used her father's intimidation tactics all of these years? She thought all of it was just due to her bad experience with Greg.

"Well, I remember the time when he thought one of his officers had taken some drug money from a crime scene. None of them would tell what really happened, so my father conveniently reassigned them to some of the worse precincts in the city."

"What happened next?"

"The money suddenly reappeared. The first time he discovered the money was missing, he came home that evening and sat at the dinner table and stared right through all five of us and said, 'I betta not ever catch none of ya'll stealin' or lyin'. Ever!' He snatched up his plate and went and ate in the dining room alone. My mother ran out and told him, 'Drake, don't intimidate these kids to make them do what you want! What's the matter with you?'"

"What did your father say to that?"

"My father sat back in his chair and looked at her sternly and said, 'They betta learn early on or they'll end up like one of my officers behind bars.' Okay, I'll admit it. You're a pretty good shrink, Marc. I can see how I have taken my father's threatening tactics and used them on the paralegals at work. Now what's next?"

Marc smiled as he did when one of his patients had a significant break. "What do you want to be next?"

"How about we not make me one of your head cases just yet? Let's talk about you," Pam said eying him cautiously.

"Well, that's fair. Hmmm, let's see. Where do I start?"

"How about your family?"

"Okay, are you sure you want to know? I mean I don't want you to change your opinion of me."

"What makes you think I have an opinion of you?" Pam joked.

"Ah ha! Well, you've got me there, Counselor. I must admit, that was a good one."

"No, seriously. I'd love to hear about your family."

"Well, my father was an alcoholic and was abusive to my whole family when we lived in California."

"Are you serious?"

"Very. Fortunately, my mother managed to escape by keeping a job as a maid without my father knowing about it. She would give her money to one of the ladies she was working for, for safe-keeping so Papa wouldn't waste it on liquor, and when she saved up enough money, she took me and my two older brothers and caught a bus to Salt Lake City, where we changed our names and started a new life."

"Now that is incredible! Your mother is a remarkable woman."

"She is. You ever heard of Shine Cleaning?"

"Yes, I've heard of them before. I hear they're an excellent cleaning service."

"I know. My mother founded the company several years after we moved over to the states. It's really well known over on the west coast, but it's spreading around," Marc said.

"Is your mom still running the business?"

"No, she eventually sold it and was able to send all three of us to Ivy League schools from the proceeds," he laughed.

"That's fantastic." Pam hesitated before she asked her next question. "So, where's your father now?"

Marc shrugged his shoulders. "Don't know and don't care."

"I see," she said as she caught him staring into her eyes.

Marc got up, tugging at her hand to pull her up from the sofa. "Enough of this heavy talking. I'm starting to feel extremely lucky tonight. Are you up for some gambling?"

"That's why I'm here."

"So, let's hit the slots, Counselor!"

Safe Return Home

Looking at Amanda with one eye open, Melvin said, "Good morning, suga."

"Hey there, you," Amanda said, hoping Melvin didn't hear the guilt in her voice.

Melvin felt Amanda's hesitancy as he leaned over to kiss her. "What's the matter, baby? Gimme some of that good kissin' I'm used to," he said pulling her face closer to his. Amanda finally gave in and kissed him tenderly. "Now, that's better. How you feelin' this mornin'?"

"Never been better," she said, pushing herself away from him as he leaned in to pull her back.

"Where are you trying to rush off to?"

Amanda smiled sheepishly. "I'm just about to make my way to the bathroom. Is that okay with you?"

"Hurry back in here, then." He patted her on her rear end as she breezed past him.

When Amanda finally reached the bathroom, she looked at herself in the mirror and was suddenly overcome with nausea. She turned on the water and vomited into the sink as quietly as she could.

"Are you all right, baby?"

She could hardly breathe. If her heaving didn't stop soon, she knew Melvin would become suspicious.

"Amanda?"

"I'm fine," she said, splashing some cold water on her face. She stared at herself again in the mirror, feeling like an adulteress, even though she wasn't married.

"Well, now, just one more day before you return back to work."

"That's right," Amanda yelled back with a mouthful of toothpaste.

"I don't know about you, but I sure am glad, because I think you were going a little stir-crazy around the house. You were starting to run out of projects."

"I can always come to work for you," she yelled back as she spit out her toothpaste and rinsed out her mouth.

"And do what?"

"Oh, I dunno, some hammering, pulling up some carpet," she said as she walked out of the bathroom and crawled back into bed.

"Oh, so is that all that you think I do all day?" he said as he grabbed her underneath the covers and nibbled on her neck.

"Melvin, stop! No!"

"No, I ain't stoppin'! You think you're so cute, don't cha," he said while crawling on top of her, pressing his face against her neck then blowing on it.

"You're acting like a fool, Melvin. Get off me!" she squealed and caught her breath as he got off her and started laughing.

"I'm only a fool when it comes to you, baby! Amanda, I need to ask you something," his voice turned serious.

Amanda patted him on his thigh. "Sure. What is it?"

"You know I'm not a man of many words, but I know what I want, right?"

"Yes," she said propping her pillow so she could look him in the face.

"Okay, here goes," he said, smiling nervously as he opened up the nightstand drawer and pulled out a black velvet box.

Amanda's stomach began to flip. "Melvin!"

He opened the box and slipped the one-carat pear-shaped diamond onto her finger. It was set in platinum with smaller diamonds around the band. "Will you marry me, Amanda? It sho' would make me a happy man," he said.

The look in his eyes turned Amanda's guilt to heartache. She wished she could erase what happened last night. She wiped away the tears that were traveling down her face. She thought about the irony of her situation. After three years of dating, Melvin had officially proposed to make her his wife. How ironic for him to ask her now.

Mile High Club

The night passed quickly while Pam played the quarter slots relentlessly and Marc played the roulette table. "Hey, Pam!" Marc yelled. "C'mon over and give me a lucky number."

Pam put another quarter in the slot. "I'll be over in a minute. I think I finally got her warmed up!"

Ding! Ding! Ding! "I won! I won! Five hundred dollars! Yes! I won!" she screamed all the way over to where Marc was. Before she caught herself, she grabbed him and hugged him. He turned around and kissed her eagerly on the lips.

"Congratulations!"

"Thanks," Pam said, caught off guard a little.

"Sam, here is my lucky charm," Marc said to the roulette table attendant.

"So, what does the charm, say, sir?"

"Five!" Pam shouted.

"Let it all roll on number five!" Marc laughed. "The lady gets half of whatever I win." Marc watched as the numbers spun, and the ball rolled directly into the five slot. "Oh yeah! I told you she was good luck! The Bellagio owes the good doctor here seven grand! Yes!"

"You gambled seven thousand dollars? Marc, are you crazy?"

"Crazy for you!" he said lifting her up to swing her around. Then he kissed her while the crowd cheered him on.

"Marc! Put me down!" Pam laughed. "You're embarrassing me!"

"Oh, I'm sorry," he said, setting her down. "Let's go and cash in!"

"This was such a great evening," Pam said as she watched the cashier count their winnings. "I can't believe you won all of that money."

"We won it."

Pam looked up at him admiringly. She couldn't remember the last time she'd had this much fun. She didn't want the evening to end.

"Pam, why don't we go back to the room and have a nightcap," Marc said almost as if he had read her mind.

"A nightcap would be good. It will help me get a good night's sleep too, especially after such a whirlwind evening in that casino."

As they rode the elevator back to their floor, Marco noticed that Pam couldn't stop smiling. "I'm glad to see you're so happy and relaxed. Vegas will do that to you," he said.

When the elevator doors opened, he took her hand and escorted her to his suite. Pam took off her shoes and sat down on the loveseat next to the window. The amazing view reminded her of the Emerald City in *The Wizard of Oz*. It would be so easy to fall in love with this city, she thought. Vegas had all of the colors, brilliant lights, and excitement.

Marco handed her a glass of cognac and took a sip of his and sat next to her. "Here, I want you to try this." He watched her take a sip and could tell she enjoyed its smooth flavor. "Good, huh?" he said as Pam nodded. "One of the things I admire about you is that you never hold back. You speak what is on your mind." His smooth accent sounded like easy listening music. She could listen to his voice all night.

"Well, thank you." Pam wasn't sure where this was leading, but she liked what she was feeling.

"I don't want you to feel uncomfortable," he said, giving her a quick peck on the lips. "Pam, I want to make love to you. Will you let me?" He felt the tension in Pam's back as she pulled away from him. She was the first woman he had ever read wrong.

"Do you always ask that question in such a formal manner?" she laughed, as she gestured to his glass insinuating that it was the cognac talking and not him.

Relieved that she still had a sense of humor, he spoke assuredly, "Usually, I don't have to ask. Believe me, you are the first," he said as he placed his hand on his heart.

Pam took both their drinks and set them on the nearby table and sat in his lap. She settled herself on his hardened bulge and seductively draped her arms around his neck. She delicately brushed the back of his hair with her fingers. Whatever had come over her, she didn't want to think about it. She wanted only to feel again.

"Show me what you've got, Doctor," she purred as she placed her fingers between his legs and unzipped his pants. He smiled obligingly, helping her with his zipper and revealed himself to her.

"Now, that's what I'm talkin' about," Pam grinned.

Marco found the zipper on her jacket and pulled it down to reveal her breasts. He bent down and gently sucked each protruding nipple, sliding his hands down her pants and slipping them down to her knees. She felt herself throbbing as his manhood rested on her leg. Marc eased her onto the sofa, carefully laid her down, and pulled her underwear and pants completely off.

"I'll be right back. Don't move," he said in a low sexy voice as he headed toward his suitcase.

"Don't worry, I'm not going anywhere," Pam said breathlessly.

He took off the rest of his clothes and pulled out a pack of condoms. "How many do you think we'll need?"

"Ummm . . . bring them all and we'll see," she moaned.

Still erect, he slipped the condom on and walked over to her as she lay naked on the couch. He sat down next to her, placing her back on his lap and skillfully moving inside of her. She felt relieved that he was not into having unprotected sex. Her moan was loud as his manhood touched her very core. It had been so long since she felt this way, as he lifted her up while still inside her, then he carried her to the large ottoman next to the bed. He laid her down, easing himself farther inside her, and then glided himself back and forth until they reached a steady rhythm.

"Ummm, Marc . . . Oooo . . ." Pam whimpered wrapping her ankles around his neck. He moved deeper inside her until he felt her warm liquids flow freely from her body.

"Pam, I don't want this feeling to end," he said, resting on top of her while gingerly kissing her lips. "I can't remember the last time I felt this way about someone."

"Uh huh," Pam managed to utter, still breathless from her orgasm. She felt his tongue make circular motions on her bare breasts while his fingers gently massaged her nipples. His tongue sampled her stomach and then her navel, making its way down toward her center of pleasure. "Oh Marc . . ." she pleaded.

"Shhh . . . just relax and let me do the work," he said placing his finger over her lips as he immersed his tongue inside of her sending her into her personal paradise.

"Marc . . . please . . . please . . . you've got to . . . to . . ."

"Got to do what? This?" he teased as he lifted her onto his rock-hard penis and penetrated her again. "Is this what I got to do, huh? Is this what you want?" he said, making his strokes longer and faster as her hands trembled, barely able to hold onto his shoulders.

"Yes! Yes! Oh my God! Yes!" she wailed as she felt another waterfall flow freely from her body.

"Oh . . . Pam," Marc moaned, shaking just before he reached his finale.

Pam looked up at him and smiled, then laid her head on his chest. "Marc," she whispered.

"Huh?" he answered groggily as he lightly kissed her ear lobe.

"I don't want this feeling to end either."

"It won't. I'll be back in Atlanta next Friday to make sure of it."

Poor Visibility

The sunrise brimmed through Amanda's window. She lifted her hand in the air and watched her ring shimmer in the light. Slowly, she put it back down and turned the diamond underneath her finger.

"All right, baby, it's hot, and it's waiting on you," Melvin said as he walked into the bedroom.

Amanda smiled at him seductively and quickly turned her ring back to its correct position. "Is that the breakfast you're speaking of or something else?"

"It's the breakfast," Melvin laughed. "C'mon out here and eat so you won't be late for work. I can't let my future wife start her day off hungry."

The thought of being Mrs. Landers made her so giddy that she even forgot to tell Tracey. She walked into the kitchen and sat down to a nice spread of assorted muffins, omelets, bacon, freshly squeezed orange juice, and a pot of coffee.

"A bride could get used to this treatment," she said, giving him an affectionate peck on the lips. She licked her lips at him and took a sip of her coffee.

"So what do you think your day will be like today?"

"Oh, I don't know. I'll probably dive right into whatever case Mr. McKesson puts me on. It's not like I've been gone that long, you know."

"What about your girl, the infamous Pam Madison?"

Amanda shrugged her shoulders and took a long sip of her juice. "I'm going to pray for her."

"Well, you need to include yourself in that prayer, too," he said, noticing that she was nervously tapping her foot. "You're not a little nervous about her comin' back to work?"

"I'm not nervous about anything, Melvin," she said confidently, immediately putting a stop to her foot tapping. "All I have to do is look at this beautiful diamond on my finger, and it will make me think of you and all of the wonderful years that we have ahead of us. Pam Madison is only a bad a memory."

"So, is that what your meetin' was about the other evening?" Amanda was caught off guard by his question. "Amanda, why are you looking at me like you don't know what I'm talkin' about?"

"Oh, yes, well the meeting was so anticlimactic in comparison to your proposal that I forgot all about it!" She'd forgotten that she lied about the other night, telling him that she had a late meeting with Bill to discuss her coming back to work at the firm.

Melvin had a peculiar look on his face as he gulped the last drop of his orange juice. "Amanda, is everything all right with you?"

Amanda could not look him in the eyes. "Of course, suga'. Why wouldn't it be?"

"All right, baby, if you say so." Melvin sounded skeptical. "Maybe you just have them prewedding jitters."

"Of course, I do," Amanda smiled nervously. "I'm going to be the wife of The Mr. Melvin Landers. Who wouldn't be a little nervous? Right?"

Melvin chuckled. "You right about that. The first and the last!" The telephone rang and startled Amanda. "I'll get it, baby. It's probably Tracey callin' to wish you good luck on your first day back at work."

"Yes, you're probably right," she said, sitting back down to sip her coffee.

"Hello. Hello, is anybody there?" Melvin spoke into the receiver.

"Who is it, Melvin?"

"I dunno. They hung up. Must have been a wrong number."

"Yeah, must have been," Amanda said sounding a little worried. "Honey, excuse me for a second, will you?"

"Sure." Melvin rose from the table along with her. She felt his eyes follow her into the bedroom and knew she must look like a bundle of nerves to him.

Amanda sat down, took a peek at the caller ID screen, and gasped.

"Hey, baby, you sure, you're okay? Melvin said as he poked his head in the doorway. "Your breakfast is getting cold."

"I'll be right there," she said, digging through the drawer of her nightstand.

"There you are," she said, opening a bottle of aspirin and popping two in her mouth, then headed back to the kitchen to finish her breakfast.

"Hey, baby, I'll rinse off the dishes and put them in the dishwasher for you, and then I gotta go."

"So soon?" Amanda said, feeling somewhat relieved.

"Yeah, I took a couple of hours off, but I've gotta be on the other side of town by 9:00."

"So, I guess I better be heading off too if I'm going to get to the firm by 8:00," she said, standing on her toes to kiss him on the lips. "Thanks for the scrumptious breakfast, Melvin. I love you."

"I love you, too, baby," he said, giving her a squeeze. "See you this evening."

Amanda closed the door behind him and leaned up against it. She took a deep breath before she walked back to her room and called the number from her caller ID.

"Hello, this is Rick."

"Rickey."

"Hey, Amanda. I thought I copied your number down wrong, 'cause I had just called you earlier but some man answered the phone."

"I know. You hung up on Melvin."

Rickey was quiet for a minute. "Hey, I didn't know—"

"Rickey, don't pretend you didn't know about Melvin."

"I wasn't. What I was going to say was that I just didn't think he would be there *this* early."

Trying to stop herself from raising her voice, Amanda was oblivious to the sound of the key in the front door.

"Hey baby, it's me," Melvin called out. "I left my wallet on the counter." He made his way back toward the kitchen. The intensity in Amanda's voice made him stop short and walk back and listen through the crack of her bedroom door.

"Listen, Rickey. We need to talk about last night."

"I agree. Things happened kind of fast."

"And they got out of control."

"I wouldn't say that, Amanda. We made love. What is so out of control about that?"

"Rickey, what happened between us cannot ever happen again."

"Why not?"

"It . . . can't," she stated, a little reluctantly.

"You said that already, but tell me why?"

"Because Melvin asked me to marry him." Her voice was nearly cracking.

"So what did you tell him?"

She could hear the anguish in his voice. "Rickey, don't make this more difficult than it already is, okay?"

"What? All I'm asking is a question. You're the one who's making it difficult."

"I told him yes."

"But how could you after what happened between us?"

"Because I love him."

"What about me. What about us?"

"That's the difficult part," she said weakly.

"What is?"

"I still love you too . . ."

Stormy Weather

Pam was back in Atlanta relaxing in her bedroom when she heard the door slam. "Dee, is that you?"

There was no answer.

"Dee?" Pam called out again. As she made her way into Dee's room, she found her friend crunched up in her chair with her face buried in her jacket, crying.

"Hey, Dee, what's going on?"

Dee could only shake her head back and forth. She waved for Pam to leave the room.

"Dee, I'm not leaving. You know that. What in the hell happened, girl?" Pam moved toward her to place her hand on her shoulders. Dee's crying turned into wailing.

"It's over, Pam. My life is a train wreck, and it's over."

"Can you tell me what is going on?"

"I've lost everybody I've ever cared about." Dee groaned in despair. She broke down and sobbed uncontrollably.

"Dee, I'm so worried about you. What are you talking about?"

"I'm so lonely, I just can't explain it."

"Well, I'm not leaving until you try."

"I haven't shared this with you, but do you know the name Chris Dickerson?"

"As in Miami Chris Dickerson?

Dee nodded.

"So, what the hell does Chris have to do with . . . oh hell, no! Don't tell me that that son-of-a-bitch did something to you! I'll sue his ass for everything he has! Just say the word."

"Pam, calm down. It's not like that."

"Well, what in the hell is it then? Are you seeing Chris Dickerson or not?"

"Yes, I mean, no . . . I was."

"How come you never told me about him?"

Dee shook her head. "I don't know. I just didn't get around to it."

"So, what happened? What did he do to you to make you this upset?"

"It's not his fault. I knew what I was getting myself into when I started dating him."

"Well, he's a fool if he let someone like you go."

"Thanks, I appreciate that."

"Well, it's true. Besides, those damn jocks think they are God's gift to women anyway. I can't imagine trying to get involved with someone like that. I say good riddance to bad rubbish!" Pam said leaning over to kiss Dee on the cheek. "He doesn't deserve you, Dee. Are you sure you don't want to talk about it?"

"No, I would really rather not."

"Well, for the record, you need someone who is honest, and who is going to love you for who you are. Don't end up like me, okay?"

"What's that supposed to mean?" she asked, pulling a crumpled tissue from her pocket and blowing her nose.

Pam inhaled deeply, pausing before she spoke. "Listen, Greg was a liar and a thief. He didn't love me for who I was. And more importantly, he didn't love me enough to trust me and tell me what was really going on with him." As Dee placed her arms around her shoulders, Pam looked up at her and formed a small smile. "Hey, it's been three years and I finally let a man hold and touch me."

"Hold up! Wait a second. Who are you talking about?"

Pam smiled like a cat that just made off with the catch of the day. Dee slapped her knees. "Look at your face! What did you do this weekend?"

"I wasn't going to tell you since I've been trying to figure it out myself. But do you remember the guy that has been sending me—"

"The exotic flower guy?"

"Well, it was purely coincidental, but when I went out to Vegas by myself, it turned out that our rooms were right across from each other's."

"No!"

"Yes!"

"You two didn't know that the other was going out there?"

"No, I hadn't even spoken with him since the day you were in my room when he called."

"That was just last week."

"Well, anyway, after thinking about my ordeal at SMS, I decided that I was going to take some time out for myself and . . ."

"That's when you flew to Vegas."

"Yes, and one thing just lead to another and before I knew it . . ."

"You got your groove on!"

"Yeah, I guess, I did."

Dee saw Pam blush for the first time in three years. "Finally!"

"Anyway, it all happened so fast."

"Well, how was it?"

"It was good, Dee. I mean really, really good. I got a chance to clear my head, too. It's amazing what a good orgasm can make you do!"

Dee laughed. It felt good. When she looked at Pam she saw something that she hadn't seen in a while—a face free of lines and anger, and happy.

"Well, did that orgasm give you some clarity about anything else?"

Pam squinted until her forehead wrinkled. She let out a huge sigh. "I know where this is going. You mean, did I have a chance to think about Amanda, right?"

Dee nodded. "Yes."

Pam began pacing as if she was about to give final arguments to a jury.

Oh boy, what have I done now? Dee thought as she started regretting the fact that she even mentioned Amanda's name.

"Yes, I gave her some thought."

Dee's eyes widened. "Really? And what did you decide?"

Pam stopped pacing and looked Dee square in the eyes. "Would you be offended if I didn't tell you?"

Dee was surprised at her answer. Since when did Pam ever care if she offended someone? "So what if I am offended?" Dee chided.

"Well, all I can say is that I do have a plan, but I haven't fully worked it out. However, when I do, I'll let you know. Deal?"

Dee smiled and got up to embrace Pam. "Deal!" She hoped that whatever her plan was that it would end this incredulous feud between her and Amanda.

"So, when do I get to meet Mr. Wonderful?" Dee asked changing the subject.

"Funny you should ask, he's coming to town on Friday. Are you flying?"

"No, I'm off this whole weekend."

"Great. Maybe you could bring a date."

"I don't think so." Dee looked at her evenly. She remembered the bet they had made about Sedrick.

It was like Pam had read her mind. "Hey, listen I may have been wrong about Sed."

"What are you talking about? Wrong about what?"

"The bet we made, remember?"

"Oh yeah, what about it?" Dee pretended that she didn't remember. She could hear hesitancy in Pam's voice.

"Well, it's just that it appears that he has a girlfriend, and it looks kind of serious."

"Really? When did you find this out?"

"He introduced her to me on the day he came by to drive me to the airport when I was off to Vegas."

"Good for Sed. Who is she?" *That leaves me off the hook!* Dee thought happily to herself.

"Her name is Miranda. She's a resident at the hospital with him. She seems to be very smart and they seem happy."

"I'm happy for him."

"I know you are, but I wanted . . ."

"I know what you wanted, but it was just never meant to be. Besides, I love Sed like a family member. Look, worry about your own love life. It sounds like you've got your hands too full to be digging into mine," Dee laughed.

"All right, I'll give you the details later about the dinner, but I'm going to remain hopeful about you and Sed. I want you to keep the thought in the back of your mind, just in case Miranda isn't THE ONE," Pam said as she started to walk out the room.

"Whatever, Pam, geez."

"Did the mail come while you were here?" Pam shouted from the hallway.

"Yes, it's on the kitchen table."

Pam scooped up the mail that had accumulated over the weekend. Just as she was about to toss out what she thought was a piece of junk mail, she noticed that the return address was from Richmond and Lieberman, a law firm in New York.

"Hmmm . . . that's strange. Why would they be sending me a letter?" She ripped open the envelope and read the first paragraph. Her breathing became labored as she grabbed the back of the chair to brace herself.

Aborted Take Off

When Amanda was about to turn into her driveway, she noticed an unfamiliar car parked next to the curb in front of her house. Cautiously, she pulled up next to it and was shocked to see who it was. She frantically pressed the button to lower her window some.

"Rickey, what are you doing here?"

"I had to see you, Amanda," he said, cutting her off.

"Rickey, have you lost all of your senses? Showing up here like this?"

"Maybe," he said, as he got out of the car and leaned in her passenger window.

"Well, maybe you have a death wish, because if Melvin sees you, he is going to kill you!"

Rickey laughed. "I'm not afraid of Melvin."

"Well, you should be!"

Rickey shook his head and laughed. "Listen, it sounds like you've got a helluva lot more to lose than I do," he said, eyeing her engagement ring as her fingers gripped the steering wheel.

Amanda took her hand off the wheel and pointed her finger in his face, speaking in a low tone. She looked around to see if anyone was watching her. "Rickey, I'm not going to discuss this with you out here."

"Good. Then let's go in the house and talk."

"In my house? You've got to be on something! I just told you . . ."

"I know you keep talking about Melvin, but I think you're using him as an excuse."

"Really, now, and why would I do that?"

"Because you won't be able to control yourself if you're alone with me."

"Rickey! Stop it!" Although she knew he was telling the truth, she still had a strong desire to slap him. Amanda tried to push the memories of their one-night stand out of her mind.

Rickey knew he had struck a chord, and he intended to play it as long and as hard as he could. "Listen, since you won't let me in your house, will you at least pull over?"

Amanda's gray eyes were now seething. She didn't know if she was angrier with him for being so presumptuous, or herself for being so weak around him.

"Now, don't look at me like that," Rickey teased.

"Rickey, you need to go home."

"Just give me a minute. And pull the car over to the curb, will you?"

Amanda reluctantly pulled her car in front of his. He darted toward the side of her car and got in on the passenger side. Her heart was pounding in double-time. *Why does my stomach still flutter when he's near? Damn you, Rickey. Why now? Why did you come back in my life and complicate matters?*

"Look at you; I'm making you nervous, aren't I?"

"Rickey, don't flatter yourself," Amanda mumbled. "I already told you, I'm en—"

"I know, I know. Engaged to Melvin."

Amanda nodded. "That's right."

"But you said you loved me."

Amanda shook her head. "I know I did Rickey, and I do, but it's a different kind of love," she said, wishing she had never told him that.

"Different how?"

Amanda sighed heavily. "We will always have a bond because of Tracey. I know that's a huge part of it. And even though I still look at the old picture of us in my wallet just about every day, I know in my heart that my life is meant to be spent with Melvin."

"See, that says a lot about how you feel about us. How can you say that your life is meant to be spent with Melvin after what we shared?"

"Because I can feel it every time he looks at me. And I don't have to wonder if he's telling me the truth. But, with you, there will always be something standing between us. I don't know; maybe just too much time has passed. We've grown our separate ways and, well, Melvin and I have grown together."

"But, Amanda, I can make up for that time. Let me prove it to you. What happened with us losing contact wasn't my fault."

"I know it wasn't *all* of your fault."

"Oh, so now you're going to make it sound like some of it was?"

"Listen, all I know is that for all of these years I raised our daughter without a father. You had a choice, Rickey."

"What choice? Mama didn't allow me to have any. She made them for me. I told you that! That's how we lost contact, that's how I lost you . . . and Tracey."

Amanda took in a deep breath. She was unprepared to tell Rickey this to his face. "Rickey, I've thought about this every hour since you and I first saw each other again." Amanda paused. "I know that your mother was sabotaging your efforts, but you could have worked harder to find us and have a relationship with your daughter."

Rickey grabbed her hand. His touch was making her so warm that she had to roll her window down further.

"Amanda, Let me make it up to you and Tracey. Tracey is willing to forgive me. Why can't you?"

"I do, I really do forgive you, Rickey. We were both so young. And young people do foolish things. But as much as I would like to, I can't go back in time. Too much has happened."

"Yes, you can, baby. You did the other night when you let me make love to you. I want you back, Amanda. I love you and I want the three of us to be a real family." He let go of her hands and cuddled her face. He kissed her with such intensity that she had chills. "Now, look at me and tell me again that you can't go back."

"Rick—"

Before Amanda could finish saying his name, her panties became moist as Rickey pulled her toward him. He playfully sucked her bottom lip and penetrated her mouth with an erotic slip of his tongue. "I love you, Amanda," he repeated as Amanda tried to catch her breath.

"Please stop. Rickey—no!" she said, trying to gain control. "You've got to stop this now, Rickey. I mean it!" she cried out, raising her hands at him.

Suddenly out of nowhere, a red pick-up truck spun in front of them. The slamming of the brakes made a loud screeching noise. Amanda nervously squirmed around in her seat and immediately started shoving Rickey toward the door. "Oh my God! Get out! Get out now! It's Melvin!"

"Damn, what's this dude got? Radar?"

Rickey barely stepped out of her car when he felt a sharp blow to the left side of his jaw. Melvin pulled his fist back to punch him again on the other side.

"Stop it! Melvin! Stop it," Amanda screamed jumping from the car.

Rickey barely had time to react as he saw Amanda jump on Melvin's back, trying to prevent him from lunging at Rickey again.

"What the hell is he doing here?" Melvin yelled.

Rickey rubbed his jaw, moving it a little to make sure it wasn't broken. "Amanda, do you want to tell him or should I?"

"Tell me what?" Melvin looked at Amanda scornfully.

"Melvin—please, honey, I can explain!"

"Explain what? That you're still in love with this no-good nigga who abandoned you and Tracey for all of these years!" Melvin's words cut through Amanda's heart like a hot razor blade. Why would he say something like that to her? Melvin would never talk to her like that unless he had good reason.

"Hey, man, why don't you get your facts right before you start accusing somebody?" Rickey looked at him as if he wanted to take a few jabs at Melvin.

"I ain't accusin' somebody, I'm accusin' you, punk!"

"Punk?" Rickey said, loosening his tie and shrugging off his blazer.

"Rickey, PLEASE!" Amanda shouted.

"Naw, nigga, show me what you got. Gone take off that $2000 suit; we wouldn't want yo' pretty-boy ass to get dirty."

"Melvin, just come on in the house. I'm warning both of you. I will call the police. The two of you are acting like juvenile delinquents!"

"Him more so than me!" Rickey said pompously.

"Why, I'll take that silk tie and tie a noose around your steroid-sized neck!" Melvin said, trying to take another swing at him. As Rickey ducked, Amanda found herself right in the middle of them.

"Rickey, GO HOME, NOW!" she shouted, looking around, hoping none of her neighbors were looking out of their window. She grabbed Melvin by the hand. Finally, he paused when Rickey jumped in his car and sped away. Amanda hurried Melvin into the house.

"Here, take this," she said, opening the freezer and handing him an ice pack for the bruise that was forming around his knuckles. Melvin flinched as it gradually numbed his sore hand.

"So why didn't you tell me that jackass was in town? Huh? Why you tryin' to hide him from me?"

"It's a long story, Melvin."

"Well, spare me the details and give me the abbreviated version! As a matter of fact, why don't we start with the conversation you had on the phone with him this morning."

Amanda was stunned. "How did you know I was on the phone this morning?"

"Cause I came back to get my wallet and I overheard you talkin' to that jerk of a daddy with the big bucks. So, now, are you gon' tell me what the hell is goin' on, or am I going to have to get it from him?"

Amanda sat down next to him and told him about their coincidental meeting at the airport and the conversation they had about Tracey over dinner. She could hardly bring herself to meet his deep disapproving gaze.

"So you mean to tell me that you've waited all this time to tell me this?"

"Yes, because I knew you would react just like you did. And I was right, wasn't I?"

Melvin got up and pushed his chair back with such force that it fell over backwards on the floor. He slammed the ice pack on top of the table, and the loud thud made Amanda jump. In all of the years she had known Melvin, she had never seen him filled with so much fury.

"Yeah, Amanda, you was right! You always are though, ain't you? You was right when you thought that cocky bastard was going to marry you when you got pregnant by him! And you was right when you decided to let him send only money to Tracey for seventeen years! And you was right when you let him seduce you after seventeen years and worm his worthless way back into Tracey's life!"

"Melvin, I didn't let him se—"

"Who you think you dealin' with, Amanda? I didn't just wake up and meet you yesterday. You've been hung up on Rickey for as long as I've known you. Hell, you been carryin' that old ass picture of you and him in your wallet since the day I met you! Bet you didn't think I knew that did you? Damn, you even startin' to get his stench!" Melvin rudely wiped his nose with his hand to show his disgust with her.

Amanda's mouth hung open from shock. "How can you talk to me like that?"

"How can you tell that classless son-of-a-bitch you love him? How do you think that makes me feel, huh? You wearin' my ring, and tellin' him that you love him! You are so caught up in Rickey's past. Mr. Big Time Football Player. Mr. Suave. Mr. GQ. Mr. Daddy Big Bucks. He sends ya' checks here and there, and you're able to lead the kind of lifestyle you want to!" He waved his hands wildly in the air. "You're okay with a check from him because he can't give you nothin' else. Well, I tell you what, Amanda, you and Rickey do as you please! I just don't want to see Tracey hurt!"

"Melvin, what are you saying?"

"All I know is that right now I don't even want to look at you. I need some space," he said as he walked to the door.

"Melvin?"

"I'll call you in a few days, and in the meantime, maybe you and Mr. Heisman Trophy can get together and work out a way not to ruin Tracey's life!" He stormed out of the house.

Amanda thought she was coming home to relax from her first day back at work, and just as she didn't think her evening could get any worse, the doorbell rang.

"Melvin?" she cried out, hoping he'd had a change of heart and came back to resolve their differences. "I'm so glad you came back!"

When she opened the door, she couldn't believe who was on the other side. She immediately flung the door, but Pam caught the handle of the door before it could close all the way.

"Amanda, please. We need to talk."

"This is the worst time you could have shown up. I don't have anything to say to you. Please let go of my door and leave."

"Okay, that's fair. I know my timing is not the best. I just saw Melvin speed out of here like a bat out of a hell, with a swollen hand that was the size of a football. I know it's none of my business, but—"

"No, it isn't! Just go away. Get out of my door before it ends up knocking you in the face, okay? I have nothing to say to you!"

"Okay, then don't say anything. Just let me talk. Will you PLEASE let me in?"

"NO!"

"All right, I promise I can say what I have to say in three minutes. I'm not leaving until you let me say what I came by to say. I can stay out here all day and wait. I've got plenty of time on my hands. So, it's up to you."

Amanda did not want to create a scene in her neighborhood. She knew Pam well enough to know that she would not leave until she had her say. She reluctantly pulled the door open and waited for the second hand on her watch to hit number 12 so she could start the count. "You have three minutes. Start."

Pam took a deep breath. "Amanda, I was so wrong to treat you the way I did." She paused and looked at Amanda, but she had no reaction. "I had no right to make your work life a living hell. You see, I have been living in hell for quite some time now, and I guess subconsciously I wanted to take you there with me. I didn't realize, nor did I care about, how unhappy I was making you and the other employees."

She took another deep breath and looked at Amanda again, hoping she would give her some eye contact. "I am turning over a new leaf starting today, and I want to make amends. I know it cannot happen overnight, but I will work at it until I can make it right."

"Are you through?"

"Yes," Pam said exhaling.

"Good. Because there are about 30 seconds left, which gives me just enough time for you to get up out of my house and shut the door behind you!"

"I understand," Pam said despairingly.

"I'm glad you do. Now, GET OUT and don't ever show up at my door step unannounced again!"

Pam started to walk back toward her car, but suddenly turned back to Amanda and whispered, "I'm so sorry. I hope that one day you can forgive me."

Amanda slammed the door, leaned up against it, and cried until there were no more tears left.

Air Sickness

Marco raised his eyebrow at Pam and asked, "We have a reservation for three?"

"Yes, three," Pam nodded.

"Has your third party gotten here yet?" the hostess asked.

"No, will that be a problem?" Pam asked, already on the defensive. She despised restaurants that held up tables until the entire party was there. She could see it if there were ten or more and only one showed up, but they were only talking about one more person.

"No, ma'am, I just was going to ask you what your friend looked like so that we could escort him or her to your table once they arrive."

"Oh, I see," Pam said, a little embarrassed. "She's a tall, medium complexion, very attractive black woman with long dark brown hair." Pam stopped mid-sentence, realizing she'd probably just described more than half of the black female population of Atlanta. The hostess looked at her and smiled. "She'll probably just call me on my cell phone when she gets here. I'll be on the lookout for her."

"Okay, I'll seat you now." The hostess walked them over to an intimate corner table facing the front window.

"Here's a good view. You'll be able to see her when she walks in," she said as she placed the menus on the table.

"Thanks," Pam said appreciatively.

"So, what is this wonderful news that you have to tell me? You sounded so elated over the phone," Marc said as he flipped through the menu.

"I got a letter from a law firm in New York."

"Oh, yeah? What for?"

"They want to discuss the possibility of me joining their firm as a partner!" She pulled the letter out of her purse and handed it to him. Marco took the letter and read it, intrigued by her good news.

"Richmond and Lieberman. I know someone who's used them before. They're excellent! They're major league, just like you," he smiled. "This is wonderful, Pam!" He bent and kissed her on the cheek.

"I know . . ."

"What's the matter?" Marco asked, as he saw her enthusiasm wane.

"I had something else happen to me earlier today."

"Sounds very dark."

"It was. I went to see Amanda today and laid all of my cards out on the table and apologized."

Marco squeezed her hand tightly. "Good for you. But I take it that it didn't go too well."

"It was about what I had expected. She kicked me out." Pam chuckled. "But, hey, I did good. I convinced her to let me in before she had a chance to kick me back out, right?"

"Well, that's a positive way of looking at it."

"Yeah, I have to stay positive. I'm not sure if she is ever going to get past this. And I can't blame her either, quite frankly."

"Give her some time to heal. She'll come back around."

"I hope so, Marc. I really do," she said looking into his eyes trying to collect her thoughts.

"Hey, Earth to Pam! Earth to Pam," Marco laughed. "Let's finish talking about this fantastic opportunity with Richmond and Lieberman. Now, that's something you should be jumping up and down about."

"I'm thrilled about the opportunity, don't get me wrong. I guess I always thought I would be here in Atlanta when I made partner. New York is a whole other world."

"Which you can take on," he grinned.

Pam smiled modestly. He was so supportive of her. "Well, it sounds great. I just wish it was here, that's all. You know, I've got to get out there and look for a place. And Lord knows, compared to how I'm living here, the rent there would be a million dollars a month!"

"You don't have to worry about finding a place to stay in New York."

"Marc, I'll be pulling down a very nice salary, no doubt. But I don't necessarily want to spend it all on rent."

He leaned over and placed his forefinger across her lips. "If you would just stop talking for a moment, please. What I'm trying to tell you is that I have a very nice apartment looking right over Central Park. I only use it when I'm there on business. It's fully furnished, has a doorman, and you could stay there rent-free as long as you like."

Was she hearing him correctly—an apartment in New York rent free, and a nice one at that? Where was all of this leading?

"Wow, I don't quite know what to say," Pam said, feeling her face flush.

"I find that hard to believe," he said teasingly.

The waiter came over and took their order. Pam rolled up her sleeves and peeked at her watch.

"What time did you tell your roommate to get here?"

"I told her 7:30."

"Well, it's only been a few minutes," he said, glancing down at his own watch. "I'm sure she'll get here."

"Yeah, she probably got caught in traffic," she said, putting her sleeve down and taking a sip of the margarita the waiter had just placed on the table.

"So, what do you think about the apartment?"

Pam hesitated for a moment before she spoke. She traced her fingers around the top of her glass. "I think it's a wonderful gesture, Marc. I have to think some more about it. I haven't even told Sterling, Mathis, and Silverman my plans. As far as they're concerned, I'm taking some long overdue vacation."

"Well, I'm sure they are sitting back and counting all of the money you made them off of that last case you won. I would love to see you go in there and tell them that you will be taking your talents elsewhere." He smiled smugly at the thought.

"I can't believe I'm hearing you say that."

"What? I know you've worked hard. I must admit that I don't always agree with your tactics, but you are paid to do a job. And you have made that firm a lot of money. And when they lose you, it will definitely hit them in their wallets."

Pam smiled and ate the calamari that was just set down on the table. "Now, I like the thought of that!" she said as she watched Marc sip his chardonnay.

"And I like the thought of you in my apartment in New York."

"Pam is going to kill me. I forgot all about this evening," Dee said glancing at the clock on the wall. "Call Pam," she said into her phone's voice activation, and then she headed out the door and down the elevator to the lobby—waiting for the valet to bring her car around. The phone rang, beeped loudly, and disconnected. Great, no battery. She had forgotten to charge the thing when she got back from her trip.

Nothing had gone right since she told Steve the truth. Her flight had been delayed because of a holding pattern in Tennessee. She'd left one of her best pair of shoes at her hotel in Salt Lake City. Also, her psychiatrist was out of town and she desperately wanted to speak with him.

What else could go wrong? At least she was only ten minutes away from the restaurant, Maggiano's. When she got to the restaurant she handed the valet her keys, then walked briskly toward the front of the restaurant where she saw someone who looked like Pam, laughing and sipping on a drink with a handsome man who looked a little familiar, but she could see only the side of his face.

"Hmmm, not bad, from what I can see here—not bad at all," she said as she walked into the restaurant and told the hostess that she was there to meet her party. As she pointed to them, she stopped abruptly as she came into full view of the new man in Pam's life. She saw him take a sip of his drink then kiss her.

She felt queasy and held her mouth. Her head was swirling as she hastily turned around and ran out of the restaurant, bumping into people as they entered. She made it outside and ran around the corner where she released the contents of her stomach. She could barely hold herself up.

"Are you all right, Miss? Can I get you some water?" asked an elderly man. Dee waved her hand to signal that she would be fine and darted toward the parking lot. The valet had not yet parked her car, and she sprinted toward him with blinding tears.

"Hey, I won't be staying," she managed to utter as she took her keys and opened her door and sped off.

"Hmmm . . . this is really strange. It's been almost an hour. It's not like her not to call if she's running late," Pam said.

"Is your cell phone's ringer on?" Marc asked.

"I thought it was. I better check." Pam pulled her cell out of her purse and looked at the screen.

"Did she call?"

"Yes, her number is in the screen, but she didn't leave a message. And of course, with all of the noise in here, I never heard the phone ring. No text either—not that she's big on texting."

"Something probably just came up, Pam. I'm sure you'll find out once you get home," he said trying to comfort her.

"Yeah, I'm sure you're right."

"Would you like to order dessert?"

"No, I'm stuffed."

"Their tiramisu is delicious you, know," he said with a tempting grin.

"I'm sure it is, but if I eat one more thing, I won't be able to fit behind my steering wheel," she chuckled patting her stomach.

"I don't think that's something you will ever have to worry about," Marc said admiring her petite frame. "Hey, are you going to stay with me tonight?" He looked at the bill and placed his tab in the bill holder. They headed out of the restaurant holding hands as Marc gave the valet their ticket.

"I want to, but I think I need to . . ."

"Go back and check on your roommate," Marco said finishing her sentence. Pam nodded reluctantly. "I understand," he said as the valet pulled the car up and opened the door for Pam.

"Thanks."

"You are welcome, ma'am," the valet responded.

Marc handed him a tip and got in the car. "And thank you, sir."

"No problem."

Pam pulled up to his hotel and parked. Marco parted her lips with his tongue and kissed her until a warm rush slid through her body. The look in his eyes was titillating. "*Arrivederci*," he said as a sexy grin spread across his face. "I'll call you later and we'll get together early tomorrow."

"Sounds good. *Arrivederci* to you, too," she said as he climbed out of the car. She noticed the fabric of his pants hugging his sexy derriere and wished she could squeeze herself in between the cloth's lining. Dee had better have a good explanation for not showing up this evening. A damn good one!

Dee sped down the freeway like she was in the Indy 500. She knew she'd better get a handle before she caused an accident. She pulled her stick shift down into second gear and coasted off the ramp, pulling into the underground parking deck of her condo. She turned off the ignition and put her head down and accidentally banged it onto the steering wheel so hard that the horn set off.

"Ouch!" she said, rubbing her forehead. "My God, what am I going to do?" She thought about all of the intimate thoughts and desires she shared with him. How long had this been going on? When did they meet? In a fit of rage, she pounded her fists on the steering wheel until the horn sounded off again. "How could he do this to me? And with all people! My best friend!"

Pam walked into the condo and saw that all the lights were turned off. She went back to Dee's room and saw her suitcase and uniform laid neatly across her bed. Good, at least she made it home. Pam walked back to her room and heard the key turn in the door. She headed toward the living room.

"Hey, it's you!" She was relieved to see that Dee was okay.

"Yes, it's me," Dee said, trying to smile. She could not bring herself to look at Pam.

"I saw on my cell phone that you called me tonight, and when you didn't show up at the restaurant I became worried and decided to cut the evening short."

Dee stared at her key chain, fumbling aimlessly with her three keys. "Yeah, you're right. My battery went dead. I tried to call you and tell you that I wouldn't be able to make it. Sorry." The key chain slipped out of her hand and onto the floor. Pam looked at her warily as Dee quickly picked it up and darted toward the hallway.

"That's okay. Is everything all right?"

"Just fine. My flight was delayed and it thoroughly threw my life off as usual." She felt the nausea creeping up again. She couldn't fake it anymore. How could she tell Pam? "Hey, listen, I'm beat. I'm going to turn in early tonight," Dee mumbled.

"All right. Get some rest. I'll talk with you tomorrow. By the way, I stopped by Amanda's today, but I'll tell you about that tomorrow."

Dee scurried to her room and slammed the door.

The Calm Before the Storm

"Sedrick, I'm telling you. It's as if Dee has become Dr. Jekyll and Mrs. Hyde. She has these crazy mood swings. I mean, just this morning, I asked her if she wanted a cup of coffee and she looked at me like I had just cut off the heels to her favorite shoes."

Sedrick laughed. "C'mon, Pam. Are you sure you two haven't had an argument or something?"

"Look, I'm telling you, I can't talk to her. She's been acting moody ever since she stood me and my friend up for dinner on Friday."

"What friend is this?"

"Oh, that's right, I didn't tell you. Everything has been happening so fast."

"Tell me what, Pam?"

"About this guy that I've been seeing."

"You?"

"Yeah, me." Sedrick gave her an odd look. "I know, I know. But he's been treating me pretty good thus far, so . . ."

"So when am I going to meet him?"

"When will you have time between work and Miranda?"

Sedrick ignored her comment and grinned.

"What does that silly look mean?"

"What it means is that I like her and all, but she's not the one who I can take home to Mama, if you know what I'm saying."

"Ooooh, so she's a ho in private *and* a ho in public." She laughed. "That's messed up. Not wifey material, eh?"

"I didn't say that."

"You didn't have to! I could tell there was something about her, but I couldn't quite figure it out when I first met her, but now I'm certain of it."

"Yeah, right."

"No, really."

"Okay, so what is that something?"

"She's mentally on your level. She's smart, pretty, and sexy, and knows all of the right things to say, and she would make a decent trophy wife, right?"

"Ah right . . . ah right."

"But, I bet she sleeps around with other good potential men, too?"

"I don't have any proof of that."

"Did she sleep with you on the first date?"

"Huh?"

"You heard me boy!" She laughed. "You know you hit it on the first date."

"Okay, you're right," he admitted, sort of embarrassed.

"So, if she let you get it on the first date, how many otha brotha's she's been doing the nasty with on the first date, huh? And that's why you can't take her home to Mama, because your Mama will know she's a doctor-scrub, stethoscope-wearing, undercover ho." Pam cracked up laughing at her analogy so hard that tears started running down her face.

"Okay, so now you're Dr. Phil, right? You analyze my relationships now in addition to practicing law?"

"Admit it, I'm right, aren't I?"

Sedrick grinned again. "Let's just get back to your Mr. Feel Good."

"The truth hurts, doesn't it, Sed?" she giggled.

"Shut up, Pam. So where does this guy live?"

"Salt Lake City."

"What? You mean to tell me with all of the men running around in the Greater Atlanta area, you couldn't find a brotha' here?"

Pam laughed. "Nope, I guess not. And guess what?"

"I'm afraid to."

Pam giggled again. "He's Italian!"

"Ital—what?"

"You heard me, silly!"

"So, you done gone the extreme makeover route on this one, huh? Never thought I'd see the day . . ."

"Oh, you've got some nerve! You are not one to talk about ethnicity with you bringing Miss Venezuela up in here."

"Touché."

"Besides, he's cool, Sedrick. I think you'll like him."

"Hey, baby, as long as you're happy. You're the one who's gotta be with him, not me," Sedrick chuckled. "So has Dee met him?"

"Naaa. She was supposed to the other night, but we missed her."

"Well, I'll talk with her and see if she'll tell me anything about what's wrong. But I must admit, I'm just as clueless as you are."

"Good, 'cause Lord knows I've got enough going on in my life without being in Dee's drama."

"Well that sounds like a major drama flick in itself," Sedrick laughed, "especially with Mr. Italia."

"You're right it is, but he's not the only thing that's going on in my life," she said handing him the letter from the New York firm.

Sedrick read it slowly. "Damn, Pam! What an opportunity!"

Pam smiled. "Yes, it is!"

"So are you going to take it?"

"I don't know. I'm really leaning toward it."

"What did Mr. Italia think about that?"

"He's happy for me. Would you please stop calling him that? His name is Marc, all right?"

"All right, I'll get back to Marc later. So, what did Dee have to say about it?"

Pam shook her head.

"You haven't told her yet?"

"No, I just got the letter, and I haven't even responded."

"What are you waiting on?"

"Well, I'm going to give them a call today and go out there and talk with them. I'll see if what they're offering is really as good as it sounds. Besides, what have I got to lose, right?"

"Right! You'll still come back for my building's ribbon cutting ceremony won't you?"

"Of course I will, Sedrick. I don't care if I'm in Australia, I'll fly back from anywhere in the world to see your butt finally open that office."

"I know. My parents feel the same way. It's been a long time coming, and I know my dad can't wait to have me to start paying him back for all the loans he and my mother took out to get me through med school. He said 'Son, I'm glad you're in a field where you can have a private practice. That way you will at least pay me back with some dividends. At least in obstetrics, women are always having babies. The cost of delivering babies is always going up, so I won't have to worry about you not having any money.'"

"Oh Sedrick, Mr. Henderson didn't say that, did he?"

"He sho' did! And he was serious," Sedrick laughed.

The door opened, and Dee zoomed past both of them.

"Hey Dee, how ya doin'?" Sedrick said, trying to sound upbeat and cordial.

"Fine," she said as she zipped through the hallway.

"Who was that, that just flew by?"

Pam looked at him, shaking her head. "I told you—that's how she's been acting lately."

Dee went into her room and caught her breath. She felt like her oxygen was being cut off, and she didn't know how to get it back. Why was Sedrick here now of all times? Her cell phone interrupted her thoughts.

"Aunt Dee?"

"Hi Tracey."

"Are you okay?"

Dee cleared her throat. "Yes, hi, Tracey. How are school and Tony? Are you two still seeing each other?"

"School's great! Tony and I are dealing with the long distance thing okay."

"I see, well, I'm glad to hear that—I really am."

"Have you spoken to Mama, lately?"

"No, is everything all right?"

"Well, have you spoken to Ms. Pam, yet?"

"Noooo. What's going on Tracey?" Dee sat on the bed and gripped the edge. Tracey sounded like she needed to brace herself.

"It's Mama and . . ."

"What about Amanda? Is she all right?"

"Calm down. Mama's fine. It's just that Ms. Pam came over the other day to see her."

"For what?" Dee said grabbing the edge of the bedspread tighter.

"To apologize!"

"Pam apologized?"

"Yes," Tracey laughed. "She apologized." Dee started shaking her head in disbelief. "Auntie Dee, are you still there?"

Dee nodded. "Yes. It just seems like every day brings in a new turn of events."

"So, Ms. Pam didn't tell you?"

"No, not yet. I think she tried to," Dee said remembering how Pam wanted to tell her something about Amanda.

"Well, it might be that she didn't tell you yet because there wasn't much to tell."

"But you said . . ."

"Mama threw her out," Tracey blurted.

Dee let out a loud giggle. She could just picture Amanda kicking Pam out of her house. "She did?"

"Yep! And I'm so proud of her."

"I bet you are. But, this is still not good because they really have to resolve this. Their problems have been going on for too long."

"I don't know if I agree with you, Aunt Dee."

"Trust me. I know what I'm talking about. You were too young to remember our closeness, but I do."

"Well, I don't know what it's going to take, but they are far away from ever being close again, according to Mama."

"I know, Tracey. Thank you for calling me."

"No problem. I'll talk with you soon."

Dee sat her phone down and was heading to the bathroom when it rang again.

"Now what?" She mumbled as she picked up the phone. "Hello?"

"Hello, Deirdre?"

"Yes, this is she."

"This is Rebecca. I'm calling to confirm your appointment this Thursday."

"I won't be meeting with him anymore."

"Ms. Bridge, is everything okay?"

"Yeah!" she said trying not to scream out of frustration.

"I see. I'm so sorry; I will give him the message. I'm sure he will want to speak with you."

"It's not necessary, Rebecca. My mind's made up. Thank you for your time."

Dee fell back into her chair and looked at the large clock on the wall. She had to be at the airport for a flight and decided that she would leave a little early to avoid any more confrontations with Pam. She changed into her uniform and pulled her suitcase out of the door, then whizzed past Pam and Sedrick again.

"Dee, where you off to?" Sedrick asked with a puzzled look on his face.

"I'm headed out for a three-day trip to Charleston, Orlando, and Tennessee. See you in a couple of days," she said as she opened the door and walked out.

Pam looked at Sedrick who was obviously baffled by Dee's reaction. "I told you."

"You're right. She is trippin."

"You know, Sedrick, I'm going to ask that you look out for her because I may not be around to do it," she said sadly as she walked over to him and gave him a hug.

"I've got her back—don't worry."

Flying High Above the Clouds

"Well, Counselor Madison, your credentials are impeccable," Adam Parks said with a satisfied look on his face.

"Your experience is extremely impressive," Mark Ward and John Lieberman, two of the firm's senior partners, chimed in. "I'm sure that Sterling, Mathis, and Silverman is shaking right about now, wouldn't you say, Adam?"

"I'm sure." Adam nodded with the same twinkle in his eye that he'd had at the beginning of Pam's interview.

Adam Parks was a shrewd man. He was in his late forties, impeccably dressed, and was anal about keeping rising attorneys on his radar. He would read about them and research their background. He kept tabs on all of their big winning cases and nabbed them before their current law firm knew what hit them. Except in this case, Pam was nabbing them. She had done all of her research and knew that they were one of the highest-ranking firms in the northeast.

"Well, your firm has a lot of positives for me, Mr. Parks."

Adam nodded. "We'd like to hear what they are."

"For one, I like the fact that your firm is not the largest."

"We hope that will change very shortly," Adam chuckled.

"I know. But for now, it's a good size firm."

John nodded in agreement.

Mark sat across from her, almost unable to contain his excitement that Pam was almost a "shoe-in."

"I especially like that your clients are so diverse," Pam laughed. "You guys range from corporate scandals, right down to major divorces. In fact, I read that most of the New York celebrities are represented by Richmond and Lieberman."

"My! You are up on the stats, aren't you?" Adam laughed.

"I do my best. By the way, congratulations on your big win!"

"Now, that was a big coup for us," Adam said proudly. "Sadly though, the whole family was devastated by that automobile manufacture's negligence."

"Yes, it was extremely unfortunate." Pam paused and looked at the three men evenly. "Gentlemen, I'm impressed with your firm and appreciate you allowing me the opportunity to come up from Atlanta and meet with you."

"We are impressed with you as well," Adam said pulling a white envelope from his jacket pocket. "Here, take a look at this, Miss Madison, and see if it meets your satisfaction."

Pam nodded as she coolly opened the flap of the envelope. Trying to keep her composure, she stared in awe at the seven figures including housing and relocation expenses. She placed the letter back in its envelope and smiled contently.

"Let me think about it, Mr. Ward, Mr. Parks, and Mr. Lieberman," she said as she stood to shake each of their hands before making her exit. Mark winked at Adam, suggesting they had won her over. The two of them escorted her out of the double mahogany doors and into the brass-coated elevator.

"It has been a pleasure, Miss Madison. We look forward to hearing from you soon."

Pam made her way down to the lobby where a black stretch limousine was waiting for her. She stepped in feeling like she was newly confirmed royalty.

A girl could get used to this, she thought as she stroked the rich leather seats that encompassed her body. She poured herself a glass of Perrier from the mini-bar and imagined herself transforming from a southern girl to a New York woman.

Emergency Exit

It was 2:00 a.m. when Sed's cell phone started buzzing.

"I thought you weren't on call tonight," Miranda said, groggily.

"I'm not. Go back to sleep," he said as he grabbed his cell phone from the nightstand. Dee had sent him a text that read: I NO ITS LATE, BUT I NEED 2 TALK 2 U. R U UP? D.

Sed chuckled.

"Where are the earplugs?" Miranda demanded. "That noise is too loud." She placed a pillow over her head while he handed her his earplugs. When Miranda was asleep, she didn't like to be disturbed at all. Sedrick found it amazing that she could sleep through a tornado, but when she was on call, she was a totally different person.

Sed texted Dee back. YES. U CAN STOP BY, S.

Suddenly, there was a loud knock at the door. He wasn't sure if he was dreaming or if Dee had been standing in the lobby sending him messages. The knock continued as he stumbled to grab his briefs off the floor. He looked over and saw Miranda's naked body under loosely draped sheets. He tiptoed out of the room and closed the bedroom door behind him.

The knock continued. "Hold on a second," he said, still trying to get his bearings as he scrambled to find his sweatpants. He opened the door and Dee raced into his trendy loft still clad in her flight attendant uniform.

"Are you just getting back or are you on your way out?"

"I've been back in town for a few hours and I've been driving around. Somehow, my car led me here."

"What kind of car is that you drive?" Sedrick said rubbing his eyes.

Dee laughed. "I know that sounds crazy. Hey, I'm sorry to bother you so late." She paused. "But I've got to talk with someone. I just can't go home until I do." Dee glanced around at Sed's classic decor and saw a woman's blouse draped across a black leather chair. "Sed, I'm really sorry. Why didn't you tell me you had company?"

"Hey, don't worry about it," he said groggily. "So, what's happening that can't wait until day break?"

"Pam and I have not been speaking to each other."

"Oh? I thought it was the other way around."

"What do you mean?"

"I mean, I thought you were the one not speaking to her."

"Is that what she told you?"

"Hey, I ain't trying to get into the middle of you two, but I saw it for myself. You were trippin' and struttin' around like you had something stuck up your behind."

Dee was silent. She felt like she was encased in a block of ice and she needed to come in from the cold to let it soften. She took off her blazer and laid it on top of Miranda's blouse.

"Hey, listen. Let me make you a cup of herbal tea."

"Oh, Sedrick, you are so good to me," she said, making herself comfortable on the supple black leather sofa.

"Not a problem. Not a problem," he said making his way to the kitchen where he brewed the tea. He handed her the cup. "Careful. That heat will take the skin right off your tongue," he joked.

"Thanks. I will." She blew gingerly into the coffee cup and set it down on the small end table next to her.

Unbeknownst to Sedrick, Miranda had turned to cuddle up to him and felt a cold set of empty sheets next to her instead of Sedrick's warm body. She took out her earplugs and heard voices coming from the living room. She tiptoed to the door and gently cracked it open.

"Now, what's got you so worked up that you have to pop over here this time of morning?"

Dee sipped on her tea and her eyes widened. "I've been going through a lot lately."

"Like what?"

Dee was silent and shook her head reluctantly. How could she tell him what had been going on with her without him thinking less of her?

"C'mon, Dee. It's old Sed, here. You can tell me anything. I won't judge you," he said tenderly, as if he already knew what she was thinking.

Dee smiled. "You always know what to say, don't you?"

Sedrick yawned. "Ah . . . ha."

"I'm so sorry to come over here like this . . ."

"Dee, stop apologizing, would you?"

"I know, but you've got company," she whispered loudly. "And . . ."

"I already said it's okay. She sleeps like a log, anyway," he said jokingly. "Just tell me what's going on so both of us can get some sleep." He popped her lightly on the shoulder with his fingers.

Dee smiled again. "You're right. That's my problem. I'm always dragging someone else into my problems."

"What problems?"

"Problems that I've been having for some time, Sedrick. I thought I could handle it all on my own, ya' know?" She stood up and paced the room as Sedrick watched her without saying a word.

"But things just started spinning out of control—my insecurities, questioning my self-worth—all of this was becoming too much for me to handle myself. Do you understand what I'm saying?"

Sedrick nodded as she slowed down to take a sip of her tea, then sat down on the couch next to him.

"Okay, I guess I'm babbling, huh?" she said. "Well, I'm saying all of this because I'm still in shock. Okay, I know what you're thinking, just get to the point, right?"

Sedrick was still silent. The subtle smile on his lips let her know that he just wanted her to tell him when she was ready to talk. He took her hands and started rubbing them.

"All right, here goes." She exhaled. "I've been seeing a psychiatrist for a few months now." Dee looked at him and waited for his reaction. To her surprise, all he did was look at her and nod for her to continue. "And now . . . now I don't even know how to say this," she said, feeling Sedrick's hands hold hers firmly, she started to relax. Dee paused. "Pam is dating my psychiatrist."

"Now, I wasn't expecting to hear that. Damn. The guy she was with in Vegas?"

"Now do you understand why I'm acting like I'm crazy?"

"Yeah," Sedrick paused. "I do, now. That's some heavy stuff to be trying to handle by yourself. Have you discussed it with your doctor?"

Dee shook her head. "I canceled my last appointment with him because I wasn't sure how to even bring it up."

"I can understand that. But you've got to let Pam know what happened. She has no idea."

"I can't, Sedrick . . ."

"Why not?"

"Because she doesn't even know that I'm seeing a shrink."

"Dee, plenty of people see psychiatrists. It's no different than going to a doctor when you're not feeling well."

"That's your philosophy."

"Listen, psychiatrists help with mental health, and then there are doctors who help with physical health. That's it. What? Do you think Pam will think you're crazy?"

"Sedrick, I just don't want her knowing that part of me. I mean, I've been involved in a lot of unsavory stuff, I'm ashamed to say." Dee hesitated as she picked up her cup and sipped the rest of her tea.

"We all have, Dee. Pam has a dark side just like the rest of us. Listen, you act like Pam is above sin. And you and I both know for a fact, she isn't."

Sedrick managed to make Dee smile as she reflected on the times when Pam didn't always make the best decisions either. Greg certainly was, by far, her worst. "But I've discussed her with him."

"So?"

"She would be angry and devastated if she knew the things that I've shared with him about her."

"Was discussing her part of your therapy?'

"She would come up from time to time as I told him about myself. I guess he was trying to understand some things about me and why certain things have happened the way they have."

"Things like what?"

"Like why she's a lawyer and I'm not."

"Is that still what you want to be?"

"I do, Sedrick. I'm more sure now than ever before. I'm just scared of taking that bar exam."

"I can understand that. I was afraid of taking a risk in opening my own practice too. But I'm doing it. We've had a few bumps here and there, but overall it's coming along pretty well. Anyway, how will Pam know any of this unless you tell her? He certainly can't tell her. Your sessions are confidential. He's bound by that doctor-patient confidentiality."

Dee pondered what he was saying for a minute, slowly feeling relieved. "You're right; I don't know why I didn't think of that before. But now when the truth comes out about her being my roommate, he probably knows more than she would be willing to share about herself."

Sedrick shrugged his shoulders. "Dee, I don't know what else to say to you. The two of them will have to work that out, baby. You just need to relax and let it go. Stop worrying. She and the good doctor will work it out. I promise."

Even though her emotions were running high, his words were very soothing. She moved closer and leaned in to him. Sedrick hugged her, and his warm touch melted the sheet of ice she had built around herself. She leaned back and looked appreciatively into Sedrick's hazel eyes and noticed he was looking at her like he had seen her for the first time. Dee snuggled in closer to Sedrick's chest. "Thank you, Sedrick." She paused. "You are the best friend a girl could have right now, and I love you for it." She moved her mouth toward his while Sedrick closed his eyes and met her halfway.

Miranda's heart sank as she watched him with Dee. She quietly closed the door and slid back into bed. She wondered why she never knew about Sedrick's feelings for Dee. Sure, she knew they were longtime friends, but now she could see that there was a lot more to their relationship then he had ever shared. Her mind played back to when she met Pam for the first time and how surprised she looked when she first saw her. That son-of-a-bitch! How did she not see this coming? And Dee was a nutcase on top of it!

Dee looked up at Sedrick again and then planted a kiss between the corner of his mouth and cheek.

Sedrick's eyes opened in wide disappointment.

"Thank you, again Sedrick."

"Hey, that's what I'm here for."

"Oh, my goodness, Sedrick," she said glancing at the clock on the wall, "I had no idea of the time. What time do you have to be at work?"

He looked at the clock on the wall. It was 4:30 a.m. "Not until 8:00."

"Oh Sedrick, I'm so sorry. I didn't mean to keep you up like this."

"It's okay, I'm used to it. I'll lie down for a little while and get back up and shower and head on out," he said with a half-smile.

"All right then. I'll talk with you later. She got up from the sofa and grabbed her jacket from the chair. Thanks for the advice."

"No problem, Dee." He opened the door and watched her until she got on the elevator, then shut the door behind him, thinking about what she said and knowing that it was no problem at all, at least not to him.

As Sedrick got back into bed, he looked at Miranda sleeping and kissed her on the cheek. He then rolled over and went to sleep while Miranda remained still.

Rough Landing

Pam wore a smile that was almost too big for her face as she retrieved the mail. She began whistling Bobby McFerrin's late '80s tune, "Don't Worry Be Happy," as she walked back to Dee's room and placed her mail on her dresser. Several days had passed, and Dee was still avoiding her. Well, it wouldn't be long. She was taking the job in New York, and she decided to stay at Marc's place. She would need some time to clean out her office at SMS. As for Dee, she would tell her today. That was if she would talk to her.

When she was ready to leave Dee's room, she heard the phone ring. "That's odd," she said as she looked at the caller ID screen. "Marco Grimaldi? Why is he calling Dee?" Pam picked up the phone.

"Hello?"

"Hello, Ms. Bridge?"

Rebecca didn't give Pam a chance to answer back. "Dr. Grimaldi asked me to give you a call. He really wants to talk with you about canceling all of your appointments with him. He asked that you please reconsider and that he will be calling you personally later today to speak with you."

Pam's jaw dropped. "All right, thank you," she managed to whisper.

"All right, Ms. Bridge, I'll let him know."

"Goodbye."

Rickey bought a pair of faded jeans, a blue denim shirt, and a pair of work boots from the local Target. He had no intention of ever wearing any of them again after today. He had taken a bold move earlier that morning and drove down to Melvin's company to inquire about the location of his next job. He pretended to be a developer wanting to speak with him regarding a planned community that was being designed around an underdeveloped area outside Atlanta. Clad in a hard hat and rolled-up faux architect plans, he convinced a newly hired intern that he needed to speak with Melvin immediately. Rickey was headed toward the address that the young man wrote down.

Rickey left the hat and the plans in the back of his cranberry Jaguar XK convertible. There was no need to pretend now. Melvin knew him for who he was, or at least Melvin thought he did.

"Hey, man, what's up?" The dark-haired man nodded as he walked past him carrying a two-by-four. "I'm looking for Melvin Landers."

"He's up on top." He pointed to the tall scaffold that seemed to line the sky.

Rickey took a deep breath, gripped the scaffold, and climbed up each rung. He dared not look down—fearing he would never be able to complete what he had set out to do. Melvin heard the sound of upcoming footsteps and slowly turned around.

"What the . . .?"

Rickey was standing eye to eye with him before he could finish his sentence. "Melvin?"

"You are a bold son-of-a-bitch," he said clenching his fists.

"Hold on, Melvin, man, you don't want to do this, do you?" Melvin looked down at his men below circling around the scaffold.

"Hey, boss! Everything okay up there?" one of the workers asked.

Melvin thought about where he was and how it was important for him to not show his anger in front of his crew. The last thing he needed was to set a poor example. "Yeah, it's cool," he said, waving his hand for them to continue working.

"Talk fast!" Melvin mumbled as his anger resurfaced.

Rickey closed his eyes for a minute to adjust them to the glaring sunlight, and then cleared his throat before speaking. "I came here today to talk with you about Amanda and Tracey."

"You got exactly one minute and then I'm gonna give you a short cut to get back down there," he said, pointing with his eyes to the hard surface below.

"All right, I can do that. I made a mistake with Amanda years ago. I loved her then, and it's true, it took me some years to realize that I still do, but she has made it perfectly clear that I have come in too late and she has moved on to be with you."

Melvin's eyes softened some, but he still looked as if he wanted to toss Rickey to the ground below. "Thirty seconds left," he said looking at his watch.

Rickey threw both his hands up. "Aight, aight . . . listen, I don't want us to be enemies. I've made a lot of mistakes in my life. The biggest one was not being a man and owning up to my responsibilities and letting someone else handle them for me. Did Amanda tell you I tried to contact her when Tracey was born?"

Melvin's eyes squinted with malice. "No!"

"I see. Did she tell you that my mother was the one who was returning all of her letters back to her and blocking mine from going out to her without me knowing about it?"

"No!" Melvin said trying to keep the bombshell that Rickey had just dropped on him from exploding. Amanda had never breathed a word to him, but then again, he hadn't given her a chance since he'd walked out on her.

"We'll, it's true." Rickey continued, unable to read Melvin's reaction one way or the other. Rickey's hands began to sweat. He looked around to see if there was anything he could grab in case Melvin decided to lose his mind again and come after him like he did before. The closest thing near to him was a metal beam. Unless he was Thor, he couldn't lift it to protect himself. Rickey paused for a moment, and prayed silently, then decided to continue. "But even though my mother had a big hand in this, I should have dug deeper to find out what was going on with my girl and my baby back then."

Melvin was silent as though his mind was spinning like a whirlpool. Why was he telling him all of this? Did he want Amanda back? Did she want him back? And where did he fall into the triangle?

"What about you and her now?" Melvin said, looking down below still trying to resist the urge to see him free falling into midair. "I . . . I heard her tell you over the phone that she still loves you."

Rickey smiled a bit, feeling his heart sinking low in his chest. Somewhere beneath the surface, his pride was trying to find its way to the top, but it too, like the look on Melvin's face, was in limbo. Rickey looked up at him more serious than he'd ever thought possible. "Yeah, she does love me, man, but not enough to leave you." Rickey sighed heavily and looked down below at his potential fate. The words he was about to say would either be his last, or Melvin would take it like a man and forgive Amanda.

"It was a seventeen-year disconnect that we made up for just that one night. I don't regret it, but she does." Melvin lunged toward him. "Because she loves you, man!" Rickey yelled before Melvin could seal his fate. "You are the one she wants to spend the rest of her life with—not me!"

Rickey's eyes pleaded for Melvin's pardon. "Listen, man, I let you get away with hitting me the other day. I felt like I deserved it, and I didn't want to create any more of a scene in front of Amanda. You were only looking out for Amanda and Tracey's best interests, and I can appreciate that. That's what real men do; that's what real fathers do. But today, I gotta say, you are looking at me more and more like you want to kill me. And I ain't interested in going out like that. I'll fight you, Melvin, if that's what you want. But I gotta say that I'd like to go down the same way I came up here, if that's all right with you."

Melvin gave him a cold stare and watched him back down the scaffold like a tortoise in high heels. *That man sho' got a lot of balls,* he thought as he shook his head and looked down at his crew staring up at him protectively.

"C'mon, now, let's get back to work! Show's over!"

Please Return to the Upright and Locked Position

When Pam heard the key jingle inside the lock, she ran from Dee's room to meet her. "Dee, we need to talk," she said, rushing toward Dee as she walked in.

Dee had lost the confidence she'd gained from speaking with Sedrick and could not bring herself to look at Pam, let alone have a conversation with her.

"I'm beat. I had to unexpectedly run back out to the airport after already leaving because I forgot my wallet. So not right now, okay? I'm going to bed." The truth was that after leaving Sedrick's, she'd been driving around all morning in hopes that Pam would be gone by the time she got home.

"Yes, now!" Pam insisted as she grabbed her arm.

Dee jerked away. "I'm not able to talk right now."

Pam's words spewed out like foam from a fire extinguisher. "Well, I can understand why, especially since you've found out that I've been in a relationship with your psychiatrist!" Dee looked at her with shock and resentment. "I didn't mean for it to come out like that," Pam said remorsefully.

"But, how'd you . . . I don't understand . . ."

"I was in your room to put your mail away and answered your phone. I thought it odd that Marc's number was coming up on your caller ID, so I answered it and his assistant assumed I was you."

"Well, did you tell her you weren't me?"

"No, I didn't get a chance to."

Dee felt her head pounding and began massaging her temples. "Well, do I need to call her and get the message or do you have that also?"

"Marc will be calling you. It seems that you have canceled all of your appointments with him." Pam's voice sounded concerned, and Dee's head was pounding even more.

Dee flopped down on the couch, opened her purse, and popped two aspirin into her mouth. She walked to the kitchen and rinsed them down with a glass of water. She knew this was going to be a long, drawn-out discussion with Pam. "I have," she said as she sat down at the kitchen table.

"So you were at the restaurant," Pam said walking toward her.

"Yes, when I got there, I saw the two of you there together in a lip-lock and, well, I just couldn't believe it . . ."

Pam sat down next to her. "Dee, why didn't you tell me you were seeing a psychiatrist?"

"Why would I tell you that?"

"Because I'm your best friend, that's why! Or at least I thought I was."

"I didn't tell you because I didn't want you to know."

"But why? What is going on with you where you feel like you need a psychiatrist? How long have you been seeing him?"

Dee's tears brimmed as she shook her head in frustration. "It's just too much to have to relive, Pam. I just don't have the energy to go into it with you." She felt the pressure in her head subside. "I've been working with him for about six months. How long have you been seeing him?"

"I've known him for about that long, I guess. But we really haven't been dating until recently."

"Recently, as in Vegas?"

Pam paused. "This is just too fucking bizarre," she mumbled.

Dee rolled her eyes. "No kidding."

"Does Marc even know?"

"No. Like I said, I have canceled all of my appointments so I haven't spoken with him."

They were both silent, and Dee had the worst sinking feeling in the pit of her stomach.

Pam went to pick up the phone. "Well, I think we both need to sit down and talk with him."

"What are you doing?"

"I'm going to call him and ask him to come to Atlanta so we can tell him what is going on."

"Oh, no you're not!" Dee demanded.

"Dee, you're being ridiculous!" Pam quickly picked up the phone and began dialing.

Dee raced toward Pam and placed her hand over the phone. "Listen, Pam. He's my doctor, okay. And believe me you don't want to do that!"

Pam put the phone down and stared at Dee. "Now I get it. You don't want me to talk to him with you, because I'm part of the reason why you've been seeing him."

Dee couldn't look at her. This was exactly why she didn't want to get into this with Pam.

"Well, are you going to say something?"

"Okay. You're right. Now, are you satisfied?"

"No! What exactly did you tell him about me?"

Dee turned her head away from Pam. Her reaction said it all.

"Dee, you didn't . . . how could you discuss my personal issues with him?"

"Listen, Pam. What I said to him was confidential, okay? I even flew to Utah every week just to keep things as private as possible."

"I know, but I'm dating him."

"Well, how was I supposed to know that? I never see you. You go to work early and come back late. You've kept your personal life a secret since Greg."

"I know, Dee. I had too. You know why. But what I don't understand is what that has to do with you talking to Marc about me."

"Everything! I never even really knew how it all added up. But after my first few months of therapy, I've realized that deep down inside I've been miserable about who I am. I look at you every day and see that you've accomplished all the things that I was supposed to."

"What? Where is all of this coming from? I never knew. I mean I had plans for all three of us opening up our own law firm together. All of us were supposed to take the bar, but—"

Dee interrupted before Pam could get her thoughts together. "Pam! Just shut up! It's not about you, and it's not about Amanda, okay! For once, it's about me!"

Pam was shocked and hurt by Dee's outburst.

"I'm sorry," Dee said. "I don't mean to go off on you like this, really. But I've been fooling myself and others for a long time, and I need to let you know how I'm feeling. Some of the stuff I've done . . . well, you just wouldn't believe it," she said, as her voice trailed off. "Doc, I mean, Dr. Grimaldi, has been helping me work through this. Sometimes I wonder if I'm ever going to get better. And now, I find out that the one person that I've been sharing all of my intimate thoughts with is dating one of the people closest to me. It's a hard pill to swallow, and I need some time to digest it."

Pam was still reeling from the large blow that had struck her and was now putting a deep wedge between them. Now, to make matters worse, Marc knew something about her that she should have been the one to tell him—not Dee.

"You know, Dee, you're right."

"Right? About what?"

"This is about you. And I think you need some time to work things out without me being around you."

"What's that supposed to mean?"

"I was wondering how I was going to tell you this, but now it seems as good a time as any. I've accepted a job offer to become a partner at Richmond and Lieberman in New York."

Dee looked at her with eyes opened wide. "Well, congratulations," she said dryly. "So this is what it comes to, huh? You find out you're dating my psychiatrist, I won't go into the specifics of why I'm seeing him, and now you plan on just leaving me high and dry?"

"No, that wasn't my plan at all," Pam answered coolly.

"Pam, you haven't grown since your breakup. You are still running away from your problems."

"What the hell is that supposed to mean? I'm taking a better job!"

"What? They wouldn't cave in to you at SMS, so instead of working out your problems, you bail and then just go to another firm?"

"Dee, you wouldn't understand—even if I tried to tell you."

"No, you're right. I don't understand you at all!"

Pam fumed at her insinuations. She knew what Dee was trying to say, but she didn't like how she was saying it. "Well, now you don't have to worry about trying to understand me, right? Especially as I seem to be the root of your problems! I'll talk to Marc on my own time," she said as she took her purse off of the kitchen table. "Here," she said, pulling out her checkbook and scribbling on the front of the check. "So you won't think I'm leaving you high and dry, I'm giving you my four months' rent. This should give you more than enough time to work things out, find another roommate, and work out your personal problems without me getting in the way!" She handed her the check and headed back to her room.

Once Pam got to her room, she sat on the bed and opened up her nightstand to look for some aspirin—Dee had just given her a headache. "Okay, I know I have some in here, somewhere," she said, as she continued to rummage through the drawer. She suddenly stopped as her fingers ran across something that she had long forgotten. *Oh no, this couldn't be!* She looked at the faded cloth that sat underneath her pillbox and removed it slowly from the drawer—the cloth that had covered a long forgotten keepsake. She sat the cloth on the bed and stared at the memento as tears slowly traveled down her face and her headache disappeared. She thoughtfully wrapped it back up again and solemnly shook her head. Things were so simple back then. She wished they were that easy now. She laid down, placed the memento close to her heart, and drifted off to sleep.

Overpriced Ticket

"C'mon, Dee. I know she didn't do that. That doesn't even sound like Pam."

"I thought the same thing, but she is, and she did."

"Well, when I spoke with her she said she was just considering taking the offer."

"Well, she considered it, and now she's taking it! And I'm stuck with trying to find a roommate within the next two weeks."

Sedrick kept shaking his head as he thought about how Pam left Dee in the lurch. "Man, I just came by to see how the two of you were doing. I had no idea it had come to this. I just can't believe she would leave you hanging like that."

"I know, and I can't afford this place by myself. The lease on this condo is two grand a month! Where am I going to find someone who wants to pay that kind of rent in two weeks?" She was lying again and to Sedrick of all people. Dee knew it was wrong, but she was hurt and angry, and wanted Pam to look bad in Sedrick's eyes.

Sedrick scratched his head, trying to come up with some type of solution. He knew that making Dee an offer to move in with him would not be a smart move. Besides, even if she wanted to, he didn't really have the space for two people. Then there was Miranda.

"Hey, take it easy. I'm sure we can come up with something." Sedrick searched through his briefcase and pulled out his checkbook ledger.

"What are you doing?"

"Let's see here. I've got some money saved up, and I was just trying to see..."

"No, Sedrick, I can't."

"Okay, if you won't let me give it to you, what about your folks?"

Dee immediately shook her head. "No way! My father is still pouting that I'm a flight attendant. I could hear him now, 'If you hadn't wasted my money on going to law school to become a flight attendant then maybe I would have some left to help you!'"

Sedrick started writing out the check. "Look, take this . . ."

"Sedrick! This will cover Pam's half for two months," she said, wishing she had the backbone to take back the lie about the rent.

"Listen, I'm not going to need that money for a while." Now he was lying. He knew he was tapping into the money he had put aside to pay his contractors for his building.

"Oh, Sedrick, I don't know what to say."

"Hey, just pay me back when your new roommate gets here. In the meantime, I'll post some flyers up around the breakroom at the hospital. Something will turn up, you'll see." He hugged her and wished he could hold her in his arms a little longer. Dee grabbed him and held him close while her heart raced and the curves of her body melded into him.

"Hey, you wanna grab some lunch?" Sedrick asked.

"Sure, let's go over to that little bistro around the corner."

"There are 500 bistros around the corner in Buckhead," Sed laughed. "Which one are you talking about?

"How about the French one called Francais Élégant. They have the best food. I had it when I was in Miami. You know the one next to the W Hotel?"

"Oh, yeah, that one. You wanna walk?"

"Sure, I'm up for the exercise."

"Ah right, then. After you," he said, as he opened the door. She locked the door behind them, and they went on their way.

"Hey, isn't that Chris Dickerson?" Sedrick said as they got closer to the restaurant.

Dee felt her stomach do a backward cartwheel. "Where?"

"He just went into Francais Élégant."

No, it can't be, Dee thought.

"Hey, I know this sounds crazy, but I'm a Chris Dickerson fan."

Great. Dee's face went flush as she watched Chris walk out to a table on the patio. Shortly after he sat down, a beautiful petite woman with long dark hair came up from behind him and started nibbling his ear. She firmly planted herself on his knee and planted a kiss on him that was so seductive that it should have been saved for a room at the hotel next door.

"Well, I can see that he hasn't wasted any time letting the grass grow under his feet!" Dee mumbled.

"Do you know this guy, Dee?"

"Yeah. Unfortunately."

"All right then, introduce a brotha."

"Listen, Sed. It's very complicated. I used to go out with Chris, and we just recently had a bad breakup."

"Get outta here! Are you serious? You and Dickerson?"

"Is that an insult?"

"No, wow! I mean, the guy's a playa. I mean look at him. Everybody knows about Dickerson. How long had you two been seeing each other?"

"Long enough to know that he was not Mr. Right."

"Gee, don't get mad at me. Look at him and that girl. He's going at it with that tongue!" Sed said, as he took a closer look at the woman. Her hair was covering the side of her face until she pulled it behind her ear and gave Sed a clear view.

"What the fu—?"

"What's wrong?" Before Dee could get a response from Sed, he had stormed over to the patio. Dee moved from the sidewalk to hide behind a nearby tree.

"Hey, Miranda," Sed said coolly. "How ya doing?"

Miranda's face looked like she had just seen a ghost.

Dee watched in disbelief. It was like a scene straight out of a soap opera. She couldn't believe this was the girl Sed had been seeing, and she hoped Sedrick would not make an embarrassing scene.

"So, you two know each other?" Chris motioned to the two of them.

"You can say that," Sedrick spoke up first. "Hey man, I'm Sedrick Henderson. And I know who you are," he said, giving him a firm handshake. "The question I have is how do you two know each other?"

"Miranda, who is he to you?" Chris queried.

"Yeah, Miranda, why don't you tell him who I am," Sedrick answered sarcastically.

"Sedrick is my b-b-boyfriend."

"Oh my God! I'm not believing this," Dee said, totally stunned. She didn't know if she should walk away to totally avoid Chris, or be a good friend to Sed and stay put for moral support.

Chris backed up his chair immediately and surrendered his hands up in the air as if he were being held at gunpoint. "No disrespect, man. I didn't know. One of my teammates introduced us. She's a doctor at Crawford Long Hospital, and he was in the emergency room. They exchanged phone numbers and that's how we met."

"Yeah, how long ago was that?"

"Hey man, it's been about a week."

Sedrick was beyond pissed. Miranda had just met this man and was already tonguing him like she had just had his first child. "Well, Miranda, you don't waste any time now do you?"

Miranda pulled Sedrick by the arm. "You should talk! I saw you the other night with your friend! You thought I was asleep, but I heard and saw everything! You'd rather be with a nutcase than me?"

Now Dee was really ready to go. She had no idea that Miranda had heard her conversation with Sedrick. Thanks to her little impromptu visit with Sed, all of her private business about seeing the psychiatrist was out. There was nothing for her to do except leave and spare herself any more humiliation. She would explain later to Sedrick.

"Dee, come over here!" Sedrick yelled just as she was set to leave.

Dee decided to be strong and walked to the patio. She was now in full view of Chris, Miranda, and Sedrick.

"Dee, what the hell are you doing here?" Chris questioned.

"She's with me, man," Sed said, coming to her defense.

"Shit, Miranda, you are right about one thing. This woman is definitely a nutcase! Damn, what on earth have I done to deserve this?" Chris shouted out to the sky.

"I'm not a nutcase!" Dee shouted.

"The hell you're not!" Chris shouted back.

"See, it's obvious, Sedrick. You are the only one who doesn't realize who you are dealing with!" Miranda said defensively.

"Oh, that's where you're wrong, baby," Sed said confidently. "I know exactly who I'm dealing with thanks to this little tête-à-tête between you and Chris. And you better stop calling Dee a nutcase," Sed said threateningly. "And to answer your question as to what you did to deserve this, Chris? This is just called fate, my man."

Dee's eyes darted between Chris and Sedrick, as Sed continued with the drama. "And Miranda, this is who you saw in my apartment the other night, correct?"

"Yes!" Miranda said in a huff. She wanted so badly to call her another name, but she didn't know how far Sed would carry his threat, so she hastily folded her arms across her chest.

"But, what you didn't see was this," Sed said. He pulled Dee toward him and pressed his lips up against hers; his tongue entered her mouth with a slow and deep thrust. Dee was breathless as he began to release her. "But, this is what should have happened, but never did." He pulled her toward him again and slowly and forcefully repeated the same motion with his tongue one more time, leaving Miranda and Chris speechless.

Dee's thoughts were rambling. *Why is Sedrick doing this to me? Oh my goodness, this man can kiss! Why am I feeling like this? This isn't happening. Sedrick and I have been friends for years.*

"I've been waiting to do that for some time now. Thank you, Miranda. And thank you, Chris, for being here today because if it weren't for the two of you coming here all hoed up like this, I don't know when I would have admitted my true feelings for this woman. Now, I'm going to leave you with some advice my brotha."

"What kind of advice could you possibly give me? If you hangin' with Dee, anything you say to me is questionable." His words were arrogant and filled with bitterness as he laughed sinisterly.

"Well, I've hit that plenty of times man," he said pointing to Miranda.

"Yeah, so? And I've hit that, too" he said, pointing to Dee.

Dee and Miranda both looked as if they wanted to find a hole and crawl up in it together.

"Well, that may be true. But Dee ain't been around like girlie girl here has, man."

"Why, you double-crossing arrogant son of a bitch!" Miranda began to lunge toward Sed as Chris pulled her back.

"Just make sure you use about two to three raincoats if you gone git with Miranda, cause she sho' has been around!" Sed warned.

Miranda picked up her glass of water and threw it at him, but missed. Sedrick gave Miranda a smirk then turned to Dee and placed his arm around her waist. "C'mon baby, let's find us another place to eat. This restaurant has a really bad smell, and I've completely lost my appetite!"

Planned Ditching

Pam walked confidently into Sterling, Mathis, and Silverman.

"Well, welcome back Ms. Madison," Carol Ann said with a southern drawl.

"Why, thank you, Carol Ann. How have things been?" Pam asked thumbing through the pile of phone messages Carol Ann had printed off her computer, stapled together, and neatly placed in an envelope.

"Things have been sort of piling up in your absence."

"I can see they have. And they are about to pile up even more," she whispered to herself, grinning broadly. As she approached her office, she saw a familiar face poring over papers in a nearby office.

Amanda looks great, she thought. *Her hair is silkier, and her body is the slimmest I have ever seen it.*

"Amanda," she said coolly.

Amanda was caught off guard by her unexpected arrival. She looked up, but quickly got her composure and started looking back down at her work again. "Ms. Madison."

"Please drop the Ms. Madison thing, okay?" Amanda acknowledged her with a nod. "Listen, I can't blame you if you never said anything else to me—ever. But I need to tell you something."

Amanda got up, opened her file drawer, took out some files, and then sat back down at her desk acting as if Pam was invisible.

"Effective today, I'm resigning from SMS and moving to New York to accept a partnership with Richmond and Lieberman. As I was going through my drawer, I came across this. She pulled out the memento that she had found hidden in her drawer. She had rewrapped it in a purple velvet cloth and handed it to Amanda. "Go ahead. Look at it," she said, as Amanda eyed her suspiciously.

When Amanda turned it over, she remembered it immediately. It was a picture of her, Pam, and Dee standing in front of the Georgia Capitol wearing their first business suits. They had met with some of the Georgia legislators after their tour and made a pact to uphold justice together, no matter what happened. They all had their hands resting on each other's shoulders and held onto a handmade sign that read "Best Friends Forever."

"I don't know what to say," she whispered as she handed it back, her hand beginning to tremble.

"No, please keep it. I made a copy of it. I wish I had found this picture three years ago. I would have brought it in here to be a constant reminder that we were best friends first and business associates second. I've been angry and hostile for a long time about the different routes our lives took. We all thought we had the same destination, but it turns out that we just chose different paths. Unfortunately, we ended up losing ourselves and our friendship along the way. I'm so sorry, Amanda. If I could get what we had back then, it would be worth starting all over. Goodbye, Amanda." Pam looked at her tearfully and turned toward the door.

Amanda couldn't keep her eyes off the photo and was caught off guard with her sudden rush of emotions. "No, wait!" Amanda shouted, as she felt her eyes welling up with tears. She raced to Pam. "Thank you. Thank you so much," she panted, as she hugged her friend for the first time in many years.

Amanda sat back down at her desk and looked at the picture one more time. Her thoughts drifted down to her hand, and she gazed at her engagement ring. Finally, she felt that Rickey had understood that her future was with Melvin. She was handling the time apart from Melvin well, but she still missed him. She needed to give him his space. She needed to believe that in time he would see that he was the only man for her.

Pam was seated at her desk when she heard a firm knock on the door. "C'mon in."

"Good morning! These are for you," Carol Ann said as she placed two dozen red and pink roses on her desk.

"Oh, my goodness, they're gorgeous!"

"Yes, they are." Carol Ann paused hoping to get a glimpse of the card.

Pam looked at the roses. They were beautiful, but not exactly Marco's taste. She hastily opened the card and smiled at the fact that the card was not intended for her to read. She definitely knew her man's taste in flowers.

"Hey, Carol Ann, let's seal this back up and make this faux pas our little secret." Pam winked. "These go to Amanda."

"Oh forgive me! I thought—"

"No, don't give it a second thought, please. It's an innocent mistake. Just take them to their rightful owner. She's going to love them."

Carol Ann was speechless. The Pam she knew would have been screaming at the top of her lungs and maybe even throwing the flowers at her! "Yes, Ms. Madison, our little secret. I'll get them to their rightful owner, right away," Carol Ann nervously winked at Pam and darted out the door with the flowers.

Watching Carol Ann swiftly move out of the office was funny to Pam. She couldn't believe how upset she used to get at her. She was going to miss Carol Ann. She hoped the receptionist at her new office was just as comical.

Carol Ann knocked on Amanda's door. "Amanda, it's me. Carol Ann, I have something for you."

"Sure, come on in. What you got, girl?"

"These!" she said as she proudly placed the roses in the middle of her desk. "Someone must love you, honey! Give him some for me too, will ya? I sure could use something to cheer up my desk," she snickered, as she left the office.

"Get outta here, Carol Ann," Amanda laughed as she watched her leave the room. She slowly stood up to open the card, took a deep breath, and closed her eyes and prayed. She opened the envelope carefully and read the card, holding her hand over her mouth to keep herself from screaming.

Let's set a wedding date! Love, Melvin

Pam knocked sternly on Bill McKesson's door. His eyes peered above his glasses. "Well, hello, Pam. When did you get back?" He got up from his desk to shake her hand.

"This is my first day back," she said with a cunning smile.

"Well, you've certainly been missed around here."

"I'm sure," she said as she looked at the mounds of paperwork on his desk.

"Well, you deserved some time off. I hope that you've had some time to rethink things," he said, extending his hand toward the chair in front of him.

"Thank you. Yes, I have."

"So, you understand why we had to hold off on your partnership?"

"Yes, I understand why you thought you had to do that."

"Well, we are looking forward to making you partner one day, Pam. We just want to make sure that this type of incident doesn't happen again."

"I understand, Bill." She gave him a stern look, but she couldn't wait to make her move. This conversation was turning into a chess match. He made his move, and she made hers. She would let him think he had her right where he wanted her—and then bam! She would checkmate his ass.

"Well, I'm glad that's settled. Have you had a chance to see your caseload since you've been back?"

"Yes, and I hear you've assigned me a new paralegal. What's her name, Helana?"

"It's pronounced Hel-ee-na. Yes, she came over here from Brad, Smith, and Torrey. The firm's up in New York."

"Yes, I'm quite familiar with them. What made her decide to come here?"

"Her husband's job transferred."

"I see." Pam shifted in her chair. She was getting really tired of this bullshit. She wanted Bill to hurry up and get it over with. "Well, since we are on the subject of transfers and New York, I've got some wonderful news!"

"You do?" He took his glasses off his nose and looked directly at her.

"Yes, I was offered a mid-level partnership with Richmond and Lieberman, and I've accepted," she said, handing him her resignation letter. Her face beamed, and anyone who saw it would realize how happy she was.

Bill's face turned bone white. "Well . . . I don't know what to say."

"Congratulations would be nice," she said, enjoying watching him stumble all over himself.

"This comes as quite a surprise. I'm sure you know that."

"Really? I can't imagine why."

"I mean, I knew you were disappointed about not getting the partnership, and there was even some underlying hint that you were thinking of suing the firm, but I felt it was just your anger talking. I figured once you had a chance to take some time off, you would come back here and . . ."

"Work just like everything was back to normal, right?"

"Well, yes, I had hoped so," Bill said, stammering.

"Well, Bill, you were right about one thing. The time off did let me cool off a bit, and I decided not to sue the firm. Even though I still feel that I would be well within my rights to do so. But I know that you guys are bigger than me. All I would be doing was setting myself up for career suicide and quite frankly, I've worked too damn hard to do that to myself."

Bill's look was sober. He wasn't quite sure where this conversation was going, but he wanted to make sure it ended amicably. After all, it was just the two of them in his office, and he had no witness to vouch for whatever allegations came out of this conversation. Pam was shrewd. Very shrewd. And he was not going to get caught up in a debate with her behind closed doors.

Pam fumed at the thought of SMS getting millions of dollars because of her expert legal strategies. If she had been a white boy and had done exactly what she did, she would be smoking an imported cigar now with her feet propped confidently across her desk in a corner office.

Pam glanced at Bill's back wall, seeing pictures of the eleven partners that lined the walls—their names shining from the light. It was blatantly obvious. There were no black partners at Sterling, Mathis, and Silverman. If someone like Pam didn't make it, then no one would.

"I know you've worked hard. You've certainly proven your abilities here," Bill conceded.

"Yes, I have, Bill, and I must say I've learned a lot. Quite a bit, in fact. And I will be able to apply it all as a partner at Richmond and Lieberman."

Bill took a silk handkerchief out of his suit pocket and wiped his forehead. The thought of losing an attorney of Pam's caliber was outrageous—and to

Richmond and Lieberman. Everyone on the east coast knew the name of the well-respected firm.

"Well, we hate to lose such a key player."

"Enough to make a counter offer?" Pam edged.

"Let me discuss it with the other partners and see what we can come up with."

Pam took a second glance at the partners' pictures on the wall. "On second thought, never mind. I think my decision is the best one for me. Goodbye, Bill."

Unexpected Passenger

Pam was dressed in a one-shoulder black-beaded evening gown that hung straight around the hips and flowed effortlessly to the floor. She looked as if she were walking on air with her head raised high above the clouds. Her double-tiered diamond necklace and matching earrings glistened against her skin as she paused for a moment to open the door for Marc.

"Wow! You look stunning! You are going to be the envy of a lot of women this evening."

Pam blushed. "Glad I meet with your approval."

"Yes, I do very much approve," he said.

"I had to make sure I represented you well tonight. After all, you are one of the American Medical Association's prestigious honorees," she said, trying to control her jitteriness.

"It's no big deal, really," he said humbly.

She gently kissed him on the forehead. "Keep telling yourself that if it will make you feel better, okay? May I get you something to drink?"

"No, I don't want to get too relaxed before the awards dinner. I think I need to continue to look as stiff as possible in this boring tuxedo," Marc laughed.

"Well, you look very handsome to me, sir. And you're wearing that Armani well this evening."

He laughed again. "You're very kind, but I hate monkey suits, no matter who the designer is. On second thought, how about some water?"

"All right. One bottled water coming right up," she said as she walked toward the kitchen, watching him casually make his way around the living room.

"Beautiful place you've got here," he said, as he walked over to the fireplace mantel and picked up a picture of Pam with another attractive woman in a flight attendant uniform. He took a second look at the photo and immediately recognized Dee. He almost dropped the picture before he could put it back in its place. Pam walked back in the room and handed him a glass and a bottle of water.

She looked at him warily. "That's my roommate."

Marc quickly took a sip of the water from the bottle, loosened his tie, and sat on the sofa. Suddenly all of his sessions with Dee flashed back like a bolt of lightning. This was Dee's roommate. The attorney. The one that made Dee feel so inadequate. The one that . . . damn it, he couldn't believe he never put this together.

Pam sat down next to him and placed her trembling hand on top of his. She could tell by the perspiration that was forming on his brow that he had figured out her and Dee's relationship.

"I know you're her psychiatrist."

Marc nodded hesitantly. "I am."

"She was at the restaurant that night. And she saw the two of us together and ran scared."

Marc only nodded and gulped down the rest of his water, wishing he had asked Pam to get him something stronger. He cleared his throat and managed to form a complete sentence. "How did you find out that she was my patient?"

Pam pulled her hand back and held it with her other one, trying to stop it from trembling. "It was a coincidence. I was in her room and your number came up on the caller ID. Your assistant assumed I was Dee when I answered the phone and—"

"And that's when you found out? When Rebecca said that she was calling to confirm Dee's appointment?"

"Yes, Rebecca was calling about Dee canceling her sessions with you," Pam responded, almost incoherently.

"This is extremely troublesome for me, Pam."

"Yes, I know. It is for all of us."

"Where is Dee now?"

"She's flying. We haven't been on the best terms since all of this happened, but I looked at her calendar and she won't be back until late the day after tomorrow."

Marc breathed a sigh of relief. "That's good, because this would really put even more of a strain on our professional relationship if she were to see me in her home with you."

"I know. I wouldn't do that. But I didn't know how else to bring this up. I knew if you came here, you would see the picture and figure it out. And that's what I need to talk to you about."

"Pam, I can't discuss my relationship with my patient with you."

"I'm not asking you to. But she told me that she discussed me with you."

"All right. That's her decision. I still can't talk about our sessions."

"Then tell me this. Whatever she told you about me—is that going to change how you feel about me?" Pam paused and looked up at him cautiously. "Can you tell me that much? I need to know because I can't move into your apartment if I know that you are uncomfortable with my past—and me, for that matter."

Marc got up nervously from the sofa and walked back toward the mantel. He looked at the picture again and shook his head as he looked over at Pam. He took in a deep breath and let out a loud sigh as he stared at the picture one more time and then placed it back on the mantel.

Pam held her breath as she waited on what was obviously the inevitable. It was okay. She was a big girl. They had a good time while it lasted. Marc paced around the room, then sat back down. His eyes seemed filled with regret, as Pam remained silent.

"So, you had decided to take me up on my offer on my apartment in New York?"

Pam nodded as he caught her chin just before it went down again. His eyes interlocked with hers as he kissed her, sucking her lips as if they were ripened fruit. This was his way of saying goodbye. She just knew it. And as much as she hated to let go, she understood it completely. Pam's heart fluttered as he smiled lovingly and then kissed her long and slow.

He paused and looked straight into her eyes and whispered, "Does that answer your question? Come on Cinderella, let's go before our chariot turns into a pumpkin."

Off Course

edrick opened his briefcase and took out one of the books he had just purchased and wrote:

Believe in yourself, because I sure do.
Love,
Sedrick.

Before he could press the button to the elevator his cell phone rang.

"Hey Sedrick. It's Pam. Did I catch you between patients?" she laughed.

"I wish. I had to take some time off and get things finalized for this grand opening. I'm practically spending the night with these contractors. If I don't stay on them, they will take their time and keep spending my money."

"I wish I was there to help put some fire under those boys. You watch 'em cause they will drag your building out for as long as they can and give you a nice bill at the end."

"I know. That's what I'm trying to avoid."

"Well, I wanted to let you know that I'm definitely going to be there. Just make sure that you email or text me the final details so I can arrange my flight. Where are you now?"

"I'm headed to check on Dee and to see how her roommate situation is coming."

"That's nice of you."

"Well, somebody has to look out for her."

"What's that supposed to mean?"

"Well, thanks to you, she was left high and dry without enough rent to cover the place until she can find a new roommate. So, I loaned her a couple of thousand dollars to tie her over." Pam was silently seething through the phone. "Pam, you there?"

"Sedrick, did you just say that you gave her some money for the rent?"

"Yes."

"Well, I'm dumbfounded as to why you did that because I gave her four thousand dollars to carry her ass until she found someone to move in!"

Sedrick put the phone down and stuck his finger in his ear and jiggled it. "What did you just say?"

"Four thousand dollars for my half of four months' rent."

"That's what I thought. Ah right. Let me call you later."

"Sed, you better talk to that woman. She sounds like she is losing her damn mind. How is she going to take money from me and then take money from you too? Between the two of us, she can go a long time without finding anybody to live with her!"

"I said let me get back with you," Sed said, trying to remain calm.

"I know this tone. All right, I'm going to hang up, but you call me as soon as you get to the bottom of it, okay?"

Sed got onto the elevator and rushed out as soon as he got to Dee's floor. He knocked on her door and took note that it was taking Dee a little longer than usual to open the door, so he put his ear to the door and thought he heard some movement. "Dee! You in there?" He knocked again.

When there was still no answer, he decided to use the spare key she had given him in case of emergencies. "Dee!" he called out again as he took out the books from his briefcase and placed them next to the door. He looked around the apartment and thought he had stepped into the wrong one. The peach-colored leather love seats were replaced with a new olive chenille sofa. The paintings on the walls had been replaced with the most unusual looking three-dimensional octagonal mirrors.

Dee walked in with a strange-looking, small-framed man dressed in lilac knit pants and a pink shirt with ruffles flowing down the front. His eyes were hard to see behind his tinted diamond studded-glasses. He reminded Sedrick of Elton John in the '70s.

"Hey, Sedrick." Dee stumbled over her words. "I didn't hear you come in. Ah, how do you like the mirrors?" she said, trying to ease the tension spreading across his face. "Sedrick, this is Omar . . ."

Sed still remained calm. "The mirrors are cool. You look familiar Omar," he said, trying not to stare at his eclectic mix of fashion. "Are you Dee's new roommate?" he said secretly hoping this was Omar's furniture.

"Oh, no! I'm helping to give the place a little face lift." Omar twisted around to shake Sed's hand.

"I see. Then whose stuff is all of this?"

"It's Miss Dee's stuff, combined with my creation," Omar admitted proudly.

That was where he knew this guy, from a picture that Miranda had taken with him at one of the home decorating shows when she was trying to convince him that they should get a place together. This guy was top notch in the decorating field.

"So, Miss Dee, what do you think you want to do in the kitchen?" Omar continued.

"Oh, this room. I like it just the way it is," she said, feeling Sedrick's eyes pierce right through her.

"Well, you've given me your budget and I can work within it, so let's get back together in a couple of days. I'll call you." He gathered up his belongings and blew her an air kiss as he headed toward the door.

"Nice meeting you, Sedrick!" He eyed Sedrick just long enough to make him feel uncomfortable.

"Same here, Omar," Sedrick said anxiously. He couldn't wait for him to leave so he could get to the bottom of Dee's sudden decorating escapade. He felt his blood pressure rising. "Dee, how'd you get the money to pay for all of this?" he asked as soon as he saw the door close behind Omar.

"Sedrick, are you hungry? I just made some killer nachos."

"Dee, answer my question," he said, evenly.

Dee looked up at him sheepishly. "My brother sent me some money."

Sedrick looked at Dee suspiciously. His voice slowly started to escalate. "Your brother? Last time we spoke, you didn't want to ask your family for any money. Now you're telling me that your brother gave you money to help decorate?"

Dee walked over to him and tried to calm him down. She took his hands and held them. "Sedrick, let me explain," she said as he yanked his hands out of her grasp and turned his back on her. "Please, Sedrick, let me talk to you," she said, placing her hand on his shoulder to get him to turn around.

Sedrick clenched his fists and looked at her with such disdain that it frightened her. He wanted to hit something. A wall. Anything that would let him release the rage festering inside him. He looked around the room again. "You're lying to me! Why would you do that? Look at this place! You're spending like you're one of them damn Atlanta housewives on that reality show, except you're on steroids with your spending! It's me, Dee. I'm not one of these brothas you can just jerk around. I didn't intend on you spending my hard-earned money like this, and I'm not payin' for this bullshit! "

"Sedrick!"

"Listen. I just got off the phone with Pam. She told me that she just gave you four thousand dollars before she left. Add my two grand, and you got six grand, according to my calculations."

"I can explain, please!"

"I don't need any explanation. What I need is my money. Save your story for Pam, because when I tell her what you've done with her money, you're going to need more than an explanation."

"But, I didn't mean to . . ."

"You heard me! I'm outta here. You've got till the end of the week!" he yelled as he picked up his briefcase and walked to the door. "Looking at you is making me sick!" He slammed the door behind him.

"Sedrick! No! Wait! Oh my God! What've I done?" She looked down and noticed the books on the floor. All were on different techniques on how to study for the bar. She opened the one on top and read his note. Her hands shook as she thumbed through the pages. She held the books against her chest and hugged them as she watched her dear friend walk out the door and possibly out of her life.

A Higher Altitude

Pam was growing accustomed to her frequent jaunts to New York. The firm was still in the process of moving her belongings to Marc's apartment, which was a New Yorker's dream. Lavishly furnished, it highlighted his rich Italian background with a large assortment of sculptures and paintings from his country.

The three-bedroom, four thousand square foot apartment overlooked Central Park. She sipped on her coffee as she sat in the bay window seat reflecting on how she finally felt like she had it all. If only her father was around to see this. He would be so proud of her.

"Penny for your thoughts," Marco's voice hummed through the room as he joined her on the window seat and stroked her hair. He was wearing a golden silk fabric monogrammed robe with nothing underneath it. "It's a lovely view, isn't it?"

"Fabulous," she said as she looked at him lovingly. "And so are you."

"New job, new home, and a great boyfriend. What more could a girl ask for, Counselor?" Marc said with a grin.

Pam hugged him. "I've never been happier. Thank you."

"Well, I'm glad you're happy." He kissed her on the forehead and held her close to him. She felt something stick her in her ribs.

"Ow, what ya got there? Is there something in your pocket or are you just happy to see me?" she said in a playful imitation of Mae West and grabbed his hardened penis.

He laughed. "I didn't think you were old enough to remember Mae West."

Pam smiled. "My father used to watch her old movies. And I've seen the reruns of Janet Jackson imitating her on *The Jackson Show* from back in the '70s."

"Well, you do a pretty good imitation yourself."

"All right, all right, you're changing the subject," she said, looking down. "What was it that just stuck me?"

"I don't know what you're talking about." Marc looked at her, pretending to be innocent. She put her hands underneath his robe and started tickling him all over his body.

"All right, I give . . . I give . . . Uncle!"

She stopped and eyed him daringly. "Give it up, mister!"

He reached down in his pocket and pulled out a small crimson velvet box. Pam was speechless as he opened the box and displayed a two-carat emerald cut diamond ring set in platinum. He slid Pam over on the seat and bent down on one knee. Pam felt tears trickling down her face as she tried to catch her breath.

"Pamela Madison, I love you. I want you to be my wife if you will have me," he said as he slipped the ring on her finger.

The diamond shimmered on her fourth finger. It was a perfect fit. Just like the two of them. Her tears were flowing down her face as Marco caught them with the back of his hand and wiped them dry. All she could do was nod over and over again. The words were stuck in her throat.

"Should I take that as a yes, Counselor Madison?"

She continued nodding her head, then pulled him up and stood on the window seat so she could look into his eyes. She kissed him with all of the passion that had been buried in her heart for years.

"Yes, Dr. Marco Grimaldi, I'll marry you."

Dream Vacation

The white sugar beach and the sky-blue backdrop of the ocean looked like a tropical paradise. The breeze swayed lightly, giving Amanda's eggshell-colored gown an elegant flair as Melvin looked lovingly at her. He gently glided her veil away from her face. To him, she looked like an angel that had just been flown down from the heavens.

"I now pronounce you husband and wife," the minister said as his white robe flapped lightly against the wind. "You may kiss your bride," he said, then closed his Bible and watched the couple prepare for their first kiss as husband and wife.

Melvin bent down and held Amanda's face tenderly in his hands. The kiss was as warm and gentle as the sea breeze that was leisurely brushing past them. As they turned around to present themselves to their audience, Amanda's parents and Melvin's mother clapped as they walked toward the couple. Tracey and Rickey followed behind them as Rickey gave Amanda a congratulatory hug and Melvin a firm handshake.

"Thanks, man," Melvin said.

"No problem. The wedding was beautiful."

"No, I mean it. You didn't have to do this. Amanda and I really appreciate it." Melvin said, referring to the fact that Rickey had flown everyone out to the Bahamas as a wedding present and a peace offering.

"Well, it's the least I could do."

Melvin nodded as Tracey came over and hugged him. "Melvin, I'm so happy for you and Mama. This is the best place to get married," Tracey said as she pulled the cell phone from her purse.

"Now, who could you possibly be calling during our wedding, Tracey?"

"Don't worry Mama. I'm going to take a picture of you and your new husband. Now smile," she said, pressing the button. "And I'm sending this to Auntie Dee! Look at how nice you two look!" she said, showing them the photo.

"That's pretty good for a camera phone," Melvin chimed in.

"I know," Tracey smiled proudly while she soaked in the view of the beautiful scenery and breathed in the fresh tropical air. "I think I want to do this too, when it's my time."

"Your time?" Amanda said.

"That will be some time from now," Rickey chimed in.

"A long, long, long, long, long, long, time!" Melvin yelled as everyone laughed and strolled down the beach to the wedding reception.

Flying Solo

The silence was deafening. Dee looked around the large condominium at all of the new furnishings within the last few days. New furniture, oil paintings, sculptures. You name it, she bought it. Her excuse was that she was trying to make it a place all her own. It had been Pam who bought most of the furniture when she was in Chicago. It was Pam's money, Pam's furniture, and everything in it had reminded her of Pam. Now it was her furniture and her taste. The only problem was that she'd squandered Sedrick's savings as well as the four months' rent that Pam had paid her. She knew she had taken advantage of them both, and an intense feeling of remorsefulness came over her.

Dee picked herself up off the steps and walked to the phone, calling the only person she knew that could help her.

"Hi, Dr. Grimaldi?" Dee wiped her running nose with her sleeve.

"Hello Deirdre, this is quite a surprise. I haven't heard from you in a while. How are you?"

Since Dee had broken all ties with him, she hadn't realized how much she missed the soothing sound of his accent. Dee swallowed the lump in her throat. "I've been trying to work things out on my own," she said as the tears flowed down her cheeks.

"I see. How's that been going?"

"Not well. That's why I wanted to talk with you. I'd like to start my regular sessions again."

There was a long pause, and Dee wondered for a moment if they had been disconnected until she heard a troubled sigh at the other end of the phone.

"Dee, I'm sorry, I don't know quite how to tell you this, but I'm retiring. And besides, it's not in your best interest for you to continue seeing me as your psychiatrist."

Dee felt like he'd pushed a knife inside her and twisted it. "But why? I don't understand."

The doctor sighed again. He could feel the strain that his words had on her. "Dee, unfortunately, a boundary has been crossed, and as a psychiatrist I can't take the chance on losing my ability to stay objective. Ethically, I just can't continue because of this dual relationship I have with you and Pam. I have to stop seeing you as a patient."

Dee's hands shook as she tried to hold the phone and herself together. How could he do this to her? She was at the end of her rope, and he couldn't see her anymore?

"Dr. Grimaldi, you have to make an exception. Please, I'm begging you."

"Dee, please. This is very difficult for both of us. But it wouldn't be right. I am confident, though, that I can recommend an excellent psychiatrist who has worked with clients with similar issues as yours."

"I can't possibly start over again with another doctor. I have to see you!"

The doctor was silent. He felt caught in the middle. He was about to marry her best friend and knew it wasn't his place to tell her. "Dee, I'm sorry. But this is the way it has to be. Do you want me to give you a list of doctors or refer you to someone? You have grown a lot from our sessions, and I am confident that this next psychiatrist can help get you over the hump."

"You are . . . leaving me . . . with no choice here, Doc," she said crying between her words.

"Dee, I am giving you my only choice."

New Route
(2½ months later)

"Good evening, Miss Madison. Here are the last of the testimonies from Tenson Enterprises."

"Thanks, Grace. Listen, it's 6:00. Why don't you take off? I can handle it from here."

Grace had been a paralegal at Richmond and Lieberman for a little over five years. Pam had only been at the firm for a couple months, but found Grace's knowledge of cases impeccable for someone who had led such a tumultuous life as a victim of spousal abuse.

"Are you sure? I don't mind, you know."

"You can go home, Grace. I'm sure your boys will be glad to see you."

Grace smiled. "All right, if you say so. I'll see you first thing in the morning."

Pam thought about how her life and her personality had changed since she'd left Atlanta and fallen in love with Marc. With his support, she was no longer inclined to resort to intimidation tactics. The new Pam Madison had empathy for Grace's situation as a single mother with two sons. She looked at the clock on the wall and decided it was time to put an end to her workday. Anything else that was left for her to do could wait until tomorrow. After all, she also had someone waiting on her at home now.

As Pam prepared to leave, her cell phone rang. She didn't recognize the number but decided to answer it anyway.

"This is Pam."

"Hi, it's me."

Pam recognized the voice right away, and for the first time in a long time she didn't know what to say. She paused for what seemed liked several minutes.

"Pam? Are you there?"

"Hi Amanda! How are you?"

"I'm doing wonderful! I must say, Melvin and I were stunned when we received your wedding gift, and quite frankly I still don't know how to react! But I do appreciate it."

Pam smiled and felt a tinge of relief go through her body. "Well, you deserve it. I realize that it won't make up for the countless hours you put up with me for the last three years."

"Yeah, but twenty-five thousand dollars is a good start, Pam. Thank you!" Amanda laughed. "But, how did you know I was getting married?"

"You know I'm not at liberty to divulge my sources," Pam snickered.

"Well, it smells like someone by the name of Carol Ann is behind this."

"My lips are sealed, sorry."

"So, how are things going with your new job and new paralegal?"

"Well, I must say that both are awesome, but you are the best and will always be. I just wish I had realized that a lot sooner than later."

"It's all good, girl. If you and Dee ever do get together and start up that law firm, I'll be glad to put my resume in for the paralegal position."

Pam chuckled. It was good to make amends with Amanda. "Well, I doubt very seriously that will be happening anytime soon. With me in New York and Dee Lord knows where, it would take a long while to make that happen. Besides, if my memory serves me correctly, the last I heard was that a person still has to pass the bar," she chuckled again. "And we both know that Dee is nowhere near close to making that happen. But, please send me your resume anyway so I can at least have it on file. You never know, I could end up back in the ATL."

"Will do. Have you spoken to Dee since you've moved to New York?"

"No, we kind of parted on shaky ground. What about you?"

"No, I was kind of hoping that she'd make an appearance at the wedding, but she sent Tracey and me a text saying the she couldn't get a flight out down here. I think everything was overbooked."

"Where's down here?"

"Oh, we're in Nassau."

"Nassau? Dee should have known to have bought a ticket instead of relying on her flight benefits. She knows those flights are always booked solid! That woman I tell you . . . listen, here I go. I just want to say congratulations to you. Nassau is a beautiful place to have a wedding."

"It is, and we love it. Well, you take care. Thank you again for the thoughtful wedding gift."

"You are welcome and best wishes to you and Melvin."

Connecting Flight
(almost 3 months later . . .)

Dee sat straight up, swung her head back, and looked Dr. Johnson right between his eyes. He was in his mid-fifties, distinguished-looking, but not nearly as handsome as Grimaldi. Dr. Grimaldi was right. He was an excellent doctor, and he'd picked right up where Grimaldi left off. She took a deep breath as she stared out the window one last time. The once snow-capped mountains were now brown, and the sun rested soothingly on top of them.

Dr. Johnson took off his horn-rimmed glasses and placed the stem in his mouth. "So, have you heard from Sedrick?"

"No, as a matter of fact, I wrote him several weeks ago, and I haven't gotten a response. I told him how wrong I had been and I would understand if he never forgave me. I took the money out of my savings to pay Sedrick back since he had given me a week to do it. I even went to my father and told him what I did, and he is loaning me the money I used to pay Sedrick back if I keep my promise. My dad's even been helping me with the rent until I find a place I can afford."

"I see," Dr. Johnson nodded. He paused and smiled reflectively while he put his glasses back on.

"Why are you smiling at me like that?"

"I'm very proud of you, Dee. I must say that you've surprised me."

Dee blushed. "Really? How's that?"

"When you first started coming to see Dr. Grimaldi, you and your father had a very strained relationship. Now, it appears that you have been able to overcome that."

"Well, I told you I had to make him a promise first."

"Yes, I know. We'll get to that. I like how you have taken charge of your responsibilities. Writing a letter to Sedrick and acknowledging your faults was a huge step. And then taking the ownership of paying him back his money—that's incredible. Look at you. You feel very confident. It shows in your mannerisms. You no longer have to stare at the floor to talk to me. And best of all, I can tell the lies have stopped."

"Yes, well, I have no one else to lie to," Dee joked. "Pam, Sedrick, Steve, and Chris. Poof! They're gone," she said, throwing her hands in the air. "I don't want to experience that type of loss again."

The doctor only nodded. "So what are your plans for Pam?"

Dee was silent. "Well, I sent Pam a letter at the same time I sent Sedrick's, and I haven't heard from her either."

"Why do you think that is?"

"I think they just need time. I've made some really bad choices, and I've hurt them. I know that I have no one to blame but me."

"Very thoughtful answer, Dee." He paused then said, "Well, it appears that all that is left now is for you to take the bar that you've been studying so diligently for all of these months."

Dee looked up at him like a doe caught in a headlight. Dr. Johnson looked concerned by Dee's reaction. "Did I say something to offend you?'

Dee was quiet and only shook her head. "I was going to tell you."

"Tell me what?"

"It's about the bar."

"You do still plan on taking it, don't you?"

"Yes, that was the promise I made to myself and to my father. I took it a couple of weeks ago."

"And you didn't breathe a word?"

"I was going to wait until I got my results back."

The doctor stood up and grabbed both of her hands. "This is remarkable, Dee. Truly remarkable. Congratulations on such a wonderful achievement!"

"Thank you," she said quietly.

"So, that's it. You've set out to do what you've always wanted to do. You realize that you can lead a life being happy with who you are, and best of all, you are on your way to doing something that will be fulfilling and that can make you proud."

Dee looked at the clock on the wall just as it was about to strike 5:00. She stood up and said, "Well, I see our session is over, Dr. Johnson."

"My, that is a switch. I usually tell the patient when the session is over."

"Well, I guess I'm no longer a patient, now am I?"

"No, I guess you're not, Dee." He smiled proudly. "You certainly are not."

Dee returned home to pack up the boxes in her sparsely furnished apartment. She was moving in a few days to something smaller and more affordable until she figured out how she would transition from flight attendant to lawyer. She unloaded the mail on the one table that was still left in the apartment and sorted through it. Tucked away inside one of the many magazines was an envelope stamped return to sender. It was the letter she wrote Pam a few weeks ago. She took her phone out of her purse and looked at Pam's contact information to verify the address. To her surprise, she'd inverted the last two numbers of the firm's address. She couldn't send it to Pam's home because she didn't know where she was living.

She threw the letter across the table in frustration and looked down at the next piece of mail. It was from the Georgia bar exam. Just as she was about to tear open the envelope she heard a loud knock at the door. Her heart stopped as she tightly clutched the letter. Maybe this was a sign that she shouldn't open it now. She opened the door and got another surprise.

"Hey!" she said, stunned.

Sedrick smiled and nodded. He was dressed in a pair of Levi's and a white t-shirt. He looked so handsome and at ease since his practice opened. She'd never thought she would miss the ribbon cutting ceremony. But Sedrick had made it perfectly clear that he didn't want anything else to do with her the last time they saw each other, even after she paid him back his money.

"Can I come in?" Dee nodded and held the door open wider for him to step inside. "I got your letter a while back. I didn't know how to react at first. But I find myself reading it over and over again."

Dee was still silent. His voice was so soothing. She thought about how much she had missed hearing it.

"I guess what I'm trying to say is . . . and I should have said this years ago, then maybe all of this would have been avoided. I love you, Dee. I always have, and if what you said in your letter is really true then I'm willing to give us a try. But I can't go back to the lies. Is it true about Dr. Johnson? You said in your letter that he felt confident that you would be able to stop therapy soon."

Dee couldn't believe what she was hearing. After all of this time, it was true. The one person that cared for her unconditionally was not in Miami or New York, but right at her back door.

Dee nodded slowly. "My last session was yesterday. I couldn't go back to the lying even if I wanted to."

"Well, if that's true, then what do you think about what I said? But I want you to know that—"

Dee stopped him midsentence and pressed her lips up against his. He welcomed Dee's tongue in his mouth, suppressing any doubts about a future with her. While still holding the envelope from the Georgia Bar Association, she placed her arms around his neck and held him close.

Final Destination

Dee's flight landed at LaGuardia Airport right on time. "245 Park Avenue, please," she announced as she slid into the backseat of the cab. The driver took a glimpse of her through his rearview mirror and then did a double take.

"I've seen you get on the crew van a few times. You're a flight attendant, right?"

"Yes, I am. For a little while longer, anyway," she remarked with a satisfied grin. The last time she was in New York she was visiting Steve. This was a new beginning. The bad luck she'd experienced with Steve couldn't possibly happen with Pam.

As she stared out at the immense buildings and long stretch of yellow cabs, she felt butterflies in her stomach. What would she do if Pam didn't want to see her? She pulled out the letter for Pam and the one from the bar association that had arrived yesterday and stared at them. If nothing else, she would leave them up front with the secretary for her to give to Pam. As the cab pulled in front of Pam's law firm, she pulled out her fare and handed it to the driver as she got out of the car.

"Thanks. Hope to see you next time you're in the Big Apple!"

Pam's building was located in one of the most prestigious areas of New York. Anything she could imagine was right outside her front door. A distinguished and portly doorman held open the door as Dee walked in and rode the elevator to the twenty-fourth floor. When she got off the elevator, she was immediately stopped by a wrinkled, gray-haired receptionist. Her voice was so irritating that it could peel paint.

"May I help you?" She looked up at Dee from her cat-eyed glasses. Her hair was piled high on her head in a beehive, reminding Dee of the lady from the old Outback Steakhouse Restaurant commercials.

"Hi, I'm Deidre Bridge. I'm here to see Pam Madison."

"Is she expecting you?" The voice pierced through Dee's ears and zipped down her spine. How could someone with such an irritating voice be at the front desk?

"No, I don't have an appointment."

"I see. Well, let me call back to her and see if she is available to speak with you."

Okay, this was where the rubber met the road. It was totally up to Pam whether or not she wanted to see her. On the other hand, if she could somehow slip past Great Grandma here, she could just walk back there and not give Pam a chance to refuse. Dee wrung her hands while the receptionist picked up the phone and called Pam's office. She felt as if she was waiting in the lobby of a hospital for the test results of a life-threatening illness.

"She'll see you now," the receptionist said.

"Excuse me? I mean, thank you." The waiting was over.

A young, slender woman walked up to meet Dee. She was wearing a charcoal gray suit with a white silk blouse. She wore a simple strand of pearls, and her auburn hair was pulled back in a taut bun. "Good morning, I'm Angelica Ashbury, Ms. Madison's secretary," she said, extending her hand to Dee.

"Hello, I'm Deirdre Bridge."

"I'll take you back to Ms. Madison's office."

Wow! Pam really hit pay dirt with this job. A gray-haired watchdog, a personal secretary, and an office to die for! As Dee walked down the winding corridors, she couldn't help but picture herself sitting in one of the elaborate offices that seemed to ooze of sophistication. What a change of pace it would be from going from a job that lifted her into the air every day to one that kept her grounded all year long. As her mind began to wander, she heard Angelica's voice.

"Here's her office," she said, knocking twice on the paneled door.

"Come in," the familiar voice answered.

Angelica opened the door and poked her head in. "Miss Deirdre Bridge is here to see you."

"Thanks, Angelica. Send her in."

Dee felt like her feet were frozen to the floor. Angelica held open the door. "You can go on in."

Pam was seated behind a desk that looked the size of her entire home office back in their old apartment. She rolled around in her leather burgundy tufted chair, stood up, and walked emotionlessly over to Dee. Her spiked four-inch heeled pumps still made her diminutive in comparison to Dee, who was statuesque even in the pair of flats she was wearing.

"So, what brings you here?"

"I know me coming here comes as quite a surprise," Dee said wringing her hands together and focusing on the two padded mahogany chairs seated in front of Pam's desk. "Do you mind if I sit down?"

"Help yourself." Pam pointed to one of the chairs nonchalantly.

Pam watched as Dee sat down and pulled two envelopes from her purse. "Listen, Pam, I know what you're thinking. Sedrick told me all about the conversation he had with you about the money. I know you were in Atlanta to attend his grand opening, too."

Pam said nothing, but she raised an eyebrow. Her hands were folded tightly behind her back.

"Sedrick and I have mended our friendship. I'm not sure how much he's told you, but I've been working really hard and getting myself back on track."

Pam still had nothing to say. Dee's words were meaningless. It sounded like a boring tune with unmoving lyrics.

Dee picked up on Pam's cool vibes instantly. If there was one thing she knew about Pam, it was that she better have some backup to go with the song she was playing. This one was falling off the charts quickly. She handed Pam the first letter, still in its original envelope.

Pam inspected the envelope carefully to make sure that she hadn't forged the words return to sender. It looked legit. She opened it and read it.

Dear Pam,

I don't know what to say, other than I have been really irrational in my thinking, lately. I'm not sure how much Dr. Grimaldi is allowed to tell you, but he recommended me to a new therapist, and I have been working with him since you left and am making strong strides in getting rid of the demons of failure that have engulfed my dreams for so long. It's too bad that I had to lose everyone I cared about or loved before I decided to stop the lying. I've lied to you, Sedrick, and many other people in my life. But, worst of all, I've lied to myself.

Pam, I hope you will eventually find it in your heart to forgive me for not using your money for what it was intended. I am sorry, and I promise that I will pay it all back to you. I have allowed your successes to fuel my insecurities for many years, and that's no one's fault but my own. I am proud of your decision to leave SMS. You have a lot more courage than I ever would have in leaving something that seemed secure and then to turn around and venture out onto the unknown. Also, congratulations on your new career and your new relationship with an honest and good man. I really do wish you and Dr. Grimaldi the best, now and forever.

As for my plans for the future, I can honestly say that I have been studying for the bar exam. I am proud to say that I have scheduled to take it within the next couple of weeks. Pam, you are, and will always be, my best friend. I only hope that one day you'll let me be yours again.

Love always,
Dee

Pam folded the letter and put it back in its envelope. Her reaction mirrored Dee's tearful one. Dee handed her the second envelope from the Georgia Bar Association and waited for Pam's reaction as she read the letter.

"I'm so proud of you! You passed!"

"And on the first try, too!"

"Man, check out these scores! They are off the charts," she said as she grabbed her friend and hugged her as if she had been lost and found after several years. They both were crying.

"Thank you, Pam! I'm so glad you approve!"

"Approve? I'm elated!" She sat down and pulled a tissue from her desk and handed one to Dee. They both blew their noses at the same time and giggled like two high school seniors who were about to embark upon their first day as college freshmen. There was a silence that filled the air and suddenly they felt like a void was between them. Dee decided to break the silence.

"I heard that you and Amanda have finally squared away your differences."

Pam nodded. "Let me guess who told you?"

Dee smiled and nodded. "Yes, it was Tracey. She emailed me this wedding picture and told me," she said showing Pam her phone.

"Oh, they look so happy!" She handed back the phone. "It felt good talking to Amanda. I must admit, I'm glad that's behind us now, and we can move forward."

"Yes, that would be a nice change."

Dee then noticed the sparkling rock on Pam's finger. "Pam, that is so gorgeous!" She grabbed Pam's hand and pulled it toward her.

"Marc asked me to marry him!"

"Oh my God!" Dee screamed again. "First Amanda, now you! Congratulations!" She grabbed her neck and hugged her. "The three of us are going to have to get together and celebrate! So, when is the big day?"

Pam shrugged her shoulders and looked giddy. "We haven't decided yet. As soon as we both find a date on the calendar when we are both available," she laughed.

"So, how is he doing?"

"Well, you already know that he's retired from his practice. Now, he's going to be taking some time off to write a book. Lately, he's been talking a lot about buying a home in Atlanta. He really loves it there."

"So what does that mean for you?"

"Well, for now, that means I'll be commuting back and forth between

Atlanta and New York. U-n-n-less . . ." Pam looked at her between giggles. "Dee, are you thinking what I'm thinking?"

"You've read my mind!" Dee squealed as they hugged each other again and screamed like two teenagers at an Usher concert.

Their long-awaited Atlanta law firm of Madison and Bridge was about to get underway, and they already had their paralegal position filled.